JUST A LITTLE KISS . . .

"What did you expect, Jesse? That I would pine for you for the rest of my days? End up an old spinster?" She moved closer to him. "You're afraid to kiss me, aren't you?"

"*What?*"

"You're plain scared . . . of what is between us."

"Friendship, Andi," he whispered. "That's all that's still between us . . ."

She lifted her chin. "Maybe. But you'll never know, will you?"

Reaching a hand out, he slid it into the hair at the damp nape of her neck and pulled her closer, closer until her body was pressed against his. Her scent drifted up to him, a heady combination of lilac water and soap. "You want me to kiss you, Andi Mae?" he asked, his mouth a whisper away from hers. "You want a kiss?"

He crushed his mouth against hers. Their breath mingled and Andi felt her insides dip and plunge. Her heartbeat raced along the edges of her nerves, awakening some long dead desire deep inside her. She tightened her arms around him, seeking to draw him even closer. His skin was smooth and hot beneath her touch.

"Oh, yes," she murmured. "I do."

PASSION BLAZES IN A ZEBRA HEARTFIRE!

COLORADO MOONFIRE   (3730, $4.25/$5.50)
by Charlotte Hubbard

Lila O'Riley left Ireland, determined to make her own way in America. Finding work and saving pennies presented no problem for the independent lass; locating love was another story. Then one hot night, Lila meets Marshal Barry Thompson. Sparks fly between the fiery beauty and the lawman. Lila learns that America is the promised land, indeed!

MIDNIGHT LOVESTORM   (3705, $4.25/$5.50)
by Linda Windsor

Dr. Catalina McCulloch was eager to begin her practice in Los Reyes, California. On her trip from East Texas, the train is robbed by the notorious, masked bandit known as Archangel. Before making his escape, the thief grabs Cat, kisses her fervently, and steals her heart. Even at the risk of losing her standing in the community, Cat must find her mysterious lover once again. No matter what the future might bring . . .

MOUNTAIN ECSTASY   (3729, $4.25/$5.50)
by Linda Sandifer

As a divorced woman, Hattie Longmore knew that she faced prejudice. Hoping to escape wagging tongues, she traveled to her brother's Idaho ranch, only to learn of his murder from long, lean Jim Rider. Hattie seeks comfort in Rider's powerful arms, but she soon discovers that this strong cowboy has one weakness . . . marriage. Trying to lasso this wandering man's heart is a challenge that Hattie enthusiastically undertakes.

RENEGADE BRIDE   (3813, $4.25/$5.50)
by Barbara Ankrum

In her heart, Mariah Parsons always believed that she would marry the man who had given her her first kiss at age sixteen. Four years later, she is actually on her way West to begin her life with him . . . and she meets Creed Deveraux. Creed is a rough-and-tumble bounty hunter with a masculine swagger and a powerful magnetism. Mariah finds herself drawn to this bold wilderness man, and their passion is as unbridled as the Montana landscape.

ROYAL ECSTASY   (3861, $4.25/$5.50)
by Robin Gideon

The name Princess Jade Crosse has become hated throughout the kingdom. After her husband's death, her "advisors" have punished and taxed the commoners with relentless glee. Sir Lyon Beauchane has sworn to stop this evil tyrant and her cruel ways. Scaling the castle wall, he meets this "wicked" woman face to face . . . and is overpowered by love. Beauchane learns the truth behind Jade's imprisonment. Together they struggle to free Jade from her jailors and from her inhibitions.

BARBARA ANKRUM

RENEGADE'S KISS

ZEBRA BOOKS
KENSINGTON PUBLISHING CORP.

ZEBRA BOOKS

are published by

Kensington Publishing Corp.
475 Park Avenue South
New York, NY 10016

First Printing: April, 1993

Printed in the United States of America

For my teacher,
Lyn Stimer,
who believed in me when I didn't believe in myself.
Thanks, Lyn.

And to my family,
who put up with a lot of restaurants for this one.
I love you guys.

Chapter One

Ohio Valley, 1864

A moan gathered at the back of her throat, low and guttural, bearing all the pain and fear that threatened to undo her. *Don't scream*, she warned herself. *Do not scream. Because if you scream you'll lose control. And if you lose control . . . you'll die.*

Andrea Carson Winslow silently repeated the litany with her eyes squeezed shut and teeth ground together. Her fingers locked around the feather pillow beneath her head. It was damp from her sweat. The pain curled harder and harder around her abdomen, while clawing her in two from the inside as if by the talons of some giant bird. The crushing ache twisted and pulled and pushed her beyond the limits she had imagined bearable.

Panic swelled in her like a living thing, consuming the courage she'd mustered. The pain peaked, then leveled, holding her captive on some invisible brink, and at the very moment the scream threatened to break loose from her throat, the contraction miraculously ebbed, then slowly, reluctantly released her.

7

Her breath scraped her parched throat as she exhaled in short, panting puffs that matched the rhythm of the shutters clattering in the wind against the house outside her window. Something about that sound kept her sane. She prayed the storm brewing outside would linger as long as she needed it and not abandon her.

That thought struck her oddly. A storm for company. A hysterical sort of laugh bubbled up in her throat. Well, that pretty much said it all. She was as alone as one person could be.

No, she corrected mentally, smoothing two palms over her swollen abdomen. Not completely alone.

The thought comforted her and made the pain almost bearable. Hearing the first drops of rain clatter against her bedroom window, Andrea pressed her head back against the pillow. The scent of the rain was earthy and fresh. For a moment she wondered if she could make it to the window to hang her head outside to catch some drops on her tongue. But she was too far gone to move. Even the thought of it made her nauseous.

Allowing her exhausted mind to wander, she closed her eyes and conjured up a picture of her child. If it was a boy, would he have his father's straight brown hair, hazel eyes, easy smile? Would his hands be the hands of a farmer, wide and blunt and gentle? Would she ever be able to tell him what a wonderful man his daddy was and how much he would have loved him if . . . if only he'd known?

Andrea reached across the small wooden end table for the picture there. The silver frame felt cold against her warm palms. Inside was an ambrotype of a man in uniform, his dark Union cap set at a jaunty angle, his smile a balm to her even now. Zach had always been able to calm her. Even when she'd been at her stubbornest, her most unreasonable. He had loved her unconditionally and had married her that way, too. Now, as his face stared silent from the frame, she wished . . . oh, how she wished she could have given him the same gift he'd given her.

Pressing the portraiture to her chest, she glanced at the small bedside clock. Almost eleven. With the back of one wrist, Andrea swept back the hair stuck to her forehead. In another two hours, Isabelle Rafferty, her neighbor to the west, would drop by with something homemade tucked in a basket. Isabelle would talk about what Andrea could expect during childbirth, having given birth to nine children of her own, or she would simply offer a sympathetic ear, as had become her habit since the day two weeks ago when they'd buried Zach's mother, Martha.

Isabelle had told her first babies came slow. She said first labors were long drawn out affairs that gave the mother time to prepare. But she'd been wrong about this one. Nothing could have prepared Andrea for the pain that had struck a mere two hours ago, low, hard, and fast.

And two weeks early.

Andrea tightened her fingers around the edge of the cotton sheet. Her waters had broken at half-past nine. No, one o'clock would be too late. She'd never last another two hours.

Thunder crackled in the distance. Perhaps Isabelle wouldn't even come because of the rain. Perhaps she would wait until it let up. Perhaps—

It started low, as it always did, curling and spiraling from the middle of her back, dragging her into its grip as inevitably as gravity pulled the drops of rain down the panes of her window. Squeezing her eyes closed, she prayed she had the strength to do this again. This one was worse. Oh, God . . . so much

9

worse than the last. She felt her fragile control slipping.

The sound seemed to come from outside her, surrounding her, echoing off the walls, mingling with the rain. But it was *her* throat that vibrated with the sound, *her* voice giving up that last thread of restraint.

And finally, she forgot to care.

Jesse Winslow pulled his Appaloosa to a stop at the hillock's crest, beneath the sheltering branches of a thick stand of boxwood and maple that lined the long dirt road leading to the house. Along the creek that ran the length of the farm, willows lined the shore, dipping their drooping branches into the water.

His wolf, Mahkwi, padded up beside him, tongue lolling out the side of her mouth. Her silver-tipped fur ruffled in the wind as she waited patiently for Jesse to move on.

The years hadn't diminished the place in Jesse's mind, though there were times he had wished he could erase his memory of it, times he actually thought he had. What lay beyond the road sent an involuntary shudder through his body.

Corn. Acre upon acre of the damned stuff.

The rigid green stalks bent and twisted with the rising wind and rattled with the sound that had filled his nightmares since he'd left the place. In all these years, he hadn't been able to force himself to eat corn, much less imagine himself here facing the prospect of working it again.

It began to rain in large fat droplets. Glancing up at the thunderous sky, he ran a nervous hand over his bearded jaw, then tugged his hat down low over his eyes. With a scowl of resignation, he nudged the gelding toward the two-story white clapboard farmhouse at the end of the lane. The wolf followed on the gelding's heels with a whining yawn.

Drawing nearer, Jesse decided it had been years since the place had seen the wet end of a paintbrush. Faded green shutters banged loosely against the house in the wind and he made a mental note to secure them. The drunken-man fence surrounding the yard was broken in places, spilling into the adjacent cornfield.

The empty yard, still planted with garden roses and grass, was overgrown and unkempt. That surprised him. It wasn't like his mother to let that go. It surprised him, too, that she hadn't appeared at the door to meet him, her gentle smile as soft as the roses she grew.

The ungodly sound stopped him.

Jesse hauled back on the reins of his horse, bringing the gelding to a stop. The wolf, with ears pricked forward, heard it too and whined. For a moment, Jesse mistook it for the howl of the wind, rising on a keening note.

Then he recognized the sound for what it was: a woman's scream.

His blood went cold. Only one thought propelled him off his horse, his feet barely touching the ground between there and the porch. *Someone was killing his mother.*

Jesse nearly ripped the door off its hinges before barreling through it, banging the heavy portal against the wall with a crash. He dragged his Colt from the cross-draw holster at his waist. "Ma?"

The screaming had stopped. Silence answered him.

"Ma!" he called again and headed from room to room searching for her, afraid of what he would find.

Oddly, nothing seemed out of place. If there had been a scuffle, it had not happened down here. His pulse thudded in his ears. God Almighty! Fifteen hundred miles and he was *one* minute too late? Impossible. His grip tightened on the Colt. *"Ma!"*

Upstairs, a board squeaked. Jesse's gaze shot to the plaster ceiling above his head—to his and Zach's old room.

Soundlessly, he moved through the kitchen to the narrow stairs leading to the second floor. It could be anyone, he told himself; raider, drifter . . . deserter from the War. Each scenario grew uglier as he considered it, so he shoved speculation from his mind.

Avoiding the squeaky board on the third step, he raced to the top, then pressed his back against the wall, listening.

He heard the harsh sound of breathing and the distinctive metallic spin of a gun's cylinder. Fury rose up in him hard and fast, replacing the terror he'd felt only seconds before. The door to his old room was half-closed, but he kicked it open with the flat sole of his boot, gun raised and ready. What he found on the other side of that door nearly made him lose his balance.

"Goddamn . . ." he said, staring at the sweat-drenched young woman in the bed against the wall. A mass of stringy hair hung down over her eyes, obscuring her face. The tangled strands trembled with each breath she took. Propped on one elbow, she held a large handgun in her shaking hands, but couldn't manage to get the small lead ball anywhere near the cylinder. Jesse's stunned gaze drifted past her hands to the thin gown stretched tautly across her swollen belly. Hellfire! She was—

The cylinder of her pistol snapped shut and she swung it up toward him. "Get out!"

Jesse's heart thudded in his ears. His gaze skimmed the rest of the room in the time it took to blink. She was alone. "What the hell is this?"

She stared through the tangle of mahogany hair that had fallen over her eyes. "What do you want?"

His gaze narrowed on the revolver he guessed was still empty.

She licked her dry lips. "What? Jewelry? Money? There's not much, but it's downstairs in the covered tin by the woodstove. Take whatever you want and go."

Jesse stared at her as the storm gathered strength against the window outside. "Who the hell are you?" he asked, tightening his grip on his pistol. "Was that you screaming a minute ago?"

The hand holding her gun shook almost as badly as her voice. "Please, just take the money and go!" Her breathing came hard and fast, and what he could see of her face was streaked with moisture.

"I don't want your money," he said, his voice dangerous and low.

"You . . . you don't want money?" She wavered on her elbow and he thought she might just fall. If she'd been scared before, a look of terror crossed her features now. "What then?"

"What's your name, and what are you doing—?"

It took both hands to pull back the hammer of her gun, but it resounded through the room with a loud click.

Jesse's eye twitched. Her gun was empty. He was almost certain. "Lady—"

"Please . . ."

13

"Look, put that thing down." He held one hand up. "I'm not going to hurt you."

She simply stared at him, breathing hard. Slowly, he lowered his own gun. "I think I have a right to know your name," he said.

"A right to—"

"Dammit, where's my ma?"

Her eyes widened as if she thought he might be crazy. "Your . . . your ma?"

"Is there an echo in here?" he asked, glancing at the ceiling. "Yes, my mother. The woman of the house—Martha Winslow."

Her mouth fell open and she stared at him so hard he wondered if she were looking right through him to the wall. Her gaze raked him from the crown of his worn hat, down the length of his beaded deerskin jacket and leather pants to the tips of his square-toed boots, then returned to his eyes. An uncharacteristic heat crept up his neck at her inspection.

Slowly, she pushed the hair off her face and shook her head with disbelief. "Oh, my God . . ."

Jesse's stomach dropped to his toes. Those eyes, violet as the wild lupine that mantled the high meadows of Montana in spring; a man couldn't forget eyes like that in a lifetime. *Andi.*

"Oh!" she cried again, more sharply this time. "Oh, my Gaaww-d—" Her empty pistol clattered to the floor as she fell back on the pillow and clutched her mounded belly. "It's . . . it's starting again . . ."

"Damn," he muttered, watching her clench up like a pulled stitch on the bed. He took a step closer, dread creeping in on him. It seemed like forever since he'd seen her. Now . . . she hardly resembled the girl she'd been when he'd left. "Tell me you're not having that baby now," he said.

She didn't answer him, only bared her teeth in a

14

grimace and panted in short, hostile breaths.

"Damn." Jesse started to sweat. "This is *not* good," he said, more to himself than to her. "This is definitely not good." He didn't have to search the house one more time to know she was completely alone here. He cursed again, then moved closer to her and holstered his gun. "Uh . . . listen . . . maybe I should, uh, ride for a doctor—"

She shook her head desperately between breaths. *"No-oo!* Don't leave . . . coming . . . soon."

"The doctor?"

She shook her head again, gritting her teeth. "The ba-baby."

He was afraid she was going to say that. Jesse bit back another curse. He was as good at delivering babies as he was at plowing corn. Where the hell was everybody? Where the hell was his mother?

"Listen," he said, trying to contain the panic in his voice, "you couldn't just . . . hold off could you?"

She shot him a murderous look.

"Right." He ground a nervous fist into his palm and scanned the room for nonexistent help. "Okay, okay that's out."

She started to moan and with a scowl he moved closer. Even through the sheet covering her, he could see her belly changing shape with the contraction. The child inside her was fighting hard to be born. He'd had experience with gunshot wounds, broken bones, and even snake bites. But the only births he'd ever witnessed had taken place in the barnyard and the progeny had had four legs.

A woman was a different matter entirely.

"Tell me what I can do," he said at last with the resignation of a man heading for the gallows.

With her back arched against the bed she panted for air. The plea in her amethyst eyes when she

15

looked up nearly undid him. "Please, ju-just hold my hand."

Jesse swallowed hard. A hand seemed little enough to offer her. He slid his long fingers around the moist warmth of hers.

"Okay. That's good," he told her sitting on the edge of the bed. "Just squeeze the hell out of my hand. It'll be over in a minute." He hoped. A bead of sweat trickled down his cheek. At least she wasn't screaming. He didn't know what he'd do if she screamed again.

Instead, as the pain seemed to reach a peak, she uttered one word like a plea.

"Jesse-eee—!"

His pulse skipped with the sound of her cry. Jesus, how had she come to this? Pregnant, alone . . . Regret knifed through him for the thousandth time in six years.

After what seemed interminable minutes, her pain seemed to ease at last and she loosened her death grip on his hand. Taking deep, exhausted breaths, she lay on the pillow with sweat beading on her forehead. Her lips were bloodless and her skin paler than alabaster save for the freckles sprinkling the bridge of her nose.

He took the edge of the sheet and dabbed her brow. Her eyes were closed, her face relaxed. She was too tired to fight him anymore, and she let him wipe away the moisture on her face without a fight. No, he thought, letting his gaze slide over her features the way a painter eyed a canvas . . . she was far from the young girl he'd left behind.

Andrea's lashes fluttered open at the touch of his hand on hers to find him half-smiling at her. She wouldn't have been surprised to discover it had all been some light-minded hallucination, but there he was. Jesse, back home again. Who would have believed it?

The years had changed him. The sun and wind had burnished his skin to a deep tan and streaked the shaggy mane of tawny hair with gold. A hairline scar, not quite healed, ran along his left cheek. It might have made him look sinister, but for the slash of dimples she could still see beneath the darker beard covering his jaw.

Montana had made him rough around the edges, but if anything, he'd become more beautiful with age, she mused. His body had grown lean and hard and strong. One thing about him hadn't changed: the way he made her heart plunge and race with a simple look from those blue sky eyes of his.

Yes, beneath all that hair, she suspected Jesse Winslow was still handsome as sin and as dangerous to her heart as the deadly-looking knife strapped to his hip. She really hated him for that.

"Andi Mae Carson," he drawled with that slow grin of his.

"Jesse." Andrea swallowed down the lump in her throat and forced a smile. "No one's called me that name since you left."

"No?"

"I'm called Andrea now."

"I like Andi Mae better," he said, his thumb tracing circles against the back of her wrist causing a ripple of heat to ebb up her arm. "But Andi'll do."

Withdrawing her hand deliberately, she settled it back over her belly. "I'm not a girl anymore, Jesse."

"Apparently not." Thunder cracked nearby followed by a streak of lightning that flickered through the lace curtains at the window.

And I'm long past the days when my knees went

weak from just being beside you, Jesse, she told him silently.

Jesse reached down for her fallen pistol on the floor at his feet. He broke open the pistol to reveal the empty chambers. "Who were you expecting?"

She twisted the quilt in her hand. "There have been some Confederate raiders hitting farms in the area." It was not untrue, she reasoned, but also not completely accurate. "When you walked in I thought—"

He frowned. "I'm sorry I scared you, but to be honest, you were the last person I expected to find here."

She released the breath she'd been holding. "And you're the last person I expected to see." She clutched the damp sheet in her hands. "But I'm not sure what would have happened if you hadn't come." She looked away, ashamed to admit what she was about to. "I . . . I'm scared, Jesse."

He shook his head and threaded his fingers around hers. "I know. I'm not going anywhere. What are you doing here all alone like this, Andi? I . . . assume you have a husband."

A soundless, mirthless laugh came from her throat. "A husband? You never knew, did you?"

He frowned. "Knew what?"

"No. Of course not. You've been gone . . . what, five . . . no, six years now?"

Jesse stiffened at the accusation in her voice. "Yeah, that's about right. What didn't I know?"

"Zach," she said. "Zach was my husband."

Jesse felt as if he'd been sucker-punched. Zach and Andi . . . married? Damn. His own brother had married and he hadn't been told? The pain that had been inside him since his mother's letter had reached him three weeks ago bubbled to the surface. Zach was dead. A statistic of a war he should never have fought in.

"Zach never wrote," he said flatly.

"Oh, he wrote. Even I wrote you a letter. But you never answered."

Jesse felt the blood leave his face. "I never got them. Are you sure?"

She stared at him coolly.

"I . . . I've moved around a lot," he said. "Mail hasn't been too reliable until the last few years up in Montana. Stage robberies, mailsacks stolen . . ."

Her gaze slid away and fixed her eyes on the gathering storm outside the window. "That must be why we never heard from you."

"I wrote. The first year. But my letters were returned unopened. The old man's handiwork, I assume," he said, standing up to escape whatever it was he saw in her eyes. "After that, I figured they knew where I was. Finally, I got a letter from Ma telling me of . . . telling me about Zach. She asked me to come home. She said the old man was sick and she needed my help. She didn't tell me about you."

She pulled at a loose thread on the quilt. "I suppose she thought the mention of my name wouldn't affect your decision one way or another." Jesse shot a look at her, but before he could reply, she added, "It must have been quite a sacrifice for you to return."

"I'm here," he said, his voice bitter.

Andi's eyes slid shut. "You should have stayed out there in your mountains, Jesse. You shouldn't have come home."

For a long moment, Jesse stared at the shuttered expression on her face, stung by her barb but unsure why. It didn't matter what she thought, or what anyone thought, for that matter. He'd come back for his mother's sake and he'd stay until she didn't need him anymore. Then, he'd damn well return to his mountains, where none of this could ever touch him again.

Glancing around the small wallpapered room, memories of the times he and Zach had shared came back to him. Gone were the squirrel's tails, kites, and turtle shells they'd collected. Gone, also, were the two narrow beds, side-by-side where he and Zach had plotted their futures by moonlight. In their place, a full-sized bed built for a man and wife, dressed with colorful handmade quilts and crisp white sheets.

Zach and Andi. Andi and Zach.

Jesse had thought of Andi Carson often in the years he'd been gone, with her rich, mahogany hair and violet eyes, but never in his mind's eye had he pictured her a full-grown woman with a husband or a child.

In the years they'd been together, she'd been there to patch his bruised ego after a bout with his father's temper, there when he thought he'd go crazy if he had to slice his blistered hands on one more corn shuck, there to lie with and enjoy the clouds on a windy day or listen to his dreams of going somewhere, *anywhere* else. So many times, he'd lost track of them.

When he'd left, she begged him not to go. But he'd been too angry with his old man to hear her, and too determined to escape to consider taking her with him to a country inhospitable to women.

He'd told her she'd get over him, even forget him in time. He'd told himself the same. And apparently, she had succeeded where he'd failed.

Zach and Andi. Andi and Zach.

He turned back to her. "Where are my parents? I can't believe they would leave you alone like this."

Her eyes were tortured as they first avoided, then met his. "Your Pa . . . Jesse, he passed on this spring—" She slammed her eyes shut as another wave of pain hit, and whatever else she'd been about to say was lost.

Jesse sank back on the chair. His father dead? Thomas Winslow the Great, dead? A strange numbness crept over him. His mother had written that his father was ill. But frankly, Jesse hadn't thought anything could kill the old bastard. He'd been too tough, too damned ornery to die and leave his blasted land.

He should feel something, he told himself. Anything. But what welled up in him was an old emptiness that not even the news of Thomas Winslow's demise could fill. And what of his mother? How had she handled her husband's death? Was that why she wasn't here? Had she gone to her sister Elda's, in Council Bluffs, leaving Andi all alone? It didn't make sense.

He did not notice when Andi's contraction peaked and ended. He didn't look at her at all until he felt her warm hand clutching his.

"Oh, Jesse," she whispered urgently, "it's happening faster now. There . . . there isn't much time. I'll need . . . some things I didn't have time to gather."

Insensibly, he tore his thoughts from his family. "Just tell me what to get."

She rattled off a list of things she'd need—boiled water, sterilized scissors, thread, towels, thick flannel sheets—and where to find them.

He was halfway up the stairs, arms full, when the moan began. *"Jess-eee!"*

He took the stairs two steps at a time, sloshing water all over the steps. When he got to her a look of

21

panic was etched across her face, but the sight of him seemed to calm her. "I'm right here, Andi. Just take it easy." He set the bucket down and dumped his load onto the foot of the bed.

"I thought—I was afraid you'd . . ." She panted as the contraction released her. Tears streamed down her cheeks.

"I'm not leaving, all right?"

She nodded, breathing like a blown-out horse. In her eyes, he could see panic edging out reason. She grabbed his hand again and pulled him to her. "Jesse—"

He crouched down lower beside her face, fear creeping up the back of his neck. "What is it?"

Her lips were nearly touching his cheek. He felt her breath, warm and sweet against him. "If . . . if I die—"

"What?" He straightened with a horrified look.

"If I do—"

"You're not going to. I won't let that happen," he promised her the way a zealot promises eternal absolution. "Look, I know you're scared—"

"Women *die* giving birth," she said breathlessly. "It happens. Yes, I am scared. It *feels* like I'm dying." Her sweat-slick hand trembled as it clutched his.

"No, what you're doin' is living, Andi Mae," he said. "And you're letting me be part of it. Now, we're going to get through it together. You need to hang onto me, then ya just hang on. That baby knows better than the both of us how to be born. All we have to do is stay calm." He flashed what he hoped was his most confident smile. "Trust me, okay?"

Trust him? He'd said that to her once before when he'd promised they'd always be together; then, that she'd forget him when he was gone. But she never had. She'd watched him ride out of her life and felt a

22

part of her go with him. *Trust him?* She didn't want to trust him, but she had no choice. She had to trust him for now. Nodding wordlessly, she closed her eyes and sank back exhausted into the pillow. If she could just rest, only for a moment or two . . .

Jesse's confident smile faded when she closed her eyes. He slipped off his beaded jacket and rolled up the sleeves on his chambray shirt. He damned well better believe all those things he was saying or she never would. But in truth, he was as scared as she was. He had no doubts he could handle a normal birth. He'd seen enough cows and horses born to know he could help her deliver a child. But if something went wrong . . .

His gaze slid to Andi's swollen belly. Zach's baby waited there to be born. The child was his blood too, he realized with a jolt. He felt his throat burn with emotion. Zach should have been here holding her hand, catching his son or daughter as she entered the world, Jesse thought. Not him.

With a sigh, he yanked from his pocket a soft square of deerskin that covered his watch. He rolled the leather tightly and tied a piece of thread around each end to hold it together.

When her eyes opened, he handed it to her.

"Wh-what is it?" she asked, fingering the soft hide.

"I've used one since a time or two myself. Bite on it."

"Oh." She looked up at him, but he busied himself setting out the scissors and knife into a neat row on the stand beside the bed. "Jesse?"

"Hmmm?"

"Thank you for . . . everything. For the . . . leather. For holding my hand . . . coming when you did."

"That was just dumb luck."

"I don't . . . believe . . . in luck." She settled back

23

and took a deep breath. Jesse was still considering her comment when her face contorted and her midsection lifted off the bed. "Oh—oh . . . J-Jesse, it's s-starting again. Oh! I don't th-think I can—" She bit down on the leather.

He grabbed her hand and she nearly took his thumb off. Her knees went up under the sheets and her back arched off the bed. She held her breath and he found himself doing the same.

"Oh, m-my Gaw-wd!"

Fear drove through him at the shrill terror in her voice. "I'm right here, darlin'. I'm right here." This contraction seemed longer and aged him with each passing second. He wiped his sweaty forehead with the back of one sleeve. How she must hurt! It was damn good men didn't have to bear children, he thought watching her, because after seeing this, he'd sure as hell never go through it. As it was, he was wringing wet with sweat. He blinked and ran a sleeve over his forehead.

Over the next few minutes, Jesse felt about as useful to her as a scythe to a grasshopper, but he held her hand and gently massaged her back until she swatted his hand away, unable to bear even the gentlest of touches.

In the moments between pains, she told him what Isabelle had told her about what to do after the baby came; how to clear the mouth, tie off the cord, make the baby breathe. Each instruction, though meant to fill Jesse with confidence, had the opposite effect. There was so much to remember and all of it crucial. He was plain scared, but he'd be damned if he'd let her see that.

The pains came almost back to back with barely time between for her to catch her breath. Finally, the pains took on a new dimension.

"Oh gaww-dd," she moaned, reaching back for the thin iron bars of the bedstead. "I have to push."

He sent up a prayer under his breath.

"It's coming, Jesse. I can feel it."

His pulse thudded in his ears. *Calm. Stay calm.* "Andi? I'm just gonna . . . pull the sheet back now. Okay?"

Andi didn't hear him, or if she did she didn't care. Her face was red and she was pushing for all she was worth. Jesse slid the sheet away from her drawn up legs. Her muslin nightrail was hitched over her knees, but covered the rest of her. "Okay . . . Andi, I need to see what's happening."

"Oh! Oh!" she panted. "God, I f-feel it. It's t-time. Jess-eee!"

Shoving the nightgown away from her, his pulse grew rapid at the sight of a tiny black-haired head crowning at the vortex of her legs. Andi's long limbs were covered in a sheen of sweat and every muscle in her body strained to the task at hand.

"I see the head, Andi! It's right there!"

She gripped the iron bedstead until he thought she'd bend the metal.

"That's it, Andi. Push. Push again!"

With a growling cry, she did. Jesse could hardly believe it as a tiny head emerged face down. Gently, he took the baby's head in his hands as it naturally rotated sideways. A perfect little face appeared, scrunched up and red. Awe filled Jesse, made his hands shake. As she'd told him to do, Jesse stuck a fingertip in the infant's mouth and cleared away any mucus. To his surprise, the little mouth clamped down momentarily on his finger.

Andi dropped back, gasping for breath. She looked too tired to go on. "Don't stop now, Andi, you've almost got it. That's it. That a girl. Here come the

25

shoulders. One more push . . ."

From somewhere, she found the strength to do as he asked. Jesse's fingers slid against the child's wet head as first one, then the other shoulder appeared. Andi gave one last push and the baby came out in a rush into Jesse's waiting hands.

Chapter Two

Jesse laughed out loud as the weight of the warm, slippery child filled his hands. The miracle of it tightened his throat and made his eyes burn. He'd never held anything so new and perfect in his life. His gaze traveled down the small length of the baby's body to the twisted cord that still linked it with Andi's body. Its tiny face was reddish purple and scrunched into an annoyed frown. Jesse cradled him upside down in both hands, silently willing the baby to take its first breath.

With a little encouragement from Jesse's gentle hand, the child opened his mouth and made a mewling sound he could only compare with a newborn kitten. *Mwa-ahh, Mwa-ahh!* The sound brought a wave of relief crashing over Jesse. Lifting the squalling infant up in his two hands, Jesse couldn't help the idiotic grin plastered on his face.

"Is it—?" Andi asked in a rasping whisper.

"It's a boy, Andi. A boy!"

Andrea fell back on the pillow, with a laugh of exhilaration. "A boy. Is he . . . is he all right?"

"Look at him, Andi." Jesse held him higher. "He's a mess, but he's perfect. Ten fingers. Ten toes.

And . . . uh, everything else that's important seems to be here, too."

Andrea burst into tears, releasing the emotions that had teetered on the brink for the last few hours—tears of relief, joy, and exhaustion. Her baby boy. Her healthy, whole son. He looked so small in Jesse's hands.

"And will you look at this hair—" Jesse ran his hand over the cap of silky hair on the baby's head. "He's got your hair. No doubt about it. Shiny as gold in moonlight."

At his touch, the baby stopped wailing. Jesse glanced down to find the baby staring up at him with wide blue eyes. The boy blinked owlishly and flailed his outstretched hands with small, jerky movements, then calmed as Jesse cradled him closer. The look on the baby's face was one few people had ever given Jesse in his life: a look of absolute trust. The realization made his heart thud against the wall of his chest. This must be what a father feels for his child when he sees it for the first time, Jesse thought. Had his father felt this way when he first held him? Had his father ever felt the emotions coursing through Jesse at this very moment?

None of that mattered. It didn't even matter that he would never be a father to this child. He only knew no matter how far apart they grew, how many miles came to separate them, he would never forget the magic of this moment, or the look in this child's eyes for as long as he lived.

Andi reached for her son. Shaken, Jesse obliged, laying the baby gently across her chest. Heartbeat to heartbeat they lay. She curled her arms around him, hardly able to believe he was hers. Running her hands over the small body, she checked that everything Jesse had told her was true. Her eyes burned with happy tears. Never in her life had she felt more alive than she did at this moment. No one could have prepared her for the exhilaration of holding the tiny life she'd helped to create in her arms . . . or for the profound love she would feel that no words could possibly describe.

Through a haze of tears, she looked up as Jesse draped a soft flannel sheet around the naked child. He was still grinning from ear to ear, though a suspicious moisture lit his eyes as well.

"Hey, you're supposed to be happy," he told her with a laugh.

"I am. Oh, I am," she said, gazing raptly at her son. "Thank you, Jesse. Thank you."

Jesse didn't reply. He was thinking he ought to be thanking her, but he didn't say so. In fact he didn't trust himself to talk at all so he grabbed the spool of thread and tied off the cord.

In the moment Andi's eyes had met his, he knew his life had been unalterably changed by what had happened here today. A bond had formed between them, as tough and tenacious as the cord he was about to cut.

He reached for the scissors, but before he could cut the cord, the bedroom door burst open with a thud.

He whirled to find a woman with hips wide as an axe handle standing agape in the doorway. It took a moment, but Jesse remembered this woman too— Isabelle Rafferty, his mother's friend and neighbor. Six years had deepened the squint lines around her eyes and bracketing her mouth, but only added to what Jesse had always considered a commanding face. Her faded blond hair was graying, and escaped the wind-blown braids wrapped double around her head. Her startled expression slid from Andi to Jesse.

"Who in tarnation are—?" Her gaze fell on the

child. "Well, slap the dog and spit in the fire!" she cried, meeting Andi's exhausted, but triumphant grin. "You went an' had that youngun' without me." Two deep dimples appeared in her cheeks. Ignoring Jesse completely, she strode toward the bed. Her heavy brown work boots clunked against the pine planking.

"I *knew* it," Isabelle said. "I just had an inklin' today was the day. But what with the rain and all . . . the wagon got stuck in the mud and the mule wouldn't move . . . I'm sorry, darlin'." She stooped to look at the baby. "Glory be, will ya look at that? If that ain't the prettiest child I ever did see. A boy?"

Andi nodded with an exhausted smile.

"Land sakes," she said, rolling up her sleeves and looking at Jesse. "An' I 'spect that'll be your wolf sitting outside the kitchen door, then."

"A wolf?" Andi repeated, glancing at Jesse.

"She's half dog," he said. "She's a pet."

Isabelle snorted without glancing at him. "Looks like a wolf to me. Round here we shoot wolves 'fore they eat our chickens. If she hadn't wagged that silver tail in my direction and backed off, I might have done just that."

Andi started to shake—violently—and clutched her belly as another contraction hit.

"Damn." Jesse moved instantly to Andi's side. "What's wrong with her?"

Isabelle glanced up at Jesse as she pulled a quilt around Andi and the baby. "I reckon it's a little late to be a'worryin' about sensibilities, but I'd be obliged if you'd excuse us ladies for a few minutes . . . she ain't quite finished here."

Jesse blinked at her dismissal. In fact, he didn't like being shunted out of the room at all. He wanted to argue that he'd been there for the beginning and he'd earned the right to see her through to the end. But the look on Isabelle's face brooked no argument. And he realized she was right. No matter what they'd been through together, Andi would be more comfortable with a woman. He rubbed at his bearded jaw and glanced at Andi whose eyes were slammed shut again in pain.

"Yeah," he said, backing out of the room. "Sure. I'll, uh, be downstairs." Bouncing off the doorjamb on the way out, Jesse righted himself and headed down the dark and narrow stairway, alone.

Twenty minutes later, after Jesse had stabled his horse and restoked the kitchen stove with wood, he sat on the worn kitchen chair sipping on a steaming mug of coffee as Isabelle came down the stairs.

His chair scraped across the wooden floor as he jumped up. He had barely opened his mouth to ask about Andi when Isabelle waved him back down in the chair.

"Don't you be worryin' now. They're both fine as frog hair, thanks to you." Isabelle sank slowly to the wooden chair opposite him, glanced out at the rain and rubbed her achy elbow. "Andrea said you were a godsend. I believe she was right."

He tightened his fingers around the warm mug. "I didn't do much."

Isabelle laughed. "I'd say you did plenty."

Jesse stood and prowled to the stove. "Do you, uh, want some coffee?" Without waiting for an answer, he reached for the blue graniteware pot and poured her a mug. He snuck a look up the stairway, feeling drawn there by some irrational need to be with her again.

"You can go up in a while," Isabelle said,

intruding uncannily on his thoughts. "She's restin'. She'll need her sleep after all she's been through."

Jesse nodded and handed her the steaming mug.

Isabelle shook her head in disbelief as she took the coffee and inhaled the rich, dark scent. "Jesse Winslow. I didn't recognize you at first. You've filled out and then some, boy. Gotten hairier, too. You remember me?"

It had been a long time since anyone had dared call him "boy," and even longer since he hadn't minded. But he did remember her, a younger her, with hoards of children tugging at her skirts. She'd always been kind to him.

"Yes, ma'am," he said. "I remember. First spread to the west of here. Best molasses cookies north of the Ohio River. Mrs. Rafferty, isn't it?"

Isabelle chuckled, a deep, throaty sound. "That's me. But call me Isabelle. It makes me feel old to have a man whose face I used to wipe still callin' me Missus Rafferty."

He took a sip of coffee to hide the unexpected heat crawling up his neck. "Isabelle. Maybe you can tell me why my sister-in-law was all alone here today. It's not like Ma to leave her alone here like this."

Isabelle took a slow sip on her coffee and settled back against her chair. "Andrea was a little pre-occupied up there to tell you."

"You mean about my father?"

Isabelle looked up with surprise. "I—well, yes. I'm real sorry about your Pa, Jesse."

"You needn't be. You knew there was no love lost between us. The whole county probably heard our arguments. My mother warned me in her letter that he was ill. It didn't come as a complete surprise."

She nodded. "Tom was hard on you. Too hard. You deserved better, bein' just a boy. So did—" She

32

cut off the thought. "But it's not my place to be speakin' ill of the dead."

Isabelle stared at the swirling coffee in her mug, her blue eyes misting. Discomfort crawled up Jesse's neck. There was more bad news, he could feel it. Outside the window, the rain thudded endlessly against the glass.

"Isabelle, where's Ma?"

She looked up through a sweep of blond lashes. Her plump face softened further as she looked at him. "Lordy . . ."

Something curled hard at the pit of his stomach.

"Jesse," she said gently, holding his gaze, "your folks both passed on. Your pa in May, your ma, just over two weeks ago. They're buried out there,"—she inclined her head toward the front window and the family plot up the hill—"alongside your brother Zach's marker."

A numbing cold seeped into his bones and seemed to freeze the surge of pain that poured through him. "*Both?*" he repeated. "Ma, too?" Shock stiffened his limbs as he staggered to his feet. Mechanically, he stood and walked to the window that overlooked the zinc-lined kitchen sink. Leaning his palms against the planked countertop, Jesse felt the world shift under his feet.

His mother gone? Impossible. He never even considered the possibility. She was too young and it had been too many years since they'd spoken, since he'd told her he—

He slammed his eyes shut. "How?"

Isabelle sighed heavily and ran a hand over her frizzled hair. "After they got word about Zach, your pa seemed to just give up. He started ailin' during the spring rains and just never got better. Your ma worried herself sick over him an' the farm. Worked

33

herself too hard, I expect, after he died. Andrea tried to take over as much as she could in her condition. I sent over my boy Gus, to help with the planting and such, but Andrea found your ma one morning in her bed. She just went to sleep an' never woke up. Went real peaceful like, if that's any comfort to you."

It was no comfort, no comfort at all. Jesse smashed his fist against the countertop and ground it there—the same countertop where his ma had worked, fixed meals, arranged her roses in her cranberry pressed-glass pitcher. He spread his fingers against the smooth, cool wood, as if by touch alone he could recapture her.

He felt Isabelle's hand on his arm, though he hadn't been aware of her walking toward him. His mind was somewhere else. Back in a time when he could have changed things, mended fences, but hadn't—couldn't.

"She told me she wrote to you," Isabelle stroked his balled fist as she might have done for her own son. "She wasn't sure you'd come. But I think if she knew, she'd be real glad, Jesse. Real glad you're home."

Jesse's eyes burned as he met Isabelle's gaze. He didn't say anything. What was there to say? That he was a bastard of a son to have let his mother work herself to death while he gallivanted across Montana, chasing the dream that had eluded him for the past six years? Oh, he'd been happy. No, *content* was closer to what he'd been. But he hadn't managed to find what he'd left the farm to search for. Freedom had its up-side, but it hadn't answered the gnawing ache that was still inside him, and it hadn't ever felt like home.

Then again, neither had this. Not for a long time before he'd left.

He picked his hat up off the table, slid it on and shrugged into his leather coat. "I'd be obliged if you could sit with Andi for a little while," he said. "I'll be back."

"You plannin' on stayin', Jesse?" Isabelle asked.

Pulling up the collar of his coat, he turned to her. "Stay here?" he asked, shaking his head. "I only came back for one reason—my mother. It's no secret I hated this place. There's nothing for me here now that she's gone. I'll probably sell the place." With that, he turned and walked out the door.

Isabelle arched one eyebrow and watched him disappear into the rain. Sell Willow Banks? She snorted. Jesse may think that's what he wanted, but he might as well be burning green wood for kindlin'. And smoke is all that idea would come to if that little gal upstairs had anything to say about it, Isabelle thought. Lots and lots of smoke.

The family plot lay at the crest of a low hill beneath an enormous oak whose branches sprawled out over the graves like protective arms, sheltering them from the steady downpour. The air was sweet and heavy with the earthy scent of the rain. A white picket fence, peeled by weather and time, but woven through with vines of morning glory, corralled the plot. Mahkwi bounded ahead of him, sniffing at the base of the oak, then wandered off in search of some long-gone animal.

And eerie light poured down through the thatch of green leaves as the sun peeked between two black clouds. Jesse stopped at the perimeter and slid his hat off, heedless of the falling rain. His boots sank deeply into the muddy earth. Moisture seeped inside the soles and the drizzle soaked the shoulders of his coat.

He scarcely noticed the chill, so cold was he at the sight of the three freshly dug graves within:

Thomas Holden Winslow
Beloved Husband and Father

A muscle in his jaw flexed, and he dragged his gaze to the next marker.

Pvt. Zachary Evan Winslow
Born July 3, 1846
Died March 1, 1864
Dearest Son, Beloved Husband
Rest in Peace

"And father of an infant son who will never know him," Jesse added bitterly. It should have been him, Jesse thought, not his brother who went, but he'd escaped the farm and the war by going west. He'd taken the coward's way out and left Zach to bear the expectations of their father alone. For that he would never forgive himself.

Dragging a hand down the moisture on his face, he turned to the newest grave where grass hadn't yet taken hold and the rain made slender rivulets in the soil.

Martha Ivey Winslow
Wife, Mother, Friend
Born September 3, 1818
Died July 14, 1864

The cold wind tore at his clothes and at the wet hair slapping his cheek. Dead. His whole family, dead. He could hardly make sense of it. Three grueling weeks had passed since he'd learned of Zach.

The pain was no less sharp now than it was the day he'd opened the letter from his ma in Seth Travers' store in Virginia City, Montana.

And now his mother. He'd missed seeing her alive by two damn weeks. Why hadn't he sent a wire to her from St. Louis when his steamboat had arrived, telling her he was catching the first train home? Or at least written to tell her he'd be there. At least she would have known.

He knew why. He hadn't wanted the old man to intercept it, or try to stop him from coming back . . . or blame his mother for asking him. Now, he could only blame himself for the unfinished business between them.

His eyes strayed to the wooden marker over his father's grave. "Well, Old Man, you finally did it. Drove her into the ground. You happy now?" Jesse's fingers tightened around a peeling picket stake until splinters dug into his hands. "You should be. You're in your element—Winslow soil. I always said the stuff ran in your veins instead of blood like the rest of us." He laughed grimly, the sound flat against the rain.

He jammed his hat back on. "I wonder if you've finally had your fill of it, old man. You know I have."

He cast one final glance at his mother's grave and made a mental note to plant some grass and maybe a rose bush or two there before he left. She always loved roses.

After checking on his horse in the leaky barn, Jesse headed into the house. The savory smell of home-made stew reached him before he'd pulled the front door fully open. Shaking the rain off his coat outside the door, he went in to find Isabelle poking a long hatpin in the floppy brimmed hat she'd settled over her thick braids. She turned and eyed him appraisingly.

"You okay, Jesse?" she asked.

"I'm fine," he answered, hanging his dripping coat on the coat rack near the door.

She nodded and turned back to the mirror hanging on the wall over the chimneypiece in the parlor. "I made a pot of stew. It's heatin' on the stove. Nappies for the youngun are stacked on the washstand in Andrea's room. You'll run out fast, so you may have to wash some tomorrow."

"Nappies," he repeated dully. He slid his hat off. Water poured off it in a stream. "You're leaving?"

"Have to." She glanced up and frowned at the puddle forming on the floor. "Don't let Andrea catch you making such a mess in her kitchen floor like that. She'll have yer hide." But it was the sight of the wolf that appeared at Jesse's side that made Isabelle draw in her chin and one apprehensive eyebrow to go up.

"But . . . you can't just leave Andi here alone," Jesse argued.

"She's not alone. She's got you."

He slapped his drenched hat across his thigh in irritation. "But . . . I told you, I'm not staying—"

Isabelle braced her fists on either side of her ample hips and searched his eyes. "You ain't leavin' tonight, are you?"

"No." He dragged a hand through his wet hair. "But what do I know about taking care of babies?"

"More than most men, considerin' what you just did up there."

"But I don't know anything about . . . nappies or—"

Isabelle laughed, a loud throaty laugh. "You men! You think you eat nails for breakfast, but when

38

it comes to somethin' like a little baby, why you'd just as soon kiss a tadpole as handle a human child. They don't break, for pity's sake. They ain't as fragile as they look. Ask my husband, John. He's had lots of experience."

"But . . . wouldn't Andi be more comfortable with you here?"

Wrapping an oversized paisley wool scarf around her wide shoulders, Isabelle shrugged with a grin. "I got a family, Jesse. Nine younguns and a houseful of chores that don't care if I got better things to do. And a husband who wants me home at night. But, if you can't stay . . . well, I reckon that's your business. We'll cart Andrea and the baby over to my place. But the ride would be awfully hard on her and what with nine children crawlin' all over her and the baby . . ."

He sighed. "Hell, I have no right to ask you to stay. It's just . . . this whole thing has kind of caught me by surprise. She's Zach's widow. That makes her *my* responsibility, not yours."

Isabelle pursed her mouth at the resignation in his voice, then laid a plump hand over his and gave it a pat. "Responsibility can be a curse or a blessing, Jesse. I reckon it's all in how you look at it." Threading a long scarf over the brim of her hat, she knotted it beneath her chin with a decisive tug.

"For the record," she continued, "I reckon I don't have to remind you to keep one floor between you at night and mind your manners. She's a lady and you're a—" her gaze drifted down his travel-weary clothes "—well, you're a Winslow. If it'll help, I'll send Etta over to fix supper and sleep over at night in the house 'til Andi's confinement's over. At least you two won't starve."

A look of doom hooded his eyes. "Etta?"

"My hired girl. With nine younguns—six of 'em

under the age of ten—there's corners of my house that wouldn't see the light of day, but once every leap year. Etta needs the work and I ain't too proud to cherish the help. Anyway, I'll send her over tomorrow if that suits you. She and Andi get along fine."

Jesse nodded numbly. He took the comforting hand Isabelle offered and gave it a squeeze. "That's generous of you, Isabelle. I . . . thanks."

She harumphed and headed for the door. Hand on the aged brass knob, she turned back to him. "It's good to see you back at Willow Banks, Jesse. And I'm—I'm right sorry about your folks. Your ma was a dear friend of mine for most of my life. You let me know if you all need anything else, you hear? I'll get word to Doc Adams to come out and check on the sprout and that little gal up there."

"I'd be obliged, ma'am."

"I'm just sorry I'll be missin' the fireworks," she mumbled, giving her hat one last good flattening with her hand.

Fireworks? Jesse frowned, pulling the door open for her. *What the hell did that mean?*

But before he could ask, she said, "You'll do, Jesse. You'll do just fine."

He stood helplessly as she headed out into the misting rain still blanketing the land. He shut the door, a sense of dread creeping in on him, trying to imagine what Chief Sun Weasel of the Blackfeet would say if he caught him washing . . . *nappies.*

Chapter Three

The scent of honeysuckle drifting through Andrea's open window awakened her. She opened her eyes to find Jesse sitting in a chair by the window, looking out over the cornfield. Beside his knee, tucked safely in an empty drawer, lay her newborn son. The sight made her pulse falter.

The reality of what had happened between them hit her like a blow: he'd been about as intimate with her as a man could be with a woman. The pain made her forget to care about such things. Now . . .

Andrea slunk lower in the covers, watching him surreptitiously. He sat with elbows braced on knees, massaging small circles at his temples with his fingertips. He hardly resembled the young man who'd left her six years ago, she thought. His features had assumed a harder edge, bronzed and weathered by the sun. His mustache covered most of his mouth and his jawline lay hidden beneath his full beard.

But his eyes, she thought, they hadn't changed. Suddenly she remembered those same eyes gazing into hers that autumn day six years ago by Willow Banks Creek—the day Jesse had left her. They'd both been young, so young then and so full of dreams and hope. That day he'd forced her to listen when all she'd wanted to do was run. . . .

His old piebald gelding had stood saddled and waiting that day, his bedroll hastily thrown across the animal's rump. Straddling the old sitting log that stretched across the water she and Jesse sat, awkward as strangers, as he sent her world crashing down around her.

"Andi Mae—" He brushed a tear off her cheek with his fingertip, "don't cry."

"Don't leave," she answered, ignoring his gentle order, letting the tears spill down her cheeks.

"Don't you see? I have to. I can't live like this anymore. I can't stay here for another day with that old bastard. I don't have to anymore."

She shook her head in confusion. "What do you mean, you don't have to?"

He clammed up and turned away from her as he always did when he realized he'd said more than he'd meant to. "Jesse?"

"Never mind," he told her. "He'll never do anything but wipe his boots on me. And on her, too."

She knew he was talking about his mother. Jesse was protective of her as only a son could be. "He's your father," she pleaded. "He doesn't hate you, Jesse. He just—"

"Don't defend him, dammit!" Jesse shoved to his feet. "Not you, too." Beneath the rolled sleeves of his shirt she could see the raised welts from Tom Winslow's strap.

Andrea got up slowly, joining him in the long drying grass that twisted around their knees. "I'm not," she said resting a comfortable hand on his arm. "Just say you won't go."

He took her shoulders in his hands. "I can't do that, Andi. I hate this place. I hate the goddamn corn,

42

and the wheat . . . just looking at the steel blades on the John Deere makes the hair rise on the back of my neck. I *can't* stay. If I do it'll be the death of me"—he gave her arms a shake—"or him. You understand?"

She did, only too well. She'd seen the trouble coming for months, but had been helpless to stop it—just as she was helpless now to stop him from going. "Then take me with you," she blurted.

He stared at her as if she'd just asked him to plow naked in the sun. *"What?"*

She swallowed hard. "I . . . I love you, Jesse."

"Aw, Andi—" His eyes rolled shut.

"I *do*."

"Christ, you're just fifteen—"

"And you're eighteen. So what? Folks marry even younger than that."

"Marry?" he gasped. Suddenly, he was looking at her the same way he looked at that old John Deere plow.

"Andi, you're young. You'll find somebody else. Someone better than me."

She grabbed his arm before he could pull away. "How would you know what I feel?"

"Let's part friends, all right?"

"Friends?" she repeated hollowly. "Friends? We talked about marriage. You yourself brought it up."

"That was . . . a mistake."

His cornflower-blue eyes had burned into her with an intensity that always made her knees go weak. "I'm sorry Andi." His hands had trembled as they held her arms.

In wanton desperation, she pressed her young breasts against the hardness of his chest. "It didn't feel like a mistake yesterday when you kissed me."

"Andi—" The word sounded strangled.

"In fact, I can still feel that kiss"—she touched her

43

lips with her fingertips—"right here. Can't you, Jesse?" And before he shoved her away as if her touch had burned him, she knew he remembered that kiss, too.

"Damn!" he cried, looking at her as if she were poison ivy. "I have to go. You have to understand—"

"I don't—"

"As soon as I'm gone, you'll forget about me. You'll see." He rubbed his temples with his fingertips. "I'm going west, as far west as I can get. I'm going to find out who the hell I really am, and I'm not taking a half-grown girl with me who's been reading too many romantic novels."

Stung, she bit back her tears and watched him get on his horse. "Is that what you think?" she cried. "Is that all I am to you? Just some half-grown pest of a girl? Well, someday I'll be fully grown and you'll be sorry you left me behind, Jesse Winslow. When you finally find yourself all alone in that wild country full of rocks wishing you had someone to talk to, you'll be sorry! And I won't think of you at all. You hear me, Jesse? I won't think of you at all!"

She turned then and ran, but through the pounding in her ears she thought she heard him call her name. It hadn't mattered. She'd lost him and nothing would ever be the same. . . .

Andi curled her hands around the covers and drew them tighter around her face, her gaze pinned on Jesse's back. Of course she'd lied about never thinking of him again. It was, in fact, years until her heart stopped aching for him or her lips ceased to tingle from that remembered kiss.

The last rays of sun were slanting through her bedroom window, and the prisms she had strung there caught that light. Rainbows danced across the wall and ceiling in the rose hues of evening and painted color on Jesse's long hair. She wondered absently what he would look like with his shaggy mane trimmed short. What had he been through since he left?

She could see the answer. He'd turned wild, she thought, like an animal let loose after years of captivity. And certainly he had no desire to find himself behind bars again.

Jesse swiveled a look at her when she rustled the sheets. "You're awake."

She smiled sleepily. "Funny, I don't even remember falling asleep."

"You've been out most of the afternoon," he said. "So has junior here. How do you feel?"

"Like a fried egg that's been run over by a wagon wheel," she replied, and he grinned. "I can only imagine what I look like." Andi's hand went self-consciously to the tangle of hair haloing her head. His slow gaze roamed over her as she pushed the mop away from her face.

"You look beautiful, Andi. Motherhood suits you."

A flush crept up her cheeks at the sincerity in his voice. "You're too kind, but you're a shameless liar. Right now, I'd kill for a hot bath and a shampoo." She settled her head back on the pillow with a tired sigh.

He stretched, raising his arms over his head. "That can be arranged."

"You didn't have to sit here with me, you know."

"I didn't mind," he said, scratching his beard. "I needed some time to think."

"Did . . . Isabelle tell you about . . . ?"

"Ma?" Jesse got to his feet and walked over to the washstand so his back was to her, but not before she saw a flash of pain in his eyes. "Yeah, she told

45

me. Seems I was a few days late and a few dollars short."

"I'm so sorry, Jesse."

He nodded. "It must have been hard on you, finding my mother like you did."

Andrea stared at his back. "I loved Martha very much. She was always like the mother I never had, even when Zach and I were just friends."

Jesse poured water into a glass from the china pitcher and handed it to her then, crossed the room and pushed aside the lace curtain to stare blindly out the window. "How long were you and Zach married?"

"Almost two years before he went off to war."

"Were you . . . happy?"

Zach's face rose up in her memory: his brown, smiling eyes . . . the way he used to laugh at her silly jokes and hold her at night when the dark made her afraid.

Had she been happy?

When she didn't answer right away, Jesse glanced back at her. "Were you?"

She met his gaze directly. "Yes, we were. What kind of a question is that?"

He shrugged. "You're right. It's none of my business."

"No, it's not. It hasn't been for a long time," she replied, controlling the urge to snap at him. He'd given up the right to ask about her happiness when he'd walked out of her life. Heart pounding, she stared at the darkening sky. The evening crickets filled the silence that stretched interminably between them.

"I left because I had to, Andi. You know that. You knew it then."

"I suppose I did," she lied. "It really doesn't matter anymore."

He massaged the palm of his right hand with his left thumb, searching for a safe topic. "Tell me, how did Zach wind up fighting in the war? Did he volunteer?"

"Conscription," she said flatly. "They took him last fall. He didn't have the three hundred dollars to hire a substitute like some men around here did. And because he wasn't technically the only son, he had no recourse." At Jesse's pained expression, she added, "Besides, I think . . . he wanted to fight. He felt as if he wasn't really doing his part here behind a plow. Although I doubt he would have left the farm if he hadn't been drafted."

Jesse snorted. "The Federals only got him with the old man kicking and screaming, I'd wager."

She smiled sadly. "Something like that. But you have to remember, Zach felt differently about this place than you did. He wasn't in a rush to leave it or me. Or even your parents."

"He was a bigger man than me."

"No," she said. "Just different."

He shrugged as if none of it mattered. "Either way, I think you should know . . . with my folks gone, I've decided to sell Willow Banks and head back to Montana."

Her pulse stalled in her chest. "You what?" Andrea pushed herself up on one elbow, and stared at him, incredulous.

"I said—"

"I heard you. I . . . I just don't believe it. Sell this place? Your parents' farm? Jesse, what are you thinking?"

"I've made up my mind," he said, slumping in the chair by the window again. The wooden legs scraped

47

against the floor with a sound she could only compare to fingernails on a slate. *Lose Willow Banks? The only real home she'd ever had in her life?*

"You know how I feel about this place, Andi," he went on as if her feelings on the subject didn't matter at all. "I've never made any secret about it."

"Hardly," she agreed, though her answer was barely audible. She couldn't hear him for the thudding in her ears.

"There's no reason for me to stay now, with Ma and Zach gone. God knows I didn't come back for the old man."

"God knows . . ."

"Hell," he pressed on, "I might as well slide a noose around my neck and kick the horse as stay chained to a plow the rest of my life."

Shaking herself out of her inertia, Andi turned to him. "My, what a colorful way you have with words, Jesse. But I'm afraid Willow Banks' future is not entirely up to you."

He narrowed a look at her. "Excuse me?"

"I mean," she said hotly, "Willow Banks is half mine now. And I, for one, have no intention of selling."

Jesse's startled expression said he hadn't even considered this possibility. "What?"

"Did you think Zach would leave his half of the farm to the state and not his wife?"

His jaw tightened. "I never intended to leave you out in the cold, Andi, if that's what's got you worried. We'll split whatever profit we make down the middle. You go your way, I'll go mine."

Andrea pushed herself up to a sitting position. "No."

"You're not telling me you expect to farm this place by yourself?"

"If I must."

Jesse let out a snort of laughter. "Pinch me if I missed something, but didn't you just have a baby?"

Her eyes flashed violet. "Well, what's that got to do with the price of beans?"

"Nothing . . . if you want those beans to rot in your fields. Geez, Andi." He turned his back on her and braced a palm against the window jamb.

"You could stay and help me," she suggested in a small voice.

"Hah! That'll be the—"

"Well, you could!"

He whirled on her and jabbed a thumb against his chest. "You mean, *I* could do it all. *I* could run the damn farm—plow, till, harvest . . . all the things that drove me out of here in the first place. And what will you be doing? Knitting booties by the fire?"

The baby, startled at his outburst, began to cry. Anger propelled Andrea halfway out of bed before she seriously regretted that action. With a sharp intake of breath, she stumbled and clutched the edge of the quilt. The pain shot up the center of her like a dagger and she let out her breath in a small, grunting gasp.

Jesse was beside her in the time it took to blink. His hands clamped around her arms, steadying her, keeping her shaky knees from sending her to the floor.

"Jesus, Andi. What do you think you're doing?"

She hissed out her inheld breath. "I didn't think—"

"You're doing a lot of that lately." He turned her in his arms, until she was nearly flush against him. Too close. For a long heartbeat, neither of them moved or even breathed. Indignation drew her eyes to his. She found his heated gaze riveted on her chest. The thin cotton fabric of her nightrail might

49

as well have been transparent for all it hid from his view.

That he'd seen pretty much all there was to see of her earlier was no consolation. In fact, the thought generated a blush that traveled from the tips of her toes to her hairline. A prickle of sweat bloomed on the palms of her hands.

"I'm fine," she insisted, trying to sound convincing.

His eyes came slowly back up to her face. "Yeah, sure."

"I—I am."

Heat flowed between them like a current of electricity at every point of contact; from the span of her fingers braced against his ironlike upper arms, to the tips of her breasts where they brushed against his chest. For a heartbeat, she thought he was going to try to kiss her.

Across the room, the baby cranked up, testing its lungs. The sound broke the moment and he edged her toward the mattress behind her knees. "Here, get back in bed," he said gruffly. Lowering her rear end to the bed, he lifted her knees under the sheets. "What do you think I'm here for anyway? My health?"

Whatever had just happened between them vanished in the space of a blink. She glared at him. "No one asked you to stay."

He slid a look at her. "As a matter of fact, you did. Twice in the space of a few hours."

She narrowed her eyes. "Oh. Well, maybe I did, but you can just forget what I said. I can manage on my own, now, thank you very much."

He sniffed and walked over to the drawer. "Sure you can."

"Well, I can. I mean . . . don't think I'm ungrateful for your help today. But if you're in such a goldanged hurry to leave, then go. Don't let me stop you.''

She heard him mutter something under his breath that sounded like ''damn stubborn females'' as he stomped over to her wailing son. Jesse stooped over the drawer, but hesitated, unsure how to get a handhold on such a miniature human being. He tried several angles then finally plunged his hands in and lifted the baby awkwardly. She couldn't help the smile that crept to her lips at the sight.

Incredibly, the baby stopped crying the minute Jesse's big hands cradled him. She watched the impact of that fact soften the anger on Jesse's bearded face. His eyes rose to meet hers with an expression close to bewilderment. The baby made soft cooing noises as his little fists opened and shut around thin air near Jesse's chest.

''I think he's hungry,'' he said, carrying him to her like precious cargo.

Andrea forgot the anger that had been between them only moments before and reached for the swaddled baby. Jesse settled him damply into her arms. ''Oooh,'' she said. ''I think he needs a change.''

That's where Jesse drew the line. He held his hands, palms up. ''Yeah, well, I won't stoop to changing wet . . . nappies,'' he told her with a scowl. ''You'll have to handle that.'' He reached over and tossed her a diaper from the washstand where Isabelle had stacked them. ''And I won't wash them either.''

''I don't recall asking you to,'' she replied without looking up.

Jesse frowned. He'd ceased to exist to Andi, who smiled raptly at her son, talking to him with low, insensible words that held no meaning except, Jesse supposed, to addlebrained women and their offspring.

51

"Well," he said, backing out of the room—he seemed to be making a lot of awkward exits lately—"we'll talk about that other thing . . . later."

"What other thing is that?" she asked absently, drawing a finger over her son's perfect little nose.

What other thing is—? He ground his teeth. "The farm, Andi. We'll talk about the farm later."

"Oh . . . uh-huh," she mumbled, but he wasn't sure if she'd even heard him.

Jesse shook his head in frustration. But he couldn't really blame her for being distracted. They made quite a picture there on the brass bed, Andi and her son, bathed in the last rosy rays of daylight, oblivious to everything but each other. An ache balled in the center of his chest and burned all the way up his throat. Zach had achieved something Jesse knew he'd never would. A child, a wife who loved him. Jesse's chest ached. But his brother hadn't even lived to see it.

"Hey—" Jesse said, bringing Andi's head up. Her smile faded. "What are you going to call him?" he asked.

She rubbed a finger over the silky cap of hair. "Zachary," she answered, returning her attention to the boy. "Zachary Evan Winslow, Jr."

"Oh." Jesse sighed, the memory of his brother's face leaping to his mind. A pang of regret shot through him. He could almost imagine the smile Zach would have smiled for his son. "That's . . . that's a real good name," he went on. "Zach would've liked that."

Andi glanced up at him, sending him a brief, tight smile then fixed her gaze once more on little Zachary.

He was a real heel for upsetting her, considering everything she'd just been through today. He hadn't meant to raise the issue of the farm, at least until tomorrow.

With a vow to let it rest until then, he left the pair cooing to each other on the bed while he made his way down the familiar stairway, his palms still tingling from the memory of Andi's child in his hands.

Andrea watched him go and dragged in a deep breath to try to calm her racing heart, thinking of the touch they'd shared only moments ago. She'd fight him every inch of the way if his intention was to remove her and her son from Willow Banks. He could go back to his damn Rocky Mountains and lose himself there for all she cared.

She smoothed a hand over her son's silky head, the gesture calming her more than anything else could. After a lifetime in shabby boarding houses and living one day to the next, never knowing where she'd be tomorrow, she was planted here, just like that corn Jesse hated so much.

She'd make a go of the farm, or die trying. She owed it to Zach Jr. and more than that, to the man who'd never raise his son on the Willow Banks land he'd loved.

The rope-springs on the old double bed in his parent's room squeaked with Jesse's weight as he flung himself off the horsehair-filled mattress and stumbled naked to the window in the moonlight. The lace curtains billowed in the damp night air. The rain had stopped, but the smell of it clung to the land. Jesse caught the filmy material in one hand and stared out into the darkness, trying to catch his breath.

A dream had awakened him and though he'd already forgotten the particulars, the feelings it invoked stayed with him still. He'd felt trapped, hemmed in by something, his feet mired in thick mud that held him relentlessly. Jesse checked the impulse to look at his fingernails to see if the mud he'd clawed in his dream was actually there.

Figuring out what that dream meant didn't take genius. His gaze went to the endless rows of corn in the distant fields, their wide leaves, glinting silver in the moonlight.

God, how he hated it.

The loathing went deeper than simple dislike, deeper even than a rational hatred. What he felt for the place was irrational perhaps, but in all the years he'd been gone, he'd never tried to make sense out of it. It was too painful to look at, or remember. Even now, he thought, pushing away from the window jamb, it was as if there was some invisible wall keeping him from gaining any kind of perspective on it.

Mahkwi, who lay curled at the foot of the bed, lifted her head in vague interest, then settled back with her nose nestled between her paws.

A sound upstairs, the small wailing of a child drew his eyes upward. A few seconds later came Andi's answering murmur. He'd put the drawer beside her bed so she wouldn't have to rise during the night. And he wouldn't have to face her in the dead of night in a setting more intimate than wise.

In his mind's eye, he pictured Andi, putting the child to her full breast—her long auburn hair drifting down across her shoulder. He imagined how she would look as her amethyst eyes rose up to meet his, soft with love for her child. Soft with love for—

For Zach, his brother.

With the back of one wrist, Jesse swiped at the sweat beading under his mustache. The urge to get outside—out where he could breathe—was suddenly great. He yanked on a pair of worn Levi's and threw a shirt on without bothering with the buttons. Barefoot, he headed down the narrow hallway and through the darkened parlor with Mahkwi on his heels.

But before he pulled open the front door, his reflection in the aged, speckled mirror in the hat tree near the door stopped him. Moonlight from the parlor window spilled across the looking glass.

The image that stared back at him made his mouth go slack and his eyes widen. Hesitantly, he brought his hand up to the rough, bearded jaw, then to his nearly shoulder length hair.

God Almighty. He looked like hell.

It had been a long time since he'd seen himself in anything but the reflection of a glassy lake or a store window. Until now, not even those glimpses had bothered him. The beard and wild sun-streaked hair made him look years older than his own twenty-five. Weathered by the sun and wind of Montana winters, his skin shone brown in the moonlight. Fine white squint lines etched the skin near his eyes and what he could see of his mouth.

His image lived up to the name his friends among the Pikuni tribe had given him, *Imoyinum*—"Looks Furry." Until this moment, he'd been perfectly content with that name and with himself. Perhaps it was only because he was seeing himself now as Andi must see him. More irritating, Jesse thought, turning from the mirror, was the unsettling realization that he gave a damn what she thought.

The door hinges complained loudly as he shoved it open and headed into the warm night air. The full moon shone down over the yard and the chest-high corn stalks threw eerie shadows across the overgrown grass.

Jesse prowled back and forth along the drunken-man fence that hemmed in the cornfields to the north, south and east of the yard. Mahkwi paced with him, stopping to sniff along the way, then bounding ahead to keep up with Jesse's thudding progress.

"Keep the farm," he muttered to the wolf. "Hellfire! What's she thinking?" Andi had grown up a town girl, in the little hamlet of Elkgrove three miles up the road, with a father who didn't know a plow from an auger. Jake Carson, a printer by trade, a drunk by choice, had barely been able to keep food on the table, much less teach her how to raise any food of her own.

"Hell. She can no more keep up a farm like this than I could crochet doilies!" He glared up at the yellow light spilling from the second story room. "She's in way over that pretty little head of hers," he said aloud.

Jesse snapped off a leaf from a corn stalk as he passed it and began to shred the tender frond, tossing the stringy pieces to the ground as he walked. His bare toes sank into the fragrant muddy ground.

Andi could live comfortably for a good time on the profits they made selling the land, he reasoned. The improvements alone should bring a tidy sum. She could buy herself a little place in town . . . raise her son. She would be happy there. She'd have people around her, unlike here. And she wouldn't have to get up at the crack of dawn to feed the chickens, plow vegetable gardens or . . . grow old before her time.

He could use the cash to open a trading post up in Last Chance Gulch up in the north country of the Montana Territory. He'd saved a little back, but not enough to set himself up the way he wanted. He'd long pictured a place like Seth Travers had down in Virginia City. A place to hang his hat for the long, frigid months out of the year. The rest of the time, he'd spend trapping and trading with the Blackfeet as he'd been doing for the past few years.

But farm again? Never. Not if the moon turned blue. Not if the Ohio River crawled over its banks and begged him to do it. He'd had enough of sod busting and stump-pulling to last him a lifetime. He'd had enough of schedules and chores and someone telling him he hadn't done it right. Never again would his hands get bloody over a harvest or blistered on the handle of a plow.

"No, dammit. She's not gonna make me stay here," he grumbled. Mahkwi woofed and perked up her ears.

Jesse glared down at the wolf. "So what the hell am I going to do with her? Throw her out of the house?" He shredded another section of the leaf in his hands with a long tearing motion.

She has every bit as much legal right to this place as I do, his conscience argued.

He stomped another few paces. "And I have every right to force her to sell." He stopped and stared at the fields. But could he do that? The answer was as plain as the full moon. He didn't need the farm or the money. He was plenty content with life in Montana. Why change things?

"I could say 'good luck, Andi,' and leave her to it," he suggested to the silent night air. The wolf skidded to a stop beside him and gave a yawning whine.

"I know, I know, she's Zach's widow . . . my sister-in-law . . . my responsibility. Who'll take care of her?"

Mahkwi padded up at him, tongue lolling pinkly out the side of her mouth in a doggie smile. Jesse scowled at her. "What are you grinning about?"

57

Mahkwi cocked her head with a wounded expression.

Jesse dropped his hand in the fur behind her ears. "Hell, what have you got to worry about? Leftover stew, a bone now and then, space to run in and you're happy. Me?" He glanced at the old plow parked under the eave of the barn roof, its blade rusting orange from exposure. *That's me after a few more years in this place,* he thought.

Isabelle's words came back to him. *Responsibility's either a curse or a blessing, Jesse. I reckon it's all in how you look at it.*

Well, this was one responsibility he'd never see as anything, but a curse. The sooner he figured a way out from under it, the sooner he'd be on his way back to Montana. And the sooner he'd forget Andi Mae Carson Winslow and the little boy with dark hair and eyes the color of the sky.

Chapter Four

A knocking sound ricochetted in his head. Jesse tried to ignore it, mashing his cheek stubbornly against the hard surface beneath his head. His outstretched hands curled around, not a pillow, but the edges of a . . . book?

He cracked open one eye and groaned to find himself half-sprawled across the kitchen table atop the farm's ledgers he'd spread out to study last night. By some miracle, he must have fallen asleep. If one could call the snatches of insensibility he'd managed sleep. Between his own restlessness and the baby's clockwork squalling, he deemed a good night's rest in Andi Carson Winslow's house impossible.

Groggy, he rubbed a hand over his eyes and sat up, wincing at the stiffness in his neck. Beside him, a kerosene lamp sputtered, nearly out of fuel. His head throbbed. Though he knew he hadn't drunk a blessed thing last night, he felt hungover. Mahkwi lay beside his chair, head on paws, following Jesse's slow movements with her eyes.

The wooden chair scraped across the floor as Jesse got up and stumbled to the sink. Giving the squeaky handle a few priming pumps, he caught the cool water in his hands and splashed it on his face. It was all he could do to stand there, hands braced against the sink, and let the water drip off his face.

The pounding came again, more insistently this time. He frowned, recognizing the sound at last. Who the hell could be knocking on the door in the middle of the night? He glanced at the soft light pouring in through the window. Morning, he corrected mentally. Hell.

He ran a towel over his face, then, pulling two hands through his long, sleep-tousled hair, walked to the door and yanked it open.

A tall, coffee-skinned, bespectacled woman stood opposite him across the threshold. Her gray-green eyes widened at the sight of him and she took an involuntary step backward. He glared at her.

"Mr. Winslow? My name is Mrs. Gaines," she announced in a voice rich as bourbon whiskey. Her gaze flicked, for the briefest of stunned moments, down the length of his unbuttoned shirt to the dry mud caked on his bare feet. Jesse pulled the edges of his shirt together and began to button it.

The morning cicadas strummed up a welcoming chorus behind her, adding to the thrumming between his ears. The air that brushed his tired face was cool and rain-fresh. In the distance he heard the retreating rattle of the wagon that had evidently dropped the negress on his doorstep.

Jesse stared blankly at her "Yeah?"

She stared back, her eyes nearly level with his own. "I'm Mrs. Gaines," she repeated more slowly, her brows dropping a fraction. "I was told you were expecting me."

He blinked. "You were? I mean . . . I was?" His gaze went from her straw hat set at a jaunty angle atop a pile of dark hair, to her starched white collar, flawless against the slender column of her neck. The horn-rimmed spectacles perched half-way down her nose made her gray-green eyes seem even larger as she peered at him.

She pushed the glasses farther up her nose with one finger. "You *are* Mr. Winslow? Mr. Jesse Winslow?"

"Winslow. Yeah, that's me."

"Perhaps there's been some kind of misunderstanding. Mrs. Rafferty said you might have need of my services. But if—"

Jesse straightened at the first thing she said that made any sense. "Mrs. Rafferty? You mean . . . Are you Etta?"

A relieved smile softened her pursed mouth. "Yes, I'm Etta Gaines."

By any standards, Jesse thought, Miss Etta Gaines would be considered a handsome woman, but she was not at all what he'd expected. Isabelle's term "hired-girl" had conjured up anything but the sophisticated thirty-five-year old woman of color who stood before him. No hint of a southern dialect softened her words. She was a northern, city-bred woman, and if he wasn't mistaken, educated, too. She stood waiting patiently for Jesse to swallow his surprise and invite her in.

"Of course Isabelle told me about you, I just . . . uh, forgive me, Miss Gaines." Jesse stepped aside so she could pass. "Please, come in."

With a curt nod, she crossed the threshold. She stopped dead at the sight of the wolf and clasped a hand to her throat.

"She's tame," Jesse assured her, "She won't hurt you."

Etta looked unconvinced. "Miss Isabelle warned me about it, but"—her gaze slid back to the wolf—"I wasn't prepared for how . . . how big it would be."

61

"Mahkwi's half dog, but she's got a wolf's speed and long legs. She has the disposition of a lamb, though . . . unless she's riled."

"Oh. I see. Well, it's not me you'll have to convince."

"You mean Andi? She loves animals. Always has."

Etta just smiled and turned to survey the mess around her. Her eaglelike gaze took in every detail of the kitchen and what she could see of the parlor. Her even expression gave away nothing, but the kitchen alone was enough to send any sane woman running, Jesse thought dolefully—dishes and pans scattered from end to end after his mad search for a pot to boil water in yesterday.

The stew pot had boiled over while he was upstairs last night arguing with Andi, and despite his valiant attempts to clean it up the smelly stuff was stuck like scorched fly paper to the black Clarion stove. And that didn't even cover the muddy footprints he'd left all over the kitchen floor after prowling outside half the night.

Unwrapping the small embroidered bag that dangled from her wrist, Etta looked for a clear spot on the table.

"A real mess, huh?" he asked, picking up the rain slicker he'd left draped over the wooden chair. "Housekeeping isn't my strong suit."

She quirked one side of her generous mouth with amusement. "I've seen worse. What nine young Raffertys can do to a clean room would make you shudder. No sir, I've seen worse than this," she said with a wink, pulling off her kidskin gloves. "At *least* by half."

Jesse caught her smile and returned it. "I'm glad to hear it. I'd hate to think I could wreak worse vengeance on housekeeping than nine small children."

Etta scooped up Jesse's dirty dishes off the table and carted them to the sink, then darted back with a wet rag—a whirlwind of efficiency. "Oh, they're not all small," she told him. "Why, Gus?—you might remember him—he's near sixteen. Joshua and Joe, the twins, are thirteen." Etta effortlessly hoisted a pile of cooking pans back into their proper places below the counter.

"Then," she went on, "there's Adeline, eleven and Cassie, nine." She counted backward on her fingers. "The rest, Levi, Noah, Gertie and little Ruthie— they're all under eight. But ages aside, twelve folks— including me—under one roof calls for organization," she said with an easy laugh. "That's what I'm there for, Mr. Winslow. Organization."

Jesse rocked back on his bare heels, not doubting her for a minute. Her voice was smooth and rich as old brandy and despite her primness, he could swear he caught a note of bawdiness underneath all that starch.

She pulled a piece of paper from her pocket, opened it and handed it to him. "Miss Isabelle isn't a slouch at organization either. She said you'd need some things in town. Supplies and such . . . for the baby. She wrote it all down for you . . ."

Jesse stared at the paper then tossed it on the table. He'd think about that later when the fog cleared out of his brain.

"How is Miss Andrea?" she asked, putting her shoulder to the water pump over the sink. The handle squeaked as the water splashed into the pot she'd placed underneath it.

"I . . . I haven't seen her yet this morning," he replied. "I uh, heard her last night, up with the baby."

Etta glanced at the dark smudges under his eyes and shook her head. "My, my. If she had the same

63

kinda night you did, I came in the nick of time." She settled the pot on the stove, then stoked the cook fire with fresh firewood. A few seconds later, the banked coals ignited the wood with a *whoosh*. "Don't you worry about a thing, Mr. Winslow. I'll take care of everything that needs doing." She stopped long enough to frown at him. "Looks like you could use some coffee."

"Actually—" he mumbled, but before he could finish, she reached for the coffee pot Jesse had left on the table, cleaned out the old grounds, and made a fresh pot. He was getting dizzy just watching her. He settled back in his chair, pressing the heels of his hands against his eyes. He decided to wait for a cup of the coffee she was brewing before he made another stab at conversation. But that plan failed when he heard Etta's gasp. "My, my . . . aren't you a sight for sore eyes?"

He looked up to see Andi standing at the foot of the stairs, looking pale and wan. Her pink calico wrapper clung to her long legs and outlined the fullness of her breasts in the morning light. The sight of her tripped his pulse. He shot to his feet. "What the hell are you doing down here, Andi?"

Andrea's throat tightened at the sight of Jesse, disheveled and bleary-eyed from apparent lack of sleep. He looked how she felt. She cinched the tie on her wrapper in irritation and glanced at his muddy bare feet. "I live here, in case you'd forgotten. I'm not an invalid, Jesse. I only had a baby." She turned to Etta and the two women met in a hug. "Etta, how can I thank you for coming?"

Etta waved a hand of dismissal. "Oh, now honey, there's nothing I like better than babies, you know that," she said patting Andrea on the back. "You feelin' all right?"

64

She nodded. "Just tired and . . . a little sore."

"Well, Lordy, I expect so!" Etta strong-armed her toward the table and forced her to sit down opposite Jesse. "Now you just stay there," Etta said. "I've got coffee brewing and oatmeal mash fixin' to cook on the stove. It'll be ready in no time. You look a little peaked."

Andrea's bare feet encountered soft, warm fur beneath the table and she jumped. "Good Lord, what's *that?*"

Mahkwi's head came up under the table with a thwack, and the animal struggled to get out from under it.

Andrea stared in disbelief at the animal whose shoulders nearly reached her hip. She backed up against the counter. The wolf's pink tongue lolled out the side of her mouth.

"A *wolf!* There's a wolf in my kitchen!"

"It's just Mahkwi, Andi," Jesse said. "She won't hurt anything—"

"Oh, no. Absolutely not. Not in my kitchen. Not in my house." Andrea pointed to the door. "There's a baby in this house, Jesse. I won't have a wild animal anywhere near him. Out!"

The wolf looked crestfallen and slunk toward the corner. Jesse sighed with resignation, walked to the door and held it open for Mahkwi. "Out, wolf."

Mahkwi padded out the door and disappeared into the yard, tail between her legs.

"And I want him tied up unless he's with you, Jesse. I can't risk having him—"

"Her," Jesse corrected.

"—*her* eating my hens or . . . or attacking my hogs or Lulabelle."

"Lulabelle?"

"My goat."

65

He gritted his teeth. The fact that Mahkwi was half dog would bear no weight with Andi. The size of the animal had her scared. Mahkwi had rarely been tethered in her life, except when they rode through towns, where Jesse didn't want people taking pot shots at her. She wouldn't take well to it now. He should have left her back in Montana, where she didn't have to worry about the constrictions of civilization. It was a piece of advice he might well have taken himself.

He sat down at the table beside her. "How's little Zachary?"

Andrea's fingers smoothed absently over the pages of the book that lay open on the table. "He's fine. He didn't—" She blinked.

It suddenly struck her what the ledgers were doing there. Yesterday's argument over the farm came back to her in a rush. "What's this doing out?"

He shrugged. "I was going over the farm accounts last night."

Andrea straightened in the chair. "Why?"

"I should think that would be obvious."

"All too obvious," she replied tightly.

Jesse got to his feet and paced to the baker's cabinet on the far side of the room. He braced a hand against the smooth oak finish. "I have a right to know where Willow Banks stands, Andi," he said, staring at the worn wood-grain dusted faintly with flour.

She slammed the book shut with a thud, bracing for another fight.

Etta stopped what she was doing and glanced at each of them warily. "I . . . uh, think now might be a good time for me to have a look at that little baby boy. I'll just . . . uh . . . go on ahead and . . ." She edged to the stairway with a finishing shrug and disappeared diplomatically up the stairs.

Jesse swiveled a hard look at Andi. "Why didn't you tell me the old man had gotten the farm into debt?"

"You're not staying. What difference would it make to tell you? Besides, it's not that bad."

A bark of laughter escaped him. "Not that bad? The price of a new tiller and a hundred additional acres of land?"

"He bought it before Zach was called up," she said, half in Tom Winslow's defense. "Before he got sick. The crop that's planted now will cover this year's payments easily. Another four or five years . . ."

He sent her a disbelieving look. "This crop may pay the loan, but what about the taxes and the seed for next year's crop?"

"The war has boosted the price of corn," she argued, feeling the dig of her fingernails against her palms. "The Union Army is clamoring for grain. Your mother said we could expect to get top dollar for this crop."

"Maybe so. But not enough to cover the debt. Certainly not if the deer make off with half the crop through the broken down fence around the south pasture. And that's saying nothing about the leaky barn that's soaking the rest of this years supply of hay."

She couldn't argue. Everything he said was true. Thomas Winslow had let the farm run down since the war had taken Zach and it had been all she and Martha could do to keep the crop going.

Turning back toward the window, he said, "The corn's only shoulder high, low for this late in the season. Why?"

"Your father was ill. It was late getting in. It almost didn't get planted at all. Isabelle sent Gus and the twins over to help. But your mother, Gus, and I planted most of it."

He straightened as if he'd butted up against a hot stove. *"What!"*

"Stop shouting."

"I'm not shouting, dammit!" The expletive rattled the walls. He paced over to the kitchen window, staring out at the corn. *"Pregnant?* You were plowing pregnant, for God's sake?"

She got to her feet, steadying herself with a hand on the smooth wood table. "I was perfectly healthy, Jesse. Just because I was pregnant, doesn't mean I was incapable of—"

He whirled on her. "You could have lost Zach's only child."

"My only child as well," she added in a tight voice. "Do you think I didn't consider that?" And angry heat crawled to her face. "I was careful. In fact, I did little plowing myself. I drilled and covered seed mostly. And as you can see, I didn't lose little Zach. But if I hadn't helped, we would certainly have lost the farm."

Jesse turned away and shook his head disgustedly. "How many acres are planted in corn?"

"Seventy."

"Wheat?"

She tightened her jaw. "Forty-five."

"What else?"

"We rotated a thirty acres of corn with alfalfa this year. Another fifty lay fallow."

He exhaled loudly. "Did you know you're months late with the payment to the bank?"

"I—" She started to lie, but decided against it. "Yes."

"Damn." The word was spit quietly and directed at the offending crop outside the window. Jesse grabbed his hat off the table, fitted it on his head, then stuffed a stray piece of paper lying there in his pocket.

"Where are you going?" she demanded getting up from the chair. The catch in her voice gave away her fear.

"To town."

She caught his arm as he brushed past her. "What for?"

Yanking the battered hat down over his brow, he frowned at her, but didn't answer. He grabbed up his mud-spattered boots sitting by the door, brushed his feet off and yanked the boots on over denim pants.

"It's not for sale," she warned, meeting his angry glare with one of her own, but the rapid rise and fall of her chest gave away her desperation.

He shouldered past her and yanked open the wooden door.

"I said it's not for sale! Damn you, Jesse—don't you do it!"

He swung around on the far side of the threshold, his face dark with some undefinable emotion. "I'm just going to town. Do I need your written permission for that, Mrs. Winslow?"

She scowled at him for a long moment, feeling lightheaded and frightened. Dizziness alone couldn't account for her overreaction, nor the fact that the next thing she did was slam the door in his face.

The buckboard's wheels jolted into the drying tracks of mud leading into Elkgrove. Jesse flicked the leather traces over the backs of the two chestnut-colored draft horses pulling the wagon.

"Gy'up, Polly . . . hy'up, Pete . . ." The pair responded like the well-trained team they were, edging to the right at the slight tug on the traces. They had, however, shied at the sight of Mahkwi, so Jesse had left the wolf tied up under the shade of the porch. Mahkwi's snout had been more than a little out of joint seeing Jesse ride off alone, but he figured the animal was safer at Willow Banks than tied to the wagon in a town full of wolf-hating farmers.

He took a deep calming breath and tugged at the buttoned cuffs of his sleeves. The five-mile ride to town had done little to calm the frustration in him. Every mile had put him closer to believing he was doing the right thing. The best thing for both of them. Andi was only one woman, and an irrational one at that.

Not that she couldn't be downright capable when she had her mind on something like giving birth to that baby he thought ruefully. But running a farm was another matter altogether. She had no idea the kind of backbreaking labor that went into a job like that. He did and that made him all the more anxious to do what he'd come here to do.

The ancient sycamores that shaded the streets of Elkgrove hadn't changed any more than the town, he mused as he passed Nate Kelder's Livery and Feed. That place had been there since Jesse was a boy. The corrals surrounding it were fragrant with clean, sun-warmed hay. The place had earned its well-deserved reputation as the best stable in Elkgrove.

Sprawled on a faded wooden bench at the open entrance of the barn, was an older-looking Nate Kelder, enjoying a cheroot beside three half-grown barn cats, preening in the morning sun. Jesse nodded to him as he passed and Nate nodded politely back, but from his frown, it was clear he had no idea who Jesse was. He felt the older man's curious stare on him as he made his way down the street.

Threading his way through the array of carriages and wagons crowding the noisy thoroughfare, Jesse passed a dozen more shops he'd been familiar with as a youth, still thriving despite the war that had cut the nation in two. He passed two Federal soldiers lounging in the early morning sun. The rich scent of coffee drifted to Jesse from the tin mugs they sipped on and he wished he'd had time for that cup Etta had offered before he'd stomped off to town.

The facades of E. A. Biddle's Mercantile and Dry Goods, and Stavely and Sons, Blacksmithing and Farriers were freshly painted and already busy for so early in the day. Jesse pulled the team over beside a half-dozen other wagons parked under a huge sycamore. He set the hand brake and jumped down to the street.

"Jesse—Jesse Winslow," came a voice from behind him. Jesse turned to find Deke Lodray, publisher, editor, and owner of the *Elkgrove Chronicle*, walking toward him. Lodray's smile expanded as he approached. "By God, I thought it was you. It's been a hell of a long time."

"Deke." Jesse smiled and shook his hand warmly. "It's good to see you. You haven't changed a bit."

Lodray laughed and ran an ink-stained hand over his thinning gray hair self-consciously. "I wouldn't go that far and I doubt the missus would agree with you," he added, patting a hand against his spreading waistline. "Good Lord, though, you have. Look at you—" His gaze went from Jesse's thick beard, then up and down his considerable height. "Some folks around here thought you were dead."

Jesse laughed in surprise as a wagon loaded with lumber rattled by. "Is that right?" He had never imagined himself rating the idle gossip of Elkgrove.

"Course, those of us who knew you never believed

the rumors." A grin cut across Lodray's handsome face. "Montana was good for you, son. You look like a damn voyager."

"I guess if I'd been born thirty years earlier that's just what I would have been," he admitted. "How's the paper? You still running it, or have you turned the reins over to Mitch?"

Lodray frowned, his gaze absently searching the crowded street. "Hell, no. I'm not ready to retire and even if I were, Mitch isn't ready for that kind of . . ." He stopped himself short of saying what he'd been about to say. "I'm not ready yet."

Jesse regarded Lodray for a moment. "Is Mitch still at Harvard?"

"No. He left the university to fight in the war, but he was wounded. They sent him home a few weeks ago." Lodray shifted uncomfortably.

"Was it bad?" Jesse asked with concern. He'd always thought Mitch Lodray a decent sort when they were in school together, except, Jesse amended, for his rather macabre habit of tearing the wings off butterflies as a boy.

Deke Lodray shook his head. "He took a minie ball in the foot, and by the Grace of God, the surgeons didn't cut his damn leg off. Hurt like hell, but it's nearly healed. The limp's hardly noticeable now. Mitch is still single, and starting back with me at the paper—advertisements, community news, that sort of thing." He slapped Jesse on the back. "And what of you, Jesse? How the hell have you been?"

"I've been well. Content." Jesse glanced at the familiar street and thought how different it was from this place. "Montana Territory is like a drug. It seeps into your blood. It's a beautiful place."

Deke nodded, picturing it in his mind's eye. "I was sorry to hear about your folks, Jesse. Both of 'em going in such a short time . . ." He shook his head. "And Zach . . ."

"Thanks." Jesse dug a toe into the rutted street. His emotions were too raw about all of it, so he changed the subject. "Say, did you find someone to replace Andi's pa after he died?"

"Sure, sure. But you know, even on one of his bad days, no one could set type as fast as Jake could. I miss the old guy. And how's Andrea doing? We don't see much of her since your ma passed on."

"She had her baby yesterday. A healthy son."

Deke smiled. "By God, tell her congratulations for me. Zach . . ." Deke's eyes flashed up to Jesse, full of irony and deep understanding, "well, Zach would have been proud as all hell and glad to know you were with her."

Of all the people in Elkgrove, Deke Lodray knew what had once been between him and Andi and what it must have cost him to leave her behind. And how it must have felt to learn that she'd married his brother.

"Give her my best, Jesse," Deke said, extending his hand once more. "You going to stick around Elkgrove for a while? Willow Banks is good land. Not as high up as Montana, but pretty all the same."

Jesse looked at the ground. "I haven't figured that out yet, sir." He lifted his gaze to the older man's clear blue eyes. Jesse knew what he was thinking. He was thinking it himself.

"I see," Lodray said, clapping him on his arm. "Well, don't be a stranger. Come in and see me sometime."

Jesse nodded and backed toward the elevated walkway. "I will. Give my best to Mitch and Mrs. Lodray."

The polished windows of Elkgrove Building and Loan glinted in the morning sun reflecting the green

73

trees and blue, blue sky. Gold leaf lettering proclaimed the bank's success. As he stepped up on the boarded sidewalk, Jesse ran a hand through his hair and took a deep breath reminding himself of his purpose. He tucked his shirttail into his denim pants, then walked through the double doors.

Chapter Five

"Mr. Bridges will be with you in a moment," said the portly fellow in spectacles who showed Jesse to a massive kneehole desk and seated him in a chair opposite.

Jesse tugged on the collar on his shirt, then flipped the top button loose. He glanced at the closed walnut humidor atop the desk, emblazoned with some fancy initials he couldn't make out upside down. The desk top was distractingly neat. Each stack of papers had a sharp edge to it, each pen perfectly lined up beside the green blotter centered on the desk.

Leaning forward, he braced his forearms on his thighs and stared at the polished wood grain floor. He felt a twinge of guilt, just a twinge, at being here at all. But the guilty flash lasted only a few seconds. He was doing the best thing for everyone concerned.

"Well, I'll be damned," came a voice from over his shoulder.

Jesse straightened to see a short fellow in banker's black skirting the corner of the desk.

"If it isn't Jesse Winslow, back from his adventure on the Great Divide." The man extended a hand to him from across the desk, causing his black frock coat to wrinkle at the shoulder. "I heard you were dead."

With a frown, Jesse got to his feet. "Apparently not," he said, then it struck him. Bridges, Ethan Bridges. Good God, the bandy-legged kid from school with a chip on his shoulder a mile wide had grown up to be a banker, for God's sake. Worse, *his* banker.

"Bridges." Jesse took the proffered hand and shook it briefly, taking in the man's thinning brown hair and the well-trimmed beard and mustache disguising a second chin starting beneath it.

Ethan Bridges settled regally behind his desk and folded his hands over the perfectly stacked paper there. His brown eyes rested appraisingly on Jesse.

"It's been a long time since we were dipping pigtails in ink wells, Winslow," he said with brotherly camaraderie.

"As I recall, ink wells were your particular forte," Jesse replied.

"Yes, perhaps they were. I was rather good at it, wasn't I? As I recall, there was only one girl who occupied your time. How is Andrea? I hear she's still living out at your folks' place."

"Fine," he answered laconically.

"I must say," Bridges continued, "you're looking . . . wild and wooly these days."

"And you're looking quite . . . planted," Jesse replied dryly, crossing one knee over the other.

Bridges chuckled. "Yes, I am quite planted, as you say. And quite successful." He gave Jesse's poor appearance a once-over and added, "What can I do for you today, Jesse?"

"I came about the farm. I understand there are outstanding loans that my father took out against the property?"

Bridges picked up a smooth black stone the size of a

quail's egg from his desk and rolled it absently in his hand. "Yes, your late father did procure a secured loan from this bank to purchase a harvester and some additional acreage . . . let's see . . . nearly two years ago. I believe he was quite certain the harvester would pay for itself in a few year's time what with the purchase of that new acreage. The increased demand for corn to supply the Union with food and forage made the risk a good one.

"But that was before that spate of bad luck that befell Willow Banks." The stone stilled in his hand for an instant. "Starting with your brother's untimely death."

"Yes. It was quite untimely," Jesse said, keeping any emotion from his voice.

"I liked Zach," Bridges went on with a shrug, smoothing a hand down his brocaded satin vest. "He paid his bills and was a good farmer, like your father." The dig was smoothly delivered. "Elkgrove has lost its share of good men in this War," he went on, drawing no reaction from Jesse. "My deepest sympathies on your losses, Winslow."

Jesse inclined his head slightly in reply.

Bridges cleared his throat and set the stone down precisely on the stack of papers to his right. "I spoke with Andrea—Mrs. Winslow—after your mother's services, about the disposition of the farm . . . and its debts . . ."

Jesse shifted in his leather upholstered chair.

"Apparently," Bridges went on with a disbelieving chuckle, "your brother's wife has some fool idea that she can keep Willow Banks going on her own. I told her she has as much chance of doing that as a block of ice would on Main Street in Jul—"

"I came to discuss selling the property," Jesse said flatly, cutting him off. He didn't like Ethan Bridges

77

any more than he had six years ago when he'd been a rooster of a boy who crowed louder than the rest just to prove he could. And despite what he thought about Andi's chances, hearing Ethan Bridges bad-mouth her made Jesse's hackles rise.

Bridges eyes widened. "I, uh, take that to mean you're not staying on?"

"That's right."

"I see. Well, Jesse, you must know that the War has affected land values and more than that, potential buyers. I'm afraid there isn't much of a market for your property right now, and damn few men around to run it if there were."

"Are you saying I can't sell it?"

The banker steepled his fingers under his chin and peered up at him through a sweep of lashes. "Lanny Hargrave's place went under three weeks ago. He'd been trying to sell it for months."

Jesse leaned deliberately toward the polished oak desk. "Lanny Hargrave has never grown anything but rocks in his south pasture and has a vertical slope of at least thirty degrees on half his acreage. Willow Banks land can hardly be put in the same class as that place."

Bridges shrugged in agreement. "True. In better times, your land would bring a prime price. But these are hard times. When the war ends . . . if it ever does . . . the price will climb again, God willing, and the Union prevails. . . . It could be years off the way things are going." He adjusted the heavily starched cravat at his throat with one hand. "Of course, if you are in a hurry to unload the land, I might be in a position to help you out personally."

Jesse didn't like the sound of that already. "How's that?"

"As I said, it's prime growing land. I'd be willing

78

to take it off your hands for a fair price."

"How fair?"

Bridges raised an eyebrow, ever so slightly. "Fifteen hundred dollars, hard cash."

Jesse surged to his feet nearly knocking his chair over. *"Fifteen hundred?* What is that, a *joke?* My farm's worth five times that. Hell, the crop in the ground alone is worth almost that much!"* Grinding his hands into fists, he glared at the banker, ignoring the stares he'd drawn from nearby customers.

Bridges chair squeaked as he leaned back with his hands folded across his stomach. "That crop's not worth squat if it rots in the fields." He let that sink in a moment before he went on. "And who will harvest it? You? You're leaving. Andrea? Last I saw her she was heavy with child. And not thinking with any more clarity than that sot of a father of hers ever did."

"Leave Andi and Jake out of this," Jesse warned with a dangerous look.

"As you wish." Bridges shrugged and shuffled one pile of papers atop another, straightening the edges. "Of course, you needn't accept my offer. That's certainly your choice." He withdrew a thick Havana cigar from the humidor on his desk and clipped off the end with a pair of silver clippers chained to his pocket. He offered Jesse his choice with a gesture of his hand. Jesse shook his head.

"Perhaps," Bridges said, "I misunderstood your desire to leave Willow Banks."

No, he hadn't misunderstood, dammit, thought Jesse, controlling the urge to shove Bridges offer and his cigar down his throat. He wanted out in the worst way, but to sell off Andi's land to this slimy land grabber . . .

Hell would grow daffodils before he'd let that happen.

"That brings us," Bridges went on, lighting his cigar, "back to our original problem. The late loan payment. I'm afraid we can't extend it until September. I was planning on riding out to her place to—"

"Why not?"

A halo of blue smoke curled incongruously around Bridges head. "Frankly," he answered, "your sister-in-law is a bad risk. And we'd just as soon cut our losses and move ahead."

"By stealing her land? You can't do that!"

"Stealing is a rather strong term, Jess. In point of fact, this bank owns a lien on the farm and she is in arrears."

"There must be dozens of farmers late with their payments because of the War. Why are you in such a hurry to close down on her?"

Bridges shrugged helplessly. "My hands are tied. If she had a man . . . potential for success . . . if she could even manage to pay off the outstanding payments—"

"One hundred and seventy-five dollars," Jesse snapped.

"Pardon me?"

"According to my books, that's the amount of the back payment, isn't it?" Jesse said. "One seventy-five?"

"Well . . . yes." The man sent him a smug grin.

Jesse pulled a drawstring antelope sack from the waistband of his belt and dropped it with a thud on the desk. "Measure it out."

Bridges stared at the bag for a moment before he picked it up, hefting the weight of it in his hand. He poured some of the gold dust out into his hand and looked back at Jesse with one eyebrow raised.

"Montana currency," Jesse told him without a hint of a smile. "There should be more than enough to cover it. Give me the rest in gold coin."

Bridges sifted the dust back into the bag and snapped the drawstring tight. "I would advise you to think carefully about throwing away your money on a losing venture."

Jesse stood, braced two hands flat on the precious, uncluttered surface of Ethan Bridges' desk and leaned over it. "Willow Banks is mine too, Bridges, in case you've forgotten. If it's going down, it won't be because I let it sink. And if I get wind of you plotting to strip my sister-in-law of her rightful land again, you'll have me to deal with. You understand? Now measure the damn gold."

Bridges rose slowly, finding himself a full head shorter than Jesse. But he gave a little knowing laugh, nonetheless, and blew out a cloud of cigar smoke in Jesse's face. "Welcome back to Elkgrove, Winslow."

Jesse watched the little bastard strut toward the scales at the back of the bank like he owned the whole damn place.

Welcome back to Elkgrove, Winslow.

Hell.

He stalked to the window, shoved his hands in his pockets and scowled out at the busy street. Crowded with women, children, and a smattering of men, some uniformed in blue, everything looked the same as it had when he'd ridden in, yet everything was different.

In his mind's eye, he pictured the wide open spaces of Montana, the freedom he'd had with only Mahkwi and his appaloosa for company. He pictured Andi, her violet eyes lonely, yet determined—expecting things from him she had no business expecting. Sharing things of which he wanted no part.

Bridges' words came back to him. *If she had a man,*

81

potential for success . . . Jesse straightened, suddenly understanding what he had to do. Only after he had accomplished it could he leave her with a clear conscience.

He had to find Andi Mae Winslow a husband.

Stepping out of the shadows beneath the portico the *Elkgrove Chronicle* shared with the Building and Loan, Mitch Lodray narrowed his eyes and watched Zach Winslow's long lost brother storm past him and climb into a buckboard parked nearby. With a silent curse, he leaned on his cane, dashed his smoke to the ground, and crushed the glowing tip to dust under the toe of his boot, ignoring the sharp pain that traveled up his foot with the pressure. Mitch had assumed, like half the town, that Jesse Winslow was dead.

Too bad the rumors proved false.

It didn't matter. He'd have what he wanted sooner or later, Jesse or no Jesse.

Brushing at the sleeves of his brown wool frock coat and snapping the white cuffs of his shirt tight, Mitch Lodray glanced at his reflection in the window of Elkgrove Savings and Loan. While he covertly watched Jesse unwrap the reins and give them an angry snap, Mitch smoothed his dark blond hair with one hand, admiring the cut Zip Timmons had given him this morning. He flashed an experimental grin to his reflection, testing and finding it lacking in conviction. Mitch turned around in time to see Ethan Bridges saunter out of the bank.

"If that don't beat all, huh?" Bridges muttered to him. "Jesse Winslow back in Elkgrove."

Mitch struck a sulphur-tipped match against the bank wall and lit another cigarette. "I thought he was dead."

The banker grinned.

"What did he want?"

"Out." Ethan said, turning a half-smile on Mitch. "Always was a frigging coward."

Mitch shot a look at Ethan, then back at Jesse's disappearing form.

"Probably doesn't want his brother's leavings," Ethan commented. "Though, he could do a hell of a lot worse than Andrea Winslow, I'll tell you . . . as long as she isn't thinking." He tossed a know-what-I-mean? look at Mitch.

Mitch took a deep drag on his cigarette. "Did he sell the place to you?"

"Not yet. But he'll come around. He can't take the farming. He'll give up on it the same way he did before."

Mitch pushed away from the bank wall as Bridges returned to the bank. He tipped his hat courteously to two women passing by them. The ladies fluttered their silk fans in the midmorning heat like a pair of flustered peahens.

"Morning ladies," he said with his most charming smile, leaning heavily on his cane for the best effect.

"How fares your poor injured foot, Captain Lodray?" asked the one with blond ringlets framing her face, a blush creeping up her plump cheeks.

"Much better, thank you, Miss Micheals," Mitch answered, flexing the appendage testingly. "Almost like new."

"I'm relieved to hear it," she replied. "My prayers have been with you." Mitch's smile grew broader. "A-and with all our local heroes to the Cause, of course."

"Of course. I'm honored to be included in your thoughts, Miss Micheals." He touched the brim of his hat.

The woman's eyes flashed briefly, adoringly, up at Mitch before the other one pulled her along down the sidewalk. Mitch's eyes followed, but his thoughts immediately dismissed Camy Sue Micheals. They settled instead beyond her on the man whose wagon was disappearing at the edge of town—and on the image of Andrea Carson Winslow's violet eyes staring up at him with something more than the adoration in Camy Sue's.

Something much more interesting.

"Mitch?" His mother's voice came from the nearby doorway. "Mitch, are you smoking those vile cigarettes again? I've been looking everywhere for you, dear."

Mitch clenched his jaw and flicked his cigarette into the street. "Coming, Mother."

"Are you hungry, girl?"

Andrea sat on the top step of the porch with a warm, cornmeal hush puppy in the flattened palm of her hand, three feet from Jesse's wolf-dog. "Come on. Take it."

Mahkwi eyed the tidbit with disinterest, her head tucked disconsolately between her huge paws.

"Just because I don't want you in my house doesn't mean I'm going to hurt you."

One silver eyebrow went up as Andrea lowered her hand to ground level, but her golden eyes slid away disconsolately. Her nose was out of joint at Jesse's departure without her this morning. Andrea had firsthand knowledge of what it felt like to be left behind by Jesse Winslow.

"He'll be back," she told the animal. "For you . . . At least he'd better be. I don't know what I'd do with a wolf."

Andrea glanced at the dirt road that led to their farm, wondering how long Jesse would stay away. Their parting had been anything but amicable this morning. He'd been angry, but so had she. Perhaps he'd been right. Perhaps she should have told him about the harvester and the late payment to the bank. Willow Banks was his too, after all. But the last thing she needed was Jesse thinking she was trying to make him feel responsible for her.

If Jesse had never come back, she would have had to solve this problem on her own. Being a woman didn't make her incapable of doing it. She'd figure some way out of her situation and save Willow Banks at the same time. She'd considered selling off the new acreage to the Raffertys. It butted up against their property. But that would mean losing the alfalfa crop planted there too, and she needed that to feed the stock for the winter.

With a sigh, she tossed the hush puppy down beside the wolf. The animal sniffed at it then proceeded to ignore it completely.

With the sun noon high, the air rippled above the yard in waves of heat. Andrea brushed the crumbs from her hands and lifted her freshly washed hair off the back of her neck. Moisture trickled down between her breasts, and she dabbed at her throat with a lace hanky she pulled from the pocket of her pale pink wrapper.

"My, my, that's one down-in-the-mouth wolf." Etta's deep voice came from behind Andrea and she turned to see her coming through the half-open Dutch door, holding little Zach against her shoulder. The sleeves of her white muslin blouse were rolled up to her elbows. Her coffee-colored skin contrasted sharply with the whiteness of the baby's complexion.

Andrea looked back at the sulking wolf. "She

won't touch it. I don't think she wants to be friendly."

"Won't even be tempted by one of my hush puppies, huh? Now that's serious."

"I think she's upset that Jesse left her here while he went into town. She's pretty though isn't she?"

Etta sniffed. "For a wolf. Lord knows why a man would take up with a wolf for company. Exceptin' if he didn't like the human kind . . . of company, that is."

"Etta, you've just defined Jesse Winslow to a tee." Andrea stood carefully, stretching the soreness in her limbs.

The other woman shook her head. "You should be in bed, resting, child. Not gallivanting around trying to feed that ornery man's equally peevish wolf."

She laughed despite herself. "No, it feels better to be up and moving. I just get stiff lying in bed. And I've slept enough in the last twenty-four hours to hold me for a week. Besides," she said, scanning the overgrown yard and the vegetable patch near the cornfield, "there is so much to do."

"Miss Andrea . . . that's what *I'm* here for. There's nothing to do that hasn't been done. For today anyway. The chickens are fed, eggs collected. Lulabelle is milked and those *nasty* hogs slopped." She made a comical face. "Little Zachary's napkins are clean and drying in the sun." Inhaling deeply, she added, "Dinner's simmering on the stove. All that's left for you is to feed this youngun. Now sit yourself down on that porch swing and—"

Andrea looked at her in shock. *"Here?"*

"Why not? Who's to see? We're two miles from anybody, and the fresh air and sunshine will do you both good." She handled the bundle over to Andrea.

The baby cooed up at her and she shrugged. "I

guess you're right. Why not? If I have to sit in that room another minute . . . Thanks, Etta."

Etta settled on the swing beside her while Andrea put the baby to her breast. "Stings a little, hm-mm?" she asked, hearing Andrea's indrawn breath.

"M-hmm, a little."

"It'll pass. It always does."

"You talk as though you've been through it, Etta. Do you have children?"

Etta's expression grew guarded. "I . . . I did have a son. Linus." She wound her fingers together. "He died four years ago. He was twelve."

"I'm so sorry, Etta. I . . . I didn't mean to—"

"It's all right. It was a long time ago. I find I can talk about Linus now without bursting into tears."

"It's odd," Andrea said, "but I didn't even know you were married."

"Was. Marcus is gone, too." She sat up straighter in the swing, until her back didn't touch the wood, as if contact with it would betray her weakness. "He was killed last July with the Fifty-Forth Colored Infantry near Charleston. He was a corporal. A good one, too." She smiled and gave a small laugh. "Or so his letters said."

"Wasn't that a Massachusetts regiment?"

She nodded. "When we heard they were forming a colored infantry, nothing I could say would stop him from joining up. Took a train all the way to Boston . . ." She swallowed hard and stared out at the cornfield.

"Marcus was second generation free like me, and school-educated, too. He could quote Shakespeare, Byron, or Homer to his students." she added with a proud smile.

"He was a teacher?"

She nodded. "We both were. But it wasn't enough

for Marcus. He felt strongly about emancipation and for colored men getting the chance to fight in this war beside whites. Said it was his duty to go.

"Besides, after Linus died, we . . . we'd sort of grown apart. He with his grief . . . me with mine." She looked down at her hands and rubbed some flour off her palm. "So afterward, when I got word about Marcus, I came to work for Miss Isabelle. It's been a comfort in a way . . . all those children keep my mind off myself. You know?"

Andrea smiled at her. "Yes, I do. Isabelle's told me she doesn't know how she ever managed without you. In fact, she's probably regretting the fact that you're sitting here with me and not there reining in that herd of hers."

Etta grinned and sniffed. "It'll do 'em good to miss me some." The woman looked at her palms, so much paler than the rest of her skin. "What about you, honey?" she asked. "It must be hard being all on your own, here. I imagine you must be happy to have Mr. Winslow here for company."

Andrea almost laughed. Happy? She would hardly go that far. "I don't think he's going to stay."

Etta raised an eyebrow. "He doesn't strike me as the sort of man who looks for rocks to slither under."

"I don't know what sort of man he is, Etta. It's been a long time. A lot of weeds have grown under our wheels since we saw each other last. If he did stay, I suppose we'd be the talk of the county, living under the same roof as we are."

"Honey, in these times, who'd fault a woman for wanting a man under her roof for protection? You know those raiders have been striking nearby. Three places in the last month, down close to the Ohio."

"Do they think it's John Morgan's Raiders again?"

"Or some of his men, sure as I'm standing here. You got a gun in the house?"

Andrea nodded, remembering of how she'd pointed that gun at Jesse when he'd surprised her.

Etta patted Andrea's thigh. "Well, you keep it loaded, you hear? And keep it beside your bed. You never know when you'll need it. I'm going to go in and straighten up before I go. You all right here?"

"I'm fine, Etta. Thanks."

The black woman winked at her and went back into the house, leaving the swing moving gently. Andrea gazed down at little Zach, rubbed a thumb over the gentle curve of his forehead, and forced dark thoughts away. She wouldn't let Jesse interfere with the joy she felt holding her newborn son. As he suckled there, she looked up to find Jesse's wolf-dog lying at full attention, ears perked forward, straining to get a look at the squirming infant in her arms.

At first the look frightened Andrea and she tightened her hold on the child. But Andrea realized it was curiosity, not malice, in the animal's eyes.

"Well," Andrea said, "not so aloof after all, are we? You'll have to stop taking lessons from Jesse if you want to be friends with me, wolf. Frankly, I don't see much hope for your master."

Chapter Six

The startling sound of someone or something crashing through the chest-high rows of Winslow corn along the road back home forced Jesse to haul back on the reins of Polly and Pete as they balked in fright.

"Whoa!" Jesse shouted and gathered the traces tight in his hands. The mare gave a shrill whinny and tossed her head. "What the hell—?" he swore fighting with the traces, imagining the whole wagonload of supplies crashing to the ground.

Before he could finish the thought, a huge black man burst onto the road from the cornfield to Jesse's right. At the unexpected sight of Jesse and his wagon, the man stumbled to a stop.

For a full five seconds, he gaped at Jesse, his black eyes wide and desperate as a rabbit caught between two foxes. His glistening chest heaved with exertion and his sweat-drenched union suit hung damply beneath a worn pair of overalls attached at only one shoulder by a knot.

The unspoken plea in his eyes robbed Jesse of speech. He had no idea what the man wanted or who he was, or what he was doing running on bloody, bare feet through the cornfield.

Before Jesse could recover enough to ask, the man tossed a terrified look back in the direction from which he'd come, and bolted again, plunging over the drunken man fence and into the opposite field.

"Hey!" Jesse called. Too late. The man disappeared into the thick hedge of green stalks. Only the rustling tips of corn betrayed his movement—directly toward Willow Banks and Andi.

Hell.

Shading his eyes against the midafternoon sun, Jesse frowned. What was that all about? Was the man a runaway? But slavery had been abolished a year ago, hadn't he heard that? So why was the man running as if the devil was chasing him?

Jesse looked up at the sound of horses. Two men mounted atop a pair of sorry-looking geldings stirred up a cloud of dust behind them as they bore down on Jesse and his wagon. He straightened, suddenly sure he was about to get answers to all his questions.

He glanced briefly at the corn, but could see no movement. Either the man had escaped or stopped dead at the sound of the men.

"Howdy, mister—" shouted the dirtiest looking one of the pair as he hauled back on the reins of his chestnut bay. He touched the brim of his filthy hat with his stained fingertips, then grabbed hold of the reins of his prancing horse with both hands. His nose looked as if it had been smashed with a board and lay peculiarly sideways on his face and his eyes were all but hidden by his hat.

"Ya'll seen a niggah runnin' 'round here? 'Bout yea tall''—he sliced a hand through the air at his waist—"an' dirty as a rag pickah?"

If Jesse had been forced to hazard a guess, that's the occupation he would have chosen for these two.

The other man pulled up beside him, out of breath. His hairy belly peeked out between the buttons of his overly tight union suit which spilled over his belt. A nasty-looking Arkansas Toothpick lay strapped along one thigh, its steel hilt glinting in the midday sun.

"He cain't be far, Lamar," the second man said, menace thick in his voice. "He's gotta be 'round heah somewheres. Dammit! Bastard's slicker'n owl shit on a glass doorknob."

Smash Nose wound up and hawked a stream of brown juice that hit the road with a splat. He narrowed a look at his partner before turning back to Jesse. "Well, mistah?"

Jesse tightened his hands on the reins. The pair looked as mean as two rattlers with their tails tied together. And no matter what the circumstance, he wouldn't relish the thought of any man being turned over to these two thugs. It wasn't unusual, this far south in Ohio, to hear their Appalachian drawl. But at this juncture in the War it surprised him.

"You say this fellow's a colored?" Jesse asked at last, rubbing a hand thoughtfully over his beard.

"Black as tar," the first replied. "Dangerous as old Satan himself. This niggah'd jus' as soon slit your throat as look at ya."

Peripherally, Jesse saw the corn move ever so slightly thirty feet away. He kept his eyes on Smash Nose's face. "Really?" he asked. "What'd he do?"

Smash Nose sent his partner a nervous look. "Well, he done kilt a white man, that's what."

Jesse whistled. "Where did that happen?"

They both answered at once:

"Nashville."

"Memphis."

The two men glared at each other then Smash Nose

snorted. "My brother cain't remember his own name half the time. It were *Nashville*," he repeated. "We been chasin' that buck for nigh on to six days."

Jesse shrugged casually. "It's no skin off my nose where it happened. Elkgrove is a good clean place. We don't want any murdering negroes around here. I think I saw your man. He was about a mile up the road, that way"—he pointed behind him—"headed north through the woods." Smash Nose's gaze narrowed in that direction.

"He tore off the road when he saw me coming," Jesse continued, "but I got a good look at him. Dirty union suit, overalls . . . that sound like him?"

A slow grin spread over Smashed Nose's face. "Yeah. Much obliged. We're just doin' our job, like y'self." He dragged his hat off his thinning brown hair and tipped it in a farce of a bow. "I thank ya . . . your neighbors thank ya."

Jesse touched the brim of his hat in reply and watched the pair whip their lathered horses into a gallop in the direction he'd sent them. He watched until they disappeared over a hill, then clucked to his team with a flick of the traces.

He hadn't gone forty feet before the man who'd disappeared into the corn materialized again on the road just ahead of him. Jesse pulled the team to a stop and eyed him warily. He was still breathing hard, but the fear Jesse had seen in his eyes only minutes ago had been replaced by suspicion.

"Why you send 'em off?" the man asked sharply. "They'd'a catched me soon enuf."

"I know." Jesse fingered the reins thoughtfully, staring at the blood encrusting the man's feet. "Did you do what they say you did?"

His jaw tightened perceptibly under the glaring sun. "No, suh. I didn't do nothin' to no white man.

93

I's a free man. I ain't got no cause to kill nobody.
They lied.''

Jesse believed him, though he couldn't say why.
Perhaps it was only because he didn't believe those
other two. He trusted his instincts enough to take a
chance on the negro. Jesse tipped the brim of his hat
back with one finger. "What's your name?"

The man hesitated just a fraction before answering. Sweat glistened on the wiry black stubble on his
face and he ran the back of his arm across it.
"Silas . . . suh. Silas Mayfield."

Jesse tipped his head toward the back of his wagon.
"Well, Silas Mayfield, I'll give you a lift if you're
going my way. You can ride in the back of the wagon.
Under the tarp might not be a bad idea," he added
pointedly.

Silas lifted his chin to the morning breeze. Pride
and desperation warred in his eyes. Glancing first in
the direction the two men had gone, his dark eyes
came back to Jesse. "Where you be goin', suh?"

With a twist of a smile, Jesse sighed. "Home. I'm
going home.''

Standing on the porch, Andrea shaded her eyes at
the sound of the wagon rumbling down the road
toward the house and searched the sea of green for a
glimpse of him. Only seconds passed before she
caught sight of him atop the benched seat of the
buckboard. A frisson of heat burned through her
that had nothing to do with the July temperature.

Head bent to the glaring afternoon sun, he rode
with elbows braced against his knees, reins held
loosely in his hands. The team was coming at a full
trot, too fast for the road conditions, she thought,
with all that mud. But the speed didn't seem to bother

94

Jesse. His knees absorbed the jolting of the wagon and he seemed too preoccupied to notice.

As he turned off the mill road, he gave the reins a little slap and her eyes unwillingly followed the strain of fabric against his upper chest and arms. He straightened then, gazing at the corn with the look a condemned man might give a gallows.

She rested a hand over the burning sensation in the pit of her stomach. She dreaded the confrontation she knew was coming, but she wouldn't back down, no matter what he said. She'd fight him if that's what he wanted. Just let him start, she thought. Just let him.

Jesse glanced up at her as he pulled the wagon to a stop in front of the house. The earthy scent of the damp ground churned by the wagon's wheels stung her nostrils. His easy, unexpected smile stung her heart.

The hand brake squeaked as he set it. Tying the traces around the handle, he jumped down. The artless grace of his movements made him all the more appealing, she thought, chewing on her lower lip. Appealing and dangerous. He glanced up at her, letting his eyes drift down the length of her calico wrapper.

"You waitin' for me, Andi Mae?"

She flinched at his cocky use of that pet name.

"Perhaps I was. Perhaps I'm waiting to see if you have a bill of sale for the farm stashed in your pocket."

A slow grin spread across his face. "You look pretty as a picture standing there all in pink." He missed her furious glare as he knelt down, roughed the wolf around her head and neck with an affectionate rub, and slipped the rope from her neck.

The wolf gazed at him with adoration and licked him in the face. Andrea shook her head at the transformation in the animal. Well, she sniffed, at least Jesse Winslow's charm was operating on one female here.

Jesse looked back up at Andrea. "Where's the baby?"

She threaded her arms across her chest. "Sleeping inside."

He moved to the back of the wagon. "Anybody else been by today? Any strangers?"

"No. Why?"

"Just wondering."

He threw back the tarp. Andrea's mouth fell open at the sight of a large black hand gripping the wood siding of the buckboard from the inside. A man sat up in the wagonbed. He was big, even bigger than Jesse, with bulging muscles straining his dirty union suit at arms and shoulders. His hair was cropped short with threads of silver stitching through it.

He looked as though he hadn't bathed in weeks. His denim overalls were near tatters. Despite all that, his dark eyes met hers almost sheepishly. Andrea dragged her gaze away and shot a questioning look at Jesse.

"You can get out now, Silas," he said, ignoring her and offering the man his hand. "This is it."

Silas looked around him, then at Jesse's hand for a heartbeat before accepting his help. He drew in a hissing breath as he slid to the ground. Andrea's eyes fell to his bare feet. An involuntary gasp escaped her.

"Mercy!"

"Mrs. Winslow," Jesse said, "this is Silas Mayfield." The negro nodded stiffly at her. "I believe," Jesse continued, "his feet could use some attention, and his empty stomach, too, if I don't miss my guess."

Silas waved a dismissing hand. "Naw, that ain't

goin' to be nes'sary. I be gittin' on down the road. I done troubled you 'nough, now." He limped backward a few steps. "I thank you kindly for what you done, suh."

"How far do you think you'll get on those feet?" Jesse asked.

"I be fine."

"For a mile, maybe two," Jesse allowed. "Just long enough for those two to catch up with you."

"Which two?" Andrea asked.

"I didn't catch their names," Jesse answered. "Did you, Silas?"

Etta came through the door at that moment, and paused mid-step with her hand still on the green painted wood. Her spectacled gaze traveled the length of Silas' considerable body and ending on his feet. "Lordy . . ."

"Silas," Jesse said, "this is Miss Etta Gaines. Etta, I'd like you to meet Silas Mayfield."

Etta gulped. So did Silas, but his distant eyes had suddenly taken on a sharper focus. "How do, ma'am."

"Mr. Mayfield." Etta's lips pursed.

"No—it . . . it be jus' Silas, ma'am," he corrected, his gaze scanning her face. "Tha'z all. Jus' plain Silas."

Etta gave him a curt nod, then cupped her flustered hands together and turned to Jesse. "I, uh . . . heard your wagon pull in. Dinner's ready if you're hungry."

"Smells mighty good," Jesse replied, inhaling an exaggerated whiff. "What do you say, Silas? I have it on good authority that Miss Etta is one of the best cooks in Adams County."

Silas' hand spread across his stomach. "Well, I . . . I reckon I is a mite hungry."

"Good. But dinner will have to wait," Jesse said,

"at least until we can get Silas' feet cleaned up and wrapped. Etta?"

She shot an almost frightened look at him, knowing what he was asking, but hid it just as quickly. "Of course. Mr. Mayfield?" Without waiting for his reply, she turned on her heel and disappeared into the kitchen.

With a final glance back at Jesse, Silas followed her, limping up the stairs. "Silas," he mumbled half to himself. "Jus' Silas."

When he'd gone, Andrea turned to Jesse, who was wrapping his arms around a crate full of supplies at the back of the wagon. "Who is he?"

He shrugged. "Dunno. That bother you?"

"I—well, maybe. I just . . . it's obvious he's in some sort of trouble."

"Yes, ma'am," he answered with a grunt, hefting the heavy crate in his arms. "But I don't think it's of his own making."

"What makes you so sure? If someone's after him, he could be dangerous."

"Just a hunch."

"A *hunch?* You brought him here to my home on a hunch?"

His cool blue eyes met hers. "It just so happened he needed a place to go and I had one." He started up the three porch steps with the crate.

"Does that mean you haven't sold the farm?"

He didn't turn. "If I'd sold the farm, you wouldn't be needing these supplies, would you?"

"Jesse—"

The word stopped him. He turned toward her slowly, sweat glistening on the sinewy muscles of his forearms. "You think I'd sell it out from under you, Andi?"

"Isn't that why you went to see Ethan Bridges?"

He watched her silently for a moment then smiled at her perceptiveness. "Who said I did?"

"Well, didn't you?"

"Yeah," he answered, setting the wooden box down by the front door. "And I didn't like him any more today than I did six years ago."

She ignored the bead of sweat rolling down between her breasts. "And?"

"And . . ." he said, staring past her, out at the fields, "I've decided not to leave . . . yet."

Relief almost made her dizzy. "I'm not asking you to stay, Jesse. Let's be clear about this."

Pulling a blue bandanna from his pocket, he wiped it across the back of his hot neck. "Are you asking me to go, Andi Mae?"

"No. I—I mean, it's your home too. If you want to stay, I have no say in it."

He came down the steps in that loose-limbed walk of his. "Good."

"How long?" She regretted the question before it was out.

His sweaty arm brushed hers as he stopped beside her. His skin was hot and the male scent of him was strong, but not unpleasant. In fact, it was downright unsettling. She held herself away from his touch, but didn't back down from the challenge in his eyes.

"Til harvest time," he replied, "Or sooner if things work out."

She braced her fists on her hips. "What things?"

"Nothing," he answered with a slight grin. "Forget it."

Frowning, she watched him climb up into the seat of the wagon. He gathered up the traces and gave them a flick. The team lumbered forward toward the barn while Andrea stood on the step, wondering what in the world he meant.

Chapter Seven

Silas swayed as he lowered himself into the rye split chair, his face suddenly a pasty color. The woven rusks creaked with his weight.

"You aren't going to faint, are you Mr. Mayfield?" Etta asked, not certain she could catch him if he did.

"No ma'am. But it shore do feel good to sit." He wiped a tattered sleeve across his sweaty face.

"You a runaway?" Etta asked directly, setting the wash basin down beside his feet. She winced inwardly at the sight of them.

"No, ma'am. I ain't no runaway. I is a free man. You a slave?"

Her head came up with a snap. "A slave! I should say not." Indignantly, she lifted one of his feet into the tepid water. He sucked in a hissing breath. "This is gonna hurt some," she said belatedly.

"Don't hurt much," he mumbled, but his dark knuckles whitened around the edge of the chair.

She sniffed. "And hogs fly south for the winter."

One side of his mouth quirked up. "Yass'm. Sometime they does."

"Do," she corrected automatically.

"Ma'am?"

She splashed the water against his swollen, bloody ankle. "Sometimes they *do*."

"Yes'm. That's what I said."

She looked up to find him smiling at her, his teeth white and straight, his black eyes amused. She felt her cheeks flush and she dropped her eyes to her task, realizing he was laughing at her.

"Dinner shore do smell fine," he said, glancing around the cozy kitchen. "You cook them vittles, ma'am?"

"Yes, I did. From the looks of you, you've been without food as long as you have without shoes, Mr. Mayfield." She slid the bar of soap over his torn-up feet and tried to keep her touch impersonal. It had been a long time since she'd touched a man so intimately.

"My friends . . . they call me Silas."

"We're not friends, Mr. Mayfield. We don't even know each other."

"Yet," he amended with a grin.

She picked up his other foot and dunked it in the water without much gentleness, ignoring his sharp inhalation of breath.

"Whoo-ee, you got's strong hands for such a prissy woman," he gritted out, digging his fingers into his muscular thighs.

She could hear the smile in his voice and didn't bother to look up again. "You don't know me well enough to call me names, Mr. Mayfield. Especially when I've got a hold of these mangled feet of yours."

He laughed then, a booming, easy sound that came from deep inside him. "Yass'm. You sho'nuff gots a point there." He was quiet a minute while she explored the extent of his cuts and abrasions. When she looked up his eyes were squeezed shut.

"You shouldn't be walking on these feet for at least a week," she pronounced at last.

"They's lots a' things I shouldn't be doin'. Don't us'ly stop me." His dark gaze drifted over her hair and face. "You got you a husband, Miss Etta?"

"Gaines," she corrected calmly, "and I hardly think that's any of your—"

"Cause if'n you do, he be one lucky man."

His words hung suspended in the air between them. There was no trace of teasing humor in his voice now. Too pragmatic to allow herself even a moment of self-pity, she shook the water from her hands.

"My husband's dead," she said, getting to her feet and walking over to the dry sink. "And well past feeling anything, especially lucky."

She heard him lift his feet out of the water and begin to dry them on the small towel she'd left there. "How long?"

"How long what?" she asked without turning around. Cranking the pump handle, she rinsed her hands and reached for another towel.

"How long he be dead?" he asked.

"One year . . . next week."

"That's a long time for a woman purty as you t' be without a man."

She whirled toward him ready to give him what-for. But he was watching her with patient, even kind eyes, eyes that belied the brutish strength of his body. She'd never been attracted to that kind of strength. And she certainly wasn't now. Marcus had been a small man, slender of build and gentle of face, who along with being capable, could manage to string whole sentences together without using double negatives and never, ever mangled the conjugation of the verb "to be."

"*Mr.* Mayfield, since we've known each other for all of fifteen minutes, I hardly think it's appropriate for you to be commenting on my situation or my state of mind—"

He grinned broadly, holding his left foot. "I shore do admire a woman can say so many ten dollar words as that. My, my, I purely do."

"—and I'll thank you to keep your opinions of me to yourself and dry your feet off on that towel so I can get on to doing what I have to do." She turned to the stove and gave the stew a jerky stir. Nine young Rafferty children didn't seem able to get her goat as quickly as this one grown man.

"Lordy," she mumbled to herself, "I never did meet a man so full of hot air in all my born days."

"Yass'm," he said with a smile still pulling at his mouth as he patted his foot dry. "But y'see, I jus' thinks to myself . . . time's short, an' there you is . . . full o' sass an' vinegar, an' purty as a striped snake on a green lawn. An' here I is, wishin' you wasn't usin' them big words likes a ol' feather duster to shoo me off." He winced, lowering his foot to the floor. "I's just a man, Miss Etta. An' you's just a woman. That's all there is about it."

Etta cheeks went hot, hearing the truth in his words. She reached for the jar of chickweed ointment she'd seen under the sink and slapped it down on the table beside him.

"Here. Make your hands useful for a change, Mr. Mayfield, instead of that mouth of yours. I has"—her eyes beseeched the heavens—"*have* more important things to do than to stand here swabbing the cuts on some fool's feet."

"Yass'm." She heard him chuckle as he unscrewed the jar lid in his big hands and slathered on some of the ointment, but felt his eyes on her as she finished the preparations for the noon meal. He'd move on after dinner and that would be that, she thought, sneaking a covert look at him.

And good riddance.

Andrea touched the edges of her mouth with the linen napkin and crumpled it in her fist, watching Silas polish off his fourth bowl of stew with sing-song moan of satisfaction.

"Fifths, Mr. Mayfield?" Etta asked with an edge of sarcasm.

"No, ma'am, I's fit to bust. That's the best squirrel stew I et in the longest time."

"It was rabbit." Etta swooped the bowl out from in front of him, and carried it to the sink.

"Oh," he said, suppressing a grin. "Well, that's the best rabbit I et in a long time, too. It was cooked partic'lar fine."

Jesse tossed an amused look at Andrea, who had made a point of avoiding his eyes throughout the meal. She could have sworn, for a moment, as his eyes met hers, that he was keeping something from her. About the farm? she wondered.

They'd barely spoken since he'd come back from unloading the wood shingles he'd bought in town, the tension between them as ripe as the bowl of strawberries sitting in the middle of the table. He'd come back a different man than he'd left. Gone was the fear she'd seen in his eyes at the thought of staying on at Willow Banks. It had been replaced with an easy good humor she couldn't account for. As if he'd resigned himself to staying on. But why?

Resting his forearms on the table, Jesse turned to Silas. "Etta thinks you should stay off those feet for a few days, until they have a chance to heal. I have to agree."

Silas shook his head and rubbed his bewhiskered chin. "I done put you folks out already, eatin' your vittles, takin' your kindness. I be movin' on directly. I ain't a man t' accept charity."

"Wouldn't be charity if you stayed on to work," Jesse observed, avoiding Andrea's look of alarm. "I can use another hand around here. Are you interested?"

Silas fingered the rim of his stoneware cup. "What kinda work?"

"You have any farming experience?"

"Farmin'?" Silas laughed. "I been tillin' the land for nigh on fifteen years, head nigger in the field, before the ol' massah give me my freedom papers in his will." Silas rubbed his calloused palms, a faraway look in his eyes. "I gots me the hands of a field worker, but the heart of a farmer. After the war, I plan on gettin' me a little piece o' land here in the north all my own, that nobody kin take away from me."

Jesse nodded. "You got money?"

"No, suh. But I got a good back and a strong will," he replied with a confident grin. "I git it someday. Somehow."

"We can't pay you much," Jesse told him, standing up and shoving his hands in his pockets. He walked to the window and looked out. "At least not until the crop is in. Room and board, a few dollars a week."

Silas watched him thoughtfully. "It's a good long time since I et a good meal or had me a roof over my head. I ain't opposed to doin' it regular."

Jesse smiled. "As you can see, we have mostly corn, some wheat, and alfalfa."

Glancing out the window, Silas nodded. "I mostly works with cotton. But cotton eats up the soil . . . leaves nothin' behind but used-up dirt. You gots to feed the soil like it was a child. Yassuh, I tilled all them other crops. An' more. You gots you a good crop o' corn, it'll see you through a year of hard times."

When Silas bent his elbow and rested them on the

table, his sleeves went up, revealing open sores in a line around both his wrists.

"Mr. Mayfield—" Andrea began, casting a silencing look at Jesse, "I don't mean to be an alarmist, but I'm concerned about the . . . situation . . . you seem to have left behind."

Silas took no offence, but followed her gaze to his wrists and lowered his arms self-consciously. "About them two fella's chasin' me?"

She nodded. "Are you in trouble with the law?"

"Not with the law. They was slave catchers, ma'am."

Her eyes widened. Even Etta turned around at his words.

"But you said you had papers," Andrea said.

Above the smooth wood grain of the table, Silas' hand tightened into a fist. "Yass'm. They's after some runaway nigger, prob'ly looks like me. I was on my way north, goin' through Kentucky, when they bears down on me with their horses. I thinks to myself, they's gonna lynch me right on this spot for bein' a nigger without a white man. So I tells 'em, 'I's a free man.' Shows 'em my emancipation papers."

"And . . . ?" Andrea prompted.

His jaw tensed with the memory. "An' they tore 'em up like they was no more'n dandelion weeds." His eyes went to his wrists. "Tied me up with a rope on my hands, and trailed me behind their hosses like I was a sack o' sorghum. I 'spect they could find some planter who didn't care what my name be, long as I got a strong back. But I got away 'fore they got too far, an' I been runnin' ever since." He shifted his gaze to Jesse. "'Til I run into you."

Andrea exchanged a look with Jesse, then turned back to Silas. "You're in the North now, Mr. Mayfield. Regardless of whether you have papers or not, you are a free man here. And no matter what that

106

black-hearted traitor, Jeff Davis, says, in Ohio, President Lincoln's Proclamation stands. But we're only a few miles from the Ohio River, this may not be the safest place for you."

"Thaz true." He took a sip on his coffee. "Now that I got no papers I 'spect I ain't safe anywheres as long as this War is goin' on. Lots of folks is hightailin' it up to Dee-troit. I 'spect that's as far as they kin run. But I hear they's no work there for nobody."

"There's work here for you if you want it, Silas," Jesse said, meeting Andi's eyes.

"We'd both be happy to have you stay on," she agreed, "if that's what you decide to do."

Silas glanced at Etta, standing by the sink so still she didn't even blink. "I reckon that's as good a offer as I'm like to get. I be obliged to stay on. These old feet'll heal up fine in a day or so, good as new. Don' you be worryin' 'bout that."

From the parlor came the sound of the little Zach's wail. Jesse and Andrea rose at the same moment, their chairs scraping loudly across the floor.

"I'll get him."

"No, that's . . . that's not necessary," she replied. "He'll be hungry. I'll have to feed him." She felt a flush creep up her neck at the strange look in Jesse's eyes as his gaze locked with hers. "Mr. Mayfield—"

"Silas," the black man corrected over the noise of the baby's wail.

She smiled and waved him back to his seat as he started to rise. "Silas, then. I'm glad you'll be staying on. I'm sure I'll see you later."

"Yes, ma'am."

Jesse watched her disappear into the parlor, and gathered his hat from the table, tamping down the desire to take a peek at that baby once more. It was probably no good to go getting too attached anyway,

107

he thought fitting his hat on.

"That a creek I seen runnin' through your land up a piece?" Silas asked him.

"That's Willow Banks Creek. Why?"

Silas rose with a grimace. "I needs t' wash some o' this trail off'n me."

Jesse nodded, flipping him a bar of soap from the sink. "You can settle in the hay mow in the barn. I'll bring a water pitcher and some blankets out later."

Silas grinned. "Yassuh. That be just fine."

"Just call me Jesse, okay?"

"Jesse," the black man repeated, trying out the sound on his tongue. He laughed, a good, deep sound like rain after a long dry spell. "Jesse, it is. Thank yuh, suh." He shrugged. "An I ain't no Mayfield, neither, suh. That be the name o' my massah—Mayfield. I took it so's I'd have one. But it ain't mine. No, suh. I's just Silas. Always been . . . always will be."

Jesse shook Silas' hand with a smile. "Pleased to meet you, Silas. Welcome to Willow Banks."

"I's right pleased to be here."

As he followed Jesse out the door, Silas winked at Etta, who was left standing in the kitchen alone, wondering how she'd possibly ignore a man who could charm the wings off a butterfly.

An hour later, Andrea heard a knock on her bedroom door. "Yes?"

Jesse poked his head in. "It's me."

Her heart stopped then started again. She'd been expecting Etta. "Come in, Jesse. I was just resting."

He eased his rangy frame into the room. He was holding a small package wrapped in brown paper. It crinkled as he leaned over the drawer to take a peek at the sleeping baby. Jesse wore a grin as his eyes met hers. "How's he doing?"

"He has a healthy appetite," she said without thinking.

Jesse's eyes strayed to her full breasts before he caught himself. "How are you, Andi?"

She swallowed hard. "Fine. Was there something you wanted?"

He set his packages down on the bed beside her quilt-covered leg. "Do I need an excuse to come and say hello?"

"No."

He returned her smile. "Actually, there is something." He handed her the packages. "I picked this up for you in town. Something for little Zach, too."

Andrea's mouth fell open and she blinked at the carefully wrapped parcels. A present? He'd bought her a present? How long had it been since someone had brought her something just for her? "Why?"

"You might call it a peace offering. Or . . . an apology. Whatever it is, I just felt like doing it. So, open 'em up."

"Which one should I open first?"

He pointed to the smallest one. It made a noise as she untied the string and unfolded the stiff brown paper.

"Oh, Jesse!" She held up a tiny silver rattle. It glinted in the afternoon sun. "It's beautiful. But it must have been—"

"My pleasure," he said, cutting off her argument. "Every baby should have one. Especially my only nephew."

Andrea blinked back tears. "Thank you."

"Open the other one now." A pleased look shone in his eyes and he leaned forward with hands pressed between his knees.

She unwrapped it slowly, savoring the anticipation of the moment. Her breath caught in her throat when she saw what he'd gotten her. The hand mirror was the most beautiful she'd ever seen, made of intricately carved pewter with flowers and birds gracefully floating about its edges. The smooth rounded handle fit the palm of her hand to perfection. She held it up and looked at herself in the clear, beveled glass.

"Mavis Broderick, down at the mercantile, said it was a lady's mirror," Jesse told her with an awkward shrug. "I thought—"

"It's beautiful, Jesse. I—" Her gaze collided with his. "I don't know what to say. You shouldn't be giving me gifts."

Jesse looked at his hands. "Zach would have . . . if he were here."

"Zach was a practical man, not given to frivolity."

"I guess that's where we were different."

No, she thought. *You're different in so many ways*.

"Anyway," he said, getting up and shoving his hands into the back pockets of his Levi's, "a hand mirror isn't frivolous for a lady, I'm told. I believe the term Mavis used was, uh, *essential*. And I didn't see one here on your table. This one doesn't have any speckles in it like all the other mirrors in this house." He smiled at her. "A beautiful woman like you deserves a fine mirror to look in now and again."

She blushed all the way to her roots and laughed. "Beautiful? Me?"

His smile had faded. "Yeah. You've turned into a real beauty, Andi. I knew you would."

She cocked her head not sure what to make of him and uncomfortable with the serious bent to the conversation. He was looking at her the way he used to, before Willow Banks had come between them. She forced a nervous smile. "Why, Jesse, if I didn't know better I might think you were trying to butter me up for something."

With one eyebrow arched, he grinned. "Not that you wouldn't be delicious buttered up," he replied lightly, drawing an indignant huff from her. He grew serious then, pulling his hands from his pockets. "No, I'm only telling the truth. Men will be lining up outside your door soon, Andi," he predicted, knowing it was true. "You might want to give some serious consideration to them when they do."

She looked stunned that he would even bring such a thing up. "I'm in mourning, Jesse. You know that. It's Zach we're talking about."

"I'm all too aware of that. But you can't afford to stand on ceremony when you've got your future to think of."

She bristled and her eyes stung with unexpected tears. "I hardly think it's sentimental to grieve over one's husband! It's your brother we're talking about, Jesse. I can't believe—"

"Take my advice. Get your grieving done and put it behind you, Andi. If you want to hang onto this place, you'll move on with your life."

Cornflower blue eyes met violet for a brief tension-filled moment. "Look, I don't want to fight," he said standing.

She lowered her eyes. "No . . . neither do I."

"I . . . hope you like the mirror."

Meeting his gaze once more she sighed and nodded. "I do. Thank you, Jesse."

He hesitated for only a fraction of a second before doing what, years ago, would have come naturally at a moment like this.

It was the briefest of kisses, a brushing of lips, a sharing of warmth. Yet, however platonic its intent, the kiss sent a bolt of desire crashing through Jesse, and he regretted taking even that small taste of her.

Eyes wide, she looked up at him with a shocked

111

expression that reflected the same shock coursing through him, the tacit understanding that what once had been a flame between them was still a live ember.

His fingers brushed the incredible softness of her arm, and he smiled, or at least tipped one corner of his mouth up in an attempt. "Night, Andi," he said, then turned and left the room.

Shock poured through Andrea as she watched him go, and she pressed her fingertips against her lips where the taste of him still lingered. His brief kiss had left her breathless, her heart hammering in her throat.

Damn him! How dare he kiss her like that? How dare he assume she would allow it?

But she had.

She pounded her fist into the feather-ticked pillow. And how dare he tell her to forget about Zach as if he were no more than a fading memory. The father of her child! The man who'd been there for her in her hour of need, when Jesse himself had run away from her like the coward he was. And now he'd kissed her as if whatever had passed between them all those years ago gave him the right. Well, it didn't and if he ever tried something like that again, she'd—

Andrea slid down on the pillow, brushing her fingertips against her mouth once more. If he ever tried that again, she thought miserably, she just might allow it. Because as much as she wanted to deny it, there was still something between them. Something every bit as powerful as the anger she felt toward him a moment ago.

Find another man. Damn him! As if she could.

As if she would.

Chapter Eight

Andrea loosened the wooden clothespin from the edge of the sheet and let the sun-bleached fabric fall against her arm. The bedding smelled of sunshine and the gentle breeze that tugged at the combs in her hair.

"Now, you give me that, honey," Etta said, taking the sheet from Andrea's hands. "You are supposed to be taking it easy. That's why I'm here, remember?"

"Oh, Etta, you've been doing nearly everything for three weeks now, and I can't stand to be idle. I'm fine. There's no sense in your working two jobs the way you do—coming here every day, when I'm perfectly capable of—"

"—of hiding those circles under your eyes?" Etta asked with a frown. She clucked her tongue. "You don't fool me child. You've been working when I'm gone and even when I'm not watching. You're dragging like the ears of an old hound dog."

Andrea couldn't help but smile. "How flattering."

"You think," Etta argued, pushing her glasses up on her nose with one finger, "I didn't notice that all the snap beans have been finding their way to the kitchen whilst I'm doing laundry? Or that a floor is scrubbed that I haven't gotten to yet?"

"I have to do something. And you shouldn't be here watching out over me when you have Isabelle's house to look after."

"That's exactly the point of my being here, Miss Andrea. Miss Isabelle wouldn't have said so if she didn't think you needed the rest. Mercy sakes, you had a baby! And without a man to spell you! You've got to take it slow at first. All new mamas think they're indestructible. But if you don't slow down, you're going to wear yourself down to a nubbin in no time."

"I feel fine," Andrea lied, tugging at the cuffs on her loose-fitting calico blouse. "Except that I'm feeling rather useless. Etta, you know how I appreciate everything you've done for me, but you simply must let me help around here. If I don't, I'll lose my mind. And if I lose my mind, I'll only prove Jesse right."

With a frown, she took an edge of the sheet back from Etta and helped her fold it. The wind caught the fabric, making it unfurl like a ship's sail.

"Prove him right about what?" Etta asked.

She shrugged. "He already thinks I'm crazy to try to hang onto this place on my own."

"Just like a man . . ." Etta mumbled.

"Exactly," Andrea agreed, dropping the sheet into the basket and reaching for the next one.

"Besides, you aren't all alone," Etta pointed out. "You've got Mr. Mayfield." Her dark-eyed gaze swept the cornfield for a glimpse of him.

Andrea flicked a curious look up at Etta. Her coffee-colored skin shone golden in the midmorning sun. "Silas? I think he's sweet on you Etta."

Flustered, Etta snapped up the edge of the new sheet. *Me?* Oh, Lordy! That man likes anything walks in skirts, that's what I think. Any fool who can flirt like that ought to be locked up for the safety of all womankind."

Andrea plucked another clothespin off the line. "Yesterday, before you came, I saw him watching the road from the cornfields all morning until Gus dropped you off." She picked a speck off the clean white cotton. "He spent the rest of the morning singing so loud I could hear him from the porch."

A pleased grin crept to Etta's mouth, despite her attempts to hide it. She slapped a handful of clothespins into the bag clipped to the line. "Mmmm-mm," she sighed, gazing at the chin-high corn. "That man sure can sing, can't he?"

"Why, Etta," Andrea gasped in feigned surprise. "I didn't think you noticed such things."

"That man's hard to miss, isn't he? 'Sides, can't hurt to listen, can it?" The woman sighed wistfully. "It's been a long time since I heard a man sing like that. Not since my Marcus . . ."

Andrea folded the sheet and tucked it in the basket. "Have you thought of remarrying, Etta?"

"I suppose I would. If the right man came along." She lifted the full hamper and moved it down the line.

"How would you know him if you found him?"

Etta regarded her seriously. "You've been married, child. I suppose you just . . . know when you know. That's all. There's no figuring to it."

She'd once thought it that easy.

"Now, take a man like your Mr. Jesse—"

"He's not mine, Etta. Not even close."

Etta smiled. "That's not what his eyes say when he looks at you."

Andrea ducked under the sheet to reach the second line. "You're imagining things Etta," Andrea scoffed, pulling the clothespins off Jesse's union suit hanging there. "The only thing Jesse sees when he looks at me is a ball and chain. He's not the marrying kind. If he were, he would have—"

115

Andrea faltered at the sight of a folded slip of paper tucked under the pin of her camisole. What in the world . . . ?

She slipped the pin off the line, and unfolded the paper. Four words were written neatly in black ink:

I've missed you, Andrea.

Her blood froze. For a moment, she forgot to breathe. She stared at the paper in her hand without really seeing it. *I've missed you.* Dear God, it couldn't be. Instinctively, she whirled around, half-expecting to see him standing behind her grinning.

Vaguely, she realized Etta had spoken to her, more than once. She stuffed the paper into the oversized pocket of her apron just as Etta popped her head between the laundry.

"Child," Etta asked with real concern, "are you all right? You look like you saw a ghost."

She snatched her hand from her pocket guiltily. "What? I—oh, I'm fine," she lied, plucking loose another pin. "It must be the heat."

Etta frowned. "Folks get red in the heat, not white. You sure you're all right?"

"Yes," she answered in a small voice. Through the fabric of her apron, her hand curled around the note in her pocket.

"Hm-mph . . ." Etta muttered. "You go on in the house now, put your feet up. You leave this laundry to Etta, now." She took the long johns and camisole from Andrea's arm and gave her a gentle nudge toward the house. "Go on."

"Etta—"

Just then, little Zachary let out a waking cry from inside the house.

"You see?" Etta asked, bracing her fists on her hips.

Andrea nodded. "All right, I . . . I'll feed Zachary, then I think I'll . . . walk some dinner out to those two stubborn men in the field. I don't believe they're going to stop for sustenance."

"I can take it to them," Etta offered.

Andrea shook her head. "I feel like a walk. Zachary could use some air, too. But thanks."

Gripping the wooden handles of the shiny new Bradley Walking Cultivator, Jesse guided the team of horses carefully between the corn rows. The tassels combed their underbellies as they trudged through the green corn. The smell of freshly turned soil lay thick in the sweltering air.

Step, step, lift. Step step, lift.

"Gee, Polly!" he called as the animals veered left. The lead mare automatically corrected her course. "Ho," Jesse intoned to straighten her.

Four steel blades straddled the corn rows, turning the soil over on either side, following the course of two iron wheels. The newfangled machine accomplished double the cultivation possible with a single horse hoe which Silas was using a few rows away. Despite his misgivings, he had to admit the new cultivator made the job easier. Together, they'd averaged eight acres a day for the past three weeks. Far more than could have been cultivated in the days he'd been working the land for the old man.

Even so, a man had to pay close attention to his work or the sharp shares would dig into the precious corn root, destroying it. Which was exactly what happened as Jesse's mind wandered and he forgot to lift.

He swore under his breath. Mahkwi, who followed his every step, rooted under the loosened soil, searching the sweet scented earth with her nose,

117

unearthing grubs or gophers or an occasional corn snake.

Step, step, lift.

Jesse ran a damp shoulder over his brow and looked behind him. Acre-long rows of fresh-cultivated corn lay behind him. Today they would finish. Then they would start shocking the wheat.

As long as the weather held.

He'd walked through the wheat yesterday and tested the ears. No longer green, the kernels had passed the doughy stage Joe Fergeson—the miller down the road—tended to prefer. It was ripening to a golden brown and had a firm pasty consistency. The Old Man had always insisted that despite his preferences, Fergeson would pay the same dollar for ripe wheat as green, and the crop would yield far more that way. That was lucky, because he couldn't have gotten to it any sooner.

It was hard, thankless work, but each acre, Jesse reasoned, put him that much closer to his goal: to return to Montana.

"Giddup, Polly, giddup, Pete," he called falling into the rhythm of the movement.

He longed for the mountains and the wind singing through the pines, and the sharp, variant land. He missed the stinging aroma of a campfire, wading hip-deep in glacial streams, and sleeping beneath the canopy of stars that seeded the black dome of sky above him. He missed not knowing what tomorrow would bring. He'd forgotten how endlessly the same Ohio seemed—rolling, flat, static . . . acre upon acre of sameness . . . and all this damned grain.

The tension between him and Andi had grown with the passing days. More times than one he'd regretted that kiss he'd given her that afternoon in her room. But neither had he forgotten the strange rush of pleasure it had given him. Andi had kept her distance from him, as aware as he of what potential lay between them. So he'd kept their conversations intentionally light, their touches—when they shared one—impersonal.

His thoughts strayed to little Zachary. The boy was a charmer, with his father's smile and his mother's eyes. Jesse felt a growing attachment to the child, despite his own warnings against it. He actually missed the kid when he spent the daylight hours in the field and found himself looking forward to the feel of Zachary's tiny hand closing around his finger at the end of the day.

Jesse frowned and concentrated on the motion of the cultivator and the jolting it gave his upper body.

The smooth hardwood handles burned the still-tender palms of his hands. He no longer got blisters. His hands were beginning to callous again. Years of trapping had softened him in some ways, hardened him in others, but hadn't lessened his distaste for this place one bit.

Beside him, two rows over, Silas worked too, wearing the new boots and pants Jesse had purchased for him in town. He sang to himself as if he were actually enjoying this:

> Chicken crow at midnight,
> It be almost day.
> Go an' get your Georgia Lover,
> 'Cause it be almost day.
> Go an' get your Georgia Lover,
> We'll dance the night away.

Step, step . . .

Silas went into the second verse humming wordlessly. Flicking the sweat off his brow, Jesse tried to shut out the sound.

Step, step, step, lift.

119

How, on God's green earth, could a man concentrate with that humming going on four feet away?

Step, step—clank.

The rock hidden beneath the soil delivered a painful jolt that traveled up his arms to his shoulders. With a curse, Jesse stopped the team and worked at the rock with the tip of his shoe, but the stone didn't budge. He got down on his knees and dug his fingers into the earth surrounding it.

What's the matter, Boy? came a voice from the dark recesses of his mind. *You ain't gonna let a little rock best you, are you?*

Jesse stiffened and looked up into the glare of the sun at the shadowy figure looming over him. A cold clamminess chased through him.

No, Papa, I can get it. I can, came another voice . . . his own. But he couldn't do it. He was eight years old and the rock was stronger. Defeat had made his young eyes sting.

Weakness will never make you a farmer, Boy. I guess I'll have to teach you a lesson.

Heart thudding in his ears, Jesse blotted out his father's image and tore the rock from the stubborn ground. He stood and threw it as far as his bitterness would carry it. The heavy stone crashed into several stalks in its wake.

His chest heaved, dark spots of memory swam before his eyes. It must be the withering heat, or the oppressive smell of the corn, making his brain go soft. He hadn't thought of that incident for years. He thought he'd put all that behind him.

"You hear me, boss?" Silas was saying, looking at him with concern.

Jesse blinked, realizing he hadn't. "What?"

"I said you all right? You don't look so good."

"No, I'm fine. Peachy, in fact," he replied, gathering up the reins again.

Silas narrowed a look at him, unconvinced. "You take a dislikin' to that partic'lar rock you just chucked, or is it my singin' botherin' you?" He grinned. "You can tell me."

"It beats me," Jesse grumbled, "how you could find anything to sing about out here."

"Singin' just comes natural," Silas told him, wiping his face on the new blue bandanna wrapped around his neck. "Hoe an' sing. Hoe an' sing. Makes it go fast an' easy. Ya'll ought'a try it."

"Nothin' would make this work go faster for me," he replied cynically, digging into the soil again, feeling Silas' stare on his back. A pair of crows circled above them cawing loudly. All around them, the cicadas chirred in the mid-day heat.

"You ain't partic'lar fond o' this here land, is you?"

They had never spoken of it, yet Jesse supposed his feelings had become fairly transparent. "No."

Silas looked truly perplexed by that. "How come? It's your land, ain't it?"

"It was my family's farm. I left it years ago with no intention of coming back."

Silas shook his head, backing down the row, coaxing the soil with the blade of his hoe. "You's here now."

"True." *The prodigal son.*

They worked in silence for a few minutes before Jesse broke it. "You've got more right to hate farming than I do, after all you've been through."

"Hate it?" Silas tossed him an incredulous look. "You mean the land?" He shook his head. "I ain't got no quarrel with dirt."

Jesse frowned and slowed his step.

"Now, folks . . ." Silas went on, "you can have a quarrel with folks. They can tell you to go one way or t' other. Sometime, it ain't the way you wants to go.

121

But the land? It be a part of me . . . who I am, what I knows."

He spread his arms and gaze to encompass the sea of green around them. "An look—no whip-holdin' overseer lookin' over my shoulder; no massah tellin' me I gots to work sunup to sundown with no break from the blisterin' sun. An' when I's done, I can lie down in a sweet mow o' hay and think on tomorrow an' what I's gonna do. No suh," he said, carrying his hoe to the next row, "I ain't got no quarrel with dirt."

Jesse plunged his hoe into the soil. Step, step, lift. Who was his own quarrel with? he wondered. A dead man? Or the legacy of pain he left behind?

"Hello, in the field!"

Jesse turned at the sound of Andi's voice drifting across the corn. Making her way through the corn rows, she carried a canteen and canvas bag on one shoulder, the baby—wearing a little knitted cap— slung across the other in some kind of contraption she'd made up with a lacy shawl. In her free hand she held two tin cups.

She looked small, slight against the solid green backdrop, the sturdy shocks of corn. If he hadn't heard her voice, he might have thought her an apparition, a trick of the eyes, like the wavy heat rising off the corn. The sight of her took him back years, when she used to cut across his father's cornfields to meet him at the creek—waving her arm above the shoulder-high corn, calling his name. . . .

Jesse blinked, shaking off the memory that left his heart beating faster. An oversized man's hat shaded her face. His gaze took in her ankle-length blue skirt, which was topped by a simple, calico blouse and cinched at the waist with a belt.

His gaze tarried there for a minute. In the three weeks since she'd given birth, she'd lost the look of pregnancy. Her stomach and hips were nearly back to normal. He didn't have to guess about that. His hand had accidentally brushed her around the waist the other day. He remembered that out of bounds touch even now. His fingers drew into a fist.

As Andrea hurried toward the men, she let out a sigh of relief. She was safe here beside Jesse, she assured herself, curling her fist around the note crumpled in her pocket. Drawing closer, she found herself unable to tear her gaze from Jesse's naked upper torso. A sheen of sweat coated his bronzed chest and arms. A dusting of darker hair covered his chest, thinning to a V past his washboard-like stomach and into the waistband of his trousers. He's beautiful, she thought, as beautiful as she remembered. His body had been sculpted by years of hard work in a place so different from this she could hardly imagine it.

"What are you doing all the way out here, Andi?" he asked with a welcoming smile.

"It's past dinnertime, or didn't you notice?" she asked. "I thought you two might be thirsty and hungry. I made you some sandwiches."

Jesse reached for the canteen and relieved her of the cups. Andrea slipped her arms around the baby, who cooed happily at her.

"You were right," he told her, unscrewing the top of the canteen and sniffing at it. "What's in here?"

Andrea jerked her gaze from Jesse's chest. "Uh . . . lemonade with, um, chipped ice from the spring house. I brought out some sandwiches too, if you're hungry."

Jesse nodded and poured a cup for Silas, who'd joined them at the promise of a cool drink.

"Lemonade—" Silas moaned. "I purely do love lemonade. My mammy used to make it for the folks up at the big house and slip us chillun some on the sly through the kitchen door." He took a long sip. "Mmm-mm, thaz fine, Miss Andi. Jus' the right amount o' sweet."

Andrea smiled. Jesse had Silas calling her Andi now too. She couldn't complain. She kind of liked the name. It was the only nickname anyone had ever given her. And Jesse had given it.

She watched him fill his own cup and slug the liquid back in four long gulps. Her eyes unwillingly followed the up and down movement of his Adam's apple and the rivulets of liquid that spilled past the corners of his mouth. "Ahhh-hhh," he sighed. His azure gaze met hers as he backhanded the moisture as it slid into his beard. She bit her lip to hide her grin of pleasure and amusement. "What?" he asked.

"Nothing."

"*What?*"

"Isn't that hot?"

"The lemonade?"

"No, the beard."

He reached up and scratched it. "I'm used to it. Why? You don't like it?"

Lifting her shoulders in a shrug that was neither approving or disapproving, she said, "No, it's fine. I mean, most men wear them. I just wondered. My hair gets hot if I don't get it off my neck. I could cut yours for you if you want." She stroked the baby's bonneted head.

Watching her, Jesse grunted noncommitally, refilled his cup, and drained it again.

Silas looked on, amused. He goo-gooed at the baby and made him smile before handing back the cup. He took the napkin-wrapped sandwich from her. "Much obliged, ma'am." He waggled his fingers at the baby.

"Jesse, Etta needs a ride back home," Andrea said. "Can you spare Silas for a few minutes? Missus Rafferty needs her help with some canning this afternoon."

"I can finish up here," Jesse told the black man. "You go on ahead. You'll have to hitch Jacksaw to the buggy, though," he said, indicating the mule hitched to Silas' plow.

"Do you mind terribly, Silas?" Andrea asked.

Silas's black eyes widened with anticipation. "No ma'am, I wouldn't mind a bit. Fact it would be my downright pleasure to do it. It shorely would." Gathering up Jacksaw's reins around his neck, he unhitched the old plow and started for home.

Andrea grinned and called after him. "You can eat first, Silas."

"Oh, no," he said half-turning. "I be savin' that for later. I just hitch up this ol' mule an' git Miss Etta where she gots t' go. Yass'm. I do that straight away." The sun glistened on his cropped black hair as he made his way through the corn, disappearing at last between the rows.

Jesse raised his eyebrows, settled down in the shade of the cornstalks and opened his sandwich. "Now there's a man happy about his work."

"I think Etta likes him."

"I think the feeling's mutual." He looked up at her. "Join me?"

She smiled. "All right." She sat down beside him in middle of the row, shaded by the tall stalks, and lay the baby across her lap.

Jesse watched her suppress a yawn and frowned. "You all right, Andi?"

"Fine, why?"

"You look worn out."

She touched her hair and glanced away annoyed he would notice. "A little tired is all. It's quite normal, I'm sure."

He studied her as he chewed his sandwich and suppressed an urge to test the tenderness of her pale cheek with the back of his finger. He glanced at her rough hands.

"You should go home and take a rest," he said. "Have you been working in the garden again?"

"Some. The beans are coming in fast."

"You shouldn't be trying to do so much. It hasn't been that long since—"

"I'm fine," she interrupted. "Really, you and Etta are a pair of worry warts." A breeze rustled the still air and she tilted her head back to receive it. "It's lovely out here, isn't it? I love the smell of corn growing and fresh-turned earth. Don't you?"

Jesse's eyes clung for a long moment to that creamy expanse of throat. His body tightened involuntarily remembering the feel of that particular patch of skin beneath his mouth. But that had been a long time ago. It didn't belong to him anymore.

"Just smells like corn to me," he grumbled and tore off a bite of ham sandwich.

Andrea glanced up with a sigh and toyed with the baby's tuft of black hair. "Remember when we used to chase each other through the fields, Jesse? When we were young?"

"Yeah . . ." A wistfulness stole into his expression for a moment. "Yeah. Seems like forever ago."

She smiled. "It was. You rarely caught me, though."

"Unless I wanted to," he added, a flash of humor crossed his face.

"Hah! Are you saying you let me win, Jesse Winslow?"

He grinned and took another bite of sandwich.

"Humph," she replied, knowing it was true. "Remember the climbing-willow up on the creek? The tree-house you and Zach and I built?"

Jesse closed his eyes, a wave of memory washing over him like rolling heat. He and Andi and Zach. Together. Laughing. "Is it still there?"

126

She nodded. "We built it like a rock into that old tree."

Jesse shook his head with a smile. "I'll never forget how mad Zach was when you brought that bucket of whitewash over and painted the fort without our knowing." He laughed. "Lord, I thought he'd have a conniption. You could see our secret fort a mile away after that through the branches of that old tree."

Laughter bubbled up in her throat, too. "I was only trying to help," she argued. "I thought it looked better white. Oohh, he was mad." They laughed together for a minute, remembering those long-gone days.

"Yeah, well," Jesse sighed, his eyes going to little Zachary. "I guess my little brother got over it."

The laughter faded in Andrea's eyes. "I . . . I guess he did." Silence stretched between them filled with unasked, and unanswered questions. "Well, I'd better go," she said, but the awkwardness of the baby made it hard to get up from the ground.

He took Zachary from her, stood and offered her his hand. She took it after a second's hesitation and let him pull her up, nearly colliding with him in the process. She caught herself, hands splayed across his hard chest. Her instinctive response to his nearness was so powerful it made her heart thud erratically and her breath catch in her throat.

Nor did he release her as soon as he might have. Instead he kept a steadying hand on her arm. *His eyes match the color of the cloudless sky*, she thought irrelevantly when his gaze rose to meet hers—deep, faraway blue. This close, she felt the heat of his skin, the dampness of his sweat. For a moment they were so close, she thought he might—

"You all right?" he asked, setting her away from him.

The sound of her heartbeat drowned out her

response but she was quite sure she said, "Yes."

She reached for her son. Jesse's large hands, brown and calloused by Winslow soil, wrapped around the babe's chest. But instead of handing the child to her, Jesse raised him in the air over his head and smiled at the cockeyed grin on Zachary's face—the one he saved mostly for Jesse.

"Hey Corncob, you're growing fast. He feels heavier to me already," he told Andi.

"He's a good eater, like his father."

Jesse lowered the boy, his eyes unconsciously falling to her full breasts, then back to her face. Gently, he handed her Zachary. "Well, I'd better get back to work."

"Me, too. We're having chicken and dumplings for supper. Do you want me to leave the lemonade?"

"Sure." His mouth was already watering for that chicken and dumplings, despite what he'd said about her taking it easy. The fields worked up a man's appetite. "We'll be in before sundown."

He watched her go, absently fingering the thick growth that covered his jaw. Maybe he did need a shave at that. And a haircut. Maybe he'd even let Andi Mae do the honors, he thought, watching the unconscious sway of her hips as she made her way through the stand of corn.

Then again, maybe he'd find a barber in town. A balding, *male* barber who didn't know chicken and dumplings from petunias—and knew nothing about shared memories of a childhood best forgotten.

Fields of wheat, edged by Queen Ann's lace, and sprays of golden tansy, sped by as the wagon wheels of the buggy rattled across the rutted dirt road. A welcome August breeze rippled the ripening fields and cut through the sweltering heat, washing over

Etta and Silas as they drove along the lane toward Isabelle and John Rafferty's place.

Etta bounced along the edge of the seat until her knee was pressed intimately against Silas' muscular thigh. With one hand plastered to her straw hat to keep it on her head, and the other firmly around the slender iron rail that fenced the seat back, Etta hauled herself back a proper five inches away from Silas Mayfield.

"You all right, Miss Etta?"

"Mr. Mayfield—!"

"Silas."

"Mr. Mayfield, are you purposely trying to find all the ruts in this road?" Her voice jiggled with the movement of the wagon.

"No, ma'am. Now why would I do that?" A gleam in his smiling eyes told her that was exactly his intent.

"I'm sure I don't know. But I'd appreciate it if—"

The wagon jolted again, this time throwing her fully against him. Stopping herself just short of mashing her face against his chest, she instead crunched the brim of her straw hat on his shoulder, skewing it over to one side of her face. Worse, her spectacles flew right off her nose and bounced off Silas' knee onto the front boot. But the most humiliating part happened when Silas drew his arm around her to steady her against him while he slowed Jacksaw.

"Whoa!" he called, drawing back gently on the reins with a chuckle. "Whoa, now. Look'it what you done, you lame-brained mule."

"Lame-brained mule!" Etta exclaimed, righting herself on the seat. "Well, I've heard of the pot calling the kettle black, but that just beats all!"

Silas couldn't help the grin that crept to his mouth. "This kettle done always been black," he

129

retorted. "But just the same, I's sorry for janglin' you that'a ways, Miss Etta." He reached down and picked up her spectacles.

"It would've been safer to walk home," she grumbled, yanking the hatpin out of her hat to re-arrange it on her head.

He rubbed the lenses with calculated slowness against the front of his pale blue cotton shirt. "It be a far piece for a woman handsome as you to be walkin' on your own."

"Don't you try to pay me any sunshine, Mr. I-can-charm-anyone-with-that-smile Mayfield. You did that on purpose." She reached for her spectacles, but instead of handing them back, he looked at her with amusement.

"Me?" He spread the fingers of one dark hand across his chest. "My, my, Miss Etta, you shore does have a suspicious nature."

"*Do* have," she corrected with exasperation. "*Do* have, Mr. Mayfield. And you're quite right, I do. And for good reason." Yanking down the pointed basque of her brown gingham gown, she glared out over the blur of wheat, waiting for him to resume driving. But he didn't. He sat staring at her. "Whatever are you looking at?"

"At you . . . without them spectacles. You gots—" he stopped, correcting himself with an effort, "*have* the purtiest eyes I ever did see on a woman. Gray like the underside of rain clouds in summer, with the color of spring grass wove through 'em." He shook his head. "Can't see that color true for them spectacles."

"I—" Struck speechless, Etta stared at him. Never had a man spoken to her in such poetic terms about the strange color of her eyes. Not even Marcus. For an uneducated ex-slave, Silas Mayfield could certainly be . . . lyrical.

She squinted, wishing she could see him clearly, see what was really in his eyes. But he was a blur. Her heart thudded like the clip-clop of hoofbeats.

"Why you need 'em?" he asked.

"I . . . I beg our pardon?"

He handed her the spectacles, his work-roughened hands brushing hers. "Why you need these?"

She gulped. "S-so I can see, of course. If you must know, I'm nearly blind without them." She fitted them tartly over the bridge of her nose. Silas Mayfield came into sharp focus. He was still grinning, but those dark eyes of his were warm and filled with something more than humor.

"Well, then," he said, gathering up the worn leather traces. "I guess you best be wearin' 'em. I wouldn't want you to be missin' the way I look at you . . . Miss I-don't-fall-for-smiles Gaines." Naturally he punctuated that jab with a smile and gave the traces a flick. "Giddap!"

They rode the remaining mile without speaking. Silas missed each and every rut in the road. Every now and then, he'd hum a little verse of a Negro spiritual and glance surreptitiously in her direction. Most of the songs he sang, she'd heard here and there. But several contained lyrics about slavery and freedom she'd never heard before. It occurred to her there was much of this man she knew nothing about. They were as different as two people of the same color could be.

She frowned, realizing the boundaries she'd already placed upon their relationship in her mind. He was an ex-slave, she an educated freewoman. Her whole life had centered on her struggle to overcome their preconceived perceptions of her as a woman of color. While Marcus, in his own way had given her a certain respectability, because of his teaching and the abolitionist articles he'd authored for the Cause in

Illinois, Etta had always craved more from her life. And long before Marcus had died, fighting for the cause in which he so dearly believed, she'd realized that while respect and love were not mutually exclusive, a couple could sadly have the first without the second.

She glanced at Silas out of the corner of her eye. With little in common, and no mutual ground, she wondered then, about the inexplicable attraction she felt for the man. Why, every time he was near her, she seemed to make a fool of herself, and found her usually glib tongue tied in knots.

She kept her eyes trained straight ahead, wishing she could think of something intelligent to say. But absolutely nothing came to mind. It seemed his very presence beside her robbed her of coherent thought and gave her the weak trembles.

All too soon they pulled into the Rafferty's yard. He parked under a spreading elm that stood at the very center of the well-kept yard, dwarfing the neat two-story farmhouse there. The children spilled out of the house, waving to her and starting an impromptu game of leapfrog beside the waving fields of wheat that spread to the horizon.

Etta sat stiffly on the seat, waiting for Silas to climb down and come around her side to give her a hand. Indeed, he walked around the wagon, but instead of taking her hand, he wrapped his big hands around her waist and lifted her down as if she weighed no more than a feather.

"Oh . . ." she gasped, "I—thank you."

"Welcome. Afternoon, Miss Etta," he said pleasantly, touching the brim of his hat with his dark fingertips.

"Good after—" she began, but he'd already hopped up into the wagon again, "—noon."

He clucked to the mule and gave the reins a quick

shake. Standing there like some pillar of stone, Etta racked her brain for something, anything to say before he left so he didn't think she hated him.

"Silas—" she called.

He pulled back on the reins and looked back at her.

She moistened her dry lips. From nearby the children's laughter rang out across the yard. "I . . . uh . . ."

His eyebrows went up expectantly.

"I like the way you sing," she blurted. Resisting the temptation to squeeze her eyes shut in mortification, she wondered why on God's green earth she'd blurted that out?

A grin spread slowly, easily across his face. "You do?"

"I—I said so, didn't I?" She fussed with her crooked hat and found it hopeless.

"Well, now, that's a start, Etta," he said, flicking the reins again. The team pulled off with jingle of metal and leather. "That's a start."

Chapter Nine

The lantern light in the barn told Andrea Jesse was still there, doing whatever it was he did out there 'til all hours of the evening. She let the faded gingham curtains slide back over the window.

What was it he did out there every night, anyway? Was he cleaning tack? Mucking stalls? Or was he simply avoiding her? The last seemed most likely. She was long in bed by the time she heard him come in from the barn most nights. Frankly, tonight she was lonely, and wished for someone besides a three-week-old baby to talk to. Zachary was sound asleep in the drawer beside the fireplace where she let him sleep in the evenings.

She glanced at the half-eaten blueberry pie sitting on the shelf. Jesse hadn't gotten a piece of it tonight. He'd excused himself after wolfing down his food and gone to the barn. She'd baked it especially for him, though Silas had, at least enjoyed it.

On impulse, she cut a generous slice and slid it onto a plate. Checking her reflection in the darkened glass pane of the window, she lifted the lighted lantern that hung just outside the kitchen door, and made her way to the barn.

Awash with a million pinpricks of light, the velvet

night sky domed over the land. Croakers chorused down by the banks of the creek with a steady hum. The familiar sound made Andrea's throat tighten as she made her way through the shadowy darkness. Willow Banks was home. Her home—as much a part of her as that baby sleeping inside. The thought of losing it was too awful to contemplate, and she thanked God for sending Jesse Winslow home to help her save it.

Slipping inside the double doors of the barn, she heard the sound of sandpaper rasping against wood and Jesse's voice. The mules shifted restively in their stalls, shuffling the straw at their feet. Jesse's appaloosa snorted over the cribbed door of his stall in welcome. Andrea moved silently to the door of the tackroom, listening for a moment.

"I know, I know," Jesse was saying. "You'd rather be off chasing females." The sound of rasping sandpaper again. *Who was he talking to?*

"It won't be long. Neither one of us was meant to be tied up to this place," he went on. "You'll have to put up with that rope for a while longer though. Andi just doesn't understand about you. Doesn't understand me either, for that matter," he muttered.

Andrea pressed her back against the wall and listened to Mahkwi's yawning whine of agreement. A smile crept to her mouth at the idea that Jesse spent his evenings in the barn talking to a wolf.

"What do you think about this tree?" Jesse asked after a few seconds. "Too big? Too small?" He sighed. "I guess it'll put her in mind of a willow, more or less."

Curiosity overcoming wisdom, she stepped into the tack room, the piece of pie clutched in front of her.

"Hi."

Jesse jumped along with Mahkwi, who had seen

135

her a split second before his master. "God Almighty, Andi. You shouldn't sneak up on a man that way." He pulled a tarp up over whatever he was working on.

"I wasn't sneaking," she retorted, trying for a look at it anyway. "I just came to bring you a piece of pie."

He eyed the slab of blueberry pie hungrily as she handed it to him. "Thanks. You didn't have to do that."

She shrugged, circling around him, her feet crunching the fragrant straw-littered floor. "I wanted to."

Mahkwi, on her feet, sniffed the air suspiciously as Andrea drew closer to her.

"So . . ." she observed, running a curious finger over the tarp covered object at the center of the room, "this is where you spend your evenings."

He nodded, his mouth full of pie.

She glanced around the tack room, noticing how orderly he had made it. Reins, traces and whips all cleaned, polished and hung from spanking-new hooks in the wall; the broken saddle-trees had been repaired and sported freshly cleaned saddles; his own and her seldom-used sidesaddle. The room smelled of saddle soap and wood shavings.

And, of course, of Jesse.

"I must say, you've made good use of your time. The tack room hasn't looked this clean since . . . well, since Zach left."

Jesse cleared a box-full of tools off a pile of grain sacks. "Here, have a seat."

"Thanks."

He settled one hip against an empty saddle tree and took a bite of pie. "M-mmm. Oh . . . this is good."

A ripple of pleasure stole through her. "It used to be your favorite."

"Still is." He shoveled in another mouthful and

moaned with pleasure. "You sure know how to bake a pie, Andi."

She smiled. "I suppose pies are few and far between in Montana."

"They opened up a mechanical bakery in Virginia City. But their pies don't compare with this." He looked up at her and shook his head. "What are you doing still up, Andi? I thought you'd be in bed by now."

She scrutinized her fingernail avoiding his eyes. "Oh, I don't know. I just felt like some company. You're always out here at night working on . . ." She frowned at the tarp-covered object. "What *are* you working on?"

"Mmph-nuphmpn," he mumbled, his mouth full of pie.

"Pardon?"

He swallowed, looking sheepish. "It's . . . uh, not finished."

She folded her arms across her chest. "What is it?"

"Well, it was going to be a surprise."

"A surprise? For whom?"

"For you. And for little Zachary."

Indeed, surprise skittered through her. Her eyes widened with excitement. "Oh, Jess, show me now."

With a grin, he slipped the tarp off.

Andrea sucked in a breath at the sight of the nearly completed cradle. Wide and perfectly formed, it had hand-carved slats of maple, each the gentle shape of a slender leaf. In the headboard he'd carved a tiny willow tree, its leafy branches gracefully brushing the ground. She was struck speechless.

With one finger, Jesse gave the cradle a push and set it to rocking. "Like it?"

"Oh, Jesse—" She moved closer, running two hands along the smooth grain. His gift moved her more than she could say. "It's . . . it's beautiful. No,

137

it's more than beautiful. It's—it's a work of art."

He laughed and buried his fingers in the thick fur at Mahkwi's neck as the wolf brought her head up under Jesse's palm. "I don't know about that . . ."

"I do," Andrea said. "I've never seen anything so fine. And for a baby."

"Not just any baby," he reminded her. "My nephew."

"Is this what's kept you out here late nights? I thought . . . that you were just avoiding me."

He shot a guilty look at her that told her she hadn't been that far off the mark. She watched as he fitted the long strip in his hands against the slats on the right side. It seated perfectly against the wood.

He knelt down to inspect the fit from underneath. Andrea's mouth went dry as she watched his shirt pull across his back, defining his hard physique. The lantern light poured over his back, burnishing his dark blond hair and casting a golden glow over the deeply tanned skin on his arms. A rush of desire tore through her so unexpectedly she leaned instinctively against the door behind her.

Unaware of her perusal, he went on. "I've been working on it in my spare time. I found the old cradle, the one Ma used for me and Zach, hanging up in the loft. Dry rot had gotten to it." Standing, he shoved his hands in his pockets. "The baby's outgrowing that drawer fast. I figured he needed a proper bed."

She traced her fingertips over the carved willow tree. "You're talented, Jesse. I never knew you could work with wood."

"Neither did I until I left here. A friend of mine taught me, an old French-Canadian trapper, Antoine Devereaux. I lived with him and his son, Creed, for several years up on the Wolf Creek in Montana Territory." He shrugged. "Antoine taught me many things about myself I didn't know. Including how to wield a carving knife."

She realized then how little she knew about what had happened to Jesse since he'd left. "You haven't told me much about your life out there."

Jesse pulled a rag from his pocket and wiped his hands on it. "I didn't think you'd be interested."

Her lips parted in surprise. "Why wouldn't I be?"

"I know how you feel about Montana."

"Oh? And how's that?" Andi rested her gaze on the wolf who had edged closer to Jesse, laying her head on her huge paws.

"You haven't made any secret about it, Andi."

She lowered her eyes and smoothed out a wrinkle in the blue calico of her dress. "I never said I hated Montana. How could I hate a place I've never seen?"

Jesse merely grunted in reply, but he could think of a reason or two. He tightened his fist around the rag. His reluctant gaze roamed over the dark braid that fell across her shoulder and molded to the shape of her breasts. He'd been here just over a month and already his memories of Montana were dulling around the edges.

With an effort he called them back; the mountains, violet and red with lupines and wild paintbrush; the Pikuni maidens balancing water paunches on ropes around their shoulders, elkskin dresses clinging to their thighs. Nights of freedom around a Blackfoot campfire; the rush of his blood at the sale of his winter pack.

Other memories came up too: the lonely isolation of the endless winters living along his trap lines; his craving for the sound of a human voice or worse, a woman's touch in the frigid dead of night. All these things he'd felt and more. But they had passed, just as the feeling he got when he looked at Andi in the lantern light would pass.

"Thanks for the pie," he said handing her the plate. "It was good. Real good."

She took it. The look on her face said she knew she was being dismissed.

"I'll, uh, bring the cradle in as soon as it's done. Tomorrow probably."

Andrea nodded with a tentative smile. "Zachary will love it. So will I, Jesse."

His eyes clung to hers for a long beat and he fought down the urge to do more than just send her off to bed, alone.

"'Night, Andi. Don't wait up for me. I'll be out here late." He bent over the cradle again, drawing the sandpaper across the already smooth wood.

"'Night, Jesse."

He listened to her footsteps as she walked away from him, and he hardened his heart against the regret that welled deep inside him.

Jesse stood watching the sun melt below the horizon, casting the field of freshly shocked wheat in vermillion. Stacked four deep and each sheaf covered by a 'top hat' of two more sheaves, the shocks reminded him of golden mushrooms sprouting from the soil. Rain clouds scudded low across the sky, trumpeting a coming storm. They'd gotten the wheat shocked just in time. Jesse exhaled with a sigh of contentment.

Every muscle in his body ached. Not, he realized, with his usual resentful tension, but with the good ache of a hard day's work. He couldn't remember ever feeling such satisfaction in all the years he'd been farming. Perhaps it was because for the first time, he'd had no one standing over his shoulder telling him how to wrap the wheat twists around the shocks or break the heads back on the top hats. With instinct born of long experience, he knew how to shock a field of wheat. And for the first time, he'd done it his way.

He'd sent Silas in for supper over an hour ago, when Andi had rung the supper bell. Now Jesse's own stomach reminded him that he'd gone too long without food.

Picking up his tools, Jesse called Mahkwi and made his way toward the house. The wolf led the way, sniffing the ground as if she were going to find some new scent that had not been there before. From a distance came a sound that brought Mahkwi's head up with a snap. Wolves. A pack of them. Their haunting sound pricked at Jesse's skin and reminded him of nights around a Montana campfire. He glanced down at Mahkwi. She took three steps in the direction of the howls and stopped.

"What's the matter, girl?" Jesse asked, breaking the spell.

Mahkwi's fervent gaze darted back to Jesse. Not for the first time, Jesse realized how out of place a wolf-dog was on the farm, and how, like himself, she must long for the freedom of the mountains. Yet, the dog part of her remained loyal to him. She was a half-breed, belonging to neither side, fitting in like a square puzzle piece in a round hole.

Like him.

"You want to go with them, huh?" he murmured, sinking his fingers into her fur.

Mahkwi whined, and nudged his hand.

"I know . . . I know," he told her as they made their way across the field to the house.

The kitchen lamp spilled light onto the porch. Jesse stepped inside. A moment of disappointment filtered through him to find the kitchen empty. Supper warmed in a pot at the back of the stove. The fragrance of stew and warming coffee filled the spotless kitchen. One place setting awaited him on

141

the table, complete with bowl and spoon and a towel-covered plate of freshly baked bread.

He took an extra bowl from the shelf, scooped some warm stew into it, then blew on it to cool it. He set it down on the floor and, with a look over his shoulder, let Mahkwi in the door. Grateful, the wolf trotted in, sniffed the air, and made a beeline, not for the stew but for the clothes basket parked near the stairwell.

"Now, where are you going, Mahkwi?"

Jesse followed her to find her nearly nose to nose with Zachary, Mahkwi's tail swishing eagerly from side to side.

"Whoa, whoa," Jesse said, his heart giving a little leap, knowing Andi's worries about the wolf.

Zachary cooed with complete unconcern.

"What's this?" Jesse asked, reaching into the basket for the baby. He lifted Zachary into his arms while Mahkwi sniffed at the baby's feet with a female's curiosity.

"Hi ya, Corncob. What are you doing in here all by your lonesome? Where's your ma?"

Zachary smiled broadly showing toothless gums and reached for Jesse's hair. The smile tugged at Jesse's heart. Gathering Zachary to him, he ducked his head into the parlor to find that empty, too.

"Andi?"

No response.

With a frown, he stood for a moment, confused. "Well, looks like it's you and me, kid."

Zachary curled his tiny fist around Jesse's ear. He laughed. "You got your daddy's grip, boy. No doubt about that." He took the child's hand in his and spread his fingers flat. "Your daddy's hands too. A farmer's hands."

The baby filled his arms with delicious weight. He'd never thought much of babies before Zachary.

142

Never given a thought to having one of his own. Having delivered Zachary himself, he couldn't imagine feeling more like a father to a child than he did this one.

A dangerous thought, he warned himself. But he allowed himself the luxury of soaking in Zachary's smiles while no one was watching and enjoying the soft pressure of his small body against his shoulder.

Andi came through the kitchen door and gasped. "Jesse Winslow! What's that *wolf* doing in my kitchen?"

Mahkwi's ears drooped guiltily.

"And get her away from Zachary. She's practically got one of his feet in her mouth!"

Jesse shook his head. "She's just curious about him. She's not going to eat him. She's gentle as a—"

"—wolf," she finished. "O-U-T." She pointed at the door. Mahkwi slunk out with a wistful glance at her dish of uneaten stew. Andi picked it up and set it outside the door then shut it after her.

Startled by the noise, Zachary's face screwed up and he started to cry.

"Oh! Now see what you've done?" She took Zach from Jesse's arms and jiggled him against her shoulder.

"*I've* done? *You* slammed the door."

"Well *you* brought the wolf in here."

"Well, you left the baby in here all by himself."

Her eyes flashed with indignation. "I had to use the privy! What did you expect me to do? Take him with me?"

"Oh."

Feeling like a real heel, Jesse looked at her closely for the first time. Fatigue bruised her eyes. He realized there were a hundred things she needed to do every day, made all the more difficult by having a baby. Alone.

Zachary carried on, his tears no doubt driven by the tension in the room.

"Listen, I'm sorry about Mahkwi," Jesse said.

She looked at him. "I . . . I'm sorry for overreacting. Have . . . have you had your supper yet?"

"No. But I'll get it. Thanks for keeping it warm. You go on to bed. You look bushed."

She nodded. "Did you finish the wheat?"

"It's all shocked. We got it in before the rain."

"Good. Well, then, goodnight, Jesse."

"See you in the morning."

She nodded and headed up the stairs, alone.

It rained the next day, and the next, but Andrea saw little of Jesse except when he came in for meals. The weather kept him out of the fields, but he spent his time in the barn, straightening out months of disorganization, cleaning rust off neglected plows, and setting things to right. But he made a habit of coming in before she rang the bell for meals to play with Zachary, leaving her hands free to get food on the table. She appreciated those moments, not only because she so desperately needed them, but because she enjoyed seeing the light shining between Jesse and her son.

Several nights later, Andrea jiggled a crying Zachary against her shoulder, desperately wishing she could find a way to comfort him. Nothing seemed to help; not food, not a clean napkin, not the lullaby she'd given up on after the tenth verse.

Her eyes blurred with tears of frustration in the dim lamplight. She couldn't make out the time on the bedside clock but by the absolute darkness outside her window, she knew she was still hours away from dawn. Exhaustion pulled at her like a heavy cloak and she wished more than anything to lie beneath the covers of her feather bed and sleep undisturbed for a day, or two, or three.

The colic that kept Zachary wakeful at night never seemed to bother him in the light of day. For that at least she was grateful. But after nights of experiments, she found that nothing short of time and her steady pacing around her small room would soothe him.

"Shhh-hh, darlin', Mama's right here," she crooned. Comforted for a brief moment, the baby snuffled tiredly against her shoulder, clutching her thin nightgown in his tiny fist. "Hush, now and go to sleep. You're so tired and so is Mama."

Did all new mothers have so much trouble comforting their children? A weepy breath hitched her chest. Whatever made her think she could do this alone? she wondered disconsolately. Maybe Jesse was right. Maybe she wasn't up to the task. Oh, how she wished Zach were there to hold her, tell her everything would be all right again as it had been once.

But it was Jesse's face that swirled in her mind.

She paced, trying to shut out his image. Her throat burned like she'd swallowed lye and an ache swelled in her chest. The War had stolen Zach from her. The damnable War with its flagrant disregard for the heartbreak it left behind. It had snatched from her the only true solace this world had ever given her, save those early years she'd had with Jesse.

But even they had been a lie. She'd been nothing more than a stop along the way for a man bound up in his dreams and his anger with his past.

She squeezed her eyes shut, allowing the breeze drifting in from the open window to caress the dampness on her cheeks. Still, she was afraid. Afraid of being completely alone; of managing the farm without a man . . . without Jesse. And worse, she feared the one who'd left the note hanging on her underthings when no one was watching.

She stopped at the window, staring down into the dark yard. The fact that she could see nothing gave her little comfort. Zachary's crying had descended into whuffling breaths and she felt him relaxing against her damp shoulder. Despite the compact warmth of him there, Andrea felt more alone than she'd ever felt in her life. She laid the baby down in the fine cradle Jesse had built, and blessedly Zachary snuggled into his bed without waking.

For a long time she stood rocking his cradle, watching her newborn son sleep. Tears, quiet and heartfelt, welled up spilled down her cheeks. She climbed into bed and buried her face in the pillow to muffle her sobs.

What she wanted more than anything was for someone to put his arms around her and hold her, tell her it would be all right, that she could do it.

She was dangerously close to believing she could not.

Jesse rolled over in the dark and looked at the clock on his bedside table—2:30 a.m. Upstairs, little Zach wailed inconsolably and Jesse heard the floorboards squeak under Andi's pacing feet.

He groaned and slid his calloused hands under his head. He was getting used to this. Though he was quiet as a lamb during the days, Zachary had yet to sleep through the night. In fact, Jesse often found himself awake automatically at feeding times listening for the baby's first stirrings. He often lay awake listening for Andi to stop pacing the floor above him with the baby, to climb back in that big bed of hers and fall asleep.

Sometimes, long after that, he would stare at the

ceiling, listening to the sound of his own heart thudding in the darkness, and imagine her there in that pale muslin nightgown he'd seen her in once. Or worse, he'd imagine himself there beside her.

He stayed away from her at night. Some unspoken agreement between them had drawn that line between propriety and common sense. Days had fallen into a routine that mimicked family life, he mused. They moved around the place as if they belonged there together, the three of them. But it was only an illusion.

On top of totally caring for the baby, Andi cooked, cleaned and put up vegetables from the garden, and though she denied it, grew visibly more exhausted each day. He and Silas sweated out in the fields, repaired fence rails, and ate the food she cooked for them.

Etta still stopped by now and then; she baked pies and bread, more now out of friendship than necessity. At night Jesse worked out in the barn until dark. Then he and Andi went to their separate rooms and, wisely, stayed there.

He sighed. Yes, what they had resembled a family life, but they weren't a family. And all of them knew it.

Jesse turned an ear to the ceiling again. The baby had stopped crying. He heard Andi stop pacing, then the creak of the ropes as she climbed back into bed.

Slapping the pillow, he dug his cheek into the softness, intent on finding sleep again. He lay there for a few minutes with his eyes closed before he recognized the other sound he heard coming through the floorboards overhead: this time, the muted sobs weren't little Zach's, they were Andi's.

Jesse sat bolt upright in bed, straining to hear the sound. She was crying softly as if her heart would break. Anger rolled through him that he hadn't seen

147

it coming. Exhaustion, loneliness, fear of losing her home, and no doubt grief over Zach's death, had caught up with her.

Without thinking it through logically, he got out of bed and pulled on a pair of pants. His only thought was to go to her, comfort her, make her hurting stop.

He walked barefoot through the kitchen and up the stairs, avoiding the squeak on the third step through old habit. At the top of the stairs he stopped to listen. Behind her closed door, he could still hear her crying, though the sound seemed even more quiet than it had in his room. It was more of a snuffling sound. Jesse's hand poised on the doorknob.

Should he knock? Should he call out to her? Should he just go in and gather her up in his arms? Tell her everything will be all right? That's what he wanted to do.

He felt the truth of that vibrate through him.

But he might as well tell her the moon was blue. What good was comfort from a man like him anyway, when his embrace might hurt her more than help?

Besides, he thought, slipping his hand off the doorknob, he wouldn't be doing her any favor exposing her now at her most vulnerable. *That's why, you dolt, she chose to hide her tears from you.*

Feeling a fool, he turned to go. The sound of her door opening behind him stopped him in his tracks.

"Jesse," she whispered. "I heard a noise and I— what are you doing? It's the middle of the night."

"I—" He fumbled for an excuse.

"Is something wrong?"

His eyes searched hers in the dark. "Are you all right?"

She sniffed and pulled the door shut silently behind her, staring at him through the darkness.

"I'm . . . fine."

"The walls in this house aren't very thick, Andi. I heard you crying."

In silhouette, he saw her reach up to run the back of one hand over her cheek, heard her hesitation. "I . . . I wasn't crying."

"Yes, you were. What's wrong?"

The velvety silence of night surrounded them, insulated them there in the dark hallway.

"Andi?"

"Oh, for heaven's sake!" She gave an annoyed sniff. "What if I was? If I feel like blubbering into my pillow in the dark I suppose I should be able to do it without an interrogation, shouldn't I?" She turned on her heel and reached for the doorknob. He stopped her with one hand.

"Andi, wait. Maybe it is none of my business, but I don't like to see you upset like this."

His touch sent heat spiraling up her arm and she tried to pull away. "You're right. It isn't any of your business. But if you must know," she lied, "Isabelle said it's quite normal for new mothers to have crying spells. That's all it is."

Jesse reached for the bowl of wooden matches on the hall table, struck one, and lit the oil sconce hanging on the wall. The golden light flared, illuminating the hallway. To his regret, her thin cotton gown became nearly translucent in the light. But Andi was looking at him wide eyed the same way he was looking at her. He became acutely aware that he'd forgotten to put a shirt on as her gaze flicked down the length of him. But his shirtless condition wasn't what really shocked her.

"Jesse," she said breathlessly. "You *shaved*."

Jesse ran a hand over his freshly shaven jaw. "Oh, that." He'd nicked the hell out of his face tonight, a direct result of his lack of practice with a straight

149

razor. "Yeah, I decided you might be right about the beard. It served a purpose in Montana, with the cold nights and all, but here it's just a nuisance."

Her gaze roamed over him. A ragged breath hitched her chest. "It looks . . . good."

"Thanks." He was thinking the same thing about her hair, lying across her breast in an auburn plait. His blood stirred to the rhythm of his thudding heart. He thought of her only minutes ago, crying as if her heart was broken. Now, only a redness around her eyes and nose betrayed her. But that was enough to make him want to reach out and protect her from that kind of pain.

She eyed him critically from several angles, then gave him a small smile. "I see you still have dimples."

"I do not," Jesse denied with an adamant frown.

"Do so."

"Never. Dimples? Come on."

"Always did. Right here"—she reached out and traced a finger over the dent in his cheek to prove her point—"and . . . and here." Her teasing grin faltered at the sudden heat in his eyes.

"Ah . . ." he added, grabbing her hand away from his sensitive skin, " . . . and the nicks. Don't forget the nicks."

Their eyes locked for the space of two heartbeats. "Well, you'll have to be more careful next time, won't you?"

He nodded slowly, without taking his eyes from hers. "Much more careful." His gaze moved to her mouth. Dangerous, was his only thought. Damned dangerous to be looking at her this way.

Close enough to feel the heat of his body, Andrea's every instinct told her to pull away from him. But she didn't. No—couldn't. He held her there with those blue eyes as surely as did his hand. She ran a tongue across her suddenly dry lips, wondering if he was going to kiss her. Wishing he would, hoping he wouldn't.

Could he hear the wild beating of her heart? The sound of it in her own ears drowned out everything else. It had been a mistake to come out in the hallway. After she'd seen it was Jesse, she should have just closed the door. Now he was so close, she could feel the heat of his body through the thin fabric of her gown. So close she felt her nipples bead and harden in response.

Jesse watched the tip of her tongue dart out to wet her full lower lip and felt his control slipping. He reached up with the hand holding hers and ran a knuckle over the smoothness of her cheek. A tremor went through her, but he wondered if the reaction was his instead. *Damnation.*

"Andi," he said low, "if I kissed you now, I'd have to stay. You know that."

Through a fringe of dark lashes her amethyst eyes glittered. "Do I?" she whispered back. "It never stopped you before."

The truth stung. "That was then."

"And now?"

"Now, you're my little brother's widow. The mother of his child. And I've got a life waiting for me out in Montana."

She pulled her hand from his and she laughed ironically. "Oh, I see. I suppose you expected me to wait for you."

"No. No I didn't."

"But you didn't expect me to marry your brother."

"It doesn't matter." Turning away from her, he stared blindly down the stairs.

"No? What did you expect, Jesse? That I would pine for you for the rest of my days? End up an old spinster? Did you think I'd wait forever for a man who never even bothered to write to tell me he was still alive?"

He turned on her. "If I'd written I—" He faltered, then changed tacks. "I'm glad you married. Glad even that it was Zach. He was crazy about you, even back then."

"You're *afraid* to kiss me, aren't you?" she taunted.

"*What?*"

"You're plain scared."

He glared at her. "Of what?"

"Of what you're afraid is still between us."

Outside the hall window, the crickets filled the empty pause as Jesse's eyes skewered hers. "Friendship. That's all that's still between us, Andi."

She lifted her chin. "Maybe. But you'll never know will you?" She took a step toward him.

"Andi, this is not a good ide—"

"Afraid to know?" she asked, arching one dark brow. "Maybe there *is* nothing. Maybe all that's left is a memory."

Damn it to hell, Jesse thought, why didn't she leave well enough alone?

"You married my brother," he said in accusation.

"Yes, I did."

"And you loved him."

Her eyes didn't flicker. "Yes . . . I did."

He felt like the worst kind of bastard to be jealous of whatever happiness Zach and Andi had found together. Nevertheless, anger was the only emotion he could allow himself to feel right now. Anger that she would push him so far. Anger that he was, in fact, afraid to be pushed.

Reaching a hand out, he slid it into the hair at the damp nape of her neck and pulled her roughly closer, closer until her body was flush with his. Instinctively, she grasped his arms to keep herself from falling. There was no fear of that. His steely grip said

152

he wouldn't let her go.

"And what if memory's all there is?" he asked.

"Then we'll know, won't we?"

He dropped his mouth an inch away from hers, but still didn't kiss her. Andi's eyes were wide with fear, or expectation, he didn't know which. Her heartbeat fluttered against the wall of his chest like a bird's. Her scent drifted up to him—a heady combination of lilac water and soap—testing his resolve.

Oh, hell. Whether it was her taunt or his own mixed-up emotions guiding him, he couldn't let her go. He'd prove to her once and for all there was nothing left between them. And then she'd let him go.

"You want me to kiss you, Andi Mae?" he asked, his mouth a whisper away from hers. She didn't answer, only stared up at him, her eyes filled with silent challenge.

He dropped his head down slowly, slowly, until his lips brushed hers with the most platonic of touches. Her mouth was unexpectedly soft and pliant, her lips warm and sweet as honey. His body tightened all over and he lingered there for a moment longer than wise. Lifting his head he glared down at her with a look that said, *"There."*

Her closed eyes fluttered open with an accusing gleam. "Coward."

He exhaled sharply at her taunt. He *was* a coward, damn him. "All right. You want a kiss?"

He crushed his mouth against hers then with all the pent-up emotion coiling inside him. He kissed her hard, grinding his lips down on hers to prove . . . hell . . . to prove himself wrong. To prove her wrong.

There was no gentleness to his kiss, Andrea thought, not even kindness. When his arms tightened around her, capturing her, she fought down a

153

moment of panic. Another man, a darker one, rose up like specter in her mind. Fighting down the picture, she opened her eyes. No, this was Jesse, she reminded herself. Jesse. Not . . . *him*.

Andrea's mouth slanted under his, opening at the insistence of his. Their breaths mingled and she felt her insides dip and plunge like a cork on water. Her heartbeat raced along the edges of her nerves, awakening some long-dead desire from deep inside her.

Invading her mouth, his tongue sought hers, then lashed the smooth surface of her teeth. Andrea tightened her arms around him, seeking to draw him closer, closer to her. His skin was smooth and hot beneath her touch as she slid her hands up his shoulders and beyond, to the silky thickness of the hair at his nape. Her fingertips raked his scalp.

A ripple of surprise went through him as she met his tongue with her own, exploring the rough texture of it the way he had discovered hers. From somewhere in his throat came a sound of need. He deepened the kiss, the anger suddenly gone from his embrace. Pulling her closer, he spread one hand across her hip until her body was flush against him as flame on a burning ember. He was strong and hard and she could feel his wanting through the thin fabric of her nightgown.

Jesse's tongue danced with hers, the tune as familiar as the one on the old music box that sat in the corner of the parlor. She remembered the taste of him, the shape of his mouth, the way it fit with hers like no one else's ever had. His hand slid intimately up the curve of her ribs to cradle the fullness of her breast. Like a river current, his touch swayed her, stole the strength from her knees, and eddied inside the very depths of her.

Here in the darkness, her body answered his the

154

way it always had, despite the years that had slipped away between them, despite the fact that only weeks ago she'd had Zach's child.

Oh, Jesse, Jesse, why did you ever leave me?

As if he'd heard her thought, Jesse pulled away from her, lifting his head only inches from hers. His breath, ragged and harsh, caressed her cheeks. His eyes, stunned and troubled, probed hers in the dim light. He swallowed hard as he set her away from him. His breath came as hard and fast as hers.

On a husky laugh, he raked one hand through his long hair. "Damn . . ."

"Yes," she agreed on a shaky breath.

He jammed his fingers into the tight back pockets of his Levi's. "So what does that prove?"

"For one, it proves you've haven't forgotten how to kiss since I last saw you." She saw in his eyes, he remembered only too well how good it had once been between them. Her thudding heart remembered it, too.

"I was hardly a monk."

"Nor was I," she replied pointedly.

"So, how do I compare?" Defensiveness edged his voice.

For an instant, she wondered if that could possibly be jealousy she glimpsed in his eyes. Zach and she had been husband and wife in every sense of the word of course, but never, in all the time they were together, had he made her tremble all over the way she was right now. She glanced down, unwilling to give him that admission with a look.

"That's hardly a fair question, Jesse."

"I suppose not. But I must admit I'm curious. After all he *was* my little brother."

"What difference could it possibly make now? Zach's dead."

He regarded her for a long moment. "No difference. Because what just happened between us was no more than just that. A kiss."

"A simple kiss," she affirmed.

He shifted in annoyance. "So, what's two?"

"I beg your pardon?"

"You said, for one, I've haven't been a monk. What's your second point?"

She shrugged. "That should be clear, even to you."

"What just happened between us only proves that I'm a healthy man and you're a healthy woman."

Her mouth tipped upward at one corner. "It proves that whatever else you feel for me," she said, turning the brass and porcelain knob on her door, and stepping into the shadows, "indifference has no part in it. Goodnight, Jesse."

She disappeared into her room, leaving him on the landing alone. He ground his teeth together, knowing she was right. Dammit! She was always right. He turned down the wick on the hall lamp and blew out the flame. He knew, too, that it was time to start putting his plan into action, before it was too damned late for either one of them.

Chapter Ten

The white clapboard Methodist church sat atop a pretty little knoll at the head of Elkgrove's Main Street. Its belled steeple, complete with huge clock, gave it the singular distinction of being official timekeeper of Elkgrove. Its rather infamous timepiece clanged religiously on the hour, every hour and at high noon, played a peal of chimes to mark the time to which everyone in town set his watch.

Jesse pulled the buggy to a stop beneath the huge white ash trees that surrounded the church, just as the bell chimed nine. He set the brake, climbed down and tied the mare to a vacant spot on the white-washed hitching rail. From within the sanctuary came the sound of voices lifted in song.

Andrea glanced down at Jesse. He looked particularly handsome in the white shirt he'd changed into, a black four-in-hand tie at his throat. She could hardly imagine him the same wooly mountain man who'd burst into her bedroom a few weeks earlier. It had been his idea to go to church instead of working today. The idea had pleased her immensely, especially since she'd hadn't been off Willow Banks since the baby.

157

"We're late," she said, handing Zachary down to him.

"They'll let us in anyway, I suppose," he replied, holding the baby awkwardly against his shoulder. Zachary seemed perfectly at home there, reaching a hand up to curl around Jesse's tie.

Offering a steady hand, he helped her dismount. "You look real pretty, Andi. Even in widow's weeds."

She laughed. "Thank you, I think. It's been a long time since I've been to church. Not since before Martha's death. What if . . . if someone makes an issue out of your staying out at the farm with me, alone?"

He glanced down at her realizing for the first time she was worried about it. "Does it bother you, Andi, my staying there?"

Her eyes met his. "No. I feel safer with you there."

"Even after last night?"

Chin up, she smiled. "Even after last night." The kiss they'd shared had proven what she'd known since that day he'd returned—time and distance had not diminished the powerful bond between them. The prospect of falling in love with him all over again didn't frighten her. Being foolish enough to risk that emotion again was what had her really scared.

"Ready?"

She nodded, threaded her arm through his and walked with him to the double doorway.

The tune to one of her favorite hymns surrounded them as he pulled open the double doors:

Amazing Grace, how sweet the sound,
That saved a wretch like me.
I once was lost, but now I'm found.
Was blind but now I see.

158

One voice in particular rose above the rest. Andrea glanced to the right. There, standing among the other coloreds along the back wall stood Silas and Etta. Silas didn't glance at the hymnal in Etta's hands. He knew all the words by heart. With a voice rich and deep, he didn't allow the fact that he'd been relegated to standing at the back of the church to dim the joy in his singing.

The air in the church was stifling, despite the dozens of ladies' fans in motion. There were tellingly few men in the congregation, but a contingent of seven Federal officers in blue uniforms took up one whole pew near the front. She supposed they were from one of the numerous companies that moved through Elkgrove on their way to nearby Cincinnati. A dark-haired lieutenant turned to catch sight of them. His lips parted in surprise when he saw her, and she wondered briefly if she knew him.

In search of an empty pew, they walked down the center aisle, she and Jesse, the baby propped still on Jesse's shoulder. Every head in the sanctuary turned to study them as they threaded their way into a pew.

She felt Jesse's fingers against the small of her back, guiding her ahead of him, reminding her that she was not alone. Andrea glanced up at him with a grateful smile for that small mercy and he nodded to her, with an almost imperceptible movement of his head. As they took their places, there among the congregation, a small part of her felt as if they belonged, she and Jesse, with Zachary snuggled against his shoulder. Almost as if they were a family. But another part of her, the logical part, told her not to wish for what could never be.

Angelina Butterworth, Loretta Pease and Camy Micheals, three old acquaintances, stood directly in front of her and Jesse. Camy's blond sausage-curls

159

bobbed perkily around her plump face as she craned her neck to catch a glimpse of the man beside Andrea. When she did, her eyes widened like a fish who'd suddenly run up on land and her voice went distinctly off key. An addlepated grin tipped the corner of her mouth when her gaze returned to Andrea. Camy waggled her finger at her before turning around.

A flash of jealousy speared through Andrea, but she concentrated on the hymn and the surprising sound of Jesse's fine, clear baritone voice joining the rest:

> Through many dangers, toils and snares,
> We have already come.
> T'was Grace that brought us safe thus far
> And Grace t'will lead us home.

The hymn seemed unusually appropriate this morning. Surely, she thought, Grace had led Jesse back to her when she needed him the most. And Grace would see her through his leaving again as well.

When the hymn ended, the stout, balding Reverend McConneghy read the names of three local young men whose lives had been claimed in recent fighting. Among them were Danny O'Dell and Pike Weaver, old friends of Andrea's who'd volunteered early on in the War. She squeezed her eyes shut at the sad news. Elkgrove was a small hamlet, and like Zach, the men who'd died were well known and liked. The war had become personal to every living citizen of the town whose numbers were shrinking weekly; hardly a family hadn't been touched by death.

Naturally, the War became the subject of McConneghy's sermon, as it had been often these many years since the conflict's beginnings. He spoke both of war and cowardice, which, in a roundabout fashion, he tied to the raiders' attacks on nearby farms. Casting an entreating look at the soldiers filling the front pew, the reverend alluded to rumblings of vigilantism. He cautioned against losing sight of both God's and man's law and encouraged prayer as the answer to the troubled town.

But as Andrea looked around the church, she noticed that few of the men appeared to be in agreement with the good pastor. Several men sat, red-necked with frustration, grumbling to each other in whispers and nods. She glanced up at Jesse to find him in tight-lipped agreement with the masses.

At the conclusion of the service, parishioners filed past Reverend McConneghy to shake his hand and thank him for his inspirational message. But it appeared that most of the men seemed inspired by something besides the Reverend's message, and outside they clustered together in small groups airing their feelings.

James McConneghy reached out his hand to Andrea as she drew near. "Ah, Andrea, my dear. It's good to see you in church again. And look at this healthy little lad." He patted little Zachary's back who was fast asleep against Jesse's shoulder. "And no doubt this is who I think it is?" he said, grinning at Jesse.

Jesse smiled and shook his hand. "Reverend?"

"I must say I'm glad to see you at long last, Jesse. We all thought you were—"

"—dead, I know." Jesse winced. "Nasty rumor."

McConneghy laughed, his gaze going back and forth between him and Andi. "I hope you're home to stay, this time, Jesse."

Jesse smiled uncomfortably avoiding Andi's eyes. "I'm afraid not, Reverend."

The reverend's gaze flicked to Andrea, who shifted her eyes to the floor. She didn't want anyone to see how deeply his answer affected her.

"I see," the reverend said. "That's too bad. All the same, it's good to see you, son."

"You, too."

They made their way out to the milling crowds in the yard. Isabelle Rafferty stood fanning herself beside her husband, John. Jesse guessed two youngsters hanging from the tails of John's frock coat were the girls Etta had told him about, and half the children nearby were likely theirs, too.

"Jesse!" Isabelle called. "It's about time you dragged that gal into town. Lemme see that youngun!"

Jesse dipped a shoulder so she was level-eyed with the sleeping baby.

Isabelle gasped with pleasure. "Oh, ain't he a button? Lookit that little face, will ya, John? Don't it just make you wanna have another one?"

Isabelle's husband was close to forty, tall as Jesse, but wiry as a bedslat. He laughed, lifting the two little girls dangling from his arms. "I don't suppose you'll ever get enough younguns, Izzy."

She chuckled and looked lovingly up at her husband. "I don't reckon I will. Can I hold him. Just for a minute?"

Jesse obliged, gently shifting the sleeping child to her shoulder.

Andrea kissed Isabelle on the cheek. "Feel free to borrow this one any time, 'Aunt' Isabelle," she teased.

Isabelle grinned with pleasure. "You're lookin' purty as a new day, Andrea. Jesse, you must be doin'

162

somethin' right with this little gal."

Andrea could have sworn he blushed.

"She, uh, doesn't need any help from me in that department Isabelle," Jesse replied, glancing at Andrea.

"Oh, for heaven's sake . . ." Andrea laughed, warmed by Jesse's words.

"Andrea! Whoo-oo! Andrea Winslow!" called a female voice from behind them. Andrea turned to see a white-gloved hand pumping in her direction from the center of a crowd of people. Camy Micheals' blond ringlets went momentarily horizontal as her head bobbed up and down over the shoulders of the crowd. "Whoo-oo!"

"Tie down the men," Isabelle told Andrea in a sotto voice. "Camy Micheals is comin'."

Andrea sighed. Everyone knew the rubenesque Camy Micheals was perpetually on the hunt for a husband. She emerged from the crowd, a cloud of pink silk, fanning herself rapidly in the morning heat, a flush rising prettily to her cheeks.

"I swear," Camy exclaimed, puffing up beside Andrea. "I thought I'd never get through that throng before you left. Hello, Isabelle, Mr. Rafferty. I was just dying to meet that new little baby of yours, Andrea," she said, unable to tear her gaze from Jesse.

"How sweet of you, Camy," Andrea said, containing the sarcasm in her voice as she tucked back the thin blanket covering Zachary's face.

"Well, he's just as cute as he can be. Why, he looks just like you, Andrea. Don't you think so?" she asked, looking with artful guilessness at Jesse.

"More and more every day," Jesse agreed, his gaze on Andrea.

"Camy," Andrea began, "I don't think you've met

163

my brother-in-law, Jesse Winslow. Jesse, Camy Sue Micheals."

"*Miss* Camy Sue Micheals," Camy amended, boldly extending her hand to him.

"Charmed," he replied, obliging the woman with a brush of his lips against the back of her hand.

"Oh, my," she gasped, and fluttered her brown eyes up at Jesse. "You *are* the mountain man we've all been hearin' so much talk about, are you not? Zach's long lost brother?"

He nodded.

"Tell me, Mr. Winslow, are all men from Montana so . . . *gallant?*" She imbued the word with a French accent so phoney that Andrea had to press her lips together to keep from smiling.

"I can't speak for any but myself, Miss Micheals," Jesse allowed, "but I'd wager you'd find a few more *'gallant'* than me." He glanced at Andrea, who fought to keep a straight face. "I am greatly relieved to know that my sister-in-law has such charming and lovely friends as you here in Elkgrove."

Camy gulped. "My, my . . . how kind of you to say so, Mr. Winslow. I'd dearly love to hear all about that wild country out West sometime if you're ever so inclined to reminisce. I'm sure you have some utterly fascinating stories to tell."

John Rafferty took hold of Jesse's arm. "I'm sure he does, Miss Camy, but right now I'm going to drag him over there for some man-talk, if you don't mind."

Looking greatly relieved, Jesse nodded. "I'd like that, John. Some other time, Miss Micheals?"

"Of course," she replied, batting her fan below her eyes with her left hand so he'd know her interest was genuine.

As Jesse and John walked toward the group of men

on the far side of the yard, Camy's gaze followed him. She sighed dramatically. "Now there's a *real* man."

Isabelle thwacked her across the arm with the tip of her fan. "Camy Sue Micheals! You're shameless."

Camy's eyes widened with pure innocence. "Well, for heaven sakes! I didn't mean anything by it." She plucked a thread from the black lace at the wrist of her pink silk gown. "It's just that we get so few through here like him. In fact, so few men around at all who aren't either soldiers or . . . or taken."

"Camy Sue," Isabelle said sternly, nodding at Jesse, "that one's taken, too."

Andrea glanced sharply up at Isabelle.

"You don't mean—Is he gonna marry you, Andrea? But . . . you're in mourning, aren't you?"

Isabelle braced her hands on her wide hips. "O'course she is, but she's got a child and a farm to look after, too. In these hard times, ain't a body in this township would blame her, nor half the widows this war's made, for marryin' up again right away."

"Well, is Mr. Winslow gonna marry you?" Camy asked Andrea.

Camy's bluntness never failed to surprise her. "I—I wouldn't know. He hasn't asked me."

"—yet," Isabelle amended. "Camy, you find somebody else to go all taffy-headed about."

Camy glared at her. "Well, I swear! He's been here near a month, Isabelle. I suppose if he was of a mind to ask her to marry up with him, he would have by now. After all, everyone knows he's got the best of both worlds without having to put a ring on her finger, with her cookin' and cleanin' and sharing her house with—"

"Camy! That's enough!" Isabelle's eyes took on a furious light. "Lord, I never met anyone who cottoned to the taste of shoe leather more'n you."

Camy clamped her mouth shut, realizing she'd gone too far. Through a fringe of brown lashes she looked up contritely at Andrea whose face was hot with anger. "Oh . . . uh, I didn't mean to say that, Andrea. Really, I *do* apologize. Sometimes, my mouth runs on . . . I—I hope you'll forgive me."

Andrea gave her a look that would freeze the steaming water in a teacup. "Camy," she said calmly, "go bang your head against a wall."

Camy's mouth fell open as she watched Andrea stalk away from her.

"Gal," Isabelle told Camy before starting off after Andrea, "I always did say you had more vines than 'taters.''

"I don't care what McConneghy says," Clyde Briggs grumbled amidst the cluster of men. He tore the hat off in frustration and slapped it against his thigh. A warm breeze ruffled his graying hair. "If we don't do somethin' soon, ain't one of our farms gonna be safe from them thievin' bushwhackers. Prayers may save our souls, but they ain't gonna protect us."

"That's right," put in the bespeckled wheat farmer, George Potts. "Why, only two days ago, they hit Cal Moore's place, a few miles down the road from me. Robbed him blind whilst he and his wife were in town, and set fire to his wheat. Darn near burnt down his barn in the process. We were up half the night tryin' to put it down."

"Anybody know who they are?" Jesse asked with a frown. "Anyone seen their faces?"

All eyes in the group turned to Jesse. The men searched his face with undisguised suspicion. John Rafferty dispelled the tension with a good-natured clap of his hand on Jesse's shoulder. "You fellas remember Tom Winslow's boy, Jesse? Well, this here is him. Back from Montana Territory to work Willow Banks. Jesse, you might remember Clyde Briggs, George Potts and Sam Eakin."

The men each nodded in turn and reached a welcoming hand out to Jesse. Potts, the oldest of the bunch, stood with his hands shoved in the pockets of his black frock coat, his thinning white hair ruffling in the hot breeze.

"So," Jesse repeated. "Has anyone gotten a good look at these men?"

"The only person to catch a look at them," Potts answered, "Was old Eli Larson. He said they all wore some sorta sacks over their heads. A couple of 'em had Butternut stripes on their trousers. They kilt a nigger at his place. Strung him up 'cause he was there, I reckon. These vermin are mean son's of guns."

That news settled in the pit of Jesse's stomach like a weight. Searching the crowd for Andi, he found her standing in a circle of women, showing off the baby. He thought of the day he'd ridden onto Willow Banks to find Andi alone, and the look of terror in her eyes when he'd burst into her room with his gun drawn. He could have just as easily been one of the raiders.

And what about Silas? His gaze found him standing in the shade of the church, deep in conversation with Etta. The truth was, Silas had no gun, nothing with which to protect himself if that gang came upon him alone, as he often walked over to Etta's place. Jesse decided he'd would have to remedy that lack right away.

"... the hell," Briggs was grumbling when Jesse's attention returned to the conversation. "They's Johnny Rebs ... or, leastwise *was*. But they ain't

167

actin' like John Morgan's bunch who come through here last summer like a plague of locusts, a thousand strong. No, these bastards don't number more'n ten from all accounts, an' are more specific in their wants.

"They ain't partial to the livestock," Briggs went on, "or foodstuffs the Southern militia is hungerin' for. Oh, they've killed their share o' hogs an' Rhode Islands, but like as not, they leave the carcass there to rot. No, they're deserters, after silver, jewelry, money where there is some. I think the fires they set are just to get us off the scent."

"If ya ask me," John Rafferty put in, "I think it's mighty peculiar they always seem to hit a place when no one's around. It's as if they know the comin's and goin's of the folks around here."

That comment brought a round of thoughtful silence. From nearby came the sounds of the children's laughter as the youngsters engaged in a lively game of tag.

"Well," Briggs said at last. "We got a choice. We can take 'em on one on one or we can try to do somethin' about 'em together. The Union Army ain't got the manpower or the inclination to spare anyone for a whistle-stop like Elkgrove. I say we try to come up with a way to protect our places— together."

Sam Eakin, who'd been silent through the conversation, cleared his throat. "And how are we supposed to protect our own places if we're off huntin' them no accounts? You got three grown sons, Briggs." He raked a hand through his thinning brown hair. "I'm a widower. I got me five younguns to chase after and a farm to keep up. I don't see how we can be two places at once."

Jesse narrowed his gaze on the man. He remem-

168

bered Sam from years ago. A few years older than Jesse, Sam had married a girl Jesse knew, Suzannah Kellogg. He was sorry to hear of her death, but the news that Sam was suddenly eligible made Jesse look at the man in a whole new light.

"Nobody's askin' you to leave your younguns, Sam," Clyde assured him as one of Sam's children came running up, crashing into his knees in a devilish hug.

"Paw, Paw!" shouted the towheaded girl dressed in a clean but worn pinafore. "Gregory won't let me have a turn wif the—"

Sam ran a hand affectionately over the four-year-old's head. "Not now, Lisbeth. You go play with your brothers. This here's man-talk."

"But, Paw . . . ith's not fair," she lisped.

"Off with ya, rascal." Scuffing her worn boots in the dirt, the girl reluctantly obeyed, then took off at a run for her brothers. Sam shouted after her. "You tell Gregory to give you a turn on that see-saw!" Satisfied, he turned back to the group.

"We all know your situation," Briggs concluded. "But there's those of us who are free to gather up in a posse and chase after them lowlifes 'fore they can hit again."

Sam scratched his head. "But Sheriff Cobb said—"

"Cobb's got his finger up his nose," Briggs said. "If he could'a stopped 'em, he'd a done it by now. These raids have been happenin' over a month now and Cobb's no closer to catchin' the culprits than he was then."

"What do you propose?" Jesse asked.

"A meeting. A *private* meeting."

"Including who?" John asked.

"Them with land to protect," Briggs replied, implicitly excluding outsiders.

169

"I'll spread the word." George Potts fitted his battered hat on his head. "Good day to you, boys."

The group broke up, and Jesse watched Sam Eakin wander toward his own wagon, where two of his boys were hanging like monkeys from the wheels.

"Jesse," John said. "When are you gonna come by with Andrea and the baby for a visit?"

Jesse wasn't sure he cared for the idea of being lumped together with Andi and her son, as if they were a family, even though it seemed that was how everyone already thought of them. "I'll try to get over soon, John."

He leaned closer. "I want you to meet Lexi."

He thought he'd heard all his children's names. "Who?"

"My draft mare." John grinned like a kid with an all day sucker. "My pride and joy. Isabelle thinks I'm crazy, but I'm buildin' a future on her and that youngun she's about to foal. Horse like that can do the work of two mules without the pigheadedness. Built her a special stall just to hold her and the foal in the barn when she delivers."

"Sounds like a lot of work."

He laughed and clapped Jesse on the shoulder. "It's good to have you back in town, Jess. Don't be a stranger, all right?"

Jesse smiled. "I won't." He excused himself from John and caught up with Sam a few steps before he reached the wagon.

"Sam!"

Sam turned and smiled at Jesse.

"Can I talk to you for a minute?"

Sam shrugged. "Sure. About what?"

"Well, it's . . ." Jesse began awkwardly, "it's a sensitive matter."

"It is?" Sam replied, interested now.

Jesse nodded. "It's about my sister-in-law, Andrea . . ."

"Well, then, don't you know," Loretta Pease droned on, "those bread and butter pickles turned out so sour even my hogs wouldn't eat them. It took me all afternoon, of course, to figure what went wrong."

"No . . ." gasped Angelina Butterworth, listening raptly to Loretta's long-winded tale.

"You'll never guess what happened . . ."

Loretta's voice faded away and Andrea suppressed a yawn searching the crowded churchyard for a glimpse of Jesse. She found him walking amiably with Sam Eakin, the widower from the other side of Elkgrove Township.

A surge of hope blossomed through her at the sight of Jesse getting reacquainted with old friends. It hadn't occurred to her before this moment, but if Jesse reestablished old friendships, he might discover he actually liked it here. The fact that he'd brought her to church today was a good sign.

In his years away, he'd become withdrawn and closed-off. Except for his growing friendship with Silas, he'd made no effort to fit in here. He did his work, ate, and slept. She supposed that was his way of keeping himself separate, aloof.

Maybe, just maybe, if she could show him that he did belong here, after all, he might reconsider going back to Montana.

He might even reconsider her.

As she watched him, deep in conversation with Sam Eakin, Jesse's head came up, absently searching the crowd. When his gaze met hers he stopped. Had he been looking for her? she wondered. The thought made her pulse pick up. His smile was the sort lovers exchange, she thought strangely. An intimate, heart-stopping smile, one that sent awareness skittering through her and made her knees weak.

For a moment, Jesse seemed to lose track of what he'd been saying, then Sam said something to him and Jesse returned to his conversation. Swallowing hard, she turned away, too, remembering the heated kiss they'd shared last night.

She realized suddenly that all the women in her group were staring at her as if waiting for a reply to some question she hadn't heard.

"Well?" repeated Angelina, her double chin wobbling as she spoke. "You heard about him didn't you?"

Andrea blinked. "Who?"

Angelina gave an exasperated sigh. "Mitch Lodray, of course. We've been admiring him for the past five minutes."

She went cold all over. "Mitch?"

"Yes, darlin'," Loretta chimed in. "Why, that's right, you two went sparkin' once or twice didn't you? Talk was, he was sweet on you. Well, he's standin' right over there and I'd say it's you he's watchin'."

Mitch Lodray was, indeed, waiting for her to meet his eye. When she did, he smiled that same smile she remembered from years ago, though it would never have the stupefying effect on her it seemed to have on the rest of the women in the church yard. It sent a chill through her.

He hadn't changed much in the intervening years. He was still tall, broad-shouldered, with steely gray eyes that seemed to reflect the daylight, so at times they appeared almost colorless. His face was gaunter than she remembered, and he leaned heavily on the cane in his right hand as he spoke with the soldiers standing beside him.

To her dismay, he started toward her, encouraged by the fact she'd met his eye. She bit back a curse and began to look for an escape route.

"Oh, sweet perdition, he's comin' this way," Loretta gushed in her ear. She grabbed Andrea's arm, effectively cutting off her getaway. "Lookit that limp. Ain't it just a shame a fine lookin' man like that has to suffer with a limp for the rest of his life simply cause he was a hero?"

Hero? Andrea nearly gagged.

"Hello," Mitch said, slipping his hat off as he reached her. His voice, deep and resonant as a well-tuned bass fiddle, sent a chill up her spine. "How wonderful to see you again. It's been . . . what? Two years?"

"Is that all?" she replied with a cool she didn't feel. "I thought it had been longer than that."

Mitch moved to kiss her cheek, but she turned her face subtly away, avoiding it. He smelled of a memory, of cigarettes and a liberal dose of bay rum, and she wished desperately for a breeze to lift the stiflingly still air surrounding them. Her stomach clenched.

"You've gotten more beautiful with the passing years, Andrea," he went on without missing a beat.

"I'm Mrs. Winslow now, Mr. Lodray," she said, fighting the nauseating sensation that the yard had begun to tilt like a wobbly top running out of spin. She braced her feet apart and tightened her grip on the baby. She would be a fool to let on to these women that anything was amiss between her and Mitch. It would all become fodder for their gossip circles.

Mitch inclined his head toward the baby, but his

eyes didn't leave hers. "Motherhood agrees with you. He's a fine-looking boy."

"I think so," she answered tightly.

"I heard you married shortly before I returned to Harvard. I was sorry to hear about Zach's death in the war."

She fixed her eyes on a shiny pebble at her feet. "Thank you."

"The conflict has stolen a lot of good men. I was one of the fortunate ones," he added, changing his grip pointedly on his cane.

"Oh, my, Mr. Lodray," Loretta sighed, "I think it's such a crime that good-hearted men like yourself oughta pay so dearly for heroism."

He tipped a charming grin her way. "It's a small price to pay for the preservation of the Union. I'll be fine I assure you, Mrs. Pease. My foot is getting better every day," he said rotating the appendage testingly. "I've been expanding my boundaries, in fact, walking a little farther on it every day. Perhaps," he suggested, glancing at Andrea, "you'd like to join me one day, Mrs. Winslow? For a walk, that is."

A cold lump caught in her throat. "No. I'm afraid I'm quite busy at Willow Banks, Mr. Lodray." Looking past him, she caught sight of Jesse again, watching her intently from over Sam Eakin's shoulder. The mere sight of Jesse calmed her, and he sent her another smile, this one reassuring.

"I'm sorry to hear that," Mitch answered, touching the brim of his hat. "Perhaps another time. After the crop is in?"

Not if the crop walked in on its own feet, Andrea thought, forcing a tight smile. "Perhaps," she said, simply to get rid of him.

"I'll look forward to that day, then . . . Mrs. Winslow." He turned, and graced Loretta with a version of the dazzle that had most of the women in Elkgrove township swooning. "Good day, ladies." He started to walk away.

"Mr. Lodray?" Batting her bright red fan beneath her nose, Loretta Pease lowered her voice, and seized the moment. "Perhaps you'd like to join the Raffertys at our house tonight for supper. Camy Micheals and her parents will be there, too."

"That's very kind of you, Mrs. Pease," he replied. "I can't think of more charming company with whom to spend an evening, but I'm, uh, afraid I have a previous engagement. Some other time?"

Loretta smiled graciously, her fan beating double time. "Oh my, of course. Any time, Mr. Lodray."

A dimple appeared in his tanned cheek. "I'll look forward to it, then. Good day, ladies."

"Good day, Mr. Lodray," they chorused as one.

His last look was for Andrea. It held both promise and threat.

She alone didn't watch Mitch limp away. Instead she searched the spot where she'd last seen Jesse and found him walking toward her and the others, his gaze on Mitch. In years past, she might have called the look on his face possessive. Today, she merely blamed it on the fierce sunlight beating down from overhead.

"Are you crazy, Andrea Winslow?" gasped Loretta. "You shouldn't turn a man like Mitch Lodray down when he's asking you to walk out with him."

Andrea sighed. "Loretta, please don't concern yourself with my social life. Or lack of it."

"Well, somebody should," Loretta retorted.

Isabelle touched Andrea's arm. "Loretta's right. You shouldn't be cuttin' yourself off from possibilities. After all, Mitch Lodray is as prime for pluckin' as any bandy rooster I ever did see. Why, one of these days he'll be taking over the *Chronicle*."

Angelina chuckled in a gossipy sort of way. "Not if his ma has any say so about it."

"Oh, phooey! If I were ten years younger and not already hooked up with Jasper," Loretta sighed, "I'd be taking a second look or two at him myself."

"Lor-retta!" Angelina gasped with an astonished grin.

"Well . . . ?" Loretta answered with a laugh.

"You should be grateful for what you've got," Andrea told them both.

The teasing smile slipped from Loretta's face. "Oh, honey, you know we all adored your Zach. But all the wishin' in the world won't bring him back. Or any of the other boys who've died for the Cause." She wrapped a sympathetic arm around Andrea's shoulder. "You've gotta move ahead with your life. You've got this sweet li'l boy to think of now. And your . . . reputation," she added pointedly, watching Jesse approach.

Andrea tightened her arms around her sleeping child and little Zach stirred in sleep. "Thank you for your concern, Loretta. I *know* you only speak out of friendship."

Loretta colored slightly and didn't say more. Andrea's gaze went to Jesse, who was approaching the group.

No one had the right to be that sinfully handsome, she mused. The sunlight gleamed on his long hair, gilding it with silver streaks making him appear more angel than devil. Her fingers itched to touch it. Saint or sinner, his effect wasn't lost on the others either.

Loretta lifted a hand to check her hair and Angelina smoothed down the ample bodice of her gray silk gown.

176

"Ready to go?" he asked, drawing up beside Andrea.

She nodded.

"Ladies?" Jesse touched the brim of his hat to Angelina and Loretta. "It's a pleasure to see you again. Come out to Willow Banks sometime and pay Andrea a visit. She's working too hard."

"Oh, we will," Loretta replied, "and it's good to have you back in Elkgrove, Mr. Winslow."

"Thank you, ma'am." Jesse flashed her a smile and steered Andrea toward their wagon at a brisk pace.

"Have fun?" he asked.

"It was nice to get out."

"Was that Mitch Lodray I saw you talking with earlier?"

She avoided his eyes. "He wasn't exactly talking to me. He was just . . . there."

"He was paying a lot of attention to you for being 'just there.'"

She felt her face heat up, surprised Jesse had even noticed. "He was admiring Zachary, like everyone else."

They reached the wagon and he lifted Zach from her shoulder, giving her a hand up. "And why not, huh, Corncob?" he asked, giving the baby a smooch on the cheek before he handed him back to Andrea. "You're an exceptionally handsome kid."

Andrea just smiled. Glancing back at the thinning crowd, the handsome, dark-haired soldier from church was standing a little apart from the crowd, watching her. He nodded to her politely and touched the brim of his hat as he caught her eye. Disconcerted, she smiled back wondering again if she knew him, then turned back to Jesse.

"I, uh, hope you don't mind," he went on,

177

climbing in after her. "I invited Sam over for dinner."

"Sam? Sam Eakin?"

"Yeah, and his kids. Is that all right with you?"

Her brain whirled. Jesse had invited a friend for dinner? She could hardly believe it. It was better than she'd hoped for. "Of course it's all right. I—I'd be happy to have Sam over. I just didn't know you were friends."

"Oh, yeah. Great friends," Jesse assured her expansively, gathering the traces from around the brake handle. "You didn't know that?"

"No."

"He lost his wife, you know. You remember Suzannah. It's probably been a while since he's had a decent home-cooked meal. Maybe you could make him one of your pies."

His rock-hard thigh brushed hers as he released the brake and gave the reins a snap. Andrea reached up and unbuttoned the top two buttons on the high neck of her black bombazine gown and lifted the damp fabric away from her skin. "I saw some ripe blackberries along the creek just yesterday."

"Mm-mmm. Sounds good."

She smiled. Jesse had always loved her pies. She remembered the October day, so long ago, when he'd outbid everyone in Elkgrove township for one of her fresh apple pies at a church bazaar. He'd paid a whole twelve dollars for it. She'd laughed then, flattered as any young girl in love would have been. But she'd wondered why he'd spent all that hard-earned money when he knew he'd be enjoying her pies for the rest of his life.

She sighed inwardly brushing a thumb over Zachary's soft cheek. Nothing had quite turned out the way she'd planned.

They started off, and Andrea stared ahead without really seeing the ribbon of dirt road snaking between the green sea of distant corn and grainfields. How silly she was to find hope in such a small thing as Jesse smiling at the thought of one of her pies, but all the same, she pressed a hand to the steady thudding of her heart. For the hundredth time since he'd returned, she cautioned herself against the foolhardiness of letting Jesse back into her heart. He'd deserted her once and in all likelihood would again. He was as wild as the tall spires of golden sunflowers that grew like scattered sunshine along the sides of the road. He craved freedom the way those flowers craved summer rain.

Yes, she'd be foolish to let him back in her heart. But the truth was, she'd never completely let him go.

Chapter Eleven

"More pie, Sam?" Jesse asked, lifting the nearly empty pie plate. Around the table, four small Eakin children inhaled the last of their slices, the youngest, Baby Benjamin, having already resorted to licking his plate clean. The fifth, two-year-old Luke, had disappeared under the table, occupied with caterpillaring his way between the chair legs.

Silas had wisely stayed at Etta's for supper. He might have gone hungry if he'd eaten here, Jesse thought, hoping Sam would turn down that last piece of pie. Jesse couldn't remember ever seeing one family pack away more food than this one just had. In fact, the Eakin children had been so intent on consuming everything in sight that they had, for a least twenty minutes, ceased whacking each other over the head with the nearest object.

Sam was another problem altogether. Nerves had apparently stolen his voice, for he'd spoken hardly two words to Andi since getting there. Who would have thought Sam Eakin tongue-tied terrified around women? Jesse ran a finger under the buttoned collar of his shirt. He'd held up his end of the conversation for most of the meal, but was running out of topics that might lead Sam to actually show interest in Andi.

"You sure, Sam?" he asked again, holding up the pie.

Sam's fork stopped halfway to his mouth. Color crept up his neck. "No, thanks." He patted his stomach. "Full."

Andrea nodded pleasantly, then sent a helpless look to Jesse. She jiggled Little Zachary against her shoulder. The baby's open mouth explored the dark burgundy paisley shoulder of her dress—a compromise Andi had made to the widow's weeds she'd intended to wear. Zachary's eyes were wide and alert at the spectacle of so many small people at his table.

"Me, me! Ith mine!" lisped four year old Lisbeth Eakin, pumping her scrawny arm in the air and peeking around the fragrant bouquet of Queen Ann's lace, wild honeysuckle and black-eyed Susans that Sam and the children had picked for Andi on the way over.

"No fair," protested five-and-a-half-year-old Gregory, his mouth and cheeks stained purple. "I'm bigger'n her an' we ain't et pie since Ma died."

"Mind your manners," Sam scolded gruffly as the child reached for the last slice of blackberry pie. "We didn't come here to eat the Winslows outta house and home."

It was the longest sentence Sam had managed to string together since arriving, except to admire the innards of the new cultivator. Jesse straightened in his seat with renewed hope.

"But Pa," Lisbeth begged, using her big gray-blue eyes to best advantage. "I'm thtill hungry."

Sam placed his hand over his daughter's in gentle warning. "Lisbeth . . ."

181

"It's okay, Mr. Eakin," Andrea said. "They're growing children. Let them have it. I made it especially for you and the children."

Sam blushed and cleared his throat as if he were going to speak, but took the plates and divided the last piece between his two oldest children.

"Andi's quite a cook, isn't she Sam?" Jesse offered with a twinkle of pride.

"Yemphn-mumm," Sam answered with a quick nod, his mouth full of food.

Trying another tack, Jesse ruffled Gregory's hair. "When I was your age," he told him with a chuckle, "my ma used to tell me I had a leg so hollow the coons were likely gonna den up in it come winter."

Gregory stared at him with wide, solemn eyes. "You had a *coon* livin' in your *leg?*"

Jesse's laughter faltered. "Well, no. It was . . . uh, just a figure of speech." He looked at Sam whose expression was equally blank. "Just a joke. You know, hollow leg . . . ?" He knocked on the wooden table. Andi was grinning openly now. "Never mind," he said. "Hey, how 'bout that corn, Sam?"

Sam ducked his head. "Looks good." A pause. "Good harvest this year." Another long pause. He squirmed in his seat and Jesse could tell he was really trying. "Been havin' some trouble with corn worms," he said at last.

Andrea pressed her fingertips against her lips and stared hard at her plate.

"*Have* you?" Jesse replied with a strangled look.

"Yup," Sam replied. "You?"

"Not too much, no." Jesse twirled the tines of his fork against his plate and listened to the slurping sounds the children were making with their pie.

Sam grunted. "Made a potion up of mashed worms, water and a little corn likker," Sam went on earnestly, wiping the beads of blackberry juice from his mustache with the edge of his sleeve. "Doused every last ear with the foul stuff. Those critters cain't abide the stink o' dead worms."

Jesse nodded, rubbing his jaw. "I've, uh, heard that." *What the hell had he been thinking, inviting Sam Eakin over here to spark Andi?*

"Drives 'em right out through the silk." Sam actually smiled. "Heck, I can give you the recipe for it. Ain't hard to make. You just gather up a mess of them little green worms in a mixin' bowl and—"

"Thanks," Jesse interrupted, pushing his plate away. "You can . . . give that to me later."

"Oh." Sam glanced up at Andi and blushed. "S-sure."

Lisbeth leaned forward with a devilish grin. "Lukey eath wormth," she lisped.

Gregory giggled. "Only live ones. Not mashed ones."

On that note, Andrea stood. "Where *is* Lukey, by the way?"

"*Ee-y-ow!*" Jesse shot out of his chair, sending it crashing to the floor behind him and reached down to rub his wounded shin. Scowling, he bent down, and pulled the culprit out from under the table. Lukey squirmed in Jesse's outstretched arms like a hooked worm himself.

"He *bit* me!" Jesse growled.

Lisbeth and Gregory convulsed into a fit of giggles, no doubt, Jesse mused darkly, glad not to have been Lukey's latest victim.

Sam clucked his tongue and reached for his son. "Sorry, Jesse. He's a biter, this one. Furniture, worms, legs . . . He'll chew on just about anything. Just like a pup."

Jesse cast a disbelieving look at Andi's amused

183

expression while he rubbed his shin, wondering if the kid had actually drawn blood.

"I have an idea," Andi suggested brightly. "Why don't we go outside where it's cooler. I made some lemonade earlier. I'll bring some out onto the porch and—"

All the children but Baby Benjamin hit the floor running for the door like a yowling herd of wild dogs.

"Great idea," Jesse replied, deadpan. "You and Sam go on and keep an *eye* on those kids. I'll bring the drinks."

"Don't be silly," she argued, with a pleading smile as Sam bent to undo Benjamin's bib and the belt that had him strapped into the chair. "I have to finish the dishes."

"Later," Jesse told her. "I'll help you with them myself. *I promise.* You've done enough today, Andi. You and Sam go on out. I'll be right there. I'm sure you and Sam can find something to talk about. *Can't* you, Sam?"

Terror crept back in Sam's expression. "Uh—"

"Good," Jesse said. His hand found the small of Andrea's back and he guided her forward, around the table toward the door. The sensation raced along her nerves like a tingling current.

"I'll be out directly," he told her.

Andrea narrowed a look at him before following Sam and little Benjamin out the door.

Evening's long shadows crawled across the yard. The air, cooler with approaching darkness, was perfumed with night-blooming jasmine and the fragrant pink-tinged roses that climbed over the porch trellis and up the side of the house. Jesse had scythed the grass earlier and the children spilled across the sweet-smelling yard, rolling and tumbling

184

in a tangle of arms, legs and giggles. They caught sight of Mahkwi, whom they'd met earlier. They made a beeline for the animal, who in turn made a beeline for the protection of the cornfield. Unperturbed, the Eakins resumed their game of tag.

Zachary cooed excitedly at the sight of the children tussling in the yard. Sam handed Benjamin down into the melee, and the baby toddled off like a wobbling top after his siblings.

A bittersweet smile curved Andrea's mouth. She had always imagined a houseful of her own children filling the yard with laughter. Perhaps she would have to settle for only one.

"You wanna, um, sit?" Sam asked, hovering near the peeling porch swing. He gave it a testing push with his hand. The chain link squeaked in rhythmic invitation.

"Sure." She sat down on the slatted wooden seat and turned Zach around in her lap so he would watch the yard. The swing creaked when Sam joined her, and he pushed off on the floor with his foot.

"It's a beautiful evening, isn't it?" she asked, gazing at the sinking sun.

He nodded. "Um-hmm."

"Your children seem to be enjoying themselves."

"Um-hmm." He wrung his hands together, staring out over the yard. Sweat beaded on his forehead and she wondered suddenly if he was feeling ill. She'd known Sam for years. Not well, of course, but they had often passed pleasantries when Andrea had run into him and his late wife, Suzannah, in town. He had always been shy and content to leave the socializing to his wife, an arrangement that had apparently worked well for both. With Suzannah gone, Sam Eakin was like a duck without pinfeathers.

The swing squeaked a steady rhythm. Tick, tock, tick, tock.

Sam cleared his throat. "It was, uh, mighty nice of you to have us out for dinner, Miss Andrea."

"Oh, it was my pleasure. Jesse was so happy to see you at church today. I never knew you two were such good friends."

He gave her a puzzled look. "Well, we *knew* each other years back, but . . . with him bein' four years younger than me . . ." He ended on a shrug.

A frown pulled at her brow. "Oh. Well, we're practically neighbors now. Maybe you two will become friends."

"I reckon. If he stays around here long enough. I, uh, heard he's thinkin' of heading back to Montana."

"Thinking and doing are two different things, Mr. Eakin," she told him with renewed hope.

He swallowed so hard his Adam's apple seemed to stick at the top of his throat. "Miss Winslow?"

"Yes, Mr. Eakin?"

"Could you . . . would you call me Sam?"

She blinked in surprise. "Well, I suppose that would be all right. Yes. Sam."

A smile stole over his face. He set the swing to rocking again with a gentle push of his foot. "It's a fine place you've got here, ma'am." Sam rubbed his hands against the shiny fabric of his worn pants.

"Thank you."

"I have me a right nice place, too. You know, down on Two Forks Creek. Not so much acreage as you," he said, staring out over the sprawling cornfields, "but I got a fine, big house. It suits me. 'Course," he sighed, "it ain't the same without a woman on the place."

"Of course," Andrea murmured. "I know what you mean."

186

"Yeah, I reckon you do." He regarded her earnestly. "These are hard times with the War and all. I got me a deferral from fightin', considering my younguns and all. I'm steady, hardworkin', loyal as the day is long."

Andrea frowned, wondering what he could possibly be leading up to.

He stared at his fingernails that looked, despite the dirt stains, as if they'd been scrubbed hard with a brush. "Got me a passel of kids that'll be helpin' with chores soon enough and well . . ."—he gestured at Zachary—"yours will be comin' up soon too."

Andrea stiffened on the benched seat and lifted one hand to the cameo pinned at her throat. "What *are* you trying to say, Mr. Eakin?"

"S-Sam," he corrected.

"Sam."

Jesse stopped just beyond the open door with the trayful of lemonade, overhearing Sam's voice. His heart skidded in his chest as he leaned against the inside of the doorway. He felt like a peeping Tom, or worse, some kind of underhanded matchmaker. God Almighty, Sam was actually going to get to the point. After the dinner debacle, Jesse hadn't given Sam a chance in a million.

Sam cleared his throat again. "I just thought . . . there you are, alone, without Zach. And here's me, without my Suzannah. We both love farmin'. I thought, m-maybe we could, uh . . . marry up and join our problems up together."

Jesse heard the swing thump against the porch rail and Andi shoot to her feet.

"Mr. Eakin!" Shock strained her words.

Sam got up, too. "Oh, now, shoot," he said. "I knew I shouldn't a brung it up so quick. Sparkin' ain't my strong suit, but I mean, I can court you if that's what you want."

Jesse's lungs froze and a tight pain cinched around his chest. He peeked around the corner to see Andi standing rigid as a board.

"No, that's not what I want," she told Sam.

"Y-you don't want courtin'?"

"No."

"More flowers?"

"No."

"Well . . ." Sam scratched his head. "I already spoke with the Reverend—"

Her eyes went round. *"You what?"*

"Well, y'know just to make sure we'd have his blessin' . . . it bein' so soon after . . . y'know, Suzannah and Zach. He said considerin' the circumstances—"

"Circumstances?"

"What with us both havin' younguns and farms to look after," Sam explained lamely. "And Jesse said—"

"You told the Reverend you wanted to *marry* me? Without so much as a word to me. Mr. Eakin, I hardly know you. How could you presume to—?"

"Aw, now, don't get mad." Sam twisted his big hands together. "I already told you my courtin' skills ain't sharp no more. I reckon I did this all upside down and backward."

Andi shook her head. "It wouldn't have mattered how you went about it. I'm not interested in marrying anyone, Mr. Eakin. My husband's only six months dead."

"And Zannah's gone only two. God rest her soul. I reckon I know as good as anyone how that sits. It don't make us miss 'em any less. But I need me a wife, Mrs. Winslow. And you? You need a husband."

Jesse heard her exhale sharply and stomp to the

rail that surrounded the open porch. Her arms were tight around her son. The scented evening breeze tugged at the tortoise-shell combs buried in her hair.

"I'm very sorry you went to all that trouble," she said with her back to him, "but I'm afraid it was all for naught."

"Y'mean, you won't consider me?" he asked in a quiet voice.

She drew her hand into a fist around Zachary's blankets. "I . . . I'm afraid not."

Jesse slunk back like a rat into the woodpile when he saw Sam's shoulders sag. *Blast your black interfering soul, Winslow.*

"It's all them younguns that puts you off, isn't it?" Sam asked forlornly.

"Of course not." Andrea turned toward him. "They're . . . why they're darling. All of them."

Except the one with teeth, Jesse thought.

"It was the worms, wasn't it?" Sam said.

She shook her head. "Worms?"

"The corn worms. I shouldn't have brung 'em up at the table. You probably think I'm"—he dipped his head with a miserable gulp—"uncouth."

"Oh, for Heaven's sake, nothing of the—"

He held two palms up, knowing the truth. "No, no, Zannah used to get riled when I talked about farmin' at table. It's just, when I get all tongue-tied, well, farmin' is about all I know."

"I certainly don't hold that against you."

Sam nodded, searching the wooden porch floor with his gaze. "Well, I . . . I'm glad of that."

"It's not personal, truly, Mr. Eakin . . . Sam. I'm sure you'll find someone happy to marry you and soon. I'm just not . . . her."

"Okay." Sam straightened his shoulders and tried

189

to smile. "You don't have to hit Sam Eakin over the head with a brick."

Jesse's jaw tightened, disappointment warring with relief inside him. It had seemed so simple when he'd considered it. Andi needed a husband, an honest, decent farmer husband who could give her the kind of life she deserved. He needed to get back to Montana, move on with his life, to put the farm and his tarnished past behind him. Right? *Right*.

So why did he feel so damn guilty about trying to arrange Andi's life to make both of them happy?

In a rush of heat came the unbidden memory of her lips, warm and pliant, surrendering to his; the soft, sweet caress of her hair against his skin; her breasts, her hips fitting against his like lost pieces to a puzzle.

He squeezed his eyes shut. Why, if leaving her again was what he really wanted, did the kiss they shared still make his chest ache, and his loins burn, and his resolve to do the right thing pale beside his damnable need?

Without an answer to that question, he stepped through the doorway onto the porch. Andi and Sam turned at the rattling clink of glass and looked about as happy to see him as two cats caught in a field full of brambles. Jesse pasted what he hoped was an innocent smile on his face and lifted his tray.

"Lemonade anyone?"

In the cozy Rafferty parlor room, Adeline Rafferty giggled as she scribbled down several words on a piece of paper, folded it in half, then stood and made a slow, calculating sweep of the circle of people cluttering the mean but comfortable furniture. The six Rafferty children old enough to participate in the game of charades bounced up and down in their places, all eager to be chosen.

Silas stared at that piece of paper, willing it to pass right on by him. Beside him, Etta giggled too, caught up in the game. He'd been lucky so far. No one had chosen him to be it. That he hadn't left already was only a testament to how good he felt to have been included at all in this family game.

Adeline passed by him, then stopped and came back. Silas gulped. Sweat beaded between his shoulder blades. With a pixyish grin, the eleven-year-old held the slip of paper out to him as if she were bestowing an honor.

"I—" Silas faltered and shot to his feet. "I gots to be goin'." He glanced at Etta, hoping she wouldn't pick this moment to correct him for speakin' wrong. She didn't. She merely looked at him in confusion.

"You don't want to play?" Adeline asked with a wounded expression. "It's only eight o'clock."

"And nearly your bedtime," Isabelle reminded her daughter.

"Oh, Ma . . ."

Silas grabbed his old hat off the hat tree. "It's kind of ya'll to let me come here tonight. An' I's obliged for supper."

Isabelle stood too, her red hair in a loose corona around her head. "Anytime, Silas. Any friend of Etta's is always welcome in our home."

"Thank you, ma'am. 'Night, folks."

They bid him goodnight, and Etta walked him outside. They stopped under the sheltering branches of the elm that stood in the center of the yard. Except for the gentle croaking of the frogs in the nearby stream, the evening was still, breezeless and warm. The place smelled of growing things and rich humus.

"I best be goin'," Silas said, not really looking at Etta.

With her hands clasped behind her back, Etta stared at the ground. "Silas?"

"Yass'm?"

"Are you really tired? Is that why you wanted to leave so suddenly tonight?"

He hesitated, uncertain what she meant. Then a smile pulled at his mouth. "Well, I ain't all that tired." He took a step closer to her, his black eyes darkening even more, if that were possible. He took her by the arms and pulled her close to him.

"Mr. Mayfield!" she gasped in a breathless whisper. "That's not what I meant." Her protest, however, lacked a certain conviction.

He slid her spectacles off her face. "No? An' here I was thinkin' you's past callin' me Mr. Mayfield." Her gray eyes captured the moonlight and Silas gazed at her as if she were a precious treasure. "I 'spect I's gonna kiss you any minute now, Mrs. Etta Gaines."

Her lips parted in a mock-outraged smile. "Well, then, I 'spect I've got no choice, but to let you, Mr. Mayfield."

He shook his head slowly. "All you gots to do is say no."

She slid her hands up his big arms. "I don't think I want to."

"Good. That's real good." Silas settled his mouth over hers in a heated, but gentle kiss. He didn't want to scare her, but he wanted her all the same. In fact, he'd never wanted a woman as much as he did this one. With all her fancy words and teacher talk, he wanted her by his side, and in his bed. As his mouth moved over hers, her tension eased into surrender, her confusion to passion.

When at last they broke apart, their breath mingled

Now you can get Heartfire Romances
right at home and save

Heartfire
Romance

Get A
Free Heartfire Novels:
A $17.00 Value!

TO GET YOUR
4 FREE BOOKS
MAIL THE COUPON BELOW.

FREE BOOK CERTIFICATE

Heartfire Romance

GET 4 FREE BOOKS

Yes! I want to subscribe to Zebra's HEARTFIRE HOME SUBSCRIPTION SERVICE. Please send me my 4 FREE books. Then each month I'll receive the four newest Heartfire Romances as soon as they are published to preview Free for ten days. If I decide to keep them I'll pay the special discounted price of just $3.50 each; a total of $14.00. This is a savings of $3.00 off the regular publishers price. There are no shipping, handling or other hidden charges. There is no minimum number of books to buy and I may cancel this subscription at any time. In any case the 4 FREE Books are mine to keep regardless.

NAME

ADDRESS

CITY _____ STATE _____ ZIP

TELEPHONE

SIGNATURE

(If under 18 parent or guardian must sign)
Terms and prices subject to change.
Orders subject to acceptance.

HF 112

GET 4 FREE BOOKS

HEARTFIRE HOME SUBSCRIPTION
SERVICE
P.O. BOX 5214
120 BRIGHTON ROAD
CLIFTON, NEW JERSEY 07015

together coming fast and hard. He looked down at her, cupping her face in his big hands. "I reckon I's fallin' in love with you, Etta Gaines."

She closed her eyes and pressed her cheek into his hand. "You . . . you hardly know me, Silas."

He hesitated, rubbing a thumb across her coffee-colored cheek. "I know enough. I reckon *I* ain't what you has in mind for a man."

"I didn't have a man in my mind."

"Maybe not. But we ain't much alike. I ain't like your husband, Marcus. I ain't so smart."

"Educated and smart are two different things." She looked up at him. "I can teach you to read if that's all that bothers you." Through the veil of night, he stared at her, silent, embarrassed.

She bowed her head. "I've offended you."

He stepped away from her and leaned one hand on the ridged bark of the white elm tree, staring out into the darkness.

"No," he said. "It's just . . . I never felt the lackin', 'til I met you, Etta. Where I growed up, none o' the slaves ciphered them chicken scratches the white folks read. But you . . . you's a colored, too. And when I hear you talk, I feels . . . I dunno . . . not good enough."

Arms akimbo, she scowled at him. "Well, now that's plain silly talk, Silas Mayfield. I won't hear it. I've taught dozens of children to read. And I can teach you."

He turned toward her, defensive. "I ain't no chile, Miss Etta."

"Of course not. That's why it will be easier for you."

He frowned and stared at the ground. "I ain't never heard o' no growed man learnin' to read."

"It's not unheard of. Besides, reading is just like

193

hoeing," she said, smiling. "The more you do it, the better you get at it."

"Well, I don't think—"

"You scared to learn to read?" she asked with a hint of challenge. "You think it's too hard for you?"

"I ain't skeered o' nothin'." He dropped his arm and took a step toward her.

"Anything," she corrected. "I'm not scared of *anything*."

He took another step, his voice deep, teasing. "Right, me neither."

She backed up a step for each one of his. "No? Then what do you say? You want to learn to read like the whites do?" Her gray eyes flashed in the moonlight and a smile widened her mouth. A breeze stirred the top of the tree, a sibilant rush of leaves in the night air. "I dare you."

He captured her with a final rush and pulled her into his arms. He grinned. "You what?"

"I . . . I dare you."

He kissed her, long and hard, then lifted his head. "A bet?"

A little breathless, she nodded. "Strictly on a teacher/student basis, of course."

"'Course. What I get if I win?"

She smiled with victory and turned toward the house. "A whole new world, Mr. Mayfield," she said. "A whole new world."

After doing the evening chores, Jesse joined Andi in the kitchen to help with the dishes as he'd promised. But they'd soon run out of inconsequential things to say. A strained silence stretched between them in the dimly lit kitchen. Only the swish of water in the dish pan and the rattle of china broke the quiet.

Finally, Andi spoke.

"Sam Eakin asked me to marry him."

She handed the last plate into Jesse's waiting dishtowel. He stared at the plate for a few seconds before rubbing it dry.

"What did you say?"

Andrea gaped at him. "What did I *say*? What do you think I said?"

He chanced a look up at her. Tendrils of her ebony hair lay damply against her skin in the evening heat. Wispy curls sprang up at nape and temple, and beads of moisture dotted her upper lip. Despite the heat, she smelled of vanilla and soap, and a sweetness that belonged only to her.

"Well," he answered, "from the way Sam lit out of here like his tail had been singed, nearly forgetting Gregory in the process, I suppose the answer was no."

She continued to stare at him, one soapy hand braced on her aproned hip. "Most certainly, *no*."

Her eyes were dark with some emotion—hurt or maybe disappointment.

"You don't even sound surprised that he'd ask," she said.

"These are hard times—"

"That's what *he* said."

"A war does things to people, Andi. Makes them hungry for things they're not sure will be there tomorrow. You could do worse."

She blinked. "Are you implying he was desperate enough to ask me after one innocent supper?"

"Hardly." He settled the flowered-painted china plate he was holding precisely atop the stack of others and considered his answer carefully before speaking.

"You're a beautiful woman, Andi. You're alone,

195

and pretty damn vulnerable. You need a husband and a father for your child. And," he added with a glimmer of a smile, "you bake a mean blackberry pie. Any man with half a brain would ask."

Her lips parted and she found she couldn't drag her gaze from his. She wondered if he could hear the heartbeat roaring in her ears. "Any man?"

He dried his hands on the towel and tossed it on the counter. "Any man with half a brain."

Andrea stared at him for a full five seconds before plunging her hands back in the water to feel for the last of the silverware. Anything to distract her from the heat creeping through her.

Jesse stood with his back to her, contemplating the darkness beyond the kitchen window. The crickets outside marked the passing seconds with their churring sound and somewhere nearby, a barn owl screeched into the night.

"Silas and I are going to start on the fences in the north pasture tomorrow."

The rag in Andrea's hands stilled on the forks she was washing. "Oh? Will you need some help?"

He gave her a strange look, then shook his head. Walking slowly to the door, he opened it on its squeaky hinge. "I'll, uh, be up and out early. Don't bother to get up. I'll fix my own breakfast."

"But I can—"

The door closed firmly behind him.

"—make it for you," she finished in a small voice. Leaning on the counter with both hands, she stared at her reflection in the window, Jesse's words flowing through her like a hot summer wind.

You're a beautiful woman, Andi. You need a husband . . . father for your child.

She closed her eyes and saw the strain etched on his face, the hint of regret filling his eyes.

Any man with half a brain . . .

"Damn you Jesse," she cursed aloud, balling her fist on the wooden counter. "Why can't you see what's right in front of you? Why can't you see that *I* love you? That I always have and always will."

Her mother had always said, "If you don't go after what you want, you'll end up sipping sorrow with a teaspoon." Well, she was tired of paying for the mistakes fate had handed her. Tired of relinquishing control of her own destiny. Fate had stolen Jesse away from her once. If the kiss they'd shared last night had proved anything, it had proved that Jesse still cared for her. Despite what he thought he felt.

All she had to do, Andrea thought, untying the apron at her back, was to make him believe it himself.

Chapter Twelve

She was killing him.

Jesse clamped five more roofing nails between his teeth and shoved the shingle into place on the barn roof.

Day in, day out, whenever he turned around, there Andi was, looking . . . well, the way she looked and doing things for him he had no business expecting and sure as hell didn't deserve. Every time he turned around, she was there, smiling at him, baking his favorite pie or meal, putting those damn, sweet-smelling roses all over his room.

Three weeks had passed since that disastrous dinner with Sam. Three weeks during which she'd managed to shut down every mangled attempt he'd made to steer her toward an eligible man. Calvin Weeks had "happened" by the next Sunday on the lame excuse of talking corn cribs and fodder with Jesse. Dressed in his Sunday best, with his hair slicked back with hands full of smelly tonic, Calvin had also, incidentally, brought along a bouquet of posies for Andrea which—with pleasant if puzzled thank you—she arranged in a glass vase, then left the two men to their talk of the animal feed market.

Calvin hadn't stayed for supper.

No, Andrea made it so plain she wasn't interested; not one of the men he'd steered toward her had dared even bring up the subject of the future. Not even the not-so-bad-looking beekeeper, Elias Mudrow, from the other side of the county, who'd come sniffing around her in town with honey under his fingernails and sparking on his mind.

Unfortunately, the beekeeper had more stock than charm. Mudrow had wound up with the honey-comb he'd tried to woo her with perched on his head.

The thought began to creep into Jesse's mind that this whole covert plan of his to find her a husband was fatally flawed from the get go.

He drove the nail home with two even strokes, spit another nail from his mouth, and pounded it in. The September sun poured over him on the shadeless roof. He welcomed the muggy heat. Maybe he could sweat out the tension that had settled between his shoulder blades like a fist.

Silas's hammer echoed the rhythm of his own from the other side of the roof. Giving the shingle a testing jiggle, Jesse reached for the next, his gaze drawn inexorably to the road which he'd been watching for the last hour, waiting for her return. She and Etta had gone to town in the buggy to do some Saturday shopping. Little Zach went along for the ride.

He pounded in another nail. He was worried for no good reason. Two women were safe enough, going the short distance between here and town, he told himself. Weren't they?

Then he thought of how she'd looked when she left—in that pretty midnight blue gown with all those rouches and tucks emphasizing the fullness of her breasts and the regained trimness of her waist. She'd worn that little navy straw hat with a cluster of fresh, bloodred roses tied to the brim, the only color in her outfit save her radiant skin, glowing with sunshine.

His fist tightened around his hammer. She'd looked, as a matter of fact, edible.

Tossing off his shirt, he glanced at the road again, imagining all the men in town that would be ogling her as if she—

That's right, Winslow, you dimwit. That's just what you wanted, isn't it?

Isn't it?

Maybe without him to get in the way, she'd find a man all on her own. Some nice farmer at the Feed and Grain, or maybe a shopkeeper, some nice steady sort who—

"Lookin' down that road won't bring her home any quicker," Silas observed with a chuckle from above him.

Jesse glared up where the black man straddled the barn's peaked roof. "I wasn't looking."

Silas smiled mildly. "An' cows give sarsaparilla." He slid gingerly down the slope on Jesse's side of the roof. "Need a hand?"

Jesse frowned. "No. You just go work on your side and I'll finish mine."

He shrugged good-humoredly. "My side's done, boss." He picked up a shingle and started in where Jesse had left off.

"Well, if you're so damned efficient, maybe *you* should just finish the roof."

Silas' eyebrows went up with amusement. "Whatever you say, boss."

"Will you stop calling me that!"

"Oooh-ee—" Silas muttered with a grin. "Who licked the red off your candy?"

"Nobody," Jesse grumbled, picking up another

200

shingle. "And what if I *was* watching for her?"

"Ain't no crime in it if you was." Silas buried the nail in the shake shingle with one clean blow and set the next. Jesse handed him a shingle from the shrinking pile.

"I'm responsible for her, after all."

"Uh-huh."

"I mean, she *is* my sister-in-law."

"That's a fact. Almost blood."

Jesse shot a look at him. "Not blood."

Silas grinned. "Oh no, suh. Not blood. Wouldn't do to have the woman you's lookin' at that way be blood."

"No," he answered distractedly, then realized what he'd said. "I mean—*No!* That's not what I mean at all."

A laugh rumbled through Silas.

"Oh, for crying out—" Jesse tossed the hammer down and it bounced over his knee and down the slope. Jesse tried to catch it, but it was no use. The hammer plunged off the side and hit the ground with a thud.

"Oh, hell." He looked up to find Silas grinning at him. "Well, what are you looking at?"

Silas wiped the sweat from his eyes with the back of his wrist. "I reckon I's lookin' at a man who don't know if'n he's comin' or goin'."

Jesse slumped to a sitting position, drawing his knees up to brace his forearms across them. "I'm going. And as soon as I can."

"Soon as you find Miss Andi a man, you mean."

Jesse shot a look at him, dismayed that he'd been so transparent. "Well, what am I supposed to do? Leave her alone here?"

"Not what I'd do," Silas muttered, more to himself than to Jesse.

"Yeah, well . . . not what I'd do either. So you see my dilemma. Anyway, it's not as simple as that."

Silas shrugged, fitting another slat of wood into place. "I reckon not."

"She's mortgaged up to here"—Jesse sliced his hand across his nose—"and that overstuffed banker, Ethan Bridges, would steal the roof from over her and Zachary's head faster than you can say 'land-grabber.' Not to mention the fact that a woman alone in these times is about as safe as a lit match in an ordinance stockroom."

Silas gave him an unreadable look. "Shingle."

"Huh?"

"Shingle," Silas requested, holding out one hand.

"Oh, yeah." He handed him the slat of wood. "I mean my only hope is to find some man willing to take on the responsibility of a woman with a young child."

"If," Silas pointed out, "that woman be willin' to look further than her own backyard . . . or barn roof."

"Andi knows I'm going."

"Maybe, but she be a woman first, logical next."

"You're wrong," he said shaking his head. "She loved my brother. Friendship is all she feels for me. Maybe she's glad for the company. She's comfortable with this arrangement. But that won't always be enough for her. She'll want more."

"'More' you don't got?" Silas stared at him.

"That's right."

"'Cause o' the farm?"

Jesse heaved an exasperated sigh, tired of trying to explain himself. "Because I can't give her what she wants. Or deserves."

Heat glistened on Silas' forehead, and his black eyes seemed to pierce into Jesse's. "That ain't what it looks like from here. I seen you with that boy—holdin' him, playin' with him when Miss Andi's too tired. You's almost like a daddy to him already. An' the way Miss Andi looks at you? Why, I reckon she'd walk to the moon for you, if'n you wanted her to. If you axted me—"

"Nobody asked you," Jesse snapped. Scowling, he shoved to his feet on the slanted roof. "I'm going to go cut some more shingles. We're running low—"

Jesse fell silent at the heart-stopping sight of a plume of black smoke rising on the horizon to the east. "What the—?"

Silas followed his gaze, getting slowly to his feet. "Jesus, God," he whispered.

Jesse's eyes widened. From their vantage point, they were too far to see the fire's origins. But he knew only one farm lay in that direction. "Isn't that—?"

"—the Rafferty place," Silas finished, real fear hitching his voice.

And almost before the words were out, both men were scrambling down the steep pitch of the roof to the ladder poised against the barn.

Once down, they raced into the paddock where Rabble and the two mules had been peacefully dozing in the late-afternoon sun. Jesse grabbed the rifle he'd left leaning against the barn and handful of worn manilla rope, then vaulted over the three-rail fence. The appaloosa reared its head but allowed Jesse to thread the lead to the rope halter around its head.

"Can you catch a mule?" he shouted to Silas as he swung up on Rabble's bare back with Mahkwi nipping at the horse's nervous heels.

"I reckon I will," he snapped, waving his arms at the brownish gray mule who'd already decided it didn't want to be caught. "You go'on. I be right behind you."

Jesse yanked the rope to the right and eased the gelding through the gate. Silas' voice stopped him before he could wheel away.

"Jesse!" Silas called.

He turned, holding back the prancing animal.

"Be careful."

Jesse nodded and dug his heels into Rabble's flanks. With Mahkwi right beside him, he took off at a gallop for the Rafferty's place with a feeling of impending doom.

He spotted the cloud of dust first, then the thunder of galloping horses. The riders passed him a half-mile to the south. Eight to ten men, as near as he could make them out, wearing hoods and riding hard. The cloud of red summer dust dissipated behind them like a ghostly veil, unlike the black cloud rising farther to the east.

Bastards! he thought, curbing the impulse to track the cowards down while he had them in his sights. But the smoke in the distance left him no choice. He'd worry about the raiders later.

Rabble's hooves beat a thudding tattoo across the land as they tore toward Rafferty's. Cornfields sped past, the low branches of a willow stung his face as he cut across a nearly dried-up creek on the edge of Isabelle and John's property. Why hadn't they rung the bell? That signal would have every farmer within hearing come running.

Jesse's heart pounded and a cold sweat had worked its way up past his spine to his clammy fingertips. Where was John? Or Isabelle? Please, God, don't let them be hurt.

Faster. Faster. Jesse kicked Rabble, spurring him on. The wolf raced on ahead of them with incredible speed. Over the crest of the hill, the whole awful picture emerged. The barn, half-engulfed in flame, was the torch that fueled the plume of black smoke. Like a roaring beast, it ate at the dry wood with a vengeance; it had already consumed one entire side of the outbuilding. The empty corn cribs were ablaze as well. Burning ash sailed across the yard toward the drying field of alfalfa to the north. But it was already too late. In the center of the field, as if someone had thrown torches, two small circles of fire were already widening.

Worse, Jesse thought, going cold, were the terrified screams of horses from within the burning barn.

Hell! What were the animals doing in the barn in the middle of the day?

"John!" he shouted, hauling his horse to a stop twenty-five feet from the barn near the rusty red water pump. He leapt off and grabbed a bucket, hanging on the fence and gave the pump three priming shoves before the water spilled out. "Isabelle! *Anybody!*"

Across the yard, the two-story house lay wide open, violated, with several first floor windows smashed and the door half ripped off its hinge. But no sign of fire.

The sound of hoofbeats brought his head around and he saw Silas galloping into the yard atop old Jacksaw, the mule.

"Check the house!" Jesse shouted to Silas as he slid off his mount. "I'll try to get the animals out." Jesse poured the bucket of water over his head, gasping with the shock and started at a run toward the inferno of a barn.

"Hey, you crazy?" Silas argued, catching Jesse's arm. "You can't go in there! It's goin' up like kindlin'."

"Let me go!"

205

"It's too late. That place'll come down on your head."

"It's my head, dammit! I have to try." Jesse yanked his arm free and ran toward the open double doors. Thick, choking smoke billowed from the portal. He pressed his sleeve against his mouth and nose, took a deep breath and ducked inside. A whooshing sound met him as the far side of the barn roof ignited, along with tinder-dry hay mow above.

From somewhere to his right, a horse screamed and kicked hard at the door of its stall. To his left, another cry, more like the baying of a wolf, sounded, and he guessed it was a cow.

He headed to the right with one hand in front of him. He couldn't really see where he was going, but he'd been in this barn before. Like most, it had a long, wide hallway down the center with a set of stalls lining each side. Overhead, the hay mow glowed eerily red through the slatted floor. The sound was deafening. Following the banging Jesse groped his way to the wall of stall doors and pulled open the first one.

Empty.

The suffocating heat bore down on him like a crushing weight, stealing strength from his limbs. Jesse coughed, unable to draw a clean breath, and pressed his nose tighter against his wet sleeve. He moved down the line, throwing open doors to the empty stalls until he came to the last.

The door banged against its frame as the horse within battered it with its hooves, her scream high-pitched and struck through with terror. Another, even shriller whinny accompanied it.

A foal. He remembered now. Silas had told him of John's prize draft mare who had foaled very late in the season. That explained why the mare was in the barn, he thought, pounding at the nearly splintered wooden latch with the heel of his hand until it came free. Like the air that seared his lungs, the wood felt hot to the touch.

Yanking the door open, he felt more than saw a hoof miss his head by inches, and he drew back. A frightened horse had the sense of a headless chicken and this one seemed on the verge of total panic. Eyes white and rolling, the huge mare banged against the far wall of her stall in confusion. Her foal was no better, but in grave danger of being crushed by its mother.

"Easy, lady," he crooned, ripping the buttons free on his shirt and stripping it off. "Easy now. I'm going to get you out of here." Coughing, he eased closer with the shirt pressed over his mouth. He had to hurry or it would be too late for all of them.

"Whoa, now, shh-hh," he said, drawing closer to the screaming mare who was disappearing in a cloud of smoke. Quickly, he wrapped the shirt over her face, blinding her, then tucked the ends under her head to use as a lead. Clucking his tongue, he led her through the open stall door, praying the baby would still have the strength and instinct to follow. Reasonably, he turned right, the opposite direction from whence he'd come, knowing there was another, closer set of doors at the far end of the corridor.

When he reached them, however, they were barred from the outside and he couldn't find the latch with all the smoke. He cursed with what little breath he had left and dragged the uneasy mare back down the long smoke-filled corridor.

The mare reared suddenly as a hot ash fell on her back, and turned Jesse in a circle trying to hold her. By the time he got her under control, he felt his strength leaving him. Light-headed and suddenly disoriented, he stopped in the center of the barn to regain his direction. The baby cowered beside him pressing her muzzle into Jesse's back. Burning ash and small fiery bits dropped all around him.

The mare let out a distressed whinny. The smoke cleared enough to see the patch of light at the end of the corridor. Jesse headed toward it. Through the smoke he saw a figure a few feet away tugging on a rope and heard Silas shouting.

"C'mon you pea-brained hunk of gleet. Git outta here!" Silas' command disintegrated into a fit of coughing. The black and white milch cow answered with a pitiful bellow.

Above them, the hay mow made an ominous groaning noise. Wood snapped like the sound of breaking bones.

Jesse ran toward Silas and the light, the mare in tow. He waved his arm frantically. "Silas! Get out, leave her!" His voice wasn't much more than a croaking rasp. "The roof's going!"

He saw Silas' gaze go up toward the roof just as a deafening noise sounded above them. Jesse slapped the mare's hindquarters and stripped away the shirt covering her eyes. The splintering roar from above swallowed her shrill scream of terror.

Etta held the buggy reins in one hand and gripped her stomach with the other as she laughed. "And did you see . . . the look . . . on Esmerelda Mastison's face when you told her she should see a . . . a doctor about that wart growing on the tip of her nose?"

Andrea giggled too, hardly able to believe she'd told the old biddy off. "She deserved it, the old witch."

"My, oh my, she did if any woman ever did," Etta

agreed with a chuckle.

Andrea straightened the brim of her straw hat and touched the wilting blooms tied there as the buggy rocked down the road toward home. The heat had taken its toll on the roses, but not on her. She felt exhilarated, alive. The outing with Etta had been just the thing she'd needed, and the scene with Esmerelda Mastison had iced the cake.

It had started in Tess MacGillen's millinery shop, where she and Etta had been window shopping, with Esmerelda making not-so-subtle insinuations about her and Jesse's living arrangements. Andrea had argued, of course, that her brother-in-law had just as much right to occupy the Winslow household as she did, a fact that hardly mitigated Esmerelda's self-righteous indignation and concern for the morals of Andrea's child. But in the end, Andrea had had the last word, leaving the prunish Esmerelda Mastison feeling the tip of her nose and looking as if she'd sucked on a lemon.

Pulling a hanky from her sleeve, Andrea dabbed at the moisture on her throat with a satisfied smile and sat little Zachary up straighter on her lap. He fussed hungrily and chewed on his fist. Andrea slid a soothing finger down his soft cheek.

"I'd say," Etta went on, smiling, "there's more than a lick or two of envy in that woman's loose lips."

"Envy?" Andrea's look was incredulous.

"That woman been's living alone so long she has nothing better to do than mind other people's business. And when that business happens to be as handsome as Mr. Jesse . . . well—"

"Etta!" Andrea's smile belied her gasp of shock.

"Aw, she's just jealous she doesn't have a man the likes of that one under her roof!"

"Etta," she repeated, struggling to keep from smiling. "Why if only Esmerelda heard you talk! It'd be you, not me, who'd be the subject of one of her Elkgrove Ladies Circle gossip sessio—" She stopped, her gaze suddenly fixed on the odd black cloud rising from the horizon. "What on earth . . . ?"

Etta looked, too, her smile fading. "Lord'a Mercy—"

Andrea grabbed Etta's hand in alarm. "Etta—!"

"I know." She gave the reins a hard slap. "Hyahh!" The horse jerked forward from its leisurely pace into a gallop as if bee-stung. Andrea grabbed the seat rail with one hand and tightened her other around Zachary, blood rushing in her ears. The Rafferty place. She'd known it from the first second she'd seen the smoke. It was too close to be the Webb farm and, God forgive her for feeling relief, too far away to be her own.

If the raiders were to blame, she prayed the family was still gone on their outing to Green Lakes.

In the time it took to cover the distance to the Rafferty place, the billowing cloud had grown ominously worse. It wasn't until they'd reached the scene that Andrea realized they'd been joined on their way by Jack Calhoun and Ezra Whitakker, who'd spotted the smoke too and were rushing to help.

The first thing they saw as they pulled up in the yard was the barn completely engulfed in flame, but Andrea's gaze found something even more dismaying—Jesse's saddleless appaloosa prancing nervously about the yard dragging a lead rope beside Andrea's mule, Jacksaw. But the telling proof was Mahkwi, who raced frantically back and forth at the barn entrance howling her panic.

"Holy hell, it's a wolf!" Ezra cried and lifted the rifle laying beside him on his wagon seat.

210

"No!" Andrea cried. "It's not a wolf. It's Jesse's dog, don't shoot her. Please!"

Ezra lowered his gun. "Where are the Raffertys? Pray the good Lord they ain't none of 'em in that hellhole."

Jumping from his wagon he ran toward the buckets stacked near the corner of the barn.

Andrea did pray, but she couldn't deny the truth. Handing the baby to Etta, Andrea leapt from the buggy. From within the barn, came the screams of animals and the roar of the hay mow going up.

Jesse! Oh, Jesse!

Ezra and Jack were dredging water from the water troughs in the paddock and splashing it futilely against the burning wood. As she reached the barn, Mahkwi leapt toward her with a desperate whine of recognition, a plea for help.

For the first time, she didn't fear Mahkwi. They shared a common terror. A common love.

Andrea raced toward the barn doors. Ezra intercepted her halfway there. "Hey, *hey!* Where do you think you're goin'?"

"Ezra, they're in there!" she cried, trying to break free.

"*Who?*"

"Jesse and Silas, I know they are. Please, we have to help them!"

Ezra tossed his bucket aside and swore. "Lookit that Goldanged mess! Ain't nobody comin' out of there alive, missy. Don't you go addin' yoreself to the list. Ain't nothin' we kin do for 'em now."

Andrea's eyes narrowed with anger that he would give up on Jesse so easily. "Please! Please, let me go."

"No, he's right," Etta said as she appeared at Andrea's side, her face pale and drawn, arms tight around a wailing Zachary. "There's nothing we can do now, but pray."

"But Etta, Silas is in there, too."

The colored woman swallowed a sob, her eyes bleak. "I know."

Refusing to be daunted, Andrea grabbed a bucket and plunged it into the nearest trough and raced toward the entrance, ignoring Ezra's shouted warnings. She couldn't just watch Jesse die without trying to do *something*. She coughed on the choking smoke, but ducked her head just inside the barn doors. "Jesse! Silas!"

Nothing.

She tried again. "Answer me, damn your ornery hides. Answer me! Jesse!"

A roaring sound came from the barn roof at almost the same moment a huge wild-eyed mare came crashing out through the curtain of smoke, with a foal close on her heels. The mare nearly knocked Andrea over, but she moved aside a second before it was too late. She staggered back, seeing a huge section of the barn roof cave in on itself, taking with it her last thread of hope.

Chapter Thirteen

She fell back from the intense heat and stumbled to the ground with her bucket of water. Despair clawed at her chest and her cry came out more like a moan.

"Jes-seee!"

Then, as if her plea had called them up from the inferno, two wraithlike forms took shape through the smoke. One was half-falling, the other supporting, dragging.

The two emerged from the smoke in a huddled mass. Jesse dragged the black man forward, beating furiously on Silas's back with his bare hand. Her reactions dulled by shock, it took her a moment to believe what she was seeing. Then Andrea realized with horror that it was the fire on Silas' shirt Jesse was trying to stamp out.

Gathering her wits, she jumped up and heaved her bucket of water over the two of them, dousing the flames. With a moan, Silas staggered another fifteen feet from the fire and dropped to the ground coughing. Jesse fell to his knees beside him, his head hanging between his outstretched hands, gasping for air. Mahkwi didn't help, planting exuberant wolfish licks all over his face.

Covered from head to toe in black soot, now dripping wet, Jesse's chest heaved as he cleared his lungs of smoke. Etta was already beside Silas when Andrea dropped down beside Jesse and threw her arms around him.

"Oh, Jesse . . . Jesse." Tears of relief streamed down her cheeks. "I thought you were dead—"

"So . . . so did I for a minute." His voice wasn't much more than a croak. "God Almighty . . ."

For a moment, he allowed her embrace, even drew her to him, as if he needed the comfort of her touch as much as she did to convince himself he was still alive. He smelled of smoke, sweat, and singed hair.

As if suddenly realizing what he was doing, he set Andrea away from him without looking her in the eye. She swallowed down a moment of hurt.

"The mare—?" he asked.

"She's safe," she assured him. "She came tearing out with her foal just ahead of you."

Jesse's shoulders relaxed a fraction, and he drew his right hand up with a wince, cradling it to his chest. "The damn cow . . . she wouldn't come."

"Never mind," she whispered. "*You're* alive."

He nodded, exhausted, and glanced at his throbbing hand. Behind them the fire roared with withering heat.

"You're hurt," she said pulling his hand to her. A large blister was already rising on the palm. "Your poor hand—"

"It's nothing," he said, taking his hand back and turning toward Silas. He didn't need to be reminded that his impulsiveness had nearly gotten Silas killed. "Is he all right?"

Silas winced, a racking cough shaking his frame. "I's fine, thanks to you," he answered hoarsely. "I 'spect . . . I be needin' a new shirt though."

214

Etta eyes glistened as she shook her head. "And some new skin, you old fool." She tightened her hold on the baby in her arms. "Lord a mercy, what got into you two, going into that fire like that? Why somebody oughta take you two over their knees and—"

"Oooh-ee," Silas said, shaking his head, "ain't she a bossy woman?" He struggled to sit up, but his attempt disintegrated into a coughing fit.

"You just stay right where you are, Silas Mayfield." Etta scolded. "You're gonna listen to some sense for a change."

Jesse glanced back to see the rest of the barn roof cave in. Several other wagons pulled into the yard, filled with neighbors ready to help. Armed with shovels and rakes, they joined Ezra and Jack in trying to contain the fire in the hayfield.

The Rafferty's wagon tore into the yard in a cloud of dust. With a look of disbelief on his face, John Rafferty stumbled from the wagon. Gus, his fifteen-year-old, followed him, his mouth slack with shock. Isabelle and the children sat frozen on the wagonbed, too overcome to move.

Jesse got slowly to his feet as John staggered toward the barn on stiff legs.

"John!" Jesse called.

John didn't seem to hear him, his gaze hardly able to take in the disaster that had befallen his family. "Somebody give me a bucket—"

"John!" Jesse grabbed his arm. "John it's too late for the barn. We have to let it go."

"Jesse—?"

"John, I'm so sorry," Jesse touching his arm. "There was nothing we could do. The bastards torched it."

"Raiders?"

215

Jesse nodded. "I saw them riding off, but they were too far away and too many. The barn was too far gone by the time we got here." He knew there'd been a full mow of hay in John's loft, meant to see his stock through the winter. But right now, the hay was the least of his losses.

John's stunned gaze took in Jesse's soot-stained clothes. "My God, you didn't—? Are you all right?"

"Yeah," he said, making a loose fist to hide the burn on his hand.

John looked up, his eyes searching the suddenly crowded yard. "Oh, my God, *Lexi*." The word was choked.

"What?"

John moved without thinking toward the burning barn. "My draft mare, Lexi. She was in the—"

"We got her out, John," Jesse told him, taking his arm. "Her and the foal, too."

John exhaled with shaky relief. "Dear God, you went in there for the horses? Lord, boy, y-you could have been killed."

"They almost were," Etta told him, looking down at Silas who was still coughing, but slowly getting to his feet.

John shook his head in disbelief. "I . . . I had a cow in there, too. Lucy. She had a cracked hoof I was treating . . ."

"We tried," Silas told him. "That cow jus' wouldn't come. I'm real sorry, Mr. Rafferty."

"No, it's . . . it's . . ." He rubbed a hand over his face as if to wipe away the horrific vision. "How can I ever thank you?"

Jesse shook his head, his eyes dark with words he couldn't find. "Don't. You would've done the same for us."

Andrea's eyes met Jesse's for a long heartstopping

216

moment. "For us," he'd said, not, "for Andi." Amidst all this destruction, Andrea felt a moment of hope. Whether Jesse wanted to admit it to himself or not, Willow Banks was every bit as much a part of him as Rafferty land was to John.

John's son appeared suddenly at his father's side. Gus Rafferty, a strapping young man, with his father's looks and his mother's dark red hair, looked uncharacteristically drawn and much older than his fifteen years. He seemed aware that his father was in shock and the responsibility had fallen suddenly and heavily upon him. Taking his father's arm, he turned John to face him.

"Pa, the alfalfa's goin' up," he said slowly, sensing his father's confusion. "There's a bunch of men out there trying to put it down. They need our help."

That seemed to snap John from his stupor. "Merciful God, the hay! We can't lose it, too!"

"They're diggin' a circle around the fire, Pa." Gus was already backpedaling toward the field.

John started automatically for the tool room of the barn where he kept his shovels. "Dammit to hell!" he cursed when he realized what he was doing.

Gus shouted to him on the run. "Ezra brought some extra shovels. Come on, Pa!"

Shaking off his insentience, John took off at a run after his son amidst the chaos.

Andrea exchanged a helpless look with Jesse. He shook his head and dissolved in a fit of coughing. Struggling to his feet, he staggered off in the direction John had gone. Andi bit her tongue to keep from calling him back. She knew better than to try to stop him.

Fighting back her tears, Andrea looked around the Rafferty's farm. All their work, their wonderful home and farm, half-destroyed. *For what?* The whim of a group of cowards intent on destroying innocent people's lives? How simple it was to undo all the hard work of a lifetime.

Behind them, the fire still raged, crackling and roaring like a victorious beast. The side wall of the blackened barn collapsed. The air, thick with biting smoke, was filled with the shouts of men, and the frantic activity that had suddenly encompassed the Rafferty yard. Isabelle had climbed down from the wagon and was running toward her ransacked house with several children tugging at her skirts.

Taking Zachary from Etta's arms, Andrea touched her shoulder. "You stay here with Silas. I'm going to see if . . . if there's anything I can do for Isabelle."

Silas waved Etta off. "I's all right. You two go on."

"You come in the house and let me put something on that burn, Silas."

He nodded, exchanging a look with Etta. "I be in directly."

But it took much longer than that. Night had long fallen by the time the barn fire had burned itself out and the men had smothered every smoldering ember in what was left of the alfalfa field. If they were lucky, they might harvest enough hay from this third cutting to last them halfway through the winter.

If they had a barn to store it in.

Already, there was talk of a barn raising, which lifted the spirits of everyone there. The thought of bringing something positive out of such pointless devastation gave everyone cause to hope. When at last the neighboring men had left, smudged with soot and exhausted, Jesse and Silas returned to the house.

Or what was left of it.

The raiders had turned the place upside down searching for anything of value and had come away with enough to make the raid worth their while.

218

Though the Raffertys were by no means well off, their farm was a prosperous one. They had found Isabelle's legacy from her mother, a silver tea service and two pair of silver candlesticks, along with her modest collection of jewelry and some kitchen money. What they hadn't found, by the Grace of God, was the secret place where Isabelle and John kept their cash—an accumulation of several years' profits from the farm—not trusting it to the banks. Had that money been gone, their sudden reversal might not have been recoverable.

Isabelle, Etta, Andrea and the older children had spent the evening putting the house to rights as much as possible. But ticks had been torn from their beds and slashed, clothes torn from drawers, and armoires overturned. The house would require more than one harried evening to sort out.

Andrea and Jesse offered to take several of the children home with them until the Raffertys were back on their feet, an offer that was met with gratitude by both Isabelle and John, and by the girls. Etta insisted that Silas stay so she could look after his back, so he bedded down on the parlor floor for the night.

After constructing a makeshift pallet in the back of the Raffertys' high-box wagon for the youngest girls, four-year-old Gertie, and Ruthie, two-and-a-half, eleven-year-old Adeline settled them and Zachary down there and stretched out beside them.

Jesse tied Rabble to the back of the wagon, and climbed into the wagon slowly, his sooty face pale and drawn. Andrea knew he hadn't taken the time to dress the burn on his hand properly and suspected he didn't want to burden John with the knowledge he'd hurt himself. His only concession to the wound was to wrap a sooty bandanna around it. Now, she could see, he was paying the price.

When he sucked in a breath as he reached for the traces, Andrea laid her hand over his. His eyes, glazed with pain, met hers with a question.

"Jesse," she said quietly, "let me drive."

He shook his head. "There's no need for—"

"Don't be stubborn. There's no one to impress here, or try to fool. Just give me the traces."

The battle of wills lasted only a few seconds, long enough for Jesse to see the sense in her words. Reluctantly, even gratefully, he did as she asked.

After a day of upheaval, little Ruthie and Gertie fell instantly asleep with the rocking motion of the wagon. Jesse did not speak to her on the way home; he seemed weighed down by the events of the day. He leaned back heavily against the wagon seat, staring almost sullenly off into the darkness. The silence between them was broken only by the night sounds of the crickets and the rumble of the high box as it made its way to Willow Banks.

Andrea tucked the edge of the blanket on Jesse's bed around Adeline, brushed her hair back, and kissed her forehead.

"Sleep well," she whispered so as not to wake the little girls sprawled beside her.

"Miss Andrea?"

"Yes, Addie?"

The young girl swallowed hard, her voice, high and small. "You . . . you don't think they'll come here . . . do you?"

Andrea squeezed Addie's hand. "No, honey. Don't you worry. We won't let anything happen to you. I promise."

Addie nodded. "Yes'm. I'll try."

"Try to get some sleep."

"Yes'm. I will."

"G'night, Addie."

"Night."

When she reached the kitchen Andi found Jesse slumped on the kitchen chair, rubbing one sooty hand over his equally sooty face. His other hand rested in a bucket of cool water. Exhaustion pulled at him. A single candle lit the room.

"I never realized what a convenience two good hands can be," he said sheepishly, looking up as she came in the room. The front of his shirt was dripping wet from a misguided attempt to manage a washcloth one-handed.

Andrea regarded him for a few seconds before making up her mind. She walked to the counter and took a sponge and a clean linen towel from the drawer near the sink. Then, crossing to Jesse, she hesitated only fractionally before reaching for the buttons on his shirt.

Jesse's reaction was swift. His hand clamped down on hers and his eyes darkened. "What are you doing?"

She shrugged off his hand. "I'm taking off your shirt."

He swallowed hard. "It's my hand that's hurt, not my . . . my chest."

She stared at him evenly. "Your hand isn't the only thing covered in soot. Do you plan to blacken my clean sofa tonight as well?"

His eyes narrowed suspiciously but he couldn't argue her logic.

"I should hope not," she finished and continued unbuttoning his shirt.

"I can do that," Jesse claimed, but when she allowed him to try, he found it nearly impossible.

221

With a small smile, she finished the job, lifting the filthy fabric of his shirt off his shoulders and past his sore hand. He sucked in a breath through clenched teeth.

Andrea dragged her gaze from his smooth sun-browned shoulders and the thick mat of hair that started on his chest and disappeared into his tapered waistband of his trousers. That he wore no union suit in this heat didn't surprise her, but he glanced up embarrassed just the same.

"Here," she told him. "Keep your hand in the water until I'm finished. You'll at least soak out whatever dirt you ground in there with your stubbornness tonight."

"Ow! That's not . . . any better," he gasped in complaint.

She soaped up the sponge with strong brown soap.

"Close your eyes."

"Andi, this is ridicu—"

"Close."

Jesse slammed his eyes shut as she came at him with the sponge, drawing the warm soapy sponge over his face in smooth, sensuous strokes: his cheek, his jaw, his throat.

He clenched his teeth. He'd half-expected her to scrub him like a child, but there was no motherliness in her approach. She bathed him as a woman would a man, in a dangerous, sensual way that made him forget the throbbing in his hand and think instead of the smokey defiance in her eyes.

He felt her lift the sponge away, heard her rinse it in the bucket. Jesse's breathing went still as her other hand came up to the hold the back of his head. Her fingers slid against his scalp, while with her other hand she rinsed the soap from his face. His body tightened involuntarily in response to the erotic

222

gentleness of her touch. He reached for the towel and wiped the moisture from his face, then dropped it strategically into his lap.

Common sense told him to put a stop to it now. Something more basic inside him didn't want her to. It had been a long time since a woman had touched him with such tenderness. Too long. He relaxed a fraction, closing his eyes, absorbing the sensations. At moments like these, he longed to stay, wished he could be part of her life . . . as if nothing before had happened. As if he was good enough for her. He wasn't. The old man had made sure of that. But that didn't mean he couldn't spend a few minutes imagining it so.

His thudding heartbeat drowned out whatever she'd just said to him. "What?"

"Your arm," she repeated softly. "Give me your arm."

"Oh." Slowly, he held it out. She took his wrist in one hand, and with the other she dragged the cool, rough-textured sponge up and down the length of his arm, following the curves and hollows of his muscles. The chilly water did little to cool the heat building within him. His pulse hammered beneath her fingertips. He wondered if she could feel it, if she knew what she was doing to him.

Her eyes stayed on his while she washed his sensitive inner arm and trailed the sponge over and between each finger. Was it his imagination, or was her hand trembling? Her chin was tilted up with just a touch of defiance, as if daring him to stop her.

He didn't.

When there were no traces of grime left, she did the same for his other arm, careful not to touch his palm.

When she turned to rinse the sponge, Jesse looked up, training his gaze on the small, thudding pulse at the base of her throat, only inches away from his face. Did it always race so? he wondered. No, he thought not. His gaze drifted inexorably south, down the curve of her breasts. Urges he had no business having made his breath come fast and shallow, and caused his heartbeat to vibrate his whole body.

In slow, deliberate circles, she rubbed the soap against the sponge. For a moment, he imagined her touching him that way with her bare hand, gliding her soapy palm, skin to skin against him—

Damn! What was he thinking?

When she pressed the cool sponge to his chest, Jesse grabbed her wrist, startling her.

"Don't—" he warned.

Her breath came unevenly, despite her attempts to control it. "Let me," she asked simply.

His fingers cut into her wrists. "What are you trying to do to me, Andi?"

"I'm trying to wash you."

"You're playing with fire."

"I'm not playing at all," she replied gravely, looking away. "I'm simply trying to—"

"Drive me crazy?"

"No."

"Well you are."

He stood up. Andrea, however, didn't move out of his way. She stood planted only inches from him, the heat from their bodies combining in the breath of space between them. "Andi—"

She lifted her chin. She looked so soft, so beautiful. He wanted to reach out and pull her into his arms, show her what it really meant to want. Instead, he said, "Thanks for the sponge, bath, but—"

"But what? You can't stand to have me touch you anymore?"

"Touch me? God Almighty, Andi, that was no

simple touch. You know what I'm talking about."

"Maybe I do. Maybe it doesn't matter *how* I touch you," she said turning away at last. "My touch obviously repulses you."

He nearly choked. *"Repulses* me?" Grabbing her with his good hand he spun her around. "You're wrong. You couldn't be more wrong."

"Am I? It seems nothing I do pleases you anymore. We used to be friends at least. Now all I see in your eyes is . . . is desperation. Why don't you just go if you can't stand to be around us anymore? If you hate this place so much."

"I haven't complained, have I?"

"You needn't put into words what I see so plainly written in your eyes every day after working in your *father's* fields." She emphasized the word, 'father' as if taunting him.

"Don't bring him into it," Jesse growled.

"Why not? He's here, isn't he? Standing in this room as if he were still alive?"

"You don't know what you're talking about."

"Don't I? I see him in your eyes every time you look at the field, or pick up a hoe or heave a maul to split a rail. I see the hatred in your eyes and . . ." she softened her voice, "the young boy who could never please his father. He's the reason you left and he'll always be alive for you, standing between you and me and the farm."

"The old man's dead," Jesse stated unequivocally. "Leave him buried."

This time she caught his arm. "Can you, Jesse?"

"Look, there is no *you* and *me*. All right. When I left this place, I left for good. I walked out on you, too," he said cruelly. "There's no turning back the clock on that. You made your choices, I made mine. You found your life with Zach—"

225

"Zach's dead."

Jesse's eyes flashed to hers. "And you're done mourning him awfully quick, aren't—"

Her palm connected with his cheek in a ringing slap, knocking his head slightly sideways.

Jesse staggered and touched his jaw. He shook his head miserably. "I'm sorry. I . . . I shouldn't have said that."

Andrea whirled away from him, tears stinging her eyes, too angry to speak, too hurt to defend herself.

With a hand on her arm, he turned her to face him, raising her chin up with his forefinger so she'd be forced to look at him. "Andi . . . I'm sorry. I know that's not true."

"You can think whatever you want of me, I don't care."

"I think of you all the time, that's the problem." His quiet admission hung in the air between them like a thread of hope. In confusion, she looked up at him, her eyes violet pools of trouble he was getting ready to dive into.

Oh, hell.

Before she could protest, he dropped his mouth against hers in a kiss that showed exactly what he meant. At first, she struggled, pushing against the wall of his chest, but he deepened the kiss, parting her lips with his tongue and proving to her that repulsed was the furthest thing from how he felt.

Andrea leaned into Jesse's kiss feeling her knees turn to jelly and her anger to dust. She'd longed for this since that first time he'd kissed her in the hallway. Thought of it every time he'd looked at her, every time she'd looked at him.

He was right.

This was what she wanted and she wouldn't apologize for it. She was a woman, not a little girl.

Her husband was dead and the man she'd spent half her life loving was holding her in his arms.

His hand slid up to cover her breast and he drew her close against him so she could feel what the towel no longer hid. Desire. Hot, longing, desire. The sweet ache between her thighs intensified and she wrapped her arms around his back, digging her fingers into the strong muscles there. She felt her nipples pucker in reply to his touch. If she could just hold him forever like this. If she could only prove to him . . .

On an angry breath, Jesse tore his mouth from hers and set her away from him, but not before she felt him quake with the power of the kiss they'd just shared.

She stared at him wordless, breathless.

"Do you know what I was thinking about when I was caught in that fire, Andi?"

She shook her head.

"You. I was thinking of you. Of this," he said, meaning the kiss, "and wondering who would take care of you if I died." He rubbed a thumb down her cheek. "Wishing that things had wound up different between us."

Things could still be different, she thought, but couldn't bring herself to beg him.

He dropped his hand away and turned toward the window. "But tonight, as I watched John's barn burn, all of his plans go up in smoke, I realized how fragile our hold is on our dreams. How useless."

"John will rebuild."

"And maybe," Jesse pointed out, "next year a tornado will get him, or a hoard of grasshoppers or—"

"Or an early frost or a thousand other things that happen to farmers," she admitted. "But he's willing

227

to risk it. It's his dream, Jesse. His land. Like this is yours. It's in his blood—"

"Dirt doesn't run in my veins, Andi. When are you going to see that?"

"When are you going to learn to put the past to rest, Jesse?" she heard herself asking. "Why can't you let your father go and move on?"

"I said to leave him out of it—" he nearly shouted.

"How can I when you can't? He's at the root of all this. Why Jesse?" she pressed. "What did he do to make you hate him so?"

He spun around to face her. "You mean what *didn't* he do?"

Confused, she shook her head. "I don't know what—"

Jesse's expression went dark. His words, when they came, were filled with venom. "He didn't *father* me, Andi. That's what he didn't do."

Her eyes went round. "Wh-what?"

His smile failed to reach his eyes. "I'm a bastard, all right? The great Thomas Winslow wasn't my father. Are you satisfied now?"

Chapter Fourteen

Andrea stared at Jesse as if she'd never seen him before. He stood, shoulders slumped in defeat, staring at the floor.

"A-are you sure?"

His ring of laughter was sharp, biting. "As sure as a bastard can be of his parentage."

"Don't call yourself that."

"That's what I am. A bastard, a by-blow, the get of some poor fool my mother had the misfortune to fall in love with."

His words, so bitter and full of anger, shocked her. It all made some kind of crazy sense now. His hatred of the land and his father. His leaving . . . not even trusting this secret to her. Not believing that she could forgive it. Had he had so little faith in her love for him? So little faith in *her*? The realization stung.

All these years and he'd never told anyone. Through a sweep of lashes, Jesse's tortured gaze rose to meet hers. Shame burned in his eyes. Suddenly, she knew what it had cost him to tell her.

The scent of honeysuckle drifted in through the open window. Lightning bugs tapped against the pane in the silence that stretched between them.

"It was that last day you found out, wasn't it?"

"Yes." His eyes held hers.

"Why? Why didn't you tell me?"

"Tell you?" He laughed humorlessly. "You think I wanted you to know that about me? That I didn't even have a decent name to give you? That the man who had pretended to be my father for my whole life had made it plain the farm I'd broken my back over would never truly belong to me because his blood didn't run in my veins?"

"Oh, Jesse . . ."

He made a fist with his good hand. "Y'know, I never knew what it was about me he hated so much." Jesse's voice shook. "He was different with Zach. Zach couldn't do anything wrong. The old man saved that damn strap for me."

"Zach loved you."

"I know that," Jesse said, shaking his head in dismissal. "I never blamed him. Zach never sided with the old man against me, in fact more than once he tried to take the blame for things I did to save me from a strapping. He was my brother regardless of the blood we didn't share."

Andrea watched him closely. "How did you find out?"

"You know that's the ironic part. I don't think the old man ever meant to tell me. I was such a convenient whipping boy . . . I guess I finally made him mad enough that it just slipped that day. That last day." He looked up at her.

Andrea swallowed the thickness in her throat and waited for him to tell her. At last.

"He was angry about some row I'd just plowed in the cornfield. It wasn't straight enough or deep enough." Jesse smiled grimly. "I disagreed. He accused me of sassin' him and started to undo the

230

buckle on his belt. I warned him against it. By then, I outweighed him by twenty pounds and was two inches taller than him. And I'd already decided, after that last time he'd whipped me, that he'd never hit me again as long as I could fight back.''

''What happened?'' she asked.

''He didn't listen. He took the belt off and started coming at me. I warned him again that he was makin' a mistake. But that only enraged him more. Told me to mind my tongue, called me gutless. Told me I'd never have the stuff it took to be a farmer.

''There I stood, covered with sweat and dirt from his goddamn field, muscles on fire from pushing that damn plow and what I wanted more than anything at that moment, was to kill him.''

Andrea shook her head. ''Did he hit you?''

''He tried. The belt came down on my arm. I yanked it out of his hand, and slugged him in the jaw.'' Jesse smiled coldly at the memory. ''He went down like a sack of grain with this . . . real surprised look on his face. It didn't last long. He sat up there in the cornfield and tore my life apart with a few words. He was in a rage. He told me it didn't surprise him that I'd shown my true colors at last and that I was no son of his.''

Jesse raked the fingers of his left hand through his hair. ''I didn't know what he meant at first, but I told him that was just fine with me if he wanted to disown me.

''He said to me, 'I don't have to disown somethin' that never belonged to me in the first place, you ungrateful little bastard.' He said I was the spawn of some other man and he'd done my ma a favor marrying her.''

''I called him a liar, but then Ma came out to try to stop the fight. One look at the two of us and she knew what he'd told me."

Jesse bent his head, his voice thick. "She followed me back to the house when I went to pack my things. She told me how sorry she was about all of it and how she'd prayed it would never come out. She took a picture out of a secret box she'd hidden under the floor boards. It was portrait of my real father. She'd kept it all that time." Jesse swallowed hard. "I realized then why Zach and I looked so different. It was like looking at a picture of myself."

"Who was he?" Andi asked.

Jesse shrugged, closing his eyes. "She said his name was John, and that he'd died in a typhoid epidemic before he could marry her. She said she'd loved him." A tremor went through him. "That she loved me."

"She did, Jesse. I know she did."

Jesse slumped back down to the chair. "I know that, too. I suppose she did what she had to do, marrying Thomas Winslow. He claimed to love her and promised to raise me as his own son. I guess he tried, but he didn't have the heart for raising another man's bastard. She tried to protect me from him a hundred times. But I think she was afraid of him."

"Zach didn't know." Andi's words were a statement, rather than a question. She felt sure if he'd known, he would have told her.

He shook his head, his hand coiling into a fist on the tabletop. "Ma asked me not to tell him. She didn't want him to know about her . . . past. I decided she was right. It was a pointless hurt."

"But why couldn't you tell *me*, Jesse?" she asked sinking to a chair across from him. Her fingers brushed his. "Why all this time?"

"Why?" A shadow of pain crossed his face. "It's pretty damned obvious, isn't it? I had nothing to offer you anymore. Not land, or a home, not even a name."

"You think so little of me that you thought it would matter—?"

"It mattered to me," he snapped. *"Me,* Andi. I'm a bastard. I had nothing. I still have nothing." He saw steel in her amethyst eyes as she watched him.

"You're Martha Winslow's son. That's something to be proud of. No matter what names Tom Winslow called you, you're as much a part of Willow Banks as Zach was. Tom can never take that away from you."

"Don't you see, Andi? He already has." Without thinking, he made a fist of his burned hand and sucked in a breath.

She stood, reaching for the jar of chickweed ointment next to the sink and the gauze bandages she kept in a drawer. She gently spread the ointment over his burn, then wrapped his hand in gauze. When she was finished, they sat staring at each other in the dark, listening to the night sounds for a long time before she spoke.

"Jesse, I'm sorry about . . . Tom," she began, choosing her words carefully. "Sorry about all of it. But that part of your life is over. Your parents are both dead." She swallowed hard. "Zach is gone. You can make what you want out of this life. You can keep stubbing your toe on that same stone, or you can cast it out of your path. It's your choice." She slowly got to her feet and looked down at him. "It's always been your choice. Good night, Jesse."

She left Jesse sitting alone in the darkened kitchen, pondering her words. Fatigue pulled over him like a worn old coat. Or maybe it wasn't exhaustion. Maybe it was self-pity weighing him down. That and the awful, niggling suspicion that the last six years of his life had been a waste.

When he'd finally vented the truth on her, he'd known what to expect in her eyes—pity, anger, even self-vindication. But he'd seen none of those emotions. Instead, he'd seen a woman who'd loved him for half her life who'd been willing, one last time, to speak the truth to him. The truth that left him nowhere to hide.

On a long sigh, he rested his head on the back of his wrists, wondering how she'd gotten so strong since he'd left.

And so damn wise.

Yanking Rabble's reins around, Jesse backtracked two rods and pulled the horse to a stop, studying the torn-up sandy soil where a half-score of horses had trampled the ground yesterday. He didn't hold out much hope of finding anything much to tell him who they were. But, all the same, he threw one leg over Rabble's flank and stepped down into the horse's shadow. He ruffled Mahkwi's fur as she came up to give him a wet, whining kiss. The wolf had barely left his side since the incident at the Raffertys yesterday. Now she seemed spooked and protective. The fact was, so did he.

Squinting into the noonday sun, he pulled the brim of his hat down over his eyes. He balanced on the balls of his feet and inspected the crisscross of hoofprints. Judging by the depth of the prints in the dusty ground, the riders had been pulling hard. That he could attest to personally. They'd been hauling ass back to the rock they'd crawled out from under.

At this point, however, the prints seemed to split up. Some heading east, some west, and one, directly toward town.

234

Jesse frowned. Why would a man who'd just ravaged a local farm show his face in town? he wondered. Why, indeed? Did he hope to hide there anonymously amongst the good citizens of Elkgrove? Make himself an alibi? Was he a stranger or one of their own?

John Rafferty's words in the churchyard came back to him in a haunting echo: *It's as if they know the comin's and goin's of folks around here.*

Kneeling on the ground, he traced a finger around the crescent-shaped print, looking for its mate further on. He found the left front print, choked with a weed buried deep into the soil. This print looked virtually the same as its partner except . . .

He frowned again.

Pacing off a few more feet, he searched the ground. There. A clearer print this time. Here, too, a half-inch-deep slash protruded from the half-moon shape mark. The shoe was about to throw a nail. The knifing metal caught the faintest edge on the ground, leaving a telltale mark like a little red flag. There was something else about it too. Oddly, the left impression seemed consistently deeper than the right. As if the rider's weight were shifted more to that side. Inexperience or a loose girth could cause that. Or half a dozen other things. The loose nail wasn't much to go on, but at least it was a tangible clue.

Jesse leaned back on his heels. What was he supposed to do, lift every left front hoof on every horse in town looking for a loose nail? No, but for what it was worth, it wouldn't hurt to give the information to Sheriff Cobb.

Gathering Rabble's reins, he nudged the gelding's head up from the thatch of grass he was enjoying and mounted up.

From his vantage point, he could just see the distant half-shingled rooftop of the barn. In his mind's eye, he pictured Andi standing in the yard, scattering cracked corn for the chickens, the child with Jesse's brother's face planted on her hip. Or, Andi bent deep over the late summer garden, yanking weeds and harvesting the fruits of her labor. But more than that, he pictured her eyes, soft amethyst eyes, telling him what she couldn't say. And he remembered her words last night.

It's your choice, Jesse. It's always been your choice.

Was it? he wondered. Was it really his choice? Or had the choices made for them both those many years ago led them irrevocably to the impasse that seemed to yawn between them now?

He kicked the gelding, and aimed him back to Willow Banks. He had the sudden urge to see her, touch her, smell the sweet familiar scent that had always belonged only to her.

Maybe he was crazy for hoping, for wondering if maybe he could have something here with her after all. Perhaps the dreams he secreted inside him were simply smoke and she would blow them away.

Then again, he considered, maybe not.

Glad to have the house to herself for a few minutes, Andrea leaned back in the old rocker and set it in gentle motion with her foot, while Zachary nursed at her breast. Contentment washed over her as she watched him take nourishment. His small hand clutched the cotton fabric of her blouse like a kitten's kneading paw, and now and then he'd pause to toss a heart-stopping smile at her.

He felt noticeably heavier in her arms, an outward sign of the daily changes in him. That she was still part of that small miracle only strengthened the irrevocable bond between them.

Soon he would be two months old. She could hardly believe it had been that long since that fateful day when Jesse had ridden back into her life. There were days that felt like Jesse belonged, as if he'd never left. And others when she half-wished he'd never come back.

She glanced out through the lace curtains at the parlor window and heard the giggles of the three Rafferty girls playing in the yard. Andrea told herself she wasn't waiting for Jesse to return, just curious where he'd gone. Perhaps he'd ridden by one of his new friends to pass the time of day. He seemed to be making quite a few new friends lately . . . if the number of fellows who'd dropped by Willow Banks was any indication. She certainly didn't mind and they were always quite pleasant to her. Even, quite thoughtfully, bringing her flowers now and then.

Though none since Sam had openly asked to court her, she suspected the men who had dropped by were all vaguely interested in that. She had, however, encouraged none of them and none had pressed his suit. And while Jesse had seemed genuinely happy to see them, their visits left him irritated and un-reasonably grumpy. It occurred to her, with the smallest glimmers of hope, that he might be jealous of the attention the men gave her.

She supposed that what he'd told her last night had everything to do with that. He'd ridden off this morning without more than a few words to her and no clue as to when he'd be back.

Andrea was hardly surprised, after what she'd said to him last night. She sighed. Sometimes the truth was well-couched in silence. Her outspokenness, was a bad habit, no doubt one Jesse neither appreciated nor needed. She'd probably driven him away . . . if he'd ever truly been here in the first place.

The truth was, his confession last night had startled her. More than that, it had answered a hundred questions that had plagued her for years. Questions about Martha and Thomas's strained relationship, of Jesse's abrupt disappearance, and questions that had plagued Jesse's only brother until the day he'd died.

A noise brought her attention to the door.

Jesse.

He stood in the doorway, lips parted as if finding her there with the baby pulling at her bare breast was the last thing he'd expected—or perhaps wanted—to see. She made no attempt to hide it from him. In fact, the tension in her shoulders relaxed at the sight of him, allowing him to drink in that part of her that nourished her son.

For a long beat, he did just that. He filled the doorway: imposing, dangerous, reined in. Yet, he stood poised there on the threshold, unsure whether to retreat or proceed.

For the first time she noticed a large pistol fit snugly into the cross-draw holster strapped to his hip. Noticed how well it seemed to fit him.

A plow boy with a gun.

No, she amended. *A mountain man with a hoe.*

Jesse's neck flushed pink under her scrutiny and he swallowed visibly. His penetrating gaze dipped to that bare breast again, then slid up to settle on her eyes. "I—" he began, then opted for retreat. "I'm sorry. I didn't—"

She tipped her chin up, heat creeping through her. "Were you looking for me?"

He nodded. A jerky movement. "You can . . . uh,

when you're done . . . I, uh, want to talk to you."

At the sound of Jesse's voice, Zachary unlatched himself and twisted to see Jesse, leaving her breast uncovered. She made no attempt to hide it. Zachary let out a coo of excitement that turned Jesse's cheeks a deeper shade of dusk. Without another word, he disappeared out the door.

Andrea sighed and redirected her attention to her son. "You happy to see Jesse, hmm-m?" she whispered catching her son's waving fist around her finger.

She glanced out through the curtains. "So am I."

Jesse cursed as he stalked out to Rabble and withdrew his Spencer Carbine Repeater from its scabbard. The metal made an angry swooshing sound against the leather.

God Almighty Winslow! Standing there like some callow schoolboy, gawking at her bare breast as if you'd never seen one before.

It wasn't *any* woman's breast you were staring at, a voice reminded.

Well, that's really it, isn't it? That's what I've come to. Catching stolen glimpses of Andi, half-naked, and not being . . . discreet enough to turn away.

Being fundamentally incapable of it, you mean.

Hell.

Jesse sat down hard on a stump in the shadow of the maple that shaded half the yard. Mahkwi whined and rested her head in his lap.

Admit it, the voice persisted. You want her.

No.

Liar.

Okay! So what? He jerked the trigger guard lever

open with a vicious snap and emptied the magazine of one spent casing.

So what's stopping you from telling her?

All of Jesse's old, tired reasons sprang to his lips but they sounded just as hollow as the cold steel barrel of his rifle. In fact, the thought of heading back to Montana alone twisted his stomach like a bad meal. He wondered how he could have thought it so easy just a few weeks ago to walk away from Andi a second time.

As if conjured from his thoughts of her, she spoke behind him.

"You said you wanted to see me?"

Jesse jumped a little, then pushed away from the sprawling tree that stood sentinel in her yard and turned around. She stood, patting Zachary's small back where he lay against her shoulder. His gaze strayed involuntarily to her breasts, then back up again. But the picture of her in that rocking chair, her white shirtwaist open at the breast, lingered. He fitted the last of his cartridges into the butt plate of his rifle.

"What's that for?" Andrea asked her eyes widening.

Jesse snapped the rifle shut and rested it, barrel up, against the trunk of the maple. "You."

"Me?" Her brows dropped in a frown.

"You know how to shoot one of these?"

"I've . . . I've never had to learn."

"Well, that just changed." He looped the long lead tied to the maple around Mahkwi's neck, and the wolf whined in complaint, making it clear she didn't think much of being left behind. Jesse dug his fingers into the wolf's fur and gave her a reassuring pat. He walked toward Andrea and scooped Zachary from her resisting arms.

"Hiya, Corncob," he said, lifting Zachary over his head. The baby let out a squeal of delight. "Puttin' on a little weight there, aren't you, boy?"

Jesse's eyes flashed to hers in a silent attempt to lighten the scene they'd just had in the house. Andrea blushed. They looked so right together, the two of them. Clearly, Zachary was as crazy about Jesse as he seemed about Zachary. Her heart gave a little jolt watching them.

Dropping a kiss on the baby's cheek, Jesse snuggled him against his shoulder and began walking toward Addie Rafferty.

"Jesse, what do you think you're doing?" Andrea asked.

"Don't worry about Corncob here," Jesse replied. "He'll be in good hands. Adeline has graciously agreed to babysit for a little while so I can corrupt you—"

Her eyes widened.

"—with some firsthand knowledge of my gun." He grinned a little wickedly.

"I don't think I want or need to know about your gun, Jesse."

"It's not optional." Adeline, on cue, walked up and held her arms out for Zachary. The baby looked as delighted to see her as he had Jesse. A line of drool followed the smile that spread over his face.

Andrea looked uncomfortable with the whole idea. "I don't know—"

"I do," Jesse cut her off. "With eight sisters and brothers you couldn't find a more qualified babysitter for Zachary, right Adeline?"

Addie grinned confidently. "Don't worry, Miss Andrea. The girls and I are just going to pick the last of those beans you've got climbing up the cornstalks

241

by the vegetable patch." She jiggled the baby against her shoulder. "I'll take real good care of him."

"Thanks, Addie. We won't be far. Just down near the creek." Jesse scooped up his rifle and box of cartridges and took Andi by the elbow. "C'mon."

"But—"

"I said"—he took her hand—"come on."

Chapter Fifteen

Dragging her by the hand, Jesse led her down the shaded creek past the rows of gracefully bent willows. Andrea nearly stumbled trying to keep up with his long-legged strides, but she didn't complain. Instead, she concentrated on the wonderfully illicit feeling of his hand holding hers. She was nearly breathless by the time they stopped at the small natural pond trapped between two hillocks and sheltered by a ring of oaks, willows, and maples. Blackbirds flitted between sturdy branches, and the creek that fed the pond made a gentle burbling sound as it rushed down the small waterfall into the pool.

"Here we are."

Her heart thumped painfully against her ribs when she saw where he'd stopped. "Why did you bring me here?"

His returning glance was puzzled. "Why not?"

Because it was our place, her mind screamed. But she merely tipped her head with feigned indifference. "I suppose one place is as good as any other."

"It's in sight of the house, but far enough so the shooting won't startle the baby."

"How thoughtful."

He frowned, and pointed to a fallen log thirty feet off where he'd set up a string of bottles and old tin cans in a tidy row. "I've set up some targets. Have you ever shot a rifle before?"

"I used your fath—Thomas's shotgun once to scare a fox away from the chickens. But I only shot it up in the air."

"A man is a much more difficult target," Jesse said. "But you'll do more damage with this than with a wavering pistol."

"I don't plan to shoot any men," she said, folding her arms.

"Planning and necessity are two entirely different things," he replied. "I want you to be prepared in case you ever have to protect yourself. I can't be at your side all the time."

Despite her unwillingness to admit the necessity for such a thing, Andrea remembered her dismal performance with the gun the day Jesse returned. If he had been a stranger . . . a raider . . . She shuddered involuntarily. "All right. What do I have to know?"

"I've already loaded it and I want you to keep it that way. But, so you know, the cartridges go in through the butt plate, here." He showed her the spot. "This gun holds seven .52-caliber rounds. The saying goes you can load it on Sunday and shoot all week. But if push came to shove, you could fire them all in less than a minute, before a man with a single shooter could get off more than a round or two. So quantity ought to compensate for what you lack in aim."

She looked doubtful as he handed her the gun with his good hand. It was heavier than she thought it would be. Deadlier.

"Rest it against the curve of your shoulder," he told her. "Here." He got beside her and nestled the butt where he wanted it. His touch sent heat soaring through her.

"Now, keep your finger off the trigger until you're ready to shoot," he warned. "Otherwise, you could cause an—"

A round exploded from the barrel, nearly knocking Andrea sideways, and found its way harmlessly into a thicket of underbrush.

"—accident," Jesse finished, one eyebrow raised in mild alarm.

"S-sorry," she stuttered on a gulp. The sound roared in her ears and left them ringing. "I-I didn't realize—"

"—how sensitive the trigger is? It is. Very. Never, *never* underestimate the danger of a gun like this. It can be your best friend or your worst enemy."

"I'm *sorry*. I won't do it again."

"All right. Let's try again."

She lifted the gun up and pointed it in the general direction of the old log. With his hand over hers, Jesse worked the trigger lever guard, locking another cartridge into place. He stood close to her shoulder, bringing his face down alongside hers. She could smell the soap he'd shaved with this morning, feel the heat from his body.

"You see this sight here, above the breech?"

Andrea nodded, unable to focus on it.

"Line up the target between the two beads here and the single one on the end of the barrel."

She nodded again and for a moment their eyes met—violet and blue. He looked away quickly, but she could feel the rapid rise and fall of his chest against her arm. Her heart drummed in her ears. Did he bring her out here for this? she wondered. She couldn't bear it if he kissed her again, only to pull away from her.

Jesse leaned closer, correcting her aim, her grip.

"Hold it steady . . . now . . . squeeze."

She did, ever so gently. The gun roared to life again, but her shot pulled wide, striking nowhere near the old log.

"Darn!" she cried, and rolled her shoulder to relieve the ache caused by the recoil.

"That's okay. That was a first shot. Let's try again."

He straightened the gun and settled it against her again. His bandaged hand covered hers. His scent— so masculine, so . . . Jesse—enveloped her. She didn't want him this close. Nor did she want him to move away. She moistened her lips and squeezed her eyes shut, trying to refocus on the gun.

"You won't hit anything that way."

Her eyes flew open and she glared at his grinning face. "I don't expect it will count anyway if you help me."

He studied her face for a moment before letting go of the rifle and gesturing that she was welcome to try.

Relieved at the distance between them, Andi brought the gun up against her shoulder once again, the need to prove him wrong outweighing her own confidence. She chose a tin can whose colorful label had half-faded, and sighted down the barrel at it, trying to ignore the feeling of Jesse's gaze on her. Holding her breath, she squeezed the trigger tighter, tighter.

The bullet exploded from the barrel and blew a chunk out of the log just below the tin, sending it flying.

She flashed a triumphant smile at Jesse.

"Not bad," he acknowledged. "Let's see you do it again."

She did, or tried, over and over again, but couldn't

come closer than random chunks out of the old deadwood. The first hit, she admitted, had been a lucky one.

Two more shots went wild, one stripping a small branch from the willow above the log. Jesse muttered something about scaring dinner out of the trees. She gave him a dirty look.

By the time she'd emptied the gun, her arms shook and her ears rang like church bells. Angry with herself, she held out the rifle to him.

"This is futile."

He handed her the box of cartridges. "Reload it."

"Me?"

He nodded. "I showed you how. What if you have to do it and I'm not here?"

"Jesse, this is a waste of time. The most I'll be able to do is blow dirt in someone's face!"

"Then hope for that," he said sharply. "These men aren't fooling around, Andi. If they caught you alone . . ."

She didn't want to think about that. Nor did she want to think about the way Jesse's eyes held hers with real concern. Grabbing the box of cartridges, she rammed them in one at a time. Then frowning in concentration, she lifted the gun once more to her shoulder. He corrected her hold on the gun one last time and drew her elbow up to the proper angle.

Taking careful aim, she squeezed the trigger.

The tin flew off the log with a satisfying *ping*. Beside her Jesse's mouth dropped open in surprise. Before he could speak, she took a bead on the next tin, braced her feet and fired.

That tin, too, disappeared off the log. She managed to wing two more of the next five tins. She lowered the gun, waved away the acrid cloud of gunsmoke and sent Jesse a smug look. "Anything else?"

"Well," Jesse said, taking the rifle from her, "never let it be said that moss grows under your feet, Mrs. Winslow."

Andrea rubbed her sore shoulder. "Are we finished?"

He raised an eyebrow. "Don't get too cocky. Shooting at tin cans and shooting at real live men are two different things."

"I pray I never have to learn that difference firsthand."

"So do I," Jesse stooped and gathered up the half-full box of cartridges.

Andrea wandered to a rock protruding from the edge of the water. "Have you?" she asked.

"Have I what?"

"Ever shot a man?"

He hesitated and kept his eyes trained on the rifle. "Yeah."

"In Montana?"

"Yeah."

It didn't surprise her. It was only another piece in the puzzle that had made Jesse the man he was today. Thoughtfully, she trailed her fingers over the sun warmed rock, leaned against it. "I suppose you had your reasons."

"Killing a man's never an easy thing."

"But you won't tell me about it?"

Jesse crossed to the rock, and leaned heavily against it beside her. "It's not something I talk about. A man does what he has to to survive. It's a rough territory."

There were more places than Montana where dangerous men hid, she mused. Today wasn't the first time she herself had considered what it would be like to kill a man. One particular man. In fact, to her shame, she'd contemplated that very thing a dozen times. But she'd always wondered . . . would she be able to do it to protect herself? Her child? Jesse?

She glanced at the scar on his cheekbone, the one that had still been angry and red on the day he'd come home. Now, it was a hairline streak of white against his deeply tanned face. Reaching up, she touched it. "Is that how you got this?"

He flinched, then seemed embarrassed by his reaction. "I got this from a man named Pierre LaRousse. He was doing his best to kill a couple friends of mine, Creed Devereaux and Mariah Parsons. And me too, while he was at it. He gun-whipped me."

Anger rose in her, swift and strong, that anyone would try to hurt Jesse. "Is that who you killed? This LaRousse?"

He shook his head. "Seth Travers had that honor. But I killed several of his men."

She heard neither triumph nor regret in his voice over the killings. So much she didn't know about Jesse's life. So many parts he'd never shared with her. She wondered about the woman he mentioned, Mariah Parsons. Was she someone he'd been involved with? Loved?

The sun beat down on them as they sat side by side on that rock. The water in the natural pond gurgled over the little fall and eddied past them invitingly. Andrea felt a bead of perspiration roll down between her breasts. "Remember when we used to go wading here?" she asked.

Startled out of his private thoughts, Jesse looked up and smiled. "How could I forget?"

"I thought maybe you had when you brought me out here."

"Some things," he murmured, looking sideways at her, "you always remember."

His words sent heat spiraling through her. Just for a moment, she wished she could erase those years that had come between them. Put them behind her as if they never existed.

Impulsively, she reached down to untie the laces on her black high-top work boots. Slipping them off along with her stockings and garters, she lifted her skirts and dipped her bare feet into the boggy edge of the water.

"What are you doing?" he asked with an incredulous laugh.

"Wading, of course!" The water lapped at the lacy edge of her pantalets, but she didn't care. The mud oozed between her toes deliciously. "Ahh-h . . . I haven't done this in years." She eased out deeper where the water crept up to her knees. "Come on in. It's wonderfully cool."

Jesse grinned, but hesitated near the shoreline. His gaze followed the hemline of her maroon cotton skirt and white petticoat as they inched up around her knees. Water soaked through her thin cotton drawers and clung to her shapely calves.

"Are you chicken?" she taunted.

"Me?" He spread five fingers across his chest.

"Yes, you. Have you grown too old and set in your ways for this sort of thing?"

"I'm hardly gray-haired yet, Mrs. Winslow."

With an impish grin, she tucked her hands under her armpits and flapped her arms heading into deeper water. *"Bwaa-auuk-buk-buk-buk."*

He lifted one eyebrow in amusement. "You think I'm afraid of a little water?"

"Bwaa-aaauuk-buk-buk," she chirped a little louder.

He nodded, grinning broadly now. "Ooo-hh . . . you're gonna regret that, Andi Mae . . ." With deliberate motions, he unfastened his gunbelt and dropped it to the ground. Pulling off his knee-high boots and socks, he rolled up his pantlegs and waded into the cool water after her. Minnows scattered at his feet. "You're going to seriously regret that."

She threw him a look of mock terror and hurried along the shallow edge of the pond. "You're too old to make me worry much," she teased, bunching her skirts higher. "Besides, I always was a better wader than you."

"Things change," he assured her, grinning with determination. Pushing against the current, he followed, drawn by the playfulness he hadn't seen in her since his return.

She brushed aside the drooping leaves of a weeping willow branch, and ducked past its meager protection, bracing herself against it. Her eyes flashed with the pleasure of the chase. "Some things change. Some things"—she let fly a slender willow shoot that nearly caught him in the face—"don't."

Jesse swept under the branch and stalked after her. "I think you need a *dip* in cool water to unswell that pretty little head of yours." He made a grab for her but she let out a shriek of laughter and darted ahead of him a few steps.

"You'll have to catch me first!" Reaching down, she arched a spray of water at him with her flattened palm.

"*Whaaa-hh!*" Jesse gasped as the cold spray hit him. He ran a hand over his dripping face. "You play dirty."

Andi's laugh rang throaty and rich. "How can you say that? The water's perfectly cle—"

She sucked in a breath as Jesse's retaliatory splash

251

hit her full force in the face.

Jesse used the moment to rush her, intending merely to lock her in his arms and claim final victory. He would have had her, too, had it not been for that sunken tree root she backed smack up against. She let out a little sound of surprise. Arms windmilling for balance, she teetered backward.

"Jesse-ee!"

He reached for her, his fingers finding hers in the last possible second, just long enough to pull him off balance, too.

He followed her into the thigh-deep water with a splash. Rolling instinctively sideways to avoid sinking her, he found purchase on the muddy bottom with his hands and pushed up. She was already sputtering when his head came out of the water. Her long hair had fallen out of its pins; it hung down her back and lay plastered against her soaked white shirtwaist. She was laughing.

"You!" she accused, slapping the water with both palms.

"*Me?* You deserved that."

Andrea threw her head back and laughed. "I guess I did, didn't I? Oh! Look at me—how shall I ever explain this to the girls?"

"You should have thought of that before you cast aspersions on my wading abilities, Mrs. Winslow." Dipping his nose under water he glided to her like a shark with only his eyes visible above the water. He came up beside her and grinned. "Personally, I think you look rather fetching soaked to the skin."

"How gauche of you to mention it, Mr. Winslow," she said, straightening the cuffs on her sleeves.

"Ah, you're right. I suppose manners really do have their place in a pond."

"They certainly do. And if you were a gentleman,

you'd help me up out of this compromising position."

"I would?"

"Absolutely."

"Well, then . . ."

He rose out of the water like some Greek hero, Andrea thought, clothes clinging to him like second skin, sun-bleached hair slicked back and wet. The endless work of summer had left him taut and hard— the lines usually hidden by his loose-fitting clothes were suddenly evident. Even his thighs, she thought, looked as if they'd been sculpted out of granite. Water lapped at his legs and sparkled on his skin. He took a step closer to her.

Andrea stared at the hand he held out to her and had second thoughts. Beyond the amused twinkle in his eyes, she saw something more. Something predatory, hungry. But she was feeling reckless and at the moment, a little wild. So, she reached out and put her hand in his.

His skin was cool from the water, but his touch was hot. He pulled her effortlessly from the water. So effortlessly, in fact, that her momentum sent her colliding into him. She gasped the moment her nipples made contact with his chest. He was flame and ice at once, friction and smooth solid mass. And the moment her hips pressed up against his she encountered the undeniable hardness at the precise point where their bodies joined. The realization took her breath away and frightened her more than any words he might have spoken.

Spreading her hands across the wall of his chest for balance, she absorbed the racing thud of his heartbeat, then pushed back. Jesse released her almost reluctantly. The suction of their wet clothes made a naughty sound.

Yet his eyes held not a trace of apology. Instead, he gazed at her with a look that set her bloodstream on fire. His chest rose and fell unevenly, and his eyes only strayed from hers long enough to drift lazily to the front of her blouse where the water had left it all but transparent.

"I guess," she said, covering her chest with her arms, "this wasn't really such a good idea."

He didn't answer. He only stared at her. Shaken, she watched his eyes change color from sky blue to a smoky lapis.

"Maybe," he suggested, "we should go."

"Maybe," she agreed, but neither of them moved. "Jesse—"

He put one silencing finger to her lips, then traced his knuckle down the hollow of her cheek and beneath her chin. He tilted her face up to him. "Do you know how you make me feel, Andi Mae?"

She shook her head, mesmerized by the intensity of his stare.

"Alive. For the first time in years, I feel like I'm part of something again." His thumb burned a path across her lips.

She closed her eyes. Weakness stole the strength from her knees. "Jesse . . ."

"I want you, Andi. I want you so much I ache with it. So much I can't think straight half the time."

Her heart raced and plunged like a frightened thing seeking escape. But escape was the last thing on her mind. Pressing her cheek into his cupping palm, she murmured, "This is all wrong—"

"Is it, Andi? Maybe its the first right thing I've done in years."

Jesse's hand slid down the column of her neck and lingered on her throat. His thumb made a slow, languorous circle in the moisture there before it moved to the back of her head to tangle in the mass of wet hair at the back of her neck. Then he drew her closer. She knew she should resist, but didn't, couldn't.

"Andi—"

Jesse dropped his head lower so his mouth hovered close to hers, so close she could feel his warm breath fan her lips. He was waiting, she realized. Waiting for her to tell him no. To stop him. The blood pounded in her ears and sang in her veins like a rush of heated wind. Stop him? She might better ask her own heart to stop beating. Whether his confession meant he'd changed his mind about staying or not, she didn't care. If only this one time, if this was all she ever had to take away with her, she wanted him . . . the way she had wanted him all those years ago—irrationally, passionately, completely.

She rose up on her tiptoes to meet him, closing the heartbeat of space between them, and brushed his lips with hers. Like a spark igniting into flame, it was all the invitation he needed.

Jesse dragged her against him. His mouth devoured hers in a kiss like no other he'd given her before: not angry, but starving, as if what had passed between them last night had only whetted his appetite. With a slow, heated slide of his tongue, the pressure of his mouth deepened, and Andrea's bones began to melt.

His hand cupped her hip, drawing her tight up against him. Sliding her upward along his thigh, he created an unbearable friction that sent fire thrumming through her veins. She heard herself moan as his hand slid to cover her wet breast, then lifted it upward like a precious gift toward his seeking mouth. Through the wet fabric of her shirtwaist, he covered her nipple with his mouth, sucking and nipping, while his fingers fumbled with the tiny buttons that ran down the front of her shirtwaist. She'd left her hated corset off today, as she did most days when she'd be stooped over the garden. Now she was doubly glad she had.

Pushing the fabric aside, he slid his hand beneath the flimsy lawn of her camisole and cupped her naked breast. His thumb raked across the aroused nipple, which beaded like a small pebble between his thumb and forefinger. "So lovely, Andi. So perfect."

"Kiss me, Jesse. Please kiss me."

Leaving a moist trail of fire behind, his mouth slid from nipple to throat, where he tortured the tender spot just below her ear. "Where? Here?"

"Yes," came her choked reply as she rolled her head back.

He moved up another inch to explore the curve of her ear. "Or here?"

"Oh . . . yes."

He kissed her eyes, her temple, her cheek. "What about there?"

She trembled like a willow in the wind. "Jesse—" she begged against his jaw, then he captured her mouth with his. His touch was a hot summer storm, driving through her like a forked streak of lightning. His mouth on hers, a need as basic as breath. She reached up and took his face in her hands, holding him closer yet. Slanting her mouth across his, she drank him in, inhaling the taste of him wantonly. Her finges slid into his nape. And when she groaned and felt her knees give in earnest, Jesse swept her into his arms and waded through the water with her to the shore.

He set her gently on the grassy slope at the edge of the water and covered her body with his own. Looking at her with such gentleness, he stroked her face and brushed a wet strand of hair from her eyes. With infinite tenderness, he kissed the drops of water from her eyelashes.

"This isn't the way I wanted it for us, Andi," he said against her neck. "When I dreamed of making love to you, it wasn't on a grassy riverbank. It was . . . special . . . right."

"This *is* right, Jesse, don't you see that? We have been destined for this place since we were young."

Jesse nestled his face between her breasts and inhaled deeply. "I'm a bastard for wanting you here. Like this. I have no right to even ask you—"

This time she put a silencing finger to his lips. "Don't talk about rights, or promises or even tomorrow. I only know that here, now, this is right. Make love to me, Jesse. I've wanted you for so long." She searched his eyes. "Does that make me wanton?"

He shook his head and dropped his mouth onto hers, in a brief, soul-wrenching kiss. "Thank God for it," he moaned against her skin.

She dragged him back to her and their mouths met with a fierceness that made breathing seem superfluous. With a nudge of his knee he spread her legs and settled between them, pressing himself there intimately while his mouth seared hers.

Finally, easing off her, Jesse freed the buttons on her shirtwaist loose and stripped her of it in one clean tug. Untying the small ribbon bow on her camisole, he freed her other breast.

His hand trembled as he ran it over the fullness of her, his mouth brushing her with the barest of caresses, then transferred his attentions to lifting her skirts up past her hips. Finding the tie that bound her drawers to her waist, he loosened it then freed her legs from them.

His hand followed the path of her drawers back up

257

her legs, dragging a palm along the sensitive inner thigh. He lingered there, drawing closer and closer to that warm, moist spot between her legs that longed for his touch. She moaned when his fingers found her at last and sank into the silken curls at the apex of her womanhood, dipping into the slick, damp heart of her. And suddenly his mouth was on hers again, claiming, demanding, seeking.

His tongue made lazy swirling motions inside her mouth and the pressure of his kiss forced her head back against the sweet-smelling grass beneath them.

Andrea's breath came in shaky gasps. Jesse shed his soaked trousers and hovered above her. She took in the sight of him and her longing became electric. The sun had burnished his skin and bleached the brown hair on his chest the same gold as the thick hair on his head. He was hard and lean but his touch belied the strength in those solid planes. His skin, when she slid her hands across it, was warm and smooth as a river-washed stone. And further down . . . Oh, my, she thought.

He was beautiful, the way a fine crystal held to the light was beautiful. Or the way a piece of music, played by someone who believed in it with his very soul, was beautiful.

That he was wholly unaware of that beauty, made him all the more attractive to her. She knew from experience that external beauty had nothing to do with a man's heart. But this man's heart was one she longed to touch.

He settled between her legs. Flesh to flesh, the tip of him seared her like a burning ember. She needed that fire inside her, mindlessly.

"Are you sure, Andi?" His words came between ragged breaths.

"Oh, Jesse, don't stop. Please—"

"In a minute, I'll be well past that point," he warned, pressing his cheek against her breast and breathing as if he'd run a long way.

Andi tangled her fingers in his hair. "I want you to. Don't you know that?"

His hands whispered across her skin as if he couldn't get enough of touching her. "You may regret it tomorrow."

She looked up at him. "Will you?"

He didn't answer her. Instead he covered her mouth with his in a kiss so heartbreakingly tender it brought tears to her eyes.

Then he entered her with a shuddering sigh of relief. Moving slowly, he gave her time to adjust to him. For Andrea, the discomfort lasted only a few seconds and then it was replaced by the unbearable rightness of having the man she'd loved her whole life inside her. He glided in and out of her, keeping his thrusts shallow, even cautious at first. Andrea arched toward him with a low moan, seeking more.

He complied with deep, sure thrusts of his powerful hips. Still, he teased her with the indolence of his movements, first burying himself deep within her then withdrawing almost completely. Over and over again, he pushed her to the brink of madness until she was writhing against him and moaning in low pants. Like an arrow seeking its mark, he drove with sure eloquence into the center of her being.

She stared up at his beautiful face, his jaw clenched, eyes squeezed shut, he grimaced in his own private agony of pleasure. He took her higher, higher until she forgot to think, forgot even the sunlight spilling through the canopy of trees above them. There was only sensation, the slick, thrusting union of two halves to make an inevitable whole.

He ground out her name, "Andi," then drove into her.

Spiraling, straining, she thrashed against his powerful thrusts as he took her to the delicate precipice between pain and ecstasy and flung her off. Airborne, on wings of coiling fire, she cried out his name. He covered the sound with his mouth. Inside her head, her blood pounded like thunder, muffling the groan of pleasure he took in seeing her climax. Andrea clung to him, drifting, soaring as Jesse gathered her close to him to find his own release.

His powerful thrust grew more intense, his hips grinding against hers harder, harder until the friction building inside her again until she thought she would die. Straining against her, head thrown back, he stiffened with a groan of release, and spilled himself into her.

Jesse collapsed against her, dropping his face into the curve of her neck. His shoulders rose and fell raggedly against her bare chest. For a long time, neither of them spoke or moved. She was too happy to do any more than cling to his damp back and hold him close. She loved the weight of him on her, the way his skin smelled, damp and sated with her.

She sighed deeply. No words of love had passed between them. Perhaps it was just as well. Tears gathered at the corners of her eyes and slid down her temples toward her ears. They were not tears of sadness, but tears of contentment. What they'd done today may have changed everything or nothing. But it didn't seem to matter to her now. She had Jesse in her arms, and he'd kissed her the way a man kisses a woman he loves.

She stared up at the treetops bending in the warm breeze and listened to the tempo of her heartbeat slow. The world filtered back, the chirp of finches, the burble of water lapping at their feet. In the tree a few feet away she glimpsed the weathered remains of the tree house they'd built all those years ago. Built in the apex of a strong tree, it had stood the test of time. It made her smile to see it now, as she held Jesse close to her at last. She wondered if she'd ever felt more complete than she did at this moment.

When he lifted his head at last, Jesse didn't attempt to break the intimate link between them. "Are you all right? Did I hurt you?"

She closed her eyes and shook her head. "No, it was . . . wonderful, Jesse. More than wonderful."

Jesse dipped down to taste her mouth again, then rolled out and off her, stretching out beside her on the bank with a sigh. It *had* been wonderful. Damn wonderful, in fact. He'd had a lot of women in his life, but never had he come close to feeling what he did with her just now. He wished he could just hold her the way he was right now, and not let life interfere.

He dropped an arm over his eyes, knowing a moment of despair. He'd spent so many years believing himself unworthy of a woman like her, and here, in a few moments, he'd taken her as if she were no better than the women he'd slept with in his travels. Self-disgust sluiced through him. To even think of her in the same moment as those others now struck him as blasphemy.

He couldn't leave her now, nor, for that matter, did he want to. He'd plow fields from dawn till dusk if he had to. But he'd taken that decision right out of her hands. She'd have to marry him whether she wanted to or not. Wouldn't she? And what about Zach? He found himself wondering if she was comparing him to Zach, unfavorably. How could he live up to a brother who'd been nearly perfect? A man Andi had

261

married, the one she'd planned on spending her life with?

"Jesse?" Andrea pushed her skirts down to her knees and rested her head on his shoulder. "What's wrong? Were you disappointed?"

He sighed and drew his arm beneath her head, pulling her close. "Disappointed? Not hardly. I—I'm still shaking." And he was.

"What then?"

"I guess I was wondering"—he lied—"a little belatedly I might add—if I . . . got you with child."

She relaxed against his shoulder. "Don't worry about that."

He lifted his head off the ground. "How can you say that? You do know where babies come from don't you?"

She exhaled a little breath of laughter. "You can ask that after delivering mine? No, I'm nursing. It's nature's preventative. So Isabelle says."

He dropped his head back against the grass with a groan of disbelief. "Oh, *Isabelle*. Isn't she the one with *nine* children? Geez, I feel so much better."

Andi laughed again, drawing circles through his chest hair with her finger. "I haven't even gotten my—" she blushed, "my curse again yet."

He relaxed a fraction. "Thank God for that."

"I used to have dreams that we had a child together. I always thought it would be a wonderful thing."

A long moment of silence had stretched between them. He sat up with his back to her.

Andi sat up silently beside him, pulled her camisole up from her waist and covered herself. She reached for her blouse. "Obviously you don't."

He grabbed her wrist and her hurt gaze met his. "No, it's not that. I . . ." He ran a hand through his hair and confessed, "I've had the same dreams."

Shocked by his confession, she stared. "You have?"

He nodded. "It's just—"

"Just what?"

"I gave up on them long ago."

Andi stroked his bare back with her hand sending shivers down him. "Things change," she said, echoing the words he'd used on her earlier.

He looked at her sideways and smiled sadly. "Some things can never be changed."

She stared at him intently. "Is it . . . Zach?"

He bowed his head unable to admit to her his fear. With shaking hands he reached for the trousers he'd discarded.

"Jesse, I don't want your brother to come between us."

"That's pretty tough, isn't it?" He stood and shrugged into the soaked pants. "I mean, you're still wearing his ring on your hand."

She stared at her hand, a little surprised to see that she hadn't removed her wedding ring. It hadn't occurred to her to take it off, nor, she supposed, would it have been proper if she had. She got to her feet beside him and touched his arm.

"Jesse, I loved Zach in a . . . special way. He was there for me when I needed him most. I'll always love him for that and for giving me my son. But . . ." she hesitated, "it's you I've always loved. I never stopped even when you left. Even after I married your brother."

His eyes rose to meet hers with a shadow of accusation . . . and hope.

"You cannot make me feel more guilty about it than I did at the time," she told him. "You broke my heart when you left. I did what *I* had to do to survive."

Jesse felt deeply sorry that his brother had never had the love he saw in Andi's eyes for him at this moment. But guilt was not only her burden, it was his. "Did he know?"

She stared at the leaf-scattered ground, tears gathering behind her eyes. "He knew. He always knew. He loved me without condition, Jesse. I loved him for that and would have been proud to be his wife for the rest of my life. I grieved deeply when he died; for myself, and because he'll never know the son he wanted so. But Zachary will know about his father. I'll tell him how funny his daddy was and how gentle and"—her voice broke—"how loyal. Zach was a wonderful man. I'll never forget him and neither will you."

Jesse nodded. He knew that only too well.

"I never wanted to want you back in my life again, but in you came. As much as I loved Zach, you've always owned my heart, Jesse. I never imagined I would trust it to you again." Implicit in her words was the fact that she had allowed herself to do just that.

He reached for her, pulling her close and dropped a kiss on her forehead. "Are you sure you should now?"

She started to reply, but the sound of approaching hoofbeats on the road to the south of the house cut her off. He peered through the trees in that direction, but could see nothing. "Riders." *Damn!*

"The children—" she gasped, her fear of the worst clearly imprinted on her face. The incident at the Rafferty place was too fresh in both their minds. With trembling fingers she buttoned the blouse and tucked it into her skirt then reached for her drawers.

Jesse was already hurrying to where he'd left his boots and guns. His thoughts ran along the same lines. Jamming his feet into his boots, he was already running for the house.

Andrea grabbed her boots, stockings, and garters. A sudden chill sliced through her, despite the warm breeze that tugged at the willow branches above her head. As she started off after Jesse, a branch snapped across the pond. She stopped dead and turned back, searching the shadowy thicket of trees. She saw nothing. Probably a squirrel, she decided, dismissing it as nothing more than imagination. Still, the coldness didn't leave her. Years of living on the edge of fear had made her skittish.

Without wasting another moment's thought on it, Andrea turned and hurried back to the children.

Chapter Sixteen

Jesse was still buttoning the last button on his shirt one-handed as he plunged over the small hillock and into the yard. Gertie and Ruthie were chasing one another through the rows of drying garden corn in a game of tag, while Addie, holding Zachary, watched the dust of the approaching riders cut a trail between the fields of man-high corn.

She turned at the sound of Jesse's footsteps, a look of fear in her eyes. "Who are they?"

He opened his mouth to tell her to get the children in the house when Sheriff John Cobb and two deputies rounded the corner of the field and trotted into the yard.

Jesse's heart gave a leap of relief. Andi appeared at his side, out of breath, and put her arm around Addie. He thought he heard her murmur a prayer of thanks at the sight of the three lawmen. But glancing at his sodden clothes, Jesse knew they couldn't have chosen a worse moment to appear.

Cobb had been Elkgrove's peacemaker since before Jesse left for Montana. Some thought that had been too long. Cobb had put on a few pounds since he'd seen him last. His barrel chest and broad shoulders gave the impression of strength, but Jesse wondered how much of that strength had turned to complacency. Still, his steely blue eyes missed nothing, and as he lifted off his hat in greeting, Jesse became all too aware of how he and Andi must look, soaked to the skin.

"Jesse?" His gaze went from Jesse's wet clothes to the rifle in his hand as he dismounted. "I'm glad I ain't who you musta been expectin'."

"Me, too. Hello, Sheriff," Jesse replied taking the man's extended hand. "Good to see you again."

"You know Jim Strands and Howard Lukes, don't ya? I've taken 'em on as deputies considerin' our . . . crisis."

The deputies nodded a greeting. Jesse nodded back.

Cobb's gaze strayed to Andi, whose cheeks had gone pink. "Mrs. Winslow. How do? We didn't, uh, catch you in the middle of somethin' did I?"

"No," she said with a nervous laugh, touching a hand to her wet hair. "Well, I mean . . . Jesse was teaching me to shoot his gun"—she held out her wet skirt delicately between her thumb and forefinger—"and, well, it's really so embarrassing. I *stupidly* slipped and fell in the water down at the pond."

Cobb raised an eyebrow and did his best not to notice the boots she concealed behind her back or her bare toes peeking out beneath the hem of her gown.

"You know," she rushed on, "that nice little natural pond we have on the, um, on Willow Creek?"

The Sheriff's bemused gaze slid back to Jesse. "Oh, yes, ma'am. An' them banks can be right slippery this time of year."

Andi rushed on, covertly picking grass from her sleeve. "Yes, well, then of course, Jesse came in to help me and then *he* fell in and so you see, w-we both

267

got soaking wet and . . . and well . . ."

Cobb rubbed his nose with his knuckle. The two deputies had the good grace to study the cloud formations.

"Actually," Jesse added, with an innocent smile, "a cool dip in the pond was quite . . . invigorating."

Andi pinched him while she smiled at the sheriff.

"Can we go swimmin', too, Miss Andrea?" Gertie piped in as she came trotting over to them.

"Yea!" chorused the two-and-a-half-year-old, Ruthie. "Thimmin!"

"Of course, dears," Andrea told them quickly.

"Why don't you let Miss Andrea go and change out of those wet things first before she catches a chill," Jesse told them. "We'll talk about swimming in a few minutes. I'm sure the sheriff didn't ride out here for nothing."

Cobb cleared his throat. "Well, now that's exactly right, Winslow. The boys and me just come from the Rafferty place and John said you seen some riders makin' tracks away from here yesterday."

Jesse glanced at Addie. "Why don't we go for a walk, Sheriff? I'll tell you what I can."

Cobb might be old, but he wasn't dense. "I reckon that's a good idea, Jesse. Boys, why don't you tie up over by the well and give the horses a drink o' that cool water. We'll be right back."

Jesse nodded. With a final look at the woman who still wore the blush of their lovemaking, Jesse walked down the road a piece with Sheriff Cobb, mentally computing the irrevocable damage he'd likely done this day to Andi Carson Winslow's already fragile reputation.

Andrea changed into a simple green muslin skirt

268

and blue paisley blouse, then cinched her waist with a belt. She hung her wet things on a drying rack in her room. A smile crept to her lips as she thought of making love with Jesse. Even now, thinking of him, an ache of wanting curled low inside her. She crossed her arms across her stomach and hugged herself as a tingle of remembrance flowed through her. The thousands of times she'd dreamed of making love with Jesse had never come close to the reality. It was beyond anything she'd ever experienced. She'd been shocked by her own response to him, by her lack of inhibition at his touch.

What they'd done today was surely sinful in the eyes of Reverend McConneghy and to most everyone else she knew. But how could something that felt so right be wrong? She reached for the portrait of Zach standing on her bedside table. She gazed at his face trying to remember how his smile dimpled his cheek and made his brown eyes twinkle.

Would he forgive her if he were somehow watching her from above? Would he understand?

Somehow, she thought he would be happy for her. That feeling brought her immeasurable comfort.

With a sigh she reached for her stockings. They were dirty. She pulled open her drawer and searched for the other pair of black ones she kept there. She found a single black stocking but not the other. Andrea frowned and dug down deeper, pushing with her hand beneath the cotton drawers and lacy camisoles. Nothing.

That's funny, she thought, she'd just washed them yesterday. She was sure . . .

She must be getting careless. The stocking was another in a long line of missing things that had cropped up in the last few months. Reaching in her drawer, she pulled her last pair. Made of white silk, she'd worn them under her wedding gown for Zach.

On second thought, she put them gently back in the drawer. She'd put the soiled ones back on and look for the lost one later.

Glancing out the window, she saw the two deputies leaning against the shade of the barn smoking cigarettes, laughing over some private joke. Her face flashed with heat, wondering if she was the subject of it.

Jesse and Sheriff Cobb were still gone. Ruthie waited patiently for her beside the chicken yard, poking her fingers through the fence for an illicit touch of the heat-dazed hens. Addie held Zachary close so he could have a good look, all the while repeating the word "chic-ken."

With a jolt of alarm, Andrea saw Gertie lying stretched out languidly in the shade beside an equally content Mahkwi. With one small hand, Gertie stroked the fur on the back of Mahkwi's head. The other absently traced the shape of some cloud she watched in the sky.

Andrea smiled and allowed herself to relax. She'd be sorry to see the Rafferty girls go home. So would Zachary. And so—perhaps most of all—would Mahkwi.

With the supper dishes done and the exhausted children tucked safely into bed, Andrea returned to the parlor to find Jesse gone. Disappointment forked through her. They'd spent the rest of the day going in separate directions. She'd taken the children to the pond and they'd spent themselves splashing in the water all afternoon.

Silas had come home, reporting that the Raffertys were slowly picking up the pieces. Etta had worked wonders on the minor burns on Silas's back with the juice of a small plant she kept growing on the windowsill. She'd sent a small one along for Andrea.

This afternoon Silas and Jesse finished what was left of the barn roof and had used the last of the light to begin threshing and busheling the cured, shucked wheat in the field. After dinner around a crowded table, Andrea began to despair of ever getting a moment alone with him.

She broke off a stalk of the plant Etta had sent and walked through the parlor to the front door. Jesse sat on the end of the porch, back braced against the house. His forearm balanced along his bent knee, he sat staring off into the darkness. A cloud of cigarette smoke escaped his lips and wreathed his head like dissipating fog.

Her heart clenched at the sight of him.

Andi opened the door. He didn't turn his head, or seem to even hear her approach.

"I didn't know you smoked," she said softly, sitting down beside him on the step.

When he looked up at her, heat lightning flashed between them, and he quickly stared down at the nearly spent stub in his fingers. "I don't usually." He sucked in a last puff then snubbed the butt out under the heel of his boot. "I guess I just felt a little restless tonight."

"Oh." She stared blindly at her hands. "I see."

"Somehow, I doubt that." After a moment's hesitation, he threaded his fingers through hers. His bandaged hand felt so large around hers. Her heart thudded like a rabbit's. Two seconds beside him and she wanted to leap into his arms and press her lips against his. *God, was it still hot out this late in the evening? Think of something else.*

271

She stared at the hand he'd woven together with hers. The bandage from his burn was shredded from a day's work.

"Your hand—"

"It's fine." With his other hand he tipped her chin up so she'd have to meet his eyes. His fingers held the faintest tremor. His eyes, a deep twilight blue, searched hers with the same intensity she'd seen there today.

On some unseen signal both seemed to hear, they met halfway, their mouths joining fiercely, hungrily as if it had been months, not hours since their last kiss. Jesse drew her to him until she was halfway across his lap. His right hand cupped her hip while his left tangled in the hair at the back of her head. Sounds of urgency came from deep in her throat; a groan came from his. She clung to him the way a drowning woman would a rescuer. She was drowning, drowning in need.

Then Jesse broke the kiss. "God almighty, Andi." With ragged breaths he raked his hand through his hair, trying to regain some modicum of control.

Stunned by what had just happened, Andi sat up too, breathing hard. Her hands shook and she pressed her palms into the hard planking of the step. Her heartbeat thudded against the wall of her chest. Dear Lord, they'd almost—

"Sorry." The word came from him in a breathless whisper.

"Don't be," she answered.

He dropped his head in both hands. "I should have never started that. I don't seem to have much control around you these days."

"Are you . . . sorry about today, Jesse?"

He closed his eyes for a moment as if gathering courage. "There are a lot of things I'm sorry about in my life. Making love to you today will never be one of them."

Andi released the breath she'd been unaware of holding. She leaned her head against his shoulder. All the mistakes they'd made, the lost years; could they ever make them up? Could they ever truly go back?

"Oh, Jess," she sighed, "we really made a mess of things, didn't we?"

A moment of awkward silence stretched between them. "I guess so."

"What shall we do?"

He untangled his fingers from hers, stiffening beside her.

"Do? I don't know, Sunshine. It's your call."

She regarded him with a frown. "Why is it my call?"

"It's your reputation on the line. You saw the look Cobb and his deputies gave us today. Do you think they believed a word of that story you fed them about falling in the creek?" He reached up and ran his thumb along her lips. "Your mouth was still bruised with my kisses, Andi. Our loving was written all over your face. Just like now."

Heat crept up her neck at the memory. "I . . . I don't care what they thought."

"Well, I do and you should." Jesse stood and stared out over the yard with his back to her. Dusk ripened the drying fields of corn a purplish blue and the ball of yellow-gold settled between the rows to the west like melting butter. The evening insects stirred the still warm air, stitching the silence gathering between them. Finally, he spoke. "If you won't say it, I will. We should get married."

On shaky legs, she stood, arms hugged to her sides. It wasn't the proposal she'd longed to hear from him.

No words of love, no bent-kneed promises. Only a single word reverberated in her mind. In a voice that sounded brittle, she asked, "Should?"

He raked his fingers through his hair. "I've given it a lot of thought, Andi."

"Have you?"

He nodded. "It's the only way."

"The only way to what?"

"To make it right."

"*It?*"

"You and me," he said, slowly as if he couldn't believe she didn't get it. "I said I wasn't sorry about today, Andi, and I'm not. But I'm a selfish man. I guess I always have been. It didn't occur to me until afterward that I'd forced you in a corner."

The crack in her heart widened. "A corner you didn't want to find yourself in either?"

He turned back to her with a frown. "I didn't say that. I didn't say that at all."

"No," she sighed and stared sightlessly past the yard. "You didn't. What about the fact that you hate farming, Jesse? What about Montana? What about your dreams?"

"Dreams are just . . . dreams. This is real life we're talking about."

"And you're willing to give them all up." It wasn't a question, but a disbelieving statement.

An angry muscle jumped in his jaw, but as his eyes flashed to hers, she saw something else; something vulnerable and wounded and scared.

"You don't want to marry me?"

She blinked, unsure what to say. *I want that more than anything in the world . . . Don't make me go on without you . . . Please say you love me. . . .*

Instead, she said, "I haven't heard a good enough reason to marry you, Jesse."

"You haven't—?" He nearly choked. "What do you mean? I just told you—"

With a shake of her head, she pressed a finger to his lips, then she kissed him. Not the heated kiss they'd shared moments before, but a light brush of her lips against his. "No, Jesse. That's not enough for me. Might as well know that much up front. It never will be again."

She dug something out of the pocket of her apron and pressed it into his palm. "This is for your hand." Without another word, she turned and hurried back up the steps toward the house and snapped the door shut behind her.

Jesse watched her go, a lifetime of doubt cresting over him like a suffocating wave. He stared at the fat green cactus leaf in his hand and cursed. Aloe vera. He'd asked her to marry him and she'd given him aloe vera! Throwing it as far as he could fling it, he turned on his heel and stalked toward the barn.

Anger warred with hurt inside him. What the hell was she thinking? What better reason for them to marry than to save her from the worst kind of humiliation once the town's gossip mill starts up. It wouldn't be long before women were sniggering behind her back and making up far worse than the truth.

Apparently, marrying him was worse.

That's not enough for me. Might as well know that up front. Her words rang in his ears, clawed at the pain in his chest. He was willing to give up everything for her . . . everything he'd thought he wanted. All the dreams that weren't worth a milk bucket under a bull to him anymore.

Maybe he should have said that. Maybe he should have told her—

Shut up, Winslow. Just shut up.

275

Why was he hurt? Hell, why was he even surprised? After what had happened between them today, he'd thought maybe . . .

But he supposed he should have known better. Despite the pretty words she'd said today about him owning her heart, despite the way she'd melted in his arms as if she were a part of him, she could never give herself completely to a man like him. A bastard. When it came right down to it, he wasn't good enough for her. He still wasn't. Hadn't the old man beaten that into him well enough, for God's sake?

He stalked into the dark barn, raided the tack room for a blanket and the bottle of the old man's rotgut he'd found hidden between the feed bins. Fortunately, the old bastard had left him a little for the road. He clambered noisily up the mow ladder. There was no way he was sleeping in the house, under the same roof with her tonight. Or any other night for that matter.

"Hey, boss. What'cha'll be doin' up here?"

Jesse jumped at the sound of Silas' voice. If he'd been thinking clearly, he would have remembered that Silas occupied the mow. As his vision adjusted, he could just make the colored man's eyes staring at him in the dark. But his mood was too black for questions. His whiskey bottle clanked against the wood as he hauled himself up into the sweet smelling loft.

"You sleepin' up here t'night?" Silas asked.

"You mind?"

"Help yourself. Be a comfortable spot right over yonder," he said pointing beside him. "I done tried 'em all. You gots enough blankets, boss?"

"I'm fine. I'm just tired. Okay?" Spreading his blanket in the hay, he flopped down on it, drew the edges over him and slammed his eyes closed. "I just

276

want to get some shut-eye."

"Right. It be eight o'clock, all right. Late."

"And I don't want to talk about it, all right?" Jesse added perfunctorily.

"Sure, boss."

Jesse uncorked the bottle with a hollow squeak and took a long pull. Instantly, he wished he had some of that fermented cactus juice called bacanora he used to import from the Utah Territory instead. Hell, this stuff was enough to kill you, he thought, exhaling sharply.

Silence presided for a full five seconds.

"Miss Andi done kicked you outta the big house, huh?"

Jesse didn't answer.

"I be noticin' things was a little sticky 'tween you two at supper. She peeved with ya'll for workin' all day with that hand o' yours? I done tol' you not to—"

"No." Jesse took another pull, this time longer. The whiskey seeped languidly through him like steam. "It wasn't my hand." Though his hand burned like the very devil.

"Ya know," Silas went on, "I 'members the time I be workin' with a blister the size a gold eagle on my—"

Jesse rolled over. "Geez, were you always this talky, or is it only since you met me?"

"Always, I reckon," Silas admitted with a smile Jesse could hear.

"Geez."

Blessed silence again. Jesse settled back and pulled the blanket over his ears.

"You drinkin' whiskey?"

A pause. "Yeah. Want some?"

"I ain't no drinkin' man."

"Good," Jesse mumbled. "There's just enough

277

here to get me piss-drunk.''

Silas grunted. "You ain't obliged to tell me nothin'."

"Thank you very much."

"'S jus' that—"

Jesse groaned.

"—my mammy always say the soul need a good airin' now an' then just to keep it honest. You reckon that true?"

Jesse threw his cover off and sat up, slightly off balance. "All right! *Aaa-all ri-ight!* We had a . . . a disagreement. A doozy. I asked her to marry me, okay? And she turned me down flat. There. Satisfied? Is my soul aired enough to suit you?"

Silence. Well, he'd finally left Silas speechless.

A minute passed. Jesse's stomach burned hotter than his hand and for the briefest of moments, imagined that this was what the old man must have felt when he was well into his cups and looking for Jesse with his strap.

Finally the colored man rolled toward him, rustling in the fragrant hay.

"You axed her to marry you an' she say no? Women. Who can figger 'em?"

"Here, here." Jesse took another swallow. The liquid sloshed musically against the bottle. He could feel the liquid fire searing his muscles, settling into his limbs with languid, paralyzing heat.

"She say how come?" Silas asked.

Jesse swallowed audibly. "Guess she didn't wanna be married to a bastard."

"Aw now, boss, you is the mos' even tempered man I ever—"

"I'm talkin' 'bout my bloodline, dammit, not my disposition. Although"—he slugged back another—"thatz in serious decline as well."

278

Another long pause as Silas lay back against the straw. "Miss Andi . . . she ain't like that."

"You're wrong there, pal. But . . . hell, it's just as well. I'm off the hook, huh? I offered di'nt I? Well I can't do any more'n that."

"No, suh."

"No siree. Thaz the last plurprosal-" he frowned, "pro-po-sal she's gettin' outta me. Let her rot here with her stinkin' corn-an'-wheat-an'-chickens-an'-hogs. Let th' bank take 'er place and the good citizens of Elkgrove snigger behind their hands cause they know we—" Jesse stopped himself before saying something he would forever regret and instead took a long, last fiery pull on his bottle. He emptied it.

He sucked on the bottle for a final drop. It slid past his lips mockingly.

Damn and double damn. He wasn't unconscious yet.

Flinging the bottle into the hay beside him, he rolled over, resting his forehead on his crossed wrists. To his dismay he discovered his cheeks were wet. He wasn't crying over her! was he?

Geez, he hated a sloppy drunk!

He sighed deeply. Tired. God Almighty, he was tired. Maybe he'd pass out after all. Yeah, maybe he'd pass out and never wake up. No . . . no, that's the liquor talkin', Winslow. You've got plenty to live for.

Plenty.

Now, if he could only remember what that was . . .

Silas lay in the dark, staring at the cracks of moonlight filtering through the barn walls. His heart ached for the man who'd become his friend. He didn't know much about what had passed between

Jesse and Andi years ago, except that Etta said they'd been close to marrying, but after Jesse left, she'd married his brother. Besides that, he'd never seen two people more bull-headed in love than Jesse and Andi, except maybe him an' Etta.

There was something missing outta what Jesse told him, something that bothered Silas into silence. And it appeared to be eatin' Jesse Winslow up from the inside out. He prayed Jesse would dig out that festering piece of his heart and get rid of it, before it was too late.

But as he heard Jesse's soft, drunken snore, he wondered if whatever had happened between them tonight hadn't already buried it too deep to find.

Andrea blew out the flame of the candle flickering beside her bed, stared disconsolately at the ceiling, and cursed Jesse Winslow for not seeing what was in his own heart. Blast his stubborn hide! He loved her. She knew it. She felt it in the way he kissed her, held her, made love to her.

Or does he just want you? a small voice asked.

She squeezed her eyes shut tight at that, her most awful fear. It wouldn't be the first time a man had used her that way.

It's not like that with Jesse, she insisted. He loves me.

Maybe he loves Montana more.

Ah, there it was. Montana, the life he'd left behind. The life he'd loved. She could never force him to sacrifice himself for her. He'd only end up hating her for it. No, if Jesse wanted her, he had to want her body and soul.

What about your dream, Andrea? Would you give up the farm for him? Would you follow him to his

280

precious Montana if that's what it takes?

For the first time, she considered that. She'd been as stubborn as he on that point. Perhaps it was time to let a few of her own dreams go, too. What was land compared with the joy she'd experienced in Jesse's arms today? At last she'd found the other half of her soul. The thought of losing Jesse to a piece of farmland seemed as impossible as losing him to Montana. Perhaps Montana was a place they could both start over—buy a new piece of land that would be Zachary's heritage. She curbed the impulse to dash out to the barn, to tell him just that.

No. She wouldn't beg him, dammit. It was his move. If he cared enough to make it.

Chapter Seventeen

Elkgrove was in a dither.

Jesse knew it as soon as he pulled the high-box wagon full of wheat bushels to a stop under Joe Fergeson's hand-lettered sign at the front of his mill at the edge of town. Clusters of people gathered here and there on the dusty street, talking with the kind of animation Elkgrove reserved for whistle-stop campaigns and visits from British royalty.

Winding the traces around the brake handle, he thought back on the time when he was twelve, a Lord-Something-or-Other from London, England had come through Elkgrove on his way West to shoot wild game with an honest-to-goodness mountain-man trapper as a guide. Perhaps that was Jesse's first glimpse of the dream that eventually led him to Montana. He'd managed to shoot his share of wild game there and become the sort of man he'd envisioned himself as being those many years ago. One wouldn't know it by looking at him now, perched on a wagon full of wheat, dressed in farmer's duds, but he'd achieved that moment of glory he'd strived for. Looking back, it hadn't been everything he'd hoped.

He wondered where that mountain man was now? Dead, perhaps, or, more optimistically, alone in some lonely cabin like the one Creed kept on the Boulder River in Montana Territory?

God, you're getting morose, Winslow.

Nearly four days had passed since his ignominious confrontation with Andi. He'd spent the first day trying to shake the head-splitting hangover he'd given himself, and the next three striving for some sort of equilibrium. He and Andi had spoken little since that day. In fact, barely five words had passed between them. Strange after the incredible intimacy they'd shared on that grassy bank.

He sucked in a deep breath. Even the wandering thoughts of that day made an ache of wanting curl inside him. Ruthlessly, he fought it down. What with Silas spending every evening at Isabelle's with Etta learning to read and Andi looking at him like something just shy of the plague, Jesse realized just how lonely a home could be.

The sound of voices brought him out of his thoughts. A pale-haired man rushed from storefront to storefront with a armload of *Chronicles*. Each stop seemed to intensify the commotion.

Jesse jumped down from the wagon as Joe Fergeson emerged from his mill with a welcoming smile.

"Jesse Winslow." Joe grabbed his hand in a bone-crunching shake. "How the heck are you, son? Got some wheat for me?"

"Sure do, Joe. You buying?"

"Always. You bring me that Hunter White again?"

"Yes, sir. It's the third season for it. As you know, the quality improves every year. This crop brought us about a hundred twenty eight grains per ear. You can't touch that size with Red."

Fergeson winked at him with a knowing smile. "Ah, you're Tom Winslow's son all right. He could sell fur to a shaggy dog."

Jesse felt himself blanch. "It doesn't take being a Winslow to know good wheat," he said more sharply than he intended. "All I ask is that you're fair with me."

Joe's brow wrinkled in a wounded frown. "Sure, Jesse, sure. I'm fair as the day is long and that's why folks bring me their wheat instead of hauling it up to Centerville."

Jesse gave his neck a small twist to work the sudden crick out. "I know, Joe. I didn't mean to snap at you."

He nodded. "It's all right. I reckon it's been hard on you, losin' your whole family like you did. You got a right to be a little testy, I reckon. I hear you got a colored fella hirin' out at your place. You should have brought him to help you with this load."

"Silas wanted to come, but I left him home with a shotgun in case we have any unexpected guests." Jesse glanced back at the crowded street. "What's all the commotion anyway? Is a circus coming to town or something?"

Joe shook his head. "Bigger. At least as far as the residents of this county are concerned. Those damn raiders made their first big mistake yesterday. Tried to make off with a small shipment of Federal gold off the Rock Island spur north of here. They managed to kill two of the guards and steal almost twenty thousand dollars worth of gold and currency before one of them was shot dead and two others wounded. The rest got clean away."

"Forgive me for pointing this out, Joe, but that sounds like bad news, not good."

"That's not the good part. The good part is the U.S. Army is so riled about this scum-sucking bunch of tuck-tail lowlifes, they've decided to assign a detachment to Elkgrove and the surrounding towns to root the cowards out of their holes. Somethin' we've been begging for fer weeks now."

Jesse smiled. "I guess the U.S. Army has its priorities. How soon?"

"Within the week they say."

"Maybe the raiders will be satisfied with all that gold and go away on their own," Jesse suggested.

"Folks are hopin' so. But nobody's countin' on it. Those bastards seem to want to squeeze Elkgrove dry." He shook his head. "Come on inside. We'll do some dickerin' on this wheat of yours. I've got some coffee on the stove."

Jesse nodded and glanced back out at the reverie on the street. The U.S. Army may make a show, but that didn't mean Elkgrove's troubles were over. If the raiders had gone beyond simple looting and pillaging to robbing gold shipments, he suspected they had just upped the ante. Unfounded though his suspicions might be, he believed that Elkgrove's problems were rooted right here and members of the gang lived here among them. That made them all the more dangerous.

Jesse deposited the draft for the wheat in the farm account at the bank and withdrew fifty dollars on-hand expense money, hoping to make it stretch until the corn harvest. He drove down to Biddle's Mercantile and Drygoods to pick up the few supplies they needed.

The bell jangled as he walked through the door. The rich scent of fresh coffee, mingled with barreled pickles, apples, and a hundred other smells, filled the air. The room was long and narrow with can-lined shelves stretching ceiling-to-floor to the back of the store. From the cross-beamed rafters overhead hung a mismash of iron cookware, tubs, and washboards. Meal and flour barrels lined the floor in front of the counter that ran halfway down the right side of the store. The portly A.E. Biddle looked up from the countertop he was dusting. His friendly smile faltered and he rubbed his palms over his ample aproned belly.

"Oh, hello, Jesse. I almost didn't recognize you without the beard. How's it going?"

"Fine. A.E. I have a list of things we need. Think you can fill this for me?"

A.E. looked down the short list. "You know I'd like to Jesse, but . . ."

"Is there a problem?"

The shopkeeper rubbed his jaw with thoughtful discomfiture. "You know I sell things on credit when times are hard, and I've done that for Miss Andrea for a while now."

Embarrassment crept up Jesse's neck. This was one bill Andi had kept from him.

A.E. continued, "But I just can't extend her credit line any more than I already—"

"How much?"

"Huh?"

"How much do we owe?"

"Uh . . ." He fumbled with his books while Jesse shifted impatiently. The bell jangled behind him and someone came in. Jesse didn't look to see who.

"Let me see now . . . here we are." A.E. jabbed a sausage-like finger at the page. "Your bill comes to forty-two dollars and sixty-three cents. I don't charge any interest on that. That's pure—"

"I'll be paying that off today," Jesse interrupted. "If you could add up the charges on my list there I'll make it right with you."

Relief spread across A.E.'s features. "Very good, Jesse. Very good. I think we can fill that up right away. Care for a cup of coffee? Or an apple? Got some real beauties down from New York State."

Another man's voice cut him off before he could answer.

"The Winslows have their own little orchard, isn't that right, Jesse?"

Jesse turned to find Mitch Lodray smiling at him companionably. He held out his hand to Jesse and limped closer.

"That's right, we do," Jesse answered, taking his hand. "But this Indian Summer we're having isn't helping to ripen them up."

The corner of Mitch's mouth twitched up in a smile. "I understand you've been removed from farming since you left Elkgrove. How do you like getting your hands dirty again?"

Jesse didn't flinch. "I like it just fine, Mitch."

"Really? I heard otherwise."

"Oh? From whom?"

Mitch grinned good naturedly. "As a newspaperman, you must know my sources are a sacred trust. But I did hear you planned on heading back to Montana. That true?"

Jesse plastered an equally good-natured smile on his face. "Is this for the record?"

"Of course not."

"Really? No comment."

Mitch laughed. "These aren't affairs of state we're talking about, Jesse. I'm just curious. After all, your return was something of an item for conversation."

"Yeah, I know. They all thought I was dead."

"Then," Mitch said, his expression growing momentarily serious, "you've decided to stay."

"Let's just say I'm thinking about my options."

Mitch gave a small nervous laugh. "You know, I knew I'd run into you sooner or later, Jesse. Strange it would be today, though."

"Why's that?"

Mitch poured himself a cup of coffee. "I was just on my way out to see Andrea, this morning—"

Jesse stiffened.

"—pay my respects. Maybe we should ride out together."

"I'm not—"

"Was that three pounds of light molasses or dark, Jesse?" A.E. called out from behind the counter.

He frowned. "I don't know."

"Go with the light," Mitch suggested casually.

For reasons he couldn't explain, he called, "Make it dark, A.E."

Mitch shrugged and stood waiting for an answer. "What do you say, Winslow? Shall we ride together or shall I go alone?"

"Andi—Andrea's staying pretty busy these days," Jesse told him. "She doesn't have much time for visiting."

Mitch raised an eyebrow. "Keeping her all for yourself, Jesse? That's not very civil of you."

His tone was strictly a jesting one, but underneath it lay something else. Something Jesse couldn't quite put a finger on. "No. Not at all," he said at last. "If Andrea wants to see you she can. I'm not her keeper."

Lodray's mouth twitched again and he slapped Jesse on the shoulder. "I'm glad to hear it."

The years had changed Mitch Lodray and not for the better, he feared. Perhaps it was the War that had hardened him or the injury to his foot that made him limp, or maybe that damn ivy league education. He watched as Lodray scanned the small glass perfume bottles along the countertop and pick one up. A cold realization began to dawn on Jesse, seeping through his bones like icy spring water.

Mitch inhaled the scent in the tiny bottle and sighed. "You don't mind if I take her a little token of our friendship do you?" He flipped three two-bit pieces on the counter.

A *token?* Flowers would have been a token. *Candy* would have been a token. Perfume was a goddamned red flag!

An unreasonable jealousy gripped him. Mitch Lodray—war hero, tall, handsome, successful. An Elkgrove resident, born and bred. Just the sort of man Andi should go for.

Just the sort of man Jesse wasn't.

"Well?" Mitch repeated.

"Like I said," Jesse answered evenly. "I'm not her keeper." She'll probably be happy to see you, he thought. Ecstatic, in fact, to have someone besides me to look at for a change. Personally, he'd rather not be there to have his nose rubbed in it.

"Well, then, I guess I'll go on out," Mitch said. "Maybe I'll see you there, Jesse?"

Consciously, he uncoiled his fists at his sides and gripped the counter behind him. "I have a few more things to do in town. I'll be home soon." He emphasized the word *home*.

"Wonderful. See you then." He flashed Jesse a sparkling smile.

Jesse couldn't resist. "Say, Mitch, it's too bad about your foot. Must make kicking up your heels a little hard."

Mitch's smile turned smug. "As a matter of fact, the women love it." He shrugged. "A wounded

289

veteran . . . you know. I can't keep 'em off me."

"Yeah . . ." Jesse nearly growled.

Mitch called out to the shopkeeper, "A.E.—I left the money for this perfume on the counter."

A.E. waved him off, trusting Mitch Lodray completely.

Jesse watched him limp down the street toward his horse, thinking he might trust a Rocky Mountain Diamondback with a sunburn more.

"A.E.—" he snapped. "Hurry up that order, will you?"

Andrea rocked the cradle in the butter churn up and down, up and down, glad to feel the cream beginning to lump. The muscles of her arm burned as it always did in this final step. She took a peek under the lid and saw little chunks of butter floating on the surface. God, she hated this job, but the end result always gratified her. It meant she wouldn't have to do this for another two days.

She glanced up at the sky. Gunmetal gray thunderheads roiled in the distance, taunting the dry land with the empty promise of rain. It had been weeks since the last rain and the unusual heat wave had taken its toll on her. She longed for autumn, with crisp nights and that peculiarly invigorating scent that belonged only to fall. It signaled a harvesting of the corn and an end to the long, hard workdays of summer.

But this fall, it would also signal an end to something else, she feared—her time with Jesse.

Four days had passed since the evening he'd proposed to her. Four days and nights of polite silence. In fact the first morning following their argument, she could have sworn he was ill, and when she'd slammed a drawer shut he'd hurried from the house holding his head. But she didn't ask him if he needed a headache powder. He'd been too rude.

She cursed him for the hundredth time for his stubbornness and herself for her pride. But how could she marry a man who didn't want to marry her? She couldn't bear the thought that his sacrifice would soon turn to bitterness and his marriage vows to resentment. She couldn't bear the thought of looking in Jesse's beautiful eyes and seeing not love, but resignation.

No, pride aside, she was right. She wouldn't allow herself or little Zachary to be lulled into a marriage that—

A low rumble in Mahkwi's throat cut off the thought. The wolf, who was lying beside Andrea on the porch, lifted her head from her paws and stared down the road. Her silvery hackles stood on end. Andrea's gaze followed the wolf's.

The trotting hoofbeats of a horse and rider coming up the road drove all thoughts from her mind. Jesse had taken the wagon. Her gaze darted automatically to where she'd last seen Silas in the south pasture, fixing a broken fence. Out of sight.

She looked back toward the road. One rider. Only one. If it were raiders, there would be more, wouldn't there? Her heart pounded as the rider rounded the curve. In her mind's eye, she pictured the rifle Jesse had so patiently taught her to shoot, leaning where she'd left it against the kitchen wall. Damn!

The man trotted into the yard, sitting tall upon a blooded bay with black fetlocks. With his hat pulled low, she didn't recognize him at first. Then, with a chill that drove right through her bones, she knew him.

She couldn't breathe. Oh, God, not him. Not now.

He pulled his horse to a stop only a few feet from the porch. "Hello, Andrea—"

Mahkwi leapt to her feet and growled a low, rumbling threat. Mitch's horse crow-hopped sideways with a whinny of fear. Andrea actually smiled to see Mitch have to grab the pommel horn to stay on.

"Jesus, Andrea, call off that wolf!"

"I don't think I will."

Mitch struggled to restrain his horse, the confident grin gone.

"What are you doing here, Mitch?"

He managed to get his horse steady. "That's not very friendly of you."

"That shouldn't surprise you. Now, turn your horse around and go home. You have no business on my place."

"That's a matter of opinion."

"Yours alone, I suspect." She tried to keep her voice even, free of the betraying terror she felt bubbling up in her.

"Perhaps."

Mahkwi growled again. Mitch tightened his hand around the reins. "I didn't come to bother you."

"Go to hell, Mitch."

"You've got me all wrong, Andrea. I've changed. I'm not the boy I was when I left here. Will you just let me talk to you?"

"No."

His eyes narrowed. "I'm getting off my horse, Andrea. Call off that wolf."

"No."

Mahkwi took a threatening step closer and Mitch's hand closed around the revolver strapped to his hip. "I can be more persuasive, if you force me."

Her eyes widened. "You wouldn't."

He shrugged. "Self-defense? Call him off, Andrea. I want to talk."

"Mahkwi! Come!" The wolf's golden eyes turned to Andrea and immediately she padded to her side. Mitch tied his bay to the snubbing post and walked to the steps. The balance of power had shifted subtly in his favor.

Andrea wondered if he could hear her heartbeat pounding in her ears. Nausea inched up her throat and she grabbed the porch rail for support. Once more her gaze scanned the corn for Silas. She couldn't see him.

Jesse! Where are you?

"Now, let's be civil, Andrea," Mitch began.

"You may be able to fool every other feather-headed woman in this town with your civility, Mitch, but you'll never again be able to fool me. I know exactly who and what you are. And if you think I believe for a minute that you've changed—"

He came up the first step.

"Don't—" she warned.

He lifted his hands as if to prove he meant her no harm. "All right, I'll talk from here."

"Say what you have to say and then get off my land."

"I want to make things right between us, Andrea."

"Things will never be right after what you did. Never."

"I've thought about you all this time. All the time I was away, it was your face I pictured. I wrote you letters, you never answered them."

"I burned them."

Surprise showed clearly on his face. "Y-you burned them? Without reading them?"

"Yes," she snapped.

His gaze drifted to the floor where he searched for

293

some kind of understanding. "I knew you were angry with me . . ."

"Angry? *Angry?*" She laughed a harsh, bitter laugh. "You were always the master of understatement. I thought you got the point when I married Zach."

"I know, but you only married him on the rebound from you and me."

She stared at him, dumbfounded. "There never was a 'you and me.'"

"You don't have to pretend with me about Zach. I knew why you married him."

"You haven't a clue about things like that."

"Ah, you're wrong, so wrong. I thought about you all these years. At Harvard, in the military . . . When I was shot in the war—"

"You probably shot yourself, you coward," she mumbled.

His face went dangerously dark. "What did you say?"

She gulped and took a step backward, knowing instantly she'd gone too far. Mahkwi growled again, baring her teeth.

Mitch's chest rose and fell in shaky anger. His mouth narrowed to a grim line. Something changed in his eyes.

"I can see you're an unforgiving woman, Andrea. A man can make few mistakes with a woman like you. Isn't that right?"

"Mitch—"

"A man could try and try to please you, couldn't he? But he'd be wasting his time with a woman as cold as you. Why he could beat his head against the wall until it was bloody"—his open palm slapped the wall hard in tempo to his words—"and it would never be enough, would it?"

Her breath froze in her throat. Inside, she heard the baby start to cry.

"Even time hasn't healed your bitterness toward me, has it? What's a man to do?" He took the next step up, reaching her level.

"Please—"

"Please? Please what, Andrea?"

"Please . . . g-go."

Mahkwi snarled openly now, but Mitch seemed not to notice.

"But I haven't finished," he said. "I have to make you understand. You think you're the only one? You think I've been alone since you? Well, you're wrong. There have been lots of women. Does that bother you?" Flecks of spittle gathered at the corners of his mouth.

She slammed her eyes shut trying not to be sick. "No."

He laughed. "I think it does. They want me, Andrea. They fall at my feet. They think I'm handsome, capable. But not you. You . . . you're just like my—" He broke off the thought, his glazed stare returning to her.

"I brought you a present," he said.

"Wh-what?"

"A present." From his coat pocket, he fished a small glass bottle of perfume and held it out to her. "For you, Andrea."

"Please—"

"Take it."

"I don't—"

"*Take it!*"

Her hand shot out and he smiled, pressing the vial into her palm. His fingers stroked the flat of her hand before she could snatch it away. Dizziness made her take a step back.

"That's better. What do you say?"

She gritted her teeth. "Th-thank you."

"Say my name Andrea. I've longed to hear it fall sweetly from your lips."

"Thank you . . . Mitch."

He gave a small shuddering sigh. "You see? Things can be pleasant between us."

"Jesse will be back any minute, you'd better go now."

"Ah, Jesse." He laughed. "Are you still waiting for him, Andrea? That loser? I've got news for you. Jesse Winslow doesn't mind that I'm here. He saw me buy the perfume for you. In fact, he encouraged me to come."

She felt the blood drain from her face. "What?"

"Me and half of Adams County." His laugh was a breath of derision. "Didn't you know he was trying to find you a man? Surely you knew he's been talking you up around the county trying to pawn you off on some man so he could run back to Montana and his Indian squaws?"

The bottle slipped from her fingers and it shattered on the floor. She gripped the porch rail harder. "Wh-what? I don't believe you. You're lying!"

A satisfied grin settled on Mitch's sculpted features. "That was rather underhanded of him, I must say, not to even confide his plan to you. But you needn't take my word for it. Ask Sam Eakin. Ask Calvin Weeks, or Elias Mudrow or any of the others who've taken a sudden interest in you. They'll all tell you the same thing."

No, her mind screamed. He's lying! Lying! But deep in her heart, some small part in her couldn't deny it. All those visits by men—'friends of Jesse.' *My God how could I have been so blind?* Something inside her tore. She looked up at Mitch Lodray, the man who nearly three years ago had almost ruined her life. Now he'd done it again. She felt brittle, like ash; one small touch and she would disintegrate.

"He's betrayed you, Andrea, just like all the others will betray you. I tried to tell you when you married Zach—"

"Don't you even speak his name," Andrea demanded in a voice she hardly recognized. "Don't you . . ." A sob tore from her throat.

Mitch's features went blurry for a moment and she blinked her eyes to clear them. He was watching her like a bird of prey watches for its supper, waiting for her to run into his arms so he could be victorious at last. He actually thought she would.

"Get . . . off . . . my . . . land!" Her whole body shook with the effort to keep control.

Real shock spread across his features. "But Andrea, don't you see—?"

"GET OFF MY LAND! Or so help me God, I'll let this wolf kill you."

Hearing her name, Mahkwi made a snapping growl and lunged in his direction.

He opened his mouth as if to say something else but snapped it shut again, giving Mahkwi an assessing glance. He walked to down the steps to his horse and mounted. Gathering up his reins he turned to her and smiled. It was the kind of smile he'd smiled for her that day . . . that day he'd changed her life. It sent shivers down to her toes.

"You're ungrateful, Andrea. Ungrateful for devotion. You pick the wrong men and wonder why your life is in a shambles. Someday soon, you'll realize it was me all along. I was the one. I hope it's not too late."

Reining his horse around hard, he took off across the yard at a lope and disappeared down the road.

Her knees gave way and she collapsed to the porch. She didn't feel the glass slice into her hand or the spilled perfume soak into the hem of her gown. It was all she could do to lean over the railing and retch over and over.

Inside she heard the baby crying, but there was nothing she could do. She didn't have the strength to get up. She wasn't sure she had the strength to go on.

Chapter Eighteen

Jesse gave the team's traces a slap as they jolted down the road toward home. Threads of a feeling akin to fear spun through him, making his heart pound. Something wasn't right. At first he'd put it off to simple jealousy, but the closer he got to home, the more he questioned that rationale. Instinct alone should have made him leave that order at Biddle's behind and follow Mitch Lodray out to Willow Banks. There seemed to be more than simple competition behind their exchange back at the store. He'd sensed a real malevolence buried under Mitch's smooth words, but it hadn't struck Jesse until he'd started on the road home that he should be worried. Now, suddenly, he was.

As if his thoughts of the man made him appear, Lodray cantered around a curve in the road.

He slowed his horse a fraction, then spurred him on again, merely touching the brim of his hat to Jesse as he passed.

With a frown, Jesse watched Lodray disappear in the churning dust. He had a bad feeling about that. Swallowing hard, he slapped the traces across the team's backs and tore the rest of the way home. When he pulled into the yard, nothing looked out of place, but that didn't diminish the awful feeling rising in his throat. Even from here, he could hear the baby crying and crying. He jumped from the wagon without even setting the brake and ran toward the house.

That's when he saw her lying on the porch floor.

"Andi!" *By God if he hurt her* . . . He ran to her and dropped down beside her. With her head hanging over the edge of the porch, she was crying . . . or sick, he couldn't be sure which. The cloyingly sweet smell of violet water stung his nostrils. His hands hovered a few inches above her trembling back, afraid to touch her. Afraid she might break.

"Andi, my God, are . . . are you hurt?" His gaze went to her hand and blood that covered her cuff. *"Jesus."* He reached for her hand, but she snatched it away.

"Don't . . . touch me."

Stunned, he sat back. "You're bleeding."

She fired an icy look at him. "Don't!"

"Okay. Okay, I won't. Talk to me Andi, did he do this to you? If he did, I'll—"

"You'll what?" she asked on a harsh sob. "Find another man better suited? One not quite so verbose, perhaps?"

Jesse felt the blood leave his face. "What are you talking about?"

"Don't insult me any more by lying about it, Jesse! How could you do that to me?"

His jaw tightened. "Do what? What did he tell you?"

Her shoulders trembled and she shook her head.

"What did he *tell* you?"

"What you should have told me long ago. Oh,

300

damn you, Jesse, why did you come back here? Why didn't you just die out in your precious Montana with . . . with your Indian s-squaws and your beautiful mountains?"

He felt the blow as if she'd struck him. And he deserved it. Every bitter ounce of her hatred. He reached out for her and she slapped his hand away.

"And *him*," she moaned. "Sending . . . him . . . out to me." She looked as if she were going to be sick again.

Jesse took her by the arms and forced her to look at him. "I didn't send Lodray here, I swear it, Andi. I saw him in town, that's all. He said he was—dammit, tell me what he did to you?" He held up her wrist. "Did he do this? Did he cut you this way?"

She winced. "Let me go."

"Not until you tell me."

"Zachary's crying."

"Let him cry for—"

She slapped his face hard with her free hand, but he didn't release her.

"Go on," he said, "hit me again if it will make you feel better. Hit me as much as you want. I probably deserve it. But I'm not letting you go until you tell me what happened."

Andrea hung her head. Her dark hair, pulled from its moorings, fell in a curtain around her face. "I feel sick."

"Give me your hand," he demanded, pulling a bandanna from his pocket. She resisted, but he captured her, pulling her closer. "Stop fighting me, dammit."

She did finally, allowing him to wrap the cloth around it to stanch the flow of blood. "Why, Jesse? Why?"

301

He stared at her hand. "You haven't told me what he said."

'I think you know." Her eyes flashed to his. "That you were talking me up around town, like—like a used piece of horseflesh, trying to—" she closed her eyes in humiliation, "trying to find someone who would marry me. Sam Eakin, C-Calvin Weeks . . ."

"Oh, Jesus, Andi." Jesse raked a hand through his hair.

"Is it true?"

His eyes searched hers and he saw that she didn't want to believe it. "It wasn't the way he made it sound—"

"I knew it." She dropped her face into her hands. "Oh, God, what a fool I've been."

"Wait a minute," he said, shaking her. "Listen to me. At first . . . God, I didn't want to stay. All I could think of was going back to Montana. I wanted nothing to do with this farm or . . . or anything else. I just wanted to get the hell out. But I couldn't just leave you here, alone. I decided—stupidly maybe—the only solution was to find a man for you. A man who could give you everything you needed and wanted."

"You bastard."

"That's right. I was. I knew you wouldn't look for a man on your own and I was desperate. But I forgot to think of one side of that equation—you." His fingers dug into her shoulders. "That was my problem, Andi. I didn't want to think of you, because I knew if I did I'd end up right here for the rest of my life."

"Let me go," she demanded.

"Listen to me, Andi—"

"Why should I?" She jerked out of his hands.

"You've made plain your intentions. How many times do I have to let myself be taken by you before I get it? How many times do you have to abandon me before I stop letting it hurt?"

"I asked you to marry me, Andrea. You turned me down flat."

She slid her eyes shut. "You wouldn't understand why."

"No, I wouldn't, so why don't you explain it to me."

She looked up at him fiercely. "I won't marry again for anything but love."

Her words hit him like a fist. "But . . . you and Zach—you said you loved him."

"Let me go, damn you!"

"No."

"It's none of your business—"

"Maybe not, but we're going to clear the air between us here if it's the last thing we do." He was nearly shouting now. "I want to know, if you didn't marry him for love, why did you marry him?"

"Protection!" she blurted.

Jesse blinked. "What?"

Tears streaked down her cheeks. "That's why Zach married me. To protect me. All right? Are you satisfied?"

"Protect you from . . . what?"

She lowered her head.

"From *what*, Andi?" he demanded with a little shake.

"Him. From him."

Jesse frowned, confused. *"Him?"*

"M-Mitch Lodray."

Jesse felt his heart sink and his body go tense all over. *No!* Dear God . . . "What . . . what did he do to you, Andrea? Tell me. Please."

303

"Two-and-a-half years ago, he . . . he tried to rape me."

Jesse slammed his eyes shut. Her admission was like a gut-punch. He swallowed down the bile that rose in his throat. His curse was low and foul. "Why didn't you tell me?"

"I never told anyone but Zach. You're the only other one who knows now."

"What happened?"

She hesitated and he could see how painful it was for her to dredge it all up. Inside, Zachary had stopped crying. Perhaps he had fallen back asleep. The cicadas hummed in the trees with the soaring heat. Jesse stared at Andi, waiting for her to speak and felt sweat inch between his shoulder blades.

She began haltingly. "Mitch came home from Harvard determined to spark me. I wasn't interested. He spoke with my father, who worked for Deke Lodray, and convinced him that it wouldn't be a bad thing for his daughter to be courted by the boss's son. Pa encouraged me. Mitch was considered a catch. Handsome, charming . . . and he wanted me." She blushed. "Still, I wasn't interested. I hadn't dated anyone since . . ." Her eyes flashed to his briefly. "But for Pa's sake, I went. We saw each other several times, at a dance, after church."

Her voice shook as she continued. "Then on a Sunday afternoon, we went for a buggy ride to Green Lakes, alone. It began innocently enough. Mitch brought a picnic. We spread a blanket and ate lunch. Then, Mitch started talking strangely about us. About how he had been thinking about me for a long time, how we belonged together, and that he believed our coming together was destined. He'd known it since we were in school together, but I was always . . . with you."

304

Jesse lowered his head, knowing if he'd stayed, none of this would have happened to her.

Andi went on. "I started to become alarmed when he put his hands on me. I told him to stop, but he didn't. He . . . started to kiss me and . . . touch me. He scared me." She stopped and shook her head.

"Go on, Andi."

"I got up and started to run away, but he caught me. He was angry that I'd run. He . . . he pinned me down beneath him with my hands over my head, and he pushed . . . my . . . skirts up. He . . . hurt . . . me." She squeezed her eyes shut. "He said I didn't understand about us. But I would and I'd know how right for each other we were. And then he . . . undid his pants and put his—" Her words fell off and she shook her head. Jesse tried to take her hand, but she pulled away. "I can't."

"Andi, you said he tried to rape you." He nearly choked on the word. "He didn't succeed?"

She swiped at the tears coursing down her cheeks. "Almost. I kicked him. Hard. When he rolled off me, I ran. As fast and as far as I could. By the time he'd recovered, he couldn't find me."

"Why didn't you tell anyone?"

She shook her head. "I was too—"

"Not even your father?"

"My father! No, I couldn't go to him. He was the one who encouraged me to go out with Mitch. I saw Mitch in town a few days later. I was so frightened, I didn't know what to do. He warned me not to go spreading any lies about him to my father or anyone else because after all who would believe me? After all, I had led him on, teased him. And a man like my father could lose his precious job easily if some kind of misunderstanding came to light."

"Sonofabitch," Jesse muttered. "How did Zach find out?"

"Mitch didn't give up. I was terrified, so I went to the shop with Pa every day. Mitch would come by and talk as if nothing had happened between us. He was so normal, so I started to wonder if it hadn't been my fault, if I'd done something to make him think . . ." She shook her head.

"Anyway, Zach found me at home one day, crying. He forced me to tell him."

"And?"

"And he married me. To keep me safe."

A heavy silence slid between them. "I would have killed the bastard," he said in a voice thick with fury. "In fact—" he added getting to his feet.

"No, you won't."

"Why the hell not?"

"Because you'll let this go. The same as Zach did."

He laughed. "Yeah? Well, apparently that's where my little brother and I part ways."

She grabbed his arm and her reddened eyes met his. "Jesse, I couldn't prove anything against Mitch then and I still can't."

"He's still after you."

"He didn't touch me today," she said.

"He didn't have to," Jesse pointed out with a feral look in his eye. "Look at you! Does he have to rape you before you try to stop him?"

Andi's fingers dug into his arm. "You *won't* kill him because he's not worth a hangman's noose."

"Then I'll see he's thrown in jail."

"Anything legal would be . . . futile. And"—she looked at her hands—"damaging. It's my word against his. That's all I have. Mitch Lodray comes from one of the best families in town. My father was a drunk. Whose word do you think they'd believe, his or mine?" She let that question hang there for a moment, then said, "If there's a shred of compassion in you, Jesse, if you still care about me, even a little, you'll just let this go."

"It's because I care about you a hell of a lot more than a little that I can't do that."

"Damn you! Don't you see? I have to live here. What do you think people would think of me if something like this came out? Even if he were convicted, which is highly unlikely, do you think I'd be able to look any of my neighbors in the eye? Do you think I'd have the chance for any sort of decent marriage? Either way I'd lose."

Jesse ground his teeth together and sat down on the step, suspecting she was absolutely right. Attempted rape was not a subject for polite conversation, but it would make her the object of malicious gossip in Elkgrove for years to come.

"Promise me, Jesse," Andi begged him. "Promise you won't do anything to make things harder for me."

Than you already have, he finished for her silently. Her plea cut into his heart with the precision of a surgeon's blade. Guilt gathered in his throat, cutting off his air. It was his fault. All of it. If he'd been man enough to stay and work out his problems with his father . . . or to have taken Andi with him when he went, none of this would have happened. And now, his conniving to find her a husband had opened the door for Mitch Lodray. God, what an idiot he'd been!

"Promise me, Jesse," she repeated.

He looked up at her reddened nose and tear-streaked face. His chest tightened with an emotion he'd not put a name to before—love. It hit him hard and low and with a clarity he'd only just acquired.

"Marry me, Andi," he said. "I won't let him hurt

307

you again. I swear to God, he won't." He reached up and touched her cheek. "I love you."

Tears trembled on her lashes and she laughed ironically as she pulled away from his touch. "You know, that's a good one. This morning, I might have even believed that."

Jesse clenched his fingers into a fist. Hurt burrowed deep inside him. "Whether you want to believe it or not, it's true."

"I'll find my own man, Jesse. Don't bother yourself trying to live up to your brother," she said. "I may have married him for protection, but in the end we had something far more precious than you and I will ever have. Trust." She got to her feet and looked down at him. "If it takes finding a husband to get you out of my life once and for all, then that's just what I intend to do. Because I . . . I wouldn't marry you now if you were the last man on earth."

She turned and fled into the house, slamming the door. He heard little Zach cry again and in a few minutes, heard him stop.

How long Jesse sat staring at the corn, he didn't know. A hollowness spread through him, stealing the strength from his legs. His mother's voice echoed in his mind. *Jesse, if you get burnt, you've gotta sit on the blister.* Well, he'd cooked himself good this time. He'd dug himself so deep he supposed there was no way out. Not for him, at least.

That sure as hell didn't mean he had to let this thing lie. He tightened his fingers into a fist. He'd abandoned her once. He wasn't about to leave her to the mercy of an S.O.B. like Mitch Lodray again.

Her words came back to him. *Promise me you'll let this go.* He hadn't promised, and he'd be damned if he'd let that bastard run roughshod over her life the way Zach had. She may have trusted his brother, but where did that leave her when Zach went off to war?

Silas's voice interrupted his thoughts. "Hey, boss, back from town so soon?"

Jesse's glare swept to the colored man, who approached from the field carrying the shotgun Jesse had left with him. Jesse rose slowly. "Yeah. And where the hell have you been?"

"Huh?"

"I told you to watch the place," Jesse snapped. "Where the hell were you?"

Silas swallowed and took a step back. "I didn't hear nothin'. I's only in the field, boss, checkin' the fencin' like you axed me to."

"Like I—" Jesse stopped himself, knowing, indeed, he had mentioned something about those bloody fences. "Your first job is to watch Andi and the boy!" he boomed. "Is that clear? The hell with the fences and anything else that has to do with the farm. When I'm gone, you're here watching over her with the gun. Nobody gets near her. Got it?"

Silas' expression flattened with Jesse's harsh words. "Yassuh. I's sorry, boss. Won't happen again. Miss Andi . . . she all right?"

Jesse exhaled sharply. "She will be. As soon as I take care of a little matter. Unhitch the team, Silas, and give them a good drink. I'm going to town. I'll be back directly."

"Yassuh."

"Don't tell Andi where I've gone."

"No suh."

"And don't let her out of your sight." Jesse hesitated beside Silas, and clapped him on the shoulder in apology. Then, he headed to the barn for Rabble.

*   *   *

Mitch Lodray fitted his hat on his head at a rakish angle and left his parent's shop feeling better than he had in years. Deciding to leave his cane behind, he stood outside on the walkway and breathed deeply before starting off for the Sunset Cafe. Things were working out quite well, all in all, he thought. He'd seen Andrea alone at last, and felt confident she'd come around.

She hadn't really meant the things she'd said to him today, he decided on the ride home. She was playing coy, toying with him. Of course, she had to *act* as if she hated him. All women played that game. He supposed he could deal with that until she finally admitted her true feelings for him.

He started down the boardwalk with a limp, nodding at several ladies who fluttered their fans at him. Mitch smiled when they glanced sympathetically at his injury. Even the bullet he'd fired into his own foot had healed well. It had been worth the price he'd paid, for it had brought him home to Andrea at last. He considered the healing a sign from God that he'd been right all along. After all, he might have lost the foot to one of those green field surgeons. But he'd considered the risk justifiable.

Not that he'd wanted to come home to his parents. His mother nearly drove him mad with her constant nagging and fawning. After three years at Harvard and two in the war, he still didn't meet her standards. Well, that was all about to change. He even thought she'd approve of his choice in women, once he could get Andrea to come around.

All the years he'd been away from Andrea, he'd done nothing but fantasize about her. In every woman's face, he saw hers. Every woman's body he'd taken had been hers. Andrea Carson Winslow had been the standard of perfection by which all others

310

were judged . . . and discarded. The apogee of womanhood. And she would be his. Then she'd forget all about Jesse Winslow.

Nothing would stop him from attaining the things he needed to convince her. She'd realize the lengths he'd gone to prove himself worthy and then she'd have to love him. Yes, things were going quite well indeed.

Passing Lawler Feed and Grain, he limped down the step at the end of the walkway and started across the dusty street. He glanced at his boots, considering whether to have them shined by the boy who sat outside the Elkgrove Hotel before his meeting this afternoon with—

A hand snaked out from the alleyway beside the shop and cinched around his arm. Taken off guard, Mitch's fragile balance failed him as he was dragged into the shadows. Helpless to stop his own momentum, he gasped in the second before he was flung against the wall with a painful smack.

Lights flashed in his head and with a groan, he slid to the ground. A metallic taste filled his mouth. His assailant bent over him in the shadows. Mitch blinked what must have been blood from his eyes, and put up his hands in self-defense, but the man grabbed his shirtfront and hauled him up behind a foul-smelling pile of refuse and empty crates stacked in the alley, out of the view of the street.

"Winslow!"

"Hello, Mitch," Jesse said just before his fist connected with Mitch's unprotected gut.

Pain exploded in his belly and he stumbled back with a gasping for air. Winslow hauled him back toward him again. Mitch managed to grab Winslow's arm to steady himself.

"What the hell . . . do you think . . . you're doing?" Mitch demanded.

"Too bad you cut your face, Mitch. Damn clumsy of you." Jesse's fist connected with Mitch's solar plexus, driving the air from his lungs.

Mitch staggered and gagged, trying and failing to suck air into his lungs. He bent over at the waist like a broken stave, clutching his belly, then dropped to his knees. With a choking gasp, he threw up his arm fending off the next blow. He was wholly incapable of defending himself against a low-down sneak attack like this and he cursed Winslow through his bloody teeth. "Jesus, Winslow—"

"The torso's the place to hit a man if you don't want to leave marks," Jesse said, grabbing his shirtfront again and dragging him halfway up to him. "How does it feel to be powerless, Lodray? To be brought to your knees?"

Mitch coughed and croaked, "You have no cause to—"

"Shut up!" He drove a fist into Mitch's kidney, sending him flying backward into the refuse. Mitch landed there with a splintering thud, falling like some damned overturned bug, helpless to get up. With a groan, he slammed his eyes shut, clutching his side.

Jesse took a step closer. "This is a warning, Lodray. You touch her again, you so much as look at her again sideways, I'll kill you. And nobody will be around to see me do it. That's a promise. Is that perfectly clear, you son-of-a-bitch?"

Mitch opened his eyes and glared at him wishing he had a gun. The toe of Jesse's boot connected hard with Mitch's thigh. He couldn't suppress a cry of pain.

"Is your hearing going, Lodray? I said is that clear?"

"I ought . . . to press charges . . . against you," Mitch gritted out bravely, grabbing for his thigh.

Jesse laughed. "Go on. I dare you. Not a man in this town would convict me of protecting Andi against a slug like you who attacks helpless women. Go on. Tell the sheriff," he said with a feral grin. "And I'll see you rot in prison."

"You don't know what you're talking about."

"Try me."

Mitch shifted on the pile of crates, his whole body aflame with pain. He tried to rise, but fell back, defeated.

"Leave her alone, Lodray, or I'll put a bullet smack between those cowardly eyes of yours." Jesse picked up a broken crate, slapped it against Mitch's chest before turning and disappearing out of the alleyway.

Mitch swore and dropped his head back against the crates with a cough, trying to gather his strength. He shouldn't have let himself be caught off guard like that by that overblown skunk-skin trader. He'd make damn sure it never happened again. And Andrea . . .

She'd told Winslow about them. His mouth twisted with the irony. He regretted that he'd have to teach her a lesson for that small betrayal. But then, life was seldom fair, he thought, shifting painfully to a sitting position on the pile of stinking crates.

As a matter of fact, life was about to become very unfair for Jesse Winslow. He'd pay for what happened here today, Mitch vowed, getting slowly to his feet. He'd see to that personally.

Chapter Nineteen

Mahkwi's yipping bark brought Andrea to the upstairs bedroom window where she looked out to see Silas holding a large-bore shotgun on a couple who'd just stepped from a hack in her yard. The man, tall with long black hair tied back from his face, wore buckskin pants and a fringed shirt. His fingers were plunged into the fur at Mahkwi's ruff, while her tail swept a happy arc into the dirt. The lovely young woman whose glorious mane of coppery hair cascaded down her shoulders and back, clutched the man's arm.

Disbelief paralyzed Andi for a moment before she could call out, "Silas! What in the world are you doing?"

"I's holdin' a gun on these two folks, ma'am."

"I can see that. Stop that this instant."

Silas darted a look up at the window. "Can't do that, ma'am."

"Why ever not?" she called.

"I is only doin' what the boss say to do, Miss Andi."

The pair glanced up at her window, perplexed, then looked back at the gun pointed at them.

314

"You're only—" Andrea sighed in exasperation. "I'll be right down."

Checking her face in the hand mirror Jesse had given her, she picked up Zachary and hurried down the stairs and out the kitchen door. No one had moved, but the handsome stranger gave her a curious look as she stopped next to Silas. His turquoise blue eyes went from her to the baby in her arms.

He touched the brim of his hat with his fingers. "I, uh, told him we were friends of Jesse Winslow's, madam," the man said with a trace of an accent, "but I don't think it made an impression."

Andi opened her mouth and closed it again. Friends of Jesse's? She moaned inwardly. If they were indeed acquaintances of his, they couldn't have picked a worse time to show up.

"The boss says to let nobody close to you or the chile," Silas explained hotly, still holding the gun on them.

She edged closer to him and said in a sotto voice, "Silas, this is not what Jesse had in mind, I'm quite certain."

Silas shrugged and muttered, "I don't reckon anybody know what's in the boss's mind these days. I's only doin' my job, ma'am."

"A little too well, I'm afraid," she whispered through her smile. "Where is Jesse now?"

"Uh, he's . . . uh . . . well, he gone."

"Gone?" she repeated loudly. "Where?" Her mind raced with possibilities. None of which she cared to consider just now.

Silas fumbled for a reply. "Uh . . . well, he uh . . ."

"Oh, never mind." She turned back to the strangers who were watching the exchange with growing discomfiture. "I do beg your pardon, I'm afraid there's been some kind of a dreadful misunderstanding, Mr.—?''

Before he could tell her his name, Jesse trotted into the yard on Rabble. As he neared, his mouth dropped open at the sight of the pair being held at gunpoint. "I don't believe it!"

Silas frowned uncertainly. "I was just doin' what you said, Boss—''

Jesse hardly seemed to hear him as he pulled Rabble up and slid off his horse, striding toward the pair with a broadening smile. "If I didn't see it with my own eyes. Creed! Mariah!"

The stranger, whose smile grew equally broad, withdrew his arm from his wife's shoulder to clasp Jesse's hand. But each pulled the other into a bear hug. Andrea stood watching the comraderie like the outsider she was.

"Jesse. It's good to see you again, *mon ami!*''

"You'll never know how good," Jesse agreed and slapped Creed on the back. He moved to draw Mariah into their circle. Silas lowered his gun.

"Hello, Jesse," Mariah said with a laugh. "We simply couldn't come this far East without stopping by to see you on our way to Texas."

"Texas?"

Creed laughed. "It's a long story."

"Very long," Mariah agreed with a tired sigh.

"Listen, I'm sorry about the gun," Jesse said. "This is Silas Mayfield, my right-hand man." Silas grinned sheepishly and shook the hand Creed offered. "Silas isn't usually this inhospitable, but he was just following my orders. I wasn't expecting you two to show up on my doorstep."

Creed frowned. "And who exactly *were* you expecting?"

"That's a long story, too." Jesse's eyes met Andi's for a brief, tension-filled moment. The words that had passed between them earlier hung heavily in the air. "Creed and Mariah, I'd like you to meet Andi Winslow, my brother's widow, and her son, Zachary."

Andrea caught the surprised look the two of them exchanged before she forced a smile and stepped forward. "I'm so happy to meet you. Jesse's spoken so fondly about you both."

Mariah smiled too, and gave Andrea an impulsive hug. "You're Zach's wife? We were very sorry to hear about your husband. It hit Jesse very hard."

"Thank you," Mariah murmured, avoiding Jesse's eyes.

Mariah went on, "I'm afraid Creed and I are horribly rude to drop in on you this way, but we had no way of getting word to you beforehand. I hope our stopping by won't inconvenience you."

"Of course not. Jesse's friends are always welcome," Andrea reassured her with a smile. "You must be tired if you've come all the way from Montana."

"A little," Mariah admitted.

"And what's this about 'stopping by'?" Jesse asked. "I hope you're planning on staying with us for a good visit."

Creed shook his head. "I'm afraid we can't. We're here for one day, two at the most. I have a job waiting for me in a little town called San Marcos."

"A job?" Jesse repeated, a frown furrowing his brow. "Bounty hunting?"

Creed glanced at Mariah and laughed. "No. A real job. Sheriffing."

Jesse pushed his hat back with his thumb. "I guess we do have a lot to talk about."

"Why don't we do that inside instead of making your friends stand out in the hot sun," Andrea

317

suggested. "I have some fresh lemonade and some iced tea made."

Mariah gasped. "Iced tea! With real *ice?* I'd absolutely kill for some."

Andrea laughed for the first time in days. "You won't have to go to such extremes, I assure you."

Jesse watched Andi and Mariah walk companionably up the steps together already falling into woman talk about the baby and the fragrant rose arbor sheltering the porch. He turned back to Creed.

"God, it's good to see a friendly face again."

"I know what you mean," Creed agreed. "How are you, Jesse?"

Jesse smiled a little sadly. "You mean for a farmer?"

"I mean for a man who didn't want to come home." Creed glanced up after Andrea. "A few surprises waiting for you, eh?"

"More than a few, it would seem," he admitted.

"Thank God life keeps surprising us," Creed murmured, his eyes following his wife. "It would get very dull otherwise."

"Funny," Jesse said, flexing his sore hand. "I was just wishing for a little bit of dull."

Creed raised an eyebrow. "By the looks of your sister-in-law, dull is something you'll never get around here."

"Too true, my friend. Too true."

Creed took a long sip of after-supper coffee, leaned back in the kitchen chair, and sighed with satisfaction. "That's the best cup of coffee I've had since we left Montana," he said, taking his wife's hand in his.

Mariah looked up at him with a sparkle of amusement in her golden eyes. "He means since he

318

met me," she corrected. "My coffee has been the butt of countless jokes since I first attempted it on a camp fire."

"I wouldn't change your coffee for all the floating grounds in the world, *ma petite*," Creed murmured with a grin.

"Good, because I'm afraid you're stuck with it for another fifty years, at least." Mariah's hand closed possessively over her husband's and the pair exchanged a look that spoke more loudly than words about the love they shared.

Andrea's gaze flicked involuntarily to Jesse, who sat across the table from her holding Zachary on his lap. She found him watching her, too. His strained expression matched her own. She looked away quickly and wondered how long they could keep up this whole charade of civility.

Except for the brief tour he'd given the Devereauxs of the farm, she and Jesse had been forced together while he and his friends reminisced about Montana and their hair-raising escape from the half-breed, Pierre LaRousse. She'd learned more about Jesse's other life in the past few hours than she had in the nearly three months since he'd been home.

Their experiences had forged the kind of bond between them that explained why Creed and his wife had traveled several hundred miles out of their way to see Jesse. It was, she suspected, a bond that Jesse had never felt with her. After today, she wondered if it had ever actually existed at all, or if she'd made it all up in her head.

Though she'd tried to keep the conversation light, the crackling tension between her and Jesse was so thick she couldn't help but wonder if Creed and Mariah noticed it. She hoped not, for their sakes, for she found herself liking the Devereauxs very much.

319

Jesse shifted in his chair, his thoughts running along the same lines as Andi's. He ran a hand over Zachary's downy head, absorbing the warmth of the child in his arms and Zachary smiled up at him, eyes full of implicit trust. The look sent a shaft of pain through him. How much longer would he be able to hold him like this? he wondered. If not for the Devereauxs showing up, would Andi have even let him back in the house? The damage between them seemed irreparable.

Yet, being with Creed and Mariah reminded him of how much the two of them had gone through to be together. The odds against them being this happy were closer to nil than his and Andi's ever were. Creed had been a bounty hunter before he'd met Mariah, a driven man with a heart full of pain. Still, they'd made it and he'd never seen Creed look happier.

"What made you pick Texas?" Andi asked, pouring more coffee in Mariah's cup.

"Texas actually picked us," Creed answered with a grin. "Fortune would have it that the War has taken San Marcos's only sheriff. They took out an advertisement in a Deer Lodge newspaper and I answered it. Apparently I fit the bill, because they replied with a letter of acceptance and money enough to get us to Texas."

Jesse shook his head. "I never thought you'd leave Montana. You love it as much as I do."

"*Oui*, that's true." Creed admitted, rubbing his thumb over the back of Mariah's hand. "But Montana winters kill the fragile and ravage the strong. It killed my mother, and I don't wish the same fate on my wife."

Mariah shook her head. "The truth is, we're both looking forward to a new start. After what happened with Seth, well . . ."

Jesse remembered the last time he'd seen Seth Travers, the man Mariah had traveled across half a continent to marry. He hadn't looked much better than Creed, whom he'd beaten bloody when he'd found out that Creed and Mariah had fallen in love with each other.

Mariah's face looked haunted for a heartbeat before she brightened. "Texas will be different, but different is not necessarily bad. We've heard it's beautiful country. And the town is providing us with a house as part of the job."

Jesse smiled. "You'll make a heck of a sheriff, Creed."

"I'd better, because I plan to keep that job for a good long time." He looked from Andi to Jesse. "What about you, *mon ami?* Ohio seems to agree with you. From what we saw your place is prospering. Have you decided to stay on and become a farmer again?"

Jesse stared first at the bruised knuckles on his hand, then up at Andi. "No," he replied flatly. "I thought for a while I might, but I guess I wasn't really cut out to be a farmer. Isn't that right, Andi?"

She looked so shocked by his blunt comment that for a moment all she could do was stare. A flush crept up her neck. Jesse was immediately and profoundly sorry for pressing her to the wall in front of his friends.

"I—yes," she said at last. "I suppose that's absolutely true." On the brink of losing her precious control, she stood, gathering up the supper dishes from the table.

Jesse stood too, his hand brushing hers on a plate. "Here, I'll help you with that," he offered.

She dropped the plate as if he'd burned her. Her

321

eyes flashed to his. "No! I mean, no thank you, I can do it."

Creed and Mariah exchanged a look and she rose beside Andi. "Why don't you men go outside and smoke your cigars or whatever it is you do after supper. I'll help Andi clean up here. We'll have it done in no time."

"You don't have to do that," Andrea protested. "After all, you came here to visit with Jesse."

"Don't be silly. It's been so long since I've had a woman close to my age to talk to I've nearly forgotten how. I'm beside myself with the need for gossip. Go on, now," she told the men. "Shoo! Let us get to work."

Andrea reached for Zachary. "Here, I'll take him."

Jesse fitted the babe against his shoulder. "I don't mind, and you've got your hands full. I'll watch him for a while, give him a little air . . . if that's all right with you."

"I—all right."

Creed and Jesse wandered out to the yard with the wolf at their heels. Mariah began to clear the dishes to the sink. "He's wonderful with your son," she said setting the dishes on the counter.

Andrea forced a smile, but could feel tears threatening. "Yes, I know. They're terribly fond of one another. He, uh . . . he helped me to deliver Zachary, you know. He rode in when I was in labor and alone."

Mariah's eyes widened. "Really? I suppose Zachary will miss him when Jesse leaves. If he goes, that is."

Andrea set her dishes down in the sink and gave the pump two priming cranks. "Oh, he's leaving. I'm sure of that. Zachary will forget him in time." *And so will I.*

"I see. That's too bad. This place seems good for Jesse."

When Andrea didn't answer, Mariah moved up beside her and set the last of the dishes on the counter. Andrea dashed the tears from her cheeks with the heel of her hand.

"Forgive me for prying, but I can see you're upset about something. I realize we don't know each other well, but sometimes it's easier to talk to a stranger."

Andrea swallowed back the emotions that threatened to undo her at Mariah's attempt at friendship. She braced her hands on the kitchen counter and stared out the window at the men walking near the barn.

"Tell me, Andi," Mariah asked her gently. "Are you in love with him?"

"You're in love with her, no? *mon ami*," Creed asked as they walked under a darkening sky.

"Well, you're direct, I'll say that for you." Jesse shook his head. "Is it that obvious?"

Creed chuckled. "A blind man could have seen it."

Jesse lifted the baby off his shoulder, and hiked him in the air over his head. Zachary opened his mouth in a squeal of pleasure. Jesse smiled. "Yes, I'm in love with her. I guess I've loved her half my life. I just didn't realize it until it was too late."

"Too late?"

"It's a long story. But I'm planning to leave as soon as I know Andi's safe and settled." He dropped a kiss on Zachary's soft cheek before settling him back on his shoulder. It had been a gesture so unconscious, so natural he felt himself color at Creed's scrutiny.

"Andrea is the one you told me about once, no?" Creed asked. "The girl you left behind?"

323

He nodded.

"And she married your brother?"

He nodded again, staring off into the distance.

"Is that the problem between you, *mon ami?*"

"In a way . . . no, not exactly . . . oh hell, you wouldn't understand."

"You don't understand," Andrea said, turning away from Mariah. "It's not as simple as whether I love him or not."

Mariah sighed. "Yes, unfortunately, love is rarely simple. In fact," she agreed, "it's usually downright complicated. That makes it more painful, but also more precious. And if I don't miss my guess, Jesse's in love with you, too. Why you could practically light a kerosene lamp with the sparks flying between you two tonight."

That was true, she knew. It had always been true between them, no matter what went wrong in their lives. "There's too much history between us," Andrea told her. "Too many hurts."

"I thought the same thing once about myself and Creed. But it's amazing what love can overcome. Who would have thought Creed and I would ever be together, as happy as we are? Certainly not me." She pressed her hand against her abdomen tenderly. "And who would have thought we'd have a baby together?"

Andi blinked. "You're with child?"

Mariah nodded. "Isn't it wonderful?"

A smile broke through Andi's tears. "Oh, Mariah, it is. Does Creed know?"

She shook her head impishly. "I haven't told him. Yet. I haven't found the right time. I think I'll wait until we reach Texas. Otherwise, he'll only worry.

You're the first to know."

"I'm so happy for you both," Andi said, drawing her close.

Mariah shook her head. "I'm sorry, Andi. It was thoughtless of me to bring that up while you're—"

"No, it's all right, really. The world doesn't stop just because my life is out of kilter." She cranked the pump handle until the water splashed into the washbasin underneath it.

"Y'know," Mariah said softly, "Jesse is very dear to me. If not for him, I don't think Creed and I would be together today. Or alive for that matter. But even in Montana, there was something missing in Jesse . . . some spark he's found here I think. To see him with you and your son . . . there's a peace within him despite whatever you two are going through. He's a wonderful man with so much to give."

Andrea sniffed and gave her a tremulous smile. "And I'm sure one day he'll find a woman to give it all to. But it won't be me, Mariah."

"She'll find herself a farmer with dirt running in his veins," Jesse told Creed, "someone who can be for her what she needs. But it won't be me. As soon as that happens, I'm going back to Montana where I belong." Zachary's open mouth found Jesse's chin with a wet squeak of delight.

Creed raised one eyebrow at the sight. "Little Zachary might disagree with you."

Jesse smoothed one hand down the boy's hair. "Yeah . . . well . . ." He pressed his lips against the boy's cheek as if to stave off that impending doom. "I'll miss him, too."

"You know, Jesse, Montana is just a place, like this place. It's never either as good or as bad as you remembered it. I never imagined myself leaving the mountains, but when I try to think of what my life would be like now without Mariah, well, it doesn't matter where I wind up. I'd go to hell and back to be with her."

"I know and I'm happy for you both." Jesse's eyes met Creed's for a long painful moment. "But I hurt Andi, Creed. Not once, but twice. Hell, I didn't mean to, but I did."

He told Creed about his misguided plan to find Andi a husband despite the fact he was falling in love with her himself. "She has every reason to hate me," he said. "I doubt she'll ever forgive me this time . . . and she's probably right."

"I'm not sure anymore what's right or wrong," Andrea told Mariah, handing her a wet plate. She buried her hands in the water and scrubbed another dish clean. "For a while, I thought I knew. I was sure he'd come to realize he loved me and give up his wandering ways. Now, I'm sure that won't happen."

"Don't give up on him, Andi," Mariah advised. "A man like Jesse is worth fighting for."

"Maybe I'm just tired of doing all the fighting," Andrea replied.

Mariah put her hand on Andi's. "I suppose I'm a hopeless romantic and I just want to see everyone find the happiness I have. But I know better than to believe it always works out that way." She gave Andi's hand a squeeze. "Whatever you do, don't let your pride stand in the way of your happiness, Andi. It would be a terrible mistake."

Jesse inhaled deeply of the scent of sun-browned

cornfields and the fragrance of roses drifting on the evening air currents.

"All these years, I've been running from something I thought I hated, only to discover it was me I was trying to get away from. The key to my life was right here all along, with Andi. I held it, Creed, right in my hand. I was this close . . ." He shook his head. "I've been a damn fool, but hell, I suppose that's nothing new. I guess I take after the old man in a way after all."

Creed leaned his forearms against the paddock rail and looked sideways at his friend. "You must do what you think is best, *mon ami*. For your sake, and hers, I only hope you don't regret your decision."

Creed and Mariah stayed that night and the next. Creed spent the day out in the hayfield with Jesse and Silas cutting and stacking hay. Mariah spent her time fussing over the baby and becoming fast friends with Andi. It had been a long time since Andrea'd had a friend to confide in. She would miss Mariah when she left.

That time came all too soon. On the morning of the third day, Creed threw the last of their bags into their rented hack. Jesse and Andi stood beside one another for the first time in days, separated by only a handspan of distance. Somehow, having Creed and Mariah there the last few days had served as a much-needed buffer between her and Jesse. Gone was the animosity that had been there earlier. What was left more closely resembled a fragile peace than real friendship, but Andrea decided she could live with that.

Creed took his hat off and smiled at her. "Andi, it has been a real pleasure getting to know you. For your hospitality, *merci*. Good luck to you and your son, *cheri*." He bent and brushed her cheek with a kiss. "If you're ever in Texas—"

"—consider our home yours," Mariah finished, hugging Andi tightly and kissing the baby in her arms. "It's been a wonderful two days. I do hope you'll come and see us if you get the chance."

"I hope so too," she answered. "You never know. Take care and be safe, you two." She winked secretly at Mariah as if to say, "you three."

"Jesse," Mariah said, hugging him, "thank you for everything. We couldn't let the chance pass to tell you how much you mean to us."

Jesse's throat tightened with unexpected emotion. "You take care of him, Mariah. See he doesn't get into too much trouble."

"Oh, he'll try, I'm sure of that." She grinned at her husband. "It's in his nature."

Creed sighed. "See what I have to put up with?" He shook Jesse's hand and clapped him on the shoulder. "Where's Silas? I wanted to say good-bye to him."

"He's over at the Rafferty's place this morning, helping John clear away what's left of his barn," Jesse said. "I'll tell him you said good-bye."

Creed nodded. *"Adieu, mon ami. Bon chance."*

"You too, my friend. Let us—me know how you are."

"I will." Creed's gaze went a little sadly from Jesse to Mariah, then to his wife. "Come on, *cheri*. San Marcos is waiting."

They climbed up into their buggy, waved good-bye and were gone before either Jesse or Andi were ready for it. For a long time, they stood there together without speaking, lost in their own private thoughts. A fickle wisp of breeze turned the hot, humid air around them.

Finally, Jesse turned to Andi. "I guess I'd better get back to the hay."

She nodded. "I liked your friends."

"They liked you. They're your friends now, too. You can bank on that."

"Jesse?"

"Yeah?"

She hesitated. "Nothing."

Jesse's gaze searched hers for a long moment before he turned to go, but the sound of approaching horses brought his head around.

They rode into the yard, three mounted soldiers in Federal blue, in a cloud of dust stirred in the dry soil. The captain and two privates pulled to a stop before them. The young officer lifted off his hat to reveal thick, dark hair and handsome features. When his eyes met hers, his lips parted in a half-smile of recognition before he caught himself. She remembered him. He was the soldier she'd seen that day at church . . . the one who had stared at her and tipped his hat.

"Mornin', ma'am, sir. Are you Winslow?" the captain asked. "Jesse Winslow of Willow Banks Farm?"

"That's me," he replied.

"Captain Micah Steele, of the 5th Illinois under Major Leland Cross. These are Privates Deeds and Johnson."

Jesse squinted at them. "How can I help you Captain?"

Steel's sharp gaze swept the house and outbuildings.

Private Deeds spoke. "That barn'll do, Captain." Steele nodded.

Jesse frowned suspiciously. "Do for what?"

"For us, Mr. Winslow," Steele answered. "We're requisitioning your barn."

Chapter Twenty

"*My barn?*" Jesse repeated incredulously. "What in the devil for?"

Steele slid his hat back on his head tiredly and dismounted. "Can we talk inside, sir? It's best if we stay out of sight as much as possible."

"Why?"

Steele smiled halfway. "Inside. Men, you get the horses in the barn while I speak with the Winslows." Deeds and Johnson obligingly headed for the barn, the captain's horse in tow.

Jesse and Andi led Steele into the kitchen, where he stood stiffly by the door until Jesse invited him to sit. Andrea noted that fatigue had etched itself in dark smudges beneath the man's brown eyes. His uniform fit him more loosely than it must have once. Despite the shiny brass buttons on his jacket, it had grown ragged about the cuffs and collar. His posture, however, betrayed none of that war-weariness, for he sat stiffly in the chair offered him as though unaccustomed to such creature comforts. His eyes met hers for a brief moment when she handed him a glass of water, then he looked at Jesse.

"I apologize," Steele began, "that you were not

informed of this turn of events sooner. However, in the interests of secrecy, you will understand why soon enough."

"Secrecy?"

Steele tipped his head. "No doubt you've heard of the robbery of a Union gold shipment only last week?"

"One would have to live in a cave not to have heard that news," Jesse admitted.

"It's hardly a secret that the Union Army has sent a detachment to investigate the murderous thugs who've been pillaging your fine county and those nearby. Those men are playing a visible role in town. Quite apart from that, my men and I, along with three other likewise small detachments of men, have been instructed to take up positions at strategic locations to lie in wait for the culprits as it were."

Jesse frowned. "You have orders stating that?"

Steele pulled a paper from his pocket and handed it to Jesse. He read it and, satisfied, handed it back.

"What makes you think my place is strategic?"

"Quite simply, it hasn't been hit yet," Steele replied. "And the corn crop you have drying in the field here makes it a prime target."

"So the Army still believes these thugs are Confederate raiders?" Andi asked. "Part of John Morgan's band?"

Steele turned to her. "John Morgan was killed at Greenville, Tennessee by Federal Cavalry on the fourth of this month. If these raiders are a splinter faction, they're being led by another man. As to their cause, if they're not Confederate Raiders, but opportunists, they've become an equal threat to the Union Army. And we mean to root them out. The Army has made them a priority."

"It's too bad the Army didn't see them as a priority before half of Elkgrove township had been torched and looted."

Steele sighed. "We're in the middle of a war, Mr. Winslow. It's unfortunate that equity has little to do with current affairs, but that's the way of it. I don't suppose you'll mind so much if we catch the scoundrels. We'll do the best we can with what we have." He pulled himself slowly to his feet.

"I assure you and your wife, you will be in no way responsible for our board while we're here, except for fodder for our mounts. We are supplied with cold rations enough to see us through several weeks if need be."

Jesse and Andrea exchanged a look. Jesse said, "I won't argue with extra protection, Captain Steele. However, I imagine there must be a more efficient way of searching out these rogues."

"With luck, the troops in town will find them before we do," the captain replied. "As far as Elkgrove knows, they are the only troops in the area. I must warn you to keep our presence here a secret. It's for your own sake as much as ours I ask it. Have I your word on that?"

Jesse nodded.

"And Captain," Andrea put in. "So there's no mistake, I *am* Mrs. Winslow, but Jesse is not my husband. He's my late husband's brother."

Jesse's eyes narrowed on hers for a brief moment before he looked away. Steele's expression, on the other hand, brightened for a moment before he checked it. "Oh, I see . . . I thought . . . well, I'm sorry for your loss, ma'am. Was your husband a soldier?"

"Yes, he was killed at Chicamonga Creek."

Steele gave Andi a look Jesse wagered held more

332

than strict sympathy.

"I am sorry," the captain said, walking to the door and fitting his hat back on his head. "You have a handsome boy, ma'am."

She smiled. "Thank you, Captain."

"Thank you both for your cooperation. My men and I will try to be as unobtrusive into your daily routine as possible."

"I hope so," Jesse said dryly.

Steele shook Jesse's hand firmly and started off across the yard for the barn.

Jesse turned to Andi with a scowl. "Why did you tell him that?"

"What?" she asked innocently.

"That you were not my wife."

"Why shouldn't I have?"

"It would have been much safer for you if those men believed we were together."

"Well, we're certainly not together, are we?" she replied with an incredulous look. "And I can't believe I'd be in any danger from a man like Captain Steele, who's been sent to protect us."

"I wouldn't be so sure about that."

"Why Jesse, with three eligible men living right here in my barn, I find it hard to believe you could find fault with that."

Jesse ground his teeth together and looked at her imploringly. "Look, Andi, I don't want to fight."

"Good, nor do I," she agreed quickly. "So let's not. Let's try to make the best of an . . . uncomfortable situation. All right?"

"All right." He started toward the door, but she called him back.

"Jesse?" She lifted her chin when he looked back at her. "When will you go?"

"Go?"

"Leave. Back to Montana."

"When I know you're safe," he replied, then turned and walked out the door.

With a bucket full of fresh spring water in one hand and several woolen blankets in the other, Andrea stepped into the dimly lit barn. Warmed by the long hot day, the air inside seemed thick and fragrant with the scent of hay. At the far end she could hear the squeaky-hinge purr of the hens as they scratched for bugs in their coop. She could see nothing, no sign of the men who were inhabiting her barn. Blinking to adjust her eyes, she rapped on the wooden door as an afterthought.

"Hello?" she called. "Captain Steele?"

"Yes?" His deep voice came from the darkness to her right, startling her. One shadow separated itself from the others near the door and caught the blankets that dropped out of her hand. His fingers brushed hers briefly with heat.

"Oh! I—I didn't see you there," she said, pressing a palm to her pounding heart.

"That's the idea," he replied with an easy smile. "Are these for us?"

"Yes . . . I thought perhaps they would make you more comfortable on the hay."

"That's very kind of you. You didn't have to do that."

"I thought it's the least I could do, considering how uncomfortable you'll be on our account." She noticed he'd removed his jacket and rolled up the sleeves of his white blouse past his elbows. A sheen of sweat stood out on his skin.

"Believe me," he said, "this place beats the hard ground I've been sleeping on for the past two years in field camps." Now her eyes had adjusted, she could see him better, as well as the other two soldiers stationed at the far end of the barn. They all looked worn out but Steele looked particularly in need of a night's rest. She wondered briefly if he was ill.

"I brought some fresh spring water for you as well."

"Thank you again. It *is* rather warm in here." He drank a dipper of water greedily, then wiped his mouth on his sleeve, watching her. "I saw you once before, you know."

"At the church in Elkgrove," she said.

He smiled, surprised. "Yes. You remember me?"

"I remember wondering if my hat was on backward, the way you were staring at me."

"Sorry. I didn't mean to make you uncomfortable. It was just that at first I thought I knew you; that we'd met before. Have we, Mrs. Winslow?"

"I don't think so, Captain. I've lived in Elkgrove all my life. Are you from around here?"

He shook his head. "Illinois. I was raised on a farm much like this one. It kind of reminds me of home."

"Perhaps I remind you of someone, too."

"Perhaps." He took another dipper of water and guzzled it down. "But I don't think that's it. A woman as beautiful as you is hard to forget."

She arched one flattered eyebrow. "Are you always this forward with women you don't know, Captain?"

"Hardly ever," he admitted with a grin.

"I'd better go," she said with a wry smile. Turning, she stepped through the barn door.

"Mrs. Winslow?" Steele said, stopping her. "When I saw you that first time in town, I thought you and your brother-in-law were . . ."

"A couple?" she supplied, looking at him.

335

He nodded. Watching her. Waiting.

"No," she replied. "We're not. Not at all. Good evening, Captain."

"Good evening, Mrs. Winslow." Steele watched her go, the corner of his mouth lifting with the first ounce of hope he'd felt in two years.

Jesse had been on his way in from the fields when he saw Andi leave the barn where the soldiers were holed up. He froze at the sight of her as she turned at something that Captain said to her. Giving her hair a little toss, she shook her head and smiled at him, saying something he couldn't make out. Then she turned and strolled back to the house. Steele hovered in the doorway, and Jesse knew he wasn't just enjoying the air.

With a curse Jesse made his way to the house. Mahkwi ran along at his heels, nipping playfully at him. He batted at her with his hand and, wagging her tail, she nipped at his fingers. He stopped at the pump outside and stripped off his shirt and then a days' worth of sweat under the cool water. The wolf stole a drink under the cool stream and then looked up at him with her wolfy smile, oblivious to the turmoil inside her master. Jesse picked up a stick and threw it hard into the cornfield. Mahkwi took off at a lope for the fallen missile, disappearing in the field of brown.

Jesse sighed. His muscles ached from cutting and shocking corn all day, but it was a good ache. Until now. Now the ache had moved low in his belly the way it always did when he looked at Andi Carson Winslow, at the sway of her hips when she walked, the tilt of her head when she talked. He wanted to drag her into his arms and force her to see what was in his heart. He wanted to prove to her that she was wrong about him, that the old man had been wrong about him, too. But that want didn't overrule the doubt that had shadowed his life, reminding him that his best would never be good enough.

Andrea stirred the fragrant chicken soup and ladled the steaming liquid into a lidded pot for the men in the barn. Though they hadn't asked her to feed them, they hadn't turned away a single dish she'd brought them over the past three days when faced with the prospect of the tinned rations they'd been given. There'd been no sign of raiders, and they grew daily more restless within the confines of the barn.

She stood and pressed her hands against the small of her back. Since the soldiers had come, she'd worked herself hard simply to keep her mind off her troubles. Jesse had made himself particularly scarce, appearing only at meals. Though they kept up a steady, even pleasant conversation, they spoke of inconsequential things. Often, she would feel his eyes on her when he thought she wasn't looking. And she would do the same.

She hadn't found it in her to forgive him yet, but seeing him through the loving eyes of Creed and Mariah had stolen some of the bitterness from her heart. She found she missed Jesse very much, but could see no road back to him.

Instead, she found herself looking forward to her brief visits with Captain Micah Steele, and enjoyed the things they shared in common. He appreciated her cooking, laughed at her jokes, and if she didn't miss her guess, he found her somewhat attractive. And though the same spark Jesse had always stirred in her wasn't there, she found his dark good looks appealing, too.

She frowned. This morning, however, when she'd brought the men some homemade porridge, the captain had been quiet and, though he'd denied feeling poorly, had looked decidedly unwell.

Packing three bowls and spoons into a canvas bag, she carried it and the soup to the barn and entered without knocking.

"Hello? Captain?"

"Over here, Mrs. Winslow," came Private Deeds's voice. "I was just about to come and get you."

"Deeds—" Captain Steele's voice croaked out.

"What is it?" Andrea asked hurrying to where Johnson and Deeds were kneeling by a stall. Her heart thumped when she saw the captain lying propped against the stall wall in the straw, his face flushed and dry. "Captain!"

"He's took real sick," Deeds said, "but he wouldn't let me come to fetch you."

"I'm all right," Steele argued feebly. "It's nothing."

Andrea set down the soup and bowls and dropped down on her knees beside him. She touched his fevered forehead with her hand. That brief contact seared her skin.

"Good Lord! You're burning up with fever, Captain!"

He rolled his head against the wall and tried to sit up. He failed. "I'm just a little under the weather, is all. I'll be fine. I could use some water though."

"Fine, my eye! Why didn't you tell me you were ill?" she replied. "You need a doctor."

He grabbed her hand. "No. You can do what has to be done. No one must know where we are."

"I'm no doctor, Captain."

"You'll do."

She sat staring at him for a moment, her hands clenched in her lap. "Gentlemen, we must get the Captain into the house at once. The barn is no place for a sick man."

He cried out as Deeds and Johnson each slid a hand under his legs. "*Stop—*" Andrea ordered, and the men released him. "Is it your leg, Captain? Are you in pain?"

He swallowed hard and nodded. "Silly."

"What's silly?"

"Didn't think . . . a bug bite could make you sick."

"Bug bite?" she repeated. "What kind of bug?"

"Spider. Small brown one. Bit me the day before I came here. It . . . seems to be . . . festering."

She turned to Private Deeds. "Do you have a knife?"

He produced one and she slipped it under the leg of Steele's trouser and long johns, and slit the seam upward. At first she could see nothing, but just below his knee on the back of his calf she found the source of his pain: a festering, red swelling the size of a child's fist. She sucked in a breath. Streaks of red radiated from the wound in both directions; a sign of blood infection.

"Gentlemen, please help him up with care and bring him into my house. That swelling must be looked after immediately."

Steele tightened his jaw. "It's still light. I can't afford to be seen outside," he protested.

"You can't afford not to, Captain."

Jesse straightened over the freshly cut corn, slipped his curved-blade corn knife into the loop at his belt and glanced toward the house. The last few days had passed with unbearable slowness. Long hours in the corn were relieved only by brief glimpses of Andi working around the yard: feeding the chickens, hoeing under the last of the summer garden, hanging laundry on the line. Sometimes she would stand staring out toward the small cemetery plot fenced in at the top of the hill, and though he never saw her go there, there were often fresh flowers on Zachary's grave.

The worst, however, was not seeing her alone, but with Captain Micah Steele, the handsome soldier ensconced in her barn. Frequently, she found excuses to bring food or drink to the men. Jesse found himself checking his watch, knowing she was taking longer than strictly necessary with the young officer. Often, when she left, she wore a smile, something Jesse himself couldn't seem to wring from her these days.

He grabbed hold of another stalk of corn and arched the corn knife, hacking through the tough stalk. It fell beside the others, and he drew them together in a shock, twisting the damp hay rope he and Silas had made around the corn. Jesse fitted the metal spiked corn-shock binder through the rope, tightened it, then sliced it with his knife.

Alongside him, Silas did the same. They'd worked hard these past few days to see that the corn was shocked before any unexpected frost hit that would ruin the crop. Silas kept a running stream of conversation going about the book Etta was teaching him to read; something by Charles Dickens, called *A Tale of Two Cities*. Jesse had listened with half an ear until now, adding his own grunting responses. Suddenly, he realized Silas had spoken to him directly.

"What?" he asked.

340

"I said I's thinkin' 'bout axing her to marry up with me."

"Who?" Jesse asked blankly.

"*Who? Who?* Who I been talkin' about for the past ten minutes? Etta o' course."

Jesse colored. "Oh, geez, Silas, I'm sorry. Of course it's Etta. I mean, of course it is. That's great, Silas. I wish you luck." *Better luck than I've had.*

His apology mollified Silas somewhat. "Well, I said I's thinkin' about it. She'd be a fool to go jumpin' over the broom with a man like me."

"Why would you say that?"

"She's used to better." He hacked at a stalk, felling it in one blow. "What I gots to offer her? I gots no house, no land, a job that cain't support both of us."

Jesse pulled the long T-shaped corn-horse from the shock he'd just made and leaned on it. "You shouldn't let that stop you, Silas. If you love her."

Silas tipped his hat back on his head with one finger and sent a doubtful look at Jesse as if to say, *strange words coming from you.* But what he said was, "Oh, I loves her all right. That woman's done sent the weak trembles through me ever since I laid eyes on her. She's contrary, an' stubborn and prissy as a old red-flannel petticoat, but I reckon she the smartest woman I knows and"—he ran a sleeve over his brow—"she fancies me, too. But I don't cotton to takin' her outta that fine Rafferty house to live in some little hovel with ol' Silas Mayfield where she gots to scratch out a livin' outen the dirt."

"A man who knows how to read won't be scratching for long," Jesse pointed out, knowing how hard Silas had been working at that. "Besides, as soon as this corn is in, I'll pay you everything I owe you. I couldn't have done it without you."

341

"Thanks, boss." Silas straightened a bit at his words. "But . . . I don' know."

"Don't give up. It'd be nice to see one happy ending in all this."

Silas smiled sadly. "Yassuh, it would. He straightened suddenly gazing over Jesse's shoulder.

"Hey, boss, look at that."

Jesse looked in the direction of the house. The two privates were hauling Captain Steele out of the barn between them like a sack of grain, with Andi following close behind.

"What the hell?" Jesse said with a frown.

"I didn't hear no guns," Silas said.

"Neither did I." Jesse looped his corn knife on his belt and started toward the house at a fast walk. He wasn't overly concerned with the good Captain, but he didn't like what he saw. Not one bit.

Chapter Twenty-one

Andrea stood beside the bed and gingerly lifted one edge of the sheet, exposing Captain Steele's naked, hairy leg. As legs went, it was a nice one, she thought, staring at it subjectively; long, well muscled . . . like the rest of him, well proportioned and lean. And infected.

Steele lay on his stomach, his eyes closed and she wondered if he had passed out. She could feel the heat he radiated even from here. While she prepared a drawing poultice, the two men had undressed him down to his union suit, and those they cut off above the bad knee and stripped the top down around his waist. She glanced uneasily at his holstered revolver hung over the bedpost near his head.

"Captain Steele?"

He stirred, opening his eyes. "Mrs. Winslow. I . . . I'm sorry."

"Don't be silly. You can't help being ill. Some people react badly to bites. But you should have told me before it got this bad."

"I thought it would get better. I'm not much use to you here." He looked at his surroundings. "Your room?"

343

It had been Jesse's room, but he hadn't slept in it for days. "No," she answered.

"Thank God for that at least."

She poured tea from a china pot she'd brought in. "I've made a poultice for your leg. I've brought you some tea for the fever. Can you manage it?"

With an effort he pushed himself to his elbows and drank the tea she'd made of feverfew and holly for fever and pain, and meadowsweet to cleanse the blood. He made a face. As he collapsed back down on the bed he muttered, "So much for impressing you."

"Impressing me?"

He gave her a sheepish grin. "How's a man . . . supposed to catch a girl's interest . . . flat on his belly on account of a bug bite?"

She blinked in surprise, not knowing what to say. So she squeezed a cloth out in the pan of cool water she'd brought up, and sponged off his back. "You've got a fever, Captain Steele. I believe you're delirious."

He swallowed thickly. "The fever's loosened my tongue, ma'am. Not my mind."

Wringing it out again, she laid it across the back of his neck. She fumbled with the warm poultice she'd wrapped in cheesecloth. "A right-minded man wouldn't have let an infection get away from him this way."

"Stupid of me."

"Foolish and stubborn," she agreed, pressing the warm compress against the back of his sore leg. He sucked in breath through gritted teeth and stiffened. "With luck," she said, "this will draw out the poison and infection."

He wrinkled his nose. "Smells like—"

"—mashed carrots. They were going to be for dinner, but they'll do more good here. There's some

344

baking soda and St. John's Wort in it, too. My tea will help the fever. You must lie still. If this doesn't work, I *will* send for the doctor whether you like it or not."

She started to rise, but he caught her hand.

"Mrs. Winslow?"

His skin was hot and dry and she was reminded, despite his banter, how sick he really was. Even so, his grip was firm, yet tender.

"Thank you, for your kindness," he said weakly.

She smiled. "You can thank me by doing as I say and getting well." She turned to find Jesse standing in the doorway, glaring at the two of them. How long had he been standing there? she wondered. Picking up the pan of water, she said, "Excuse me, Captain."

She met Jesse at the doorway and walked past him into the kitchen. He followed on her heels. "So? What happened?"

"He's sick."

"Sick? Sick, how? With what? Is he contagious?"

"No," she replied, turning toward him. "He was bitten . . . by a spider."

Jesse's scowl slid into a disbelieving grin. "A *spider?*"

She lifted her chin. "Yes, a *spider!* Some people have serious reactions to them. Captain Steele simply let it go. His leg is quite infected."

Jesse swatted irritably across the top of a freshly baked loaf of bread cooling on the table. "Well, at least that's pretty damned convenient for him isn't it?"

"Convenient?"

"He comes here to protect you and winds up right here under your roof, half-naked, getting your undivided attention . . ."

"Do you think I planned this?" She tossed the

345

water out the kitchen door and stalked back to the pump, cranking the handle three times.

"No, but maybe *he* did."

"Oh, come on—"

"Hey, I've seen him making calf-eyes at you all week—"

She turned on him, eyes wide with insult. "That's ridiculous."

"—and you've been making them right back."

"I have not!"

He smiled grimly. "You're blushing, Andi."

Her hand went automatically to her hot cheek, then she glared at him. "What if I am? And what if he is interested in me? What difference could that possibly make to you? In fact, I think it should fit into your plans for me rather nicely." She turned and primed the pump again. The water went splashing into the metal bowl with a musical ping.

Jesse clenched his fists, wondering if she wasn't absolutely right. "You're so worried about what people think, how will it look having a strange man under your roof while you're alone in this house?"

"You slept here," she pointed out, her back firmly to him.

"Yeah, but I'm not a stranger."

She looked at him sideways. "That's a matter of opinion."

He smiled humorlessly. "The fact is, this is my house, too. My bed, as a matter of fact."

"*You're* sleeping in the barn remember?" she retorted.

"Not exactly out of choice."

She lifted the enameled bowl. "Oh? I thought everything you did was out of choice, Jesse."

He swallowed hard. "Some choices are not as wise as we might have wished they'd been."

346

"Unfortunately, that's true," she said lowering her head.

Jesse knew instantly what she thought he meant. He took a step closer to her wanting to reach out and draw her in his arms. "I didn't mean about making love to you, Andi."

She met his gaze evenly. "Is that what it was?" She started to go, but he stopped her, taking the bowl of water from her and setting it on the table.

He took her shoulders in his hands. "You know damn well it was."

She shook her head. "I've got to get back."

"Andi," he said almost desperately, "what can I say?"

"There's nothing *to* say."

He released her. "You mean, there's nothing you want to hear. From me, at least."

She bowed her head again. Her voice, when she spoke was controlled and low. "Let's not hurt each other by saying more, all right? I'm going to go back and tend to Captain Steele. Despite what you think of him, he's a very nice man, Jesse. I like him and I'm going to make sure he gets well. And if, by the Grace of God, something good comes of his presence here, then maybe, just maybe I'll be happy. Is that so bad?"

Something shrank inside him. "No. That's not bad. Not at all."

He turned and walked out the door. His feet covered the yard in ground-eating steps, but he shoved down the urge to run, as far and as fast as he could.

That evening, Andrea sat up with Captain Steele, sponging him off, changing the poultice. The swelling on his leg began to respond by nightfall, but

347

the fever stubbornly remained. He slept most of the time, often waking only to drink the teas she brewed for him.

By the next afternoon, his fever was down some as well, though not gone completely, but he was able to sit up in bed and feed himself the soup she'd brought him. When he'd finished, Andrea set his bowl back on the tray and rose to go.

"I know I've already demanded too much of your time, Mrs. Winslow, but can you stay for a minute?"

She smiled down at him. "Yes, Captain, what is it?" She sat down again, her knees brushing the colorful sunflower-pattern patchwork quilt covering his bed.

"I don't know how to thank you for everything you've done for me."

"There's no need for that."

"I mean, I'm a stranger to you. You didn't owe me that kind of care."

She shook her head. "I would have done the same for anyone in your situation."

"I know. That's my point exactly." His brown eyes searched hers. The flecks of gold that swam in his irises were fringed by thick dark lashes that seemed to make his paleness all the more stark. Two days growth of beard shaded his jaw.

"You're a remarkable woman, Mrs. Winslow," he said.

Andrea smiled and touched his forehead with the backs of her fingers. "Are you sure that fever isn't still making you ramble, Captain?"

He caught her hand and brought her fingers to his lips. With a brush as gentle as a hummingbird wing, he kissed her. His whiskers tickled her skin.

"Captain!" she scolded in breathy surprise, pulling her hand from his.

Humor curved his mouth. "Forgive me for taking liberties with your fingers, Mrs. Winslow. But I can hardly bear the thought of losing your gentle touch."

Andrea pressed her hands in her lap and looked at the floor.

"I've embarrassed you," he said.

She shook her head. "I'm a grown woman, Captain, without schoolgirl fantasies. And I'd be lying if I said your sentiments didn't flatter me. But we hardly know one another."

He nodded with fatigue, and picked at a thread on the quilt beneath his hands. "You know, I've been fighting in this war for nearly two-and-a-half years now. I've seen men come into my unit and die the same day. I've had lifelong friends killed before my eyes. And I've come to know others better in the space of an hour on a battlefield than I might have in years were it not for our situation.

"I feel that way with you," he went on. "An experience like this one can cut propriety to the bone, and can certainly dispense with the kind of limitations society places on friendship between men and women."

She regarded him for a long moment. "What exactly are you trying to say, Captain? That we're friends?"

He sighed. "Actually, I'm beginning to feel something more than simple friendship for you. In fact, that first day I laid eyes on you in town, I felt an attraction. Does that frighten you?" He gave a nervous laugh. "Repulse you?"

She smiled. "No."

Encouraged, he sat up straighter against the pillows, wincing at the pain in his leg. "Mrs. Winslow, I haven't time or inclination to be backward about this. God only knows how much

349

longer this war will last, or if all your work here will be undone by one untimely bullet when I go back into battle. But it would give me great comfort, should I be so fortunate as to escape unscathed, that I might come back this way, and perhaps you would not be too unhappy to see me."

Andrea felt the room press in on her and her pulse thud in her ears. She let her gaze drift away from the Captain and settle on Jesse's spare shirt hanging from a peg across the room.

Micah Steele's words didn't come as a complete surprise, though hearing them now, she didn't know what to say. He asked for no more than friendship: no commitment, no promise; simply a thread of hope that when, or if, the time came she'd receive him kindly.

And why not? she asked herself. Was he not exactly the sort of man she should be looking for? Steady, kind, even handsome? A man who'd been raised on a farm and didn't hate every spadeful of dirt he'd ever turned? Yes, she'd be a fool to say no. Even though she felt nothing more than friendship for him now, there was nothing to say she wouldn't some day feel more. And to deny that eventuality before it had a chance to bloom would be not only foolhardy, but idiotic.

When she didn't reply right away, Steele's weary gaze dropped to his hands. "Mrs. Winslow, I certainly understand if you don't want to—"

"No, Captain," she said, stopping him by placing her hand over his. "As a matter of fact, I hope very much that if you should ever pass this way again you would consider me friend enough to remember me with a visit."

"You do? You would?"

"Yes, I would," she answered with a smile.

Steele swallowed hard, visibly relieved. She noticed his cheeks had flushed again with unnatural heat.

"That's . . . well . . . that's fine," he said. "I'll surely . . . try my best to keep that promise to you, Mrs. Winslow."

"God willing, you shall." She got to her feet. "But if you don't get some rest, that may never come to pass." She touched his forehead once more and found it slightly warmer. "Now I must go. My son will be waking any minute hungry and I have a thousand things that need doing."

"Of course," he said, slipping down on his pillow as if the conversation had sapped him of strength. "I'll be out of here by tonight. My men—"

"—are managing quite well without you believe it or not," she told him. "You need another day in bed at least, until that fever is completely gone. You get some rest, Captain."

He watched her, lids growing heavy. "Maybe just a little rest . . . just for a few more . . . hours . . ." His words drifted off and she could see he had fallen asleep where he lay.

Andrea took up the tray with a satisfied smile and headed with it back into the kitchen. Her smile faded when she came face to face with Jesse, who'd been leaning over the kitchen table making himself a sandwich out of leftover chicken and fresh bread.

"Jesse."

"You don't mind if I help myself do you?" he asked with a hint of sarcasm, scanning the empty kitchen. "I never heard the dinner bell and I'm hungry."

She set the tray down on the table, guilt rushing through her. She'd been so busy with Captain Steele and Zachary she hadn't had time to make more than the soup still warming on the stove. "Here, I can do that," she told him.

"Never mind. I'm done," he said, tearing off a bite of sandwich.

"There's soup on the stove."

"Broth," he corrected. "For a sick man. Not for a man who's still got a day's work ahead of him." He leaned one hip against the counter, watching her. His hands and face were the only clean parts of him. A day in the cornfield had left him sweaty, covered with dirt and smelling of the fields, but eternally, damnably handsome.

"I'm sorry, Jesse," she said, casting those thoughts away. "I'll make something for you right now."

He tore another bite from his sandwich. "This will do," he said with his mouth full.

She poured him a glass of buttermilk from the cloth-covered jug and set it on the counter beside him. He chugged it down immediately, then tore another bite from his sandwich, all the while staring at her. Busying herself with the Captain's dishes, she felt Jesse's gaze burning into her back.

"By the way, have you seen Mahkwi?" he asked.

"No, I thought she was with you."

He glanced out the window. "No . . . she's probably off carousing or hunting up moles. She's been cutting out far afield lately."

From the parlor came the sound of Zachary's wakeful cries. Andrea reached for a towel to dry her hands, but Jesse stuffed the last bite in his mouth and held out an arm to stop her. "No, I'll get him."

Surprised, Andrea nodded and went back to her dishes. With one ear cocked to the other room, she waited for Jesse and the baby to return. When five minutes passed, she wiped her hands on the towel anyway and walked quietly to the parlor door. She found Jesse leaning over Zachary, fastening—with some difficulty—a clean nappy around the baby's hips. The wet one lay in a soggy pile on the floor, but Andrea didn't think to complain.

Instead, she found herself mesmerized by the sight of the two of them together, man and child, communicating with smiles. Zachary stared raptly at a smiling Jesse, fists waving in the air.

"Now, doesn't it feel better to have dry britches, Corncob?" Jesse asked, and frowned at the stubborn clasp.

"Da-da-da-da!" Zachary cried.

Jesse froze and swallowed heavily.

"Da-da!"

Andrea's hand went involuntarily to her mouth. It wasn't the first time her son had strung that sound together by accident—and since she'd never used the word "daddy" for Jesse, she was certain it was just that—but Zachary had never done it for Jesse before. The effect was startling.

Jesse wiped his hands on his back pockets and stared at Zachary as if he'd bit him. "Hey, Corncob," he said warily. "That's no way to be talking to your uncle. Say Jesse? *Je-sseee?*"

"Da-da-da-da!"

"No, kid. *Je-sseee.*"

Zachary blew a bubble.

Andrea forced a bright smile and stepped into the room. "Well you two, what's going on in here?"

Jesse straightened guiltily and looked at her. "I was just . . . ya know . . . he was, uh, wet."

Andrea reached for the diaper, fastened it and lifted Zachary into her arms with a flourish. "Thanks, Jess." She rubbed her nose against her son's chubby belly, evoking a giggle from him. "Did Uncle Jesse change your nappies, sugar plum?" Her eyes met Jesse's for a fleeting moment. "Wasn't that nice of him?"

353

Jesse shifted uncomfortably beside her as Zachary reached out for him.

"What?" Andrea asked. "You want Jesse back?"

"Da-da-da-da-da!" Zachary exclaimed, obviously enjoying the clucking noise his tongue made against the roof of his mouth.

Jesse smiled uncomfortably. "He's got a good strong voice."

"Yes, he does."

He reached out and allowed the baby to curl his fist around one large finger. "I gotta go, Corncob, but I'll see you later." He pried the small fist loose to the protest of Zachary.

"How's the harvest coming?" Andrea asked, following Jesse back into the kitchen.

"We're still shocking. We'll start husking the seed corn by the end of the week. Another five or six days . . . we'll be done." He fitted his hat on his head and sent her a half-hearted smile.

"Oh," she replied.

Silence stretched between them, then they both spoke at once. "Well, I guess—" he began.

"Supper will be—"

They both stopped mid-sentence and looked uncomfortable. "You go," he prompted.

"Supper will be ready when you are," she promised.

He nodded. "Oh, yeah, Silas told me to tell you he'd be eating at the Rafferty's tonight. So it's just you and me for supper." He opened the door and looked back at her. "And, of course, the U.S. Army."

Silas sat down beside Etta on the circular wrought-iron bench that surrounded the old elm tree in the Rafferty yard. The moonlight spilled down on them through the swaying branches above. Leaning his head back against the bark of the tree, he stared at the three-quarter moon.

"You reckon that ol' moon looks the same up in the North as it do right here?" he asked Etta.

She nestled her head against his shoulder and nodded. "We're in the North, Silas."

"I mean . . . the truly North. Like . . . Dee-troit."

"It looks just the same," she said slowly. "Why?"

"'Cause, I'd sorely miss seein' it if it don't."

She sat up at that and stared at him. "What are you talking about?" She shook her head disparagingly. "Dee-troit . . . why there's nothing there, but a lot of people and buildings and shops where folks like us sweat sixteen hours a day."

"For money," Silas added.

"Not enough money. Not enough to make it worth living like that. I've been there. Air smells like a smokestack, and the rooms folks live in are crowded and bug-infested. Silas, you're not thinking of—"

"I's thinkin' of a lot of things," he said, looking down at her. "Mostly, how I can keep a woman like you happy."

She shook her head. "You old fool. Don't you know I *am* happy? Can't you see it on my face? It's been a long time since I've been happy like this."

He smiled when she threaded her arm through his and leaned her head back against his shoulder. "I don't mean jus' for today, Etta," he said softly. "I mean . . . for the rest o' our days."

She went rigid beside him, but didn't look up. "A-are you asking me to marry you, Mr. Mayfield?"

"I reckon so, Mrs. Gaines."

She sat up slowly. She pushed her spectacles up on her nose with one finger and looked him in the eye. "You mean it? You're not just joking with me are

355

you? 'Cause if you were, I—''

He silenced her with a kiss, wrapping his big hand around the back of her head and pulling her close. His mouth moved over hers with the sweet pressure of desire. "That feel like a joke?" he asked when he released her.

Stunned, she shook her head. "No." Then a slow smile spread over her face. "No," she repeated and pressed her full mouth against his once more.

Silas drew her into his arms and held her tight against him. "My feelin's for you ain't nothin' I cares to joke 'bout, Etta."

"Nor do I. Oh, Silas, I never thought I'd feel this way again." She sighed. "It makes no sense, because we're as different as day and night."

"Apples an' oranges," he agreed.

"Scissors and paper," she added. "But maybe that's why it's good, you know? Maybe my late husband, Marcus, and I were too much alike. We thought alike, taught alike, spoke alike . . .''

He laughed. "You ain't gots to worry about that with me."

"No, I don't. And if you can stand my—as you call it—'prissiness,' I can certainly stand your conjugations."

"My *what?*"

"Never mind." She smiled and tightened her arms around his chest.

"Only thing is," he said, "I ain't got no notion how we's gonna live. You go to Dee-troit with me?"

"We don't have to go to Dee-troit. I've got a job . . . and you've got a job . . .''

Silas scoffed. "We ain't never gonna get ahead that way. And how we gonna live? Me there, an' you here?''

Her thumb trailed absently back and forth across

his sleeve. "Mr. John, he was just saying the other day—like he does at harvest time every year—how he couldn't handle all the land he had. He was thinking of selling some of it off."

"I can't buy it."

"No," she agreed, "not now. But there's not much market on land now either. Maybe he'd let you work it for a few years, and share the profit with him until you can pay it off. I read there's talk of that sort of arrangement already cropping up in the South."

Silas frowned, considering it. "I don't know."

She sat up, excited. "Why not? I've got some money put aside. We could build ourselves a little house on the land and I could keep working for the Raffertys and you could keep working for the Winslows. We'd make it. I know we would."

"You think Massah John would do somethin' like that?"

"There's only one way to find out," she said, kissing Silas on the cheek. "We ask him."

Chapter Twenty-two

Silas gave Jacksaw's traces a little shake as he drove the buckboard home in the moonlight. He felt light. Lighter than air. Why if he didn't concentrate on keeping his seat on the wagonbench, he might just float home and the mule would have to find his own way.

Etta's gonna marry me! Me. Silas Mayfield, ex-slave. A woman like her could turn a man's whole life around, he thought. The way she thought things up . . . like the land-sharing idea with the Raffertys. Who would'a thought a fine man like John Rafferty would trust someone like him to farm a piece of land on his own. It was more than he'd ever dared hope for.

The sound of that was so sweet, Silas could almost taste it! He sucked in a lungful of night air. Ah, freedom! It had been a lucky day, that day he'd stepped in front of Jesse Winslow on this very road. He sent up a silent prayer of thanks to God and gazed at the glowing moon. There'd be no stoppin' him and Etta now. All he had to do was—

A high-pitched sound coming from close by made Silas draw Jacksaw to a stop. He tipped his head, trying to catch the sound again. Standing utterly still, he heard the rustle of evening air through the rattling stalks and the call of an owl in the distance. That must'a been it, he decided, and clucked to Jacksaw.

As soon he started, he heard it again. A whine? It came from across the road, near the ditch that ran beside the corn. Darkness kept him from seeing anything clearly.

Cautiously, he climbed down from the wagon, and moved toward it. The sound came again, louder this time. Silas fingered the collapsible pocketknife Jesse had given him for protection. He never carried a gun off the farm. Any colored man caught carrying one would like as not be hung, even in the North.

"Who's in there?" he asked in a soft voice, hoping no one answered. "I got me a knife."

The sound came again, this time at his feet. Silas swallowed and looked down into the shadowy ditch. What he saw sent his heart to his throat.

"Oh-hh, Lord a mercy, no."

Jesse helped himself to more potatoes and ladled another spoonful of brown gravy over them. As he ate, he watched Andrea jiggle Zachary on her lap while she tried to enjoy her own meal. The baby's fussy time always seemed to coincide with supper. His gaze traveled over her face, appreciating the crescent of shadow her lashes made against her cheek as she studiously avoided meeting his eye.

He returned his gaze to his food, wishing talking hadn't become so hard between them. He missed her company, and more than that, he missed her smile.

He'd made the mistake of practically walking in on them when he'd come back today for lunch. He'd seen Andi holding the soldier's hand and laughing with him over something he'd said. It had been all he could do to contain the flash of jealousy that sight provoked and make it back to the kitchen to slap a sandwich together. But he hadn't gotten the picture out of his head all day.

"More sausage?" she asked, noticing he'd finished his.

He shook his head.

"Captain Steele is doing much better," she said brightly.

"Oh?" he replied dispassionately.

"M-m-hmm. As a matter of fact, his fever is nearly normal again. But it left him weak. He wasn't well enough to join us for supper tonight."

"What a shame. Does that mean he'll be out of here soon?"

Andrea took a bite of hash. "He offered to leave tonight—" Jesse looked up hopefully, "but I told him he needed another day to recover his strength. I've given him something to help him sleep."

Jesse tightened his grip on his fork. "Yeah, well, tomorrow, I may just ride into town and have a talk with his superior officer."

"What?"

"Captain Steele is doing no one here any good. You're working twice as hard to feed the three of them, not to mention the extra work of caring for a sick man. Besides, this whole idea of laying in wait for the raiders is ridiculous. They're not going to hit while the soldiers are in the area."

"That didn't deter them from robbing that train shipment. Captain Steele thinks—"

Jesse slammed his fork down, about to tell her exactly how he felt about what Steele thought when Silas burst through the door, eyes wide and troubled.

"Boss—"

"What is it, Silas?" he asked getting to his feet.

He swallowed hard. "Better come. It's Mahkwi. I found her on the road. She been hurt bad."

Jesse grabbed the lantern from the shelf near the door and was out the door before he could finish.

The wolf lay on the wagonbed of the buckboard. She lifted her head with a whine of pain when Jesse approached. Jesse held the lit lantern aloft. He could see the sheen of blood glistening on her shoulder. He could even smell it.

"Easy girl," he murmured. A wolf, or any animal who'd been injured, could be dangerous even to a friendly hand.

Silas came up behind him. "I be afraid she bite my hand off when I took her up in my arms, but she didn't. I reckon she was happy to see a friendly face."

"She's been shot," Jesse replied flatly. "The bullet's still in her shoulder from what I can see."

"Poor thing. Who would do something like that?" Andrea asked drawing near the circle of light.

Jesse's eyes met hers, filled with the only answer that came to mind.

"Oh—" Andrea said, "you don't think—"

"I don't know what else to think."

"It could have been anyone, Jesse. Someone who thought she was a rogue wolf."

"I doubt it."

Andrea looked down at Mahkwi again. "What can we do? We can't take that bullet out."

Jesse's expression had descended into fury. He stalked back to the house and returned with his gunbelt strapped to his hips and his rifle in his hand. Climbing into the drivers seat of the buckboard, he said, "I'm going to take her into town. Maybe Doc Adams can do something. Silas you stay here and watch out for Andi and the baby. Tell the men in the barn what happened. I'll be back as soon as I can.''

"But I treat people, Jesse," Doc Adams protested, standing over the buckboard in his nightshirt and cap. His breath smelled vaguely of whiskey. "Nope, I don't work on animals. Especially . . . a wolf.''

"I know that," Jesse answered patiently. "But I'm asking you to make an exception. And she's half dog.''

Adams shook his head, his whiskered jowls jiggling in the moonlight. "You'd be better off to put the animal out of her misery.''

"No!" Jesse growled. "She doesn't deserve that. None of this is her fault." He raked a hand through his hair. "Dammit, Doc, it can't be that different cutting a bullet out of a dog than a man. I'll pay you whatever you want.''

"It's not the money," Adam's hedged. "She, uh . . . she might bite me—''

"I'll make sure she doesn't.''

"And I . . . well, if it ever got around I was workin' on animals, it might, you know, raise some eyebrows. Plus I'd have every farmer from here to New Richmond bringing' me their cows and horses and—''

"Twenty-five dollars, cash," Jesse said.

"—goats to unplug a teat or some such nonsen—'' Adams stopped. "You say twenty-five dollars?''

"And my word of absolute silence about the matter.''

"I see." The doc rubbed his jaw. "Well . . . then again, I might be able to help the poor animal at that. Now, that's no guarantee mind you . . .''

"Twenty-five," Jesse repeated grimly, "no matter what the outcome.''

Doc stuck out his smooth hand. "I'll do my best, son. You can carry her into my examining room. . . ."

Tension worked its way up Jesse's spine as he neared the Lodray's house on the corner of Third and Oak. He pulled the mule to a stop at the hitching rail and climbed down. A deep breath did nothing to calm the roiling anger inside him. Damn the bastard, he thought. He was worse than a coward, taking his retribution out on a dumb animal.

A pain fisted in his chest and burned there like an ember. Mahkwi was more than just an animal to him. She was a true and loyal friend. More loyal than any people he'd ever known. Her loyalty was wholly unconditional. It didn't matter if he made mistakes, used bad judgment, or didn't pet her when she thought he should. She forgave him everything.

And he'd let that bastard hurt her. After checking her over, Doc Adams had assured him that the bullet hadn't hit anything vital. She'd recover with time and care. Though his relief had been great, the fact that Lodray hadn't outright killed her changed nothing. He intended to make him pay for it. Dearly.

The Lodray house sat nestled behind a neat hedgerow of boxwood. The lantern that hung outside the door was still lit. White-winged moths hurled themselves mindlessly toward the flame, their wings making a whirring, futile ping against the chimney glass.

Jesse knocked on the door. When no one came, he knocked again. Deke Lodray opened the door, pushing his reading spectacles down on his nose and looking up at Jesse with a pleased smile. A half-spent cigar dangled from his fingertips.

"Jesse! What a surprise."

363

"Deke?" Jesse's attempt at a smile was a bad one.

"What brings you out tonight?" Deke asked. "Come in, come in." He ushered Jesse into the house. The furnishings befitted a successful newspaper editor. Burgundy velvet upholstered sofas and chairs beckoned from the parlor, heavy brocaded drapes curtained the windows, imported rugs covered the floor. The parlor shelves were covered with an assortment of bric-a-brac that would have driven any sane man running for an uncluttered space.

Jesse removed his hat, but stayed by the door, not wanting his mission here to be mistaken for a social call.

"Mother—" Deke called into the other room, "Look who's here!"

"Is it Mitchell?" Sarah Lodray, Deke's wife appeared at the door, a look of disappointment spreading across her aging features. "Oh. Jesse Winslow. I was hoping it was—"

"Your son?" Jesse finished with a frown. "He isn't home then, I take it?"

"No. Why? Did you come to see him?"

"Yes," Jesse replied without a trace of a smile. "Do you know where I can find him?"

Sarah's eyebrows knitted together. "No, I don't as a matter of fact. I didn't realize you and Mitchell were friends."

"We're not."

Deke's expression descended into concern. "Then why do you want to see him?"

"It's a personal matter. Between your son and me."

"I see," Deke said.

"Anything you have to say, you can say to us," Sarah announced, pulling a perfume-scented lace hanky from her sleeve. She tore nervously at the delicate tatting with her fingertips. "Mitchell

364

keeps no secrets from us."

Jesse slid his hat back on his head. "I'm afraid you're wrong about that, Mrs. Lodray."

Deke put a restraining hand on his arm. "Jesse, wait. Won't you tell us what has you so riled up? The truth is, we've been a little worried about Mitch lately ourselves."

"Deke!" Sarah turned to her husband, obviously appalled that he would share such private concerns.

"Well, it's true, Mother, and we might as well come out and say it here. Why, just the other day, Mitch came home with a black eye and moving real slow as if he'd been hurt. He said he'd had a riding accident, but—"

"Of course he did," Sarah affirmed. "That's what he said, wasn't it? He's a good boy. Always has been."

"Pardon me, Mrs. Lodray, but your son is no 'boy,'" Jesse pointed out. "He's fully grown and responsible for his own actions."

"Jesse's right," Deke told her, then looked at Jesse. "But he doesn't tell us where he's going or who he's going with. Has something happened, Jesse?"

Sarah stepped in front of her husband. "I'm afraid we can't help you, Mr. Winslow. When Mitch gets home, we'll tell him you were looking for him."

Deke looked at his shoes, a muscle twitching in his jaw. Sarah's haughty invective made it plain that Jesse had overstayed his welcome. "There's no need for that, Mrs. Lodray. I'll find Mitch on my own."

"I'll walk you out," Deke said firmly, taking Jesse's arm.

"I don't think—" Sarah began.

"I *said*, I'm walking our guest out, Sarah. And that's exactly what I intend to do. I'll see you in a moment."

Put in her place for once, Sarah could do no more

365

than sniff as she turned around and left the men to themselves.

Deke followed Jesse down the porch steps. "I want to know what this is all about, Jesse. Is there bad blood between you and Mitch?"

"He shot my dog tonight."

Deke blanched. "I'm sorry, but I find it hard to believe that Mitch—"

"He was paying me back. There was no riding accident, Deke. I gave Mitch that little warning a few days back after he came out to our place and bothered Andi."

"Andi? I'm surprised at you, resorting to violence," Deke said in a reprimanding tone.

"Sometimes, a fist makes a bigger impression than words."

Deke's dark eyes flashed momentarily, but he checked his temper. "That's what this is all about isn't it? Andrea Winslow?"

"Yes."

Deke rubbed a hand over his jaw. "I've known for some time that Mitch was in love with her. One of the reasons we sent him off to Harvard was to get him away from her. She wasn't interested, in fact she married Zach, but he didn't seem able to accept it."

"He still hasn't."

Deke shook his head. "Since he came home, I thought he had. Frankly, I was relieved. There was something not quite right about the way he idolized that girl. Sarah convinced herself there was nothing amiss in the boy, but I . . . well . . ." He looked off into the darkness. "Then earlier this afternoon, an unsavory-looking sort of fellow came to the house asking for Mitch. I didn't tell Sarah this, but I'd seen Mitch with that man once before. Of course, we're appalled by his choice of friends, but

366

as you say, he's a grown man."

"Did he say anything about where he was going. Anything at all?"

Deke scuffed his foot in the dirt, sending up a cloud of parched dust. "He did mention something about Andrea again," he admitted reluctantly.

"What?" Jesse's whole body went rigid. "He mentioned her by *name?*"

"Not to me, but to his mother. Something . . . something about proving Andrea wrong about him."

Jesse felt as if the earth shifted under his feet.

"What do you think he meant by that?" Deke asked, honestly perplexed.

He didn't want to think about it, or imagine what Mitch's out-of-kilter mind had planned, but a bad feeling had begun to take hold. Jesse climbed into the buckboard and gathered up the reins. "I have to go," he told Deke.

Concern creased Deke's brow. "Maybe I should come with you."

"I can handle Mitch. Thanks anyway."

Deke laid his palm on the mule's rump. "Jesse, whatever your problem is with my son, I want you to know he's not bad. But I . . . well, I know, well . . ." He swallowed visibly, struggling to hold his emotions in check. "I'm asking you to settle things between you peaceably. Please, if you find him . . . don't hurt him."

Jesse's expression grew dark. "I'm sorry, I can't promise that. But out of respect for you, Deke, I'll try."

Andrea tucked a fast-asleep Zachary into his cradle in her bedroom and covered him gently with a blanket. She smiled down at the cherubic face, remembering Zachary and Jesse together tonight. In her dreams, before everything had gone so wrong, she had imagined them together as a family: her and Zachary and Jesse. Certainly, the baby had accepted Jesse into his life as if he belonged there and would miss him when he left.

She would miss him, too.

That came as no surprise, but it had been days since she'd allowed herself to admit that Jesse had insinuated himself back into her life in ways from which she wasn't sure she could ever fully recover.

She picked up a large turning key from her dresser and began tightening the loosened ropes beneath her mattress. Certainly her romantic fantasy about never marrying again for 'anything but love' was a useless old adage, one no doubt made up by some spinster who never found that perfect, elusive happiness. Because she would never feel about another man the way she did about Jesse despite what had happened between them. It was as simple as that.

The farther away she'd gotten from that horrible day when Mitch had come by—when he'd told her what Jesse had been doing behind her back—the more she came to believe that Jesse had never intentionally meant to hurt her. Just as she'd also begun to suspect she'd let her own stubbornness keep her from seeing the truth.

Mariah Devereaux's words came back to her. *Don't let your pride stand in the way of your happiness,* she'd said. *It would be a terrible mistake.*

Had she done that after all? she wondered. Had she been so stubborn and prideful she couldn't see the gift he'd offered her? Not once, but twice he'd asked her to be his wife. Why was it so easy for her to believe the bad about him, and so hard to believe the good?

Pulling the edges of her wrapper together, Andrea walked to the window and pushed aside the lace curtain, hoping to see Jesse's wagon on the road home. Mahkwi's shooting had cut him to the bone and she worried he might do something foolish—like look for Mitch Lodray himself.

She could see no sign of him. The barn lights were out. Silas and Private Johnson were inside. Deed's had been assigned watch. She could just see him posted in the shadows outside the barn.

She would wait up for Jesse, no matter how long it took. She'd make a cup of tea and keep the water hot for him. Maybe when he came home, they could talk. Maybe even . . .

A sound downstairs cut off her thought. She frowned, wondering if it was the captain. But he'd been asleep the last time she checked. She could hardly believe the decoction she'd given him to help him sleep hadn't put him right out.

Barefoot, she crossed the room and padded silently down the steps, her wrapper billowing behind her. She'd left a light on in the kitchen when she'd come upstairs, but now that light had gone out. Strange. She'd just refilled the fuel in that lamp yesterday. Perhaps the captain had gotten up and turned it down, thinking she'd forgotten it.

In the dark, she made her way to Jesse's old bedroom and opened the door a crack. Moonlight spilled through the open curtains onto Captain Steele's sleeping features. His chest rose and fell in the slow, steady rhythm of deep sleep. Confused, she eased the door shut and started back for the kitchen.

A dark silhouette of a hooded man emerged from the shadows of the hallway, a mere arm's reach away.

Chapter Twenty-three

A scream bubbled up in her throat, but it came to nothing as the man leaped for her and clamped his hand over her mouth. She slammed against the wall behind her from the force of his weight. A breath-stealing pain shot through her head and back. The fingers of his left hand dug into her cheeks and she stared wide-eyed at the rough burlap sack that covered his face. Two holes for his eyes were all that made his appearance human. The cold steel of his revolver pressed against her arm.

A gunshot shattered the quiet outside. Shouting erupted. Men's voices, she couldn't tell how many, echoed on the night air.

Raiders! The frantic realization struck her as the man pulled her back against him and began dragging her to the back of the house toward the rear door.

Her first thought was for Zachary, alone upstairs. *Oh, my God! What if they burn the house? What if they don't even know he's there?*

More shots rang out outside.

Andrea kicked at him and struggled in his arms, but his arms pinioned hers like iron.

"Don't struggle," came her captor's hoarse whisper.

She was too terrified to listen. She tried to bite his hand, but couldn't. She screamed, but the sound wasn't more than a muffled grunt.

His fingers tightened against her mouth and he gave her head a retaliatory jerk. "Stop it!" he hissed and dragged his gun up to her temple. "I don't want to hurt you, Andrea."

His words made her go absolutely still in his arms. Bile rose in her throat and her stomach took a sickening plunge. It was Mitch. She would know his voice anywhere.

"Now," he said with a grunt, yanking her toward the door, "we're just going to take a little walk. Just you and me. Open the door," he commanded, releasing her arm.

It seemed too much to hope that Captain Steele would come roaring out of his bedroom with his gun blazing to save her from this madman. Desperate, she thought of Jesse in town. He'd been right. Mitch must have shot Mahkwi to get her out of the way. Oh, Jesse!

"Do it!" he repeated.

With a trembling hand, she reached for the knob.

Mitch pushed her out the back door and down the two steps there. With his gun pointed at her temple, he dropped his mouth close to her ear. "I'm going to take my hand away from your mouth now. Don't make a sound, you hear?" His tone was peculiarly entreating and vicious.

She shook her head with a promise not to. But as soon as his hand lifted away from her mouth, she screamed as loud as she could.

*   *   *

Jesse heard the shots as he rounded the bend in the road approaching Willow Banks. His heart leapt to his throat. Damn it to hell! He was too late.

Hauling back on the reins, he reached for his rifle tucked under the benched seat. He jumped to the ground. Hastily tying off the mule on a fencepost, Jesse took off at a run through the dry cornfields to his right.

As he kept low and traversed the field in ground eating strides, he cursed Mitch Lodray. He'd expected trouble tonight, but he hadn't expected gunplay. He heard the retort of at least seven guns. More than was possible from the three soldiers, Silas, and even Mitch. That could mean only one thing. Mitch hadn't come alone.

Jesse plunged onward. Dried cornstalks crackled against him, tore at his face, and sliced into his hands as he straight-armed a path for himself. When he got closer he stopped and crouched down with a full view of the yard. The house was pitch dark. Flashes of gunpowder accompanied each shot, illuminating the darkness briefly. From his position, he could see that at least four men were positioned opposite the barn directing their fire there: one behind the buggy, another two crouched behind the well. A fourth darted between the split-rail fencing and the barn wall, his rifle trained on the wide open loft door. Something in their silhouettes was wrong.

Then it struck him—they all wore hoods. Hell, he thought, confused. Maybe it was actually the raider attack the soldiers had been expecting and not Mitch at all. Maybe, Jesse thought, Mitch had nothing to do with what was going on here.

Instinct refuted that speculation.

No, he knew with a deep down gut feeling Mitch was part of this. And he was after Andi. If that was true, his original theory about an insider had been right. Mitch Lodray was responsible for the terror Adams County had been under for the last few months.

Jesse's gaze darted downward. In the shadow of the barn lay a crumpled figure. It was too dark to see who it was or which side of the fight he'd been on. Jesse prayed it wasn't Silas as he lifted his own rifle and took a bead on the man edging toward the barn.

His shot found its mark, and the man was lifted to his toes with a groan before dropping heavily to the ground. A shout went up from one of the men in the yard and a bullet sailed by Jesse's ear, close enough for him to feel its heat. He flattened himself to the ground and crawled through the corn to a safer position. The sound of his own ragged breathing and his thudding heart echoed in his ears.

Another bullet plowed into the dirt four feet from him. They couldn't see him. Not clearly anyway, he reasoned. Jesse raised his head and looked toward the house. He knew only one thing—he had to get to Andi. If Mitch was indeed involved in this, he would be trying to make his way to her.

Another bullet exploded a stalk ten feet away. He smiled grimly. They were guessing. If he kept moving, they wouldn't be able to find him. He got to his feet in a crouch and ran, seeking the cover of the corn. Thirty feet away, he stopped, took aim again, and fired at the man crouched by the well. His bullet struck the man in the arm, forcing him to drop his rifle.

Jesse got to his feet again and ran. The ensuing gunfire burrowed into the dirt at his heels. He prayed Andi had had the good sense to grab the baby and run out the back when she'd heard the gunfire. Maybe she had and was halfway to the Rafferty place by now.

That thought gave him a brief moment of hope. He stopped again and took a quick aim on the raider.

The sound of a scream reached him through the din of gunfire. God Almighty—Andi's scream.

"Shut up!" Mitch's closed fist connected with her cheek, and the barrel of the gun glanced off her forehead, cutting off her cry and nearly knocking her to the ground. His hand around her upper arm was the only thing that saved her from a fall. Her breath came fast and shallow. Pain radiated across her face.

"That was foolish. *Foolish*, Andrea!" Mitch nearly shouted.

Yes, she thought with numbing clarity. It was foolish. No one would hear her. No one could possibly hear through the sound of gunfire. She was alone with the monster who'd haunted not only her dreams, but many of her waking hours for the last three years.

He smelled of sweat and bay rum and cigarettes. She slid her eyes shut, thinking of her son, lying unprotected in her room. She felt nauseous and filled with a sense of rage.

"Are you going to throw me down and try to rape me again, Mitch?" she asked, glaring at his masked face.

His thumb stroked her windpipe. "Ah, so you know me. I knew you would."

"I won't let you do it, Mitch. I swear I'll kill you before I let you do that to me again."

He looked down at her through the holes in his burlap hood. "You still haven't learned, have you darling? You can't escape from me. I know you don't even want to."

"Take your hands off me!"

His hand tightened around her arm and he gave it a brutish jerk. "As soon as we're away from here, Andrea," he said dragging her toward the horse he'd tied by the spring house. A thick cloud passed over the moon, making the going awkward and suddenly dark.

"You're a coward is what you are," she accused.

That seemed to touch a nerve in him. He yanked her closer to his chest. Tearing the sack off his head, he leaned closer so his lips touched her ear. "Everything I did I did for you!" he gritted out in a harsh whisper. *"Everything."* He swept an arm toward the gunfire in the distance. "Even that. Even the raiding . . . All for you. For *us.* It wasn't easy, you know. It took imagination; brilliance, even. But I did it. *She* never would have believed it," he added with a bitter smile, "but I knew I could do it. I'm rich now, Andrea. Don't you see? You and I can go away together now."

Andrea felt his breath on her, steamy in the cool night air. Fear sliced through her sharply. *She?* Who did he mean? His mother? Was all of this about her?

Good Lord, he was deranged.

"I—I don't want to go anywhere with you, Mitch," she pleaded more calmly than she felt. "Please . . . please just let me go. I won't press charges. I won't even tell you were here—"

He yanked her harder. "Don't say that."

"Mitch, for the love of God—"

"Shut up! You're coming. It's . . . . it's all planned. You'll like it when we get there. I know you will. You just need some time—"

She shook her head and grasped his arm that had drawn tightly around her throat. *"I* didn't plan it. Do you think I'll love you for this? Do you think I can ever forgive you for taking me away from my home? My son?''

"He'll just be a burden to you. When we get to where we're going, I'll give you another son, as many as you want. And they'll be ours. Not Zachary Winslow's . . . And not that sonofa—" He turned back to her, the whites of his eyes glistening in the dark. "Not Jesse's."

His thumb stroked the back of her neck sending shivers up her spine. "He's not good enough for you. You should know that by now."

"No, you—you've got it all wrong, Mitch. We're not together."

"Andrea," he said in a disappointed tone. "You're not going to lie to me again? Not now. Not when I've gone to all this trouble just for you?"

"I—I don't know what you mean."

He started pulling her again. The acrid smell of gunpowder drifted by them on the night breeze. Gunshots were close and peppered the night with deafening sound. And in the momentary silence that came between shots, she heard her baby crying. Her heart sank.

"You think I didn't see what he was trying to do?" he demanded. "To get back into your good graces again after he ran out on you once before? That bastard doesn't deserve you."

She shook her head in disbelief.

"He'll pay for that, too, I promise you."

She struggled futilely against him, lashing out with her feet.

He leaned close to her ear again, tightening his muscled arm brutishly around her throat. "I'll always be stronger than you. You know that, don't you?" His hand drifted down over her breast. On an indrawn breath, Andrea froze. Nausea inched up her throat.

Mitch's chest rose and fell faster against her back. "I've waited so long for this, Andrea. I have all your things right here with me. You'll feel more at home when we get to where we're going."

"Th-things?"

"Your glove, your stocking, your hairbrush . . ."

Her knees went weak. *He'd been in her house* touching her things. All those things she'd thought she'd misplaced, it had been Mitch all along.

". . . even a camisole from that day I left the note for you. I knew you'd need it when I took you. It was so beautiful, I fantasized about seeing you in it."

She pressed her lips together to keep from getting sick.

"Let her go, Lodray." Jesse's voice came from the darkness behind them. Relief tore through her. She recognized the controlled rage behind his quiet command.

Mitch spun around, his pistol aimed at Jesse.

"Ah, it's Jesse Winslow, here at last to save his damsel in distress. Your armor's looking a little tarnished, Winslow."

"Let her go. *Now*," Jesse ordered.

Mitch laughed. "Or what?" He lifted her chin with his forearm. "You'll shoot me? How? Through her?"

"Jesse—" Andrea choked out. "Don't."

"You see?" Mitch said. "She wants to come with me. Isn't that right, Andrea?"

Andrea slid her eyes shut while Mitch nodded her head with an up-and-down motion of his arm.

"I think you'd better drop your gun," Mitch suggested through gritted teeth as he settled the gun against her temple. "Unless you want to lose her to a bullet instead of to me."

377

Jesse's forehead glistened in the pale moonlight. He hesitated, torn. "Let her go!"

"Drop the gun, Winslow!"

"You sonofabitch—"

"Drop it now!"

Jesse uncocked the hammer, and tossed the rifle on the ground. "There! It's down. It's dropped!" He did the same with the pistol strapped to his hip.

Silence, sudden and stark stretched between them. The shooting had stopped in the distance. Andrea's heartbeat rushed in her ears, pounding against her temples and against Mitch Lodray's steely arm.

"You won't get away with this, Lodray," Jesse told him. "I'll find you wherever you go. I swear to God."

"I don't think so," Mitch replied, taking casual aim at Jesse who stood defenseless before him.

"No-o-oo!" Andrea's scream coincided with the explosion of Mitch's gun. Jesse tried to dive out of the way, but too late. With a groan, he twisted and dropped to the ground with the impact of the bullet.

Rage, hot and mindless bubbled up inside her. *Jesse! Dear God help him!* Face down on the ground, Jesse drew himself up on his knees, clutching the small, crimson stain spreading across his upper shoulder. His pain-filled eyes met hers with regret.

Mitch dragged her toward Jesse. He pulled the hammer back again. The noise seemed unreasonably loud. "You won't be looking for anyone, Winslow. Because I'm gonna kill you."

Unconsciously, he loosened his arm around her throat and took aim again. Rage welled in her throat as Andrea twisted and grabbed his shooting arm, yanking it down. The pistol went off harmlessly into the ground as Andrea brought her knee up hard into Mitch's unprotected crotch.

Caught completely off guard, Mitch groaned and

doubled over, clutching himself. Andrea wrestled the gun from his hand and stumbled backward with it, as surprised as Mitch at the turn of events.

Mitch coughed, and dropped to his knees, his dark eyes furious. "Damn you, woman. You'll regret that. That's . . . the . . . last time you'll ever do that . . . to me."

Andrea's breath came hard and fast. She lifted the gun in his direction. "I don't think I'll regret it." She pulled back the hammer with both hands.

Mitch's eyes met hers in pained confusion. "Give me that gun, Andrea," he choked out.

"No." She lifted the barrel toward his face. Andrea cradled the heavy gun in her hands, feeling the real power of it for the first time. Within her grasp was the means of ridding herself and the world of Mitch Lodray.

He shook his head. "You don't know what you're doing."

"Jesse?" she called with her eyes on Mitch and her back to Jesse. "Are you all right?"

"Yeah," he answered weakly. "Good girl. Now . . . give me the gun."

"No." The years of harassment, she thought, the months of pain; the days and nights he'd stolen from her . . . never to be recovered. It had taken her months to feel clean after he'd touched her the first time. Now, he'd touched her again and even worse, he'd shot Jesse.

Mitch's eyes widened as he grasped her intent.

"Andi, don't—" Jesse called.

"He deserves to die," she announced with a quiet certainty that belied the tearing emotion behind the thought.

"Yes, he does," Jesse told her, "but not by your hand."

"Andrea," Mitch pleaded, "you couldn't shoot me."

"Couldn't I?" She smiled grimly through the tears that clouded her eyes. His taunt hardened her resolve. "This gun can't be much different from the one you taught me to shoot, is it, Jesse? You just pull the hammer back and tighten your finger around this little piece of metal here."

Her finger coiled around the trigger. The spring creaked ominously. "I suppose this gun is just as touchy as Jesse's. Remember how it went off in my hands before I was even ready to shoot? That could happen here, couldn't it? One little touch and I could blow your head off, Mitch. And who would blame me? No one."

The house door slammed and Captain Steele staggered out the door, his nightshirt hastily tucked into a pair of soldier blues, his gun in hand. He raised it immediately at Mitch, trying to take in the circumstance. "What the hell's going on?"

"Andi, give me the gun," Jesse told her, getting to his feet. "We'll let the law take care of him."

Her laugh was angry. "The law? You mean the same law that scoffs women like me into silence and allows men like him to roam free? You mean the law who's here protecting us now? I don't think I trust them to take care of him. I don't think I trust anyone to make him leave me alone." Tears leaked down her cheeks. "I'll never let him m-make me feel helpless again."

"Mrs. Winslow—" Steele called, walking closer. "Let me take him. He'll hang for treason if nothing else."

"Will they make him suffer the way he has me?" she asked.

Mitch squeezed his eyes shut like a doomed man.

380

"No," Steele answered, curling his lip in Mitch's direction. "But he'll die just the same. I'll see to it."

"That's not good enough." Andrea tightened her finger around the trigger. The gun leapt in her hand with an explosive roar. The shot went intentionally wide, tearing a furrow in the ground a few feet behind Lodray.

Mitch gasped, then glared, ashen faced at Andrea.

"Damn, I missed," she said shakily. "I'm not a very good shot, Mitch. Jesse will tell you. This could take a while." She pulled back the hammer again with trembling hands and fired again. This time, the gravel at his feet jumped and sprayed him in the face.

He blinked hard and wiped his face on his sleeve. Mitch shook his head. "You don't understand. I would have taken care of you."

From out of the darkness, Silas and Deeds appeared. Deeds's thigh was covered with blood and he leaned on the colored man.

Jesse tossed them a look, then, clutching his shoulder, walked closer to her. "Andi, give me the gun."

"No. I'm going to kill him."

Jesse shook his head slowly. "It's not worth it. He's unarmed. It would be murder."

"That's . . . that's what he tried to do to you," she said, arms straight, gun trembling.

"Andi." He covered her hand gently with his. "I love you." She turned her head slightly as his words sank in. "He's not worth the price," he went on. "Give me the gun. Give us a chance. I'll never let him hurt you again. I swear it."

A tremor went through her body, starting at her toes and ending in her fingertips. She wanted so much to do as he said, but her hand seemed frozen around the gun. If she didn't kill him, would she ever feel safe again? Would she if she did?

Then through her tears, she saw Silas walk directly into the path of her gun and haul Mitch to his feet with one burly arm.

"Boss?" Silas looked questioningly at Jesse's shoulder.

Jesse nodded as Steele stepped forward and took Lodray's other arm. "Where are the others?"

"Dead," Silas answered.

"Get him out of here," Jesse told them. Turning back to her, he eased the hammer down on the pistol in Andrea's hands and pried it from her stiff fingers. He tossed it to the ground behind him and hauled her hard against him with his good arm. "Andi—"

She wrapped her arms around his waist. "Oh, Jesse, Jesse . . . I'm sorry."

"For what?" he murmured against her hair.

"F-For everything."

"Shh-hh. It's all over. It's going to be all right now. We'll never see Lodray again."

She leaned back in his arms. "Your shoulder—"

"It's not bad, a flesh wound. Thank God he's a bad shot."

"Oh, God, Jesse, when I saw him fire at you, I thought—"

"That bastard," he muttered under his breath. "I wanted to kill him myself. Did he hurt you, Andi?"

She shook her head. "He wanted to take me away with him. He thought . . . he'd convinced himself I was in love with him."

"He's sick, Andi. His mind's twisted. He won't hurt you or anyone else again."

She pressed her face against his shirt absorbing his strength. He'd taken a bullet for her, stood up for her against hopeless odds. How could she have ever doubted his love for her?

382

"Jesse?"

"Yeah?" His lips brushed her hair.

"Is it too late to change my mind?"

"About what?"

"Marrying you." She pressed her forehead against his chest, unable to look him in the eye. "I love you Jesse. More than you'll ever know. I was wrong about you, about everything. If you can forgive me for being so stubborn and hard-headed—" She swallowed. "I want to be your wife . . . if you'll still have me."

He tightened his arm around her and his inheld breath went out in a sigh. He tipped her chin up so she'd have to look at him. "If I'll still *have* you?" He laughed with relief. "I would have *walked* clear back from Montana to hear those words."

She hugged him tightly, pressing her cheek against the hard expanse of his chest. "I'll give up the farm," she promised. "We don't even have to live here. We can go wherever you want. Montana, Texas . . ."

"Right here will do just fine." He smiled, taking her in with his gaze. A cool night breeze tugged at his hair and sent it wisping across his forehead.

Andi brushed it away with her fingers. "But I thought—"

"I was wrong, Andi. Wrong about this place, and how I felt about it. I'd given it more power over me than it had ever demanded. Silas was right when he said Willow Banks was just a piece of dirt. But it's not the Old Man's piece of dirt any more. It'll be ours. We'll *make* it ours. And little Zachary's, too. And all our other children I'll have the pleasure of catching as they come into this world."

Her throat tightened with tears. "What about Montana? Won't you miss it?"

A smile warmed his eyes. "It's a beautiful place. I'll take you there someday. But it's not my home. It never was. I've spent the last six years of my life running: from the old man, from myself, from you. I'm tired of running." He tightened his arms around her. "I need you, Andi. I realized after I'd made an ass out of myself that I could never let you marry another man. But I thought it was too late."

She shook her head. "I never could have married anyone else. I told you once, I'd never marry again for anything, but love. It's you I love." She hugged him tightly, her throat tight. "Ah, Jesse, promise you won't ever leave me again."

He dropped his mouth on hers and kissed her hard and deep. Andrea felt her body go warm as candle dip as she leaned into his kiss. Meeting him with a need as old as time, she cherished the joining, knowing at last the utter rightness of it.

Love, that most delicate and tenacious of emotions, welled between them again like the gentle breeze stirring the ripening stalks of corn on Winslow land. Their land. Their future.

Jesse lifted his head, his mouth curving into a grin. "Does that feel like I'm going anywhere, woman?"

A smile warmed her eyes. "That felt kinda permanent to me." She threaded her arm around his waist. "C'mon, plow boy. Let's go home."